WHISPERS

Feathers and Fire Book 3

SHAYNE SILVERS

ARGENTO PUBLISHING

CONTENTS

Shayne Silvers

Whispers

Feathers and Fire Book 3

A TempleVerse Series

ISBN: **978-1-947709-08-9**

© 2018, Shayne Silvers / Argento Publishing, LLC

info@shaynesilvers.com

THE VATICAN IS BROKEN...

And Callie's hearing Whispers in the dark corners of her mind...

One of the Vatican's most infamous Shepherds has been murdered, and Callie's friends are the prime suspects. To prove them innocent, Roland and Callie must risk their very souls...

Because Callie can't reveal that she's hearing strange Whispers when she uses her magic, or that she's harboring an Angel's Grace. And if the Shepherds discover the hellish bargain Roland made, the streets of Rome will flow with blood as brother turns against brother.

And with the Antipope pressuring the Vatican for change, and Nate Temple arriving unannounced to demand an audience with the Shepherds, things couldn't get any more chaotic.

Until Callie learns of an ancient order of traitors hiding in the Vatican, and they'll do anything to bring it down – brick by brick.

The only way to find the traitor, keep her secrets, and save those she loves is to raise her blade against these Holy warriors of God, shattering the Vatican itself.

And the Whispers in her head find all of this so terribly...*amusing*.

<u>DON'T FORGET!</u>

VIPs get early access to all sorts of book goodies, including signed copies, private giveaways, and advance notice of future projects. AND A FREE NOVELLA! Click the image or join here:
www.shaynesilvers.com/l/219800

FOLLOW AND LIKE:

Shayne's FACEBOOK PAGE:

www.shaynesilvers.com/l/38602

I try my best to respond to all messages, so don't hesitate to drop me a line. Not interacting with readers is the biggest travesty that most authors can make. Let me fix that.

I

I stared down the big, hairy, mouth-breather. "Bring it on," I growled menacingly.

All one thousand pounds of Kenai, a shifter grizzly bear, barreled straight at me like a snowplow, ignoring petty laws like physics. The beast rose up on two tree-trunk thick legs, towering over me as he roared.

Starlight, the impish black bear, clapped excitedly from the sidelines, and Claire emitted a nervous gasp. I was still unsure where Starlight stood in the hierarchy of the bears. The Cave of shifters listened to his opinion even when it contradicted Armor, their Alpha, who was sitting beside Starlight in bear form, leaning forward as he watched. He was a ten-foot-tall brown bear, but his hair was longer and shaggier than a typical bear. More than a dozen other bears watched the bout from various places around the ring.

Claire was the referee for this particular matchup, one of many that would progress throughout the day. Their idea of a relaxing vacation. Kenai's jaws were alarmingly wide, and his long, ivory fangs were designed to rend flesh from bone. Standing against him in the ring was my fault. Too many drinks last night at the campfire had made this encounter inevitable. Drunken pride had brought me to this place.

A figurative cage-match in the middle of the snowy Alaskan tundra with a freaking grizzly bear. The upside was that shifters healed fast, and they had

Claire in case I got too overzealous. On the other hand, I had no such protections. I hoped that wouldn't be my downfall.

He swiped at me, testing my fear.

Rather than staying back, I lunged within his swipe and scored a direct hit on his inner thigh with my blade. I wasn't using magic... yet. I wanted to push myself, and using magic seemed unfair – even though he was ten times my weight. Still, I wanted to wait as long as possible because Beckett was sparring next, and he had none of my special abilities since he was a Regular human. He wasn't a wizard, so no magic. He also didn't have ties to Heaven.

He only had those ancient abilities that had boosted mankind for thousands of years.

The instinct for self-preservation, improvisation, and sheer grit.

Kenai roared at the slash of pain, but I was already rolling away, using the hilt of my dagger to hammer into his hamstring on my way by. His stance faltered, and I ended up behind him. I immediately sliced and stabbed into his thick hide, knowing that the layers of fat would protect him from serious injury. Still, if I took it too easy on him I would look weak to the rest of the Cave – the term they used for a group of shifter bears – and he would likely beat me, making me look even more unfit to be the self-imposed protector of Kansas City.

Like all men seemed to think, I needed to finish this fast and hard.

Too distracted by my thoughts, I missed the backhanded swipe of his massive paw and he scored a solid blow to my chest, making the belts and buckles of my Darling and Dear coat clank together. I didn't know much about Darling and Dear, other than that they made magical gear with various types of leather. They had given me the coat and a pair of boots for doing them a favor, and that was good enough for me.

My boots were a thing of beauty. If I focused, I could change them into different shapes and styles, but right now they were calf-high riding boots, because I hadn't wanted to get snow inside them and soak my socks. Priorities.

The coat was like an armor of sorts, but Kenai's blow still hurt like a mother-lover. As I flew through the air, I immediately decided to forego my abstinence on magic in favor of survival, casting a blanket of air before me so that the approaching tree didn't break my face.

I bounced off, landing lightly in the snow, my Darling and Dear boots cushioning my fall. I lifted a smirk to Kenai – the big hairy lout. His eyes narrowed, noting my use of magic, but he didn't call me out on it. Bears were like that. Honorable, respectable, and not inclined to belittle someone for a mistake – unless there was a lesson to be learned. Still, we both knew I had resorted to magic. Not that it counted against me, but that it was something we were both aware of. Just another fact on the table.

He settled his weight evenly across his four legs, debating whether to attack or wait.

I solved his moral dilemma and charged. Before he could react, I threw one of my blades at the ground near his lead foot, making him flinch in that direction to defend himself as I simultaneously ran up the nearby tree on his opposite side. He was so stunned by the fact that I had given up one of my weapons – and missed – that he didn't see what I had intended.

I took three steps up the tree trunk and catapulted myself off, flipping backwards to avoid the instinctive swipe of his inches-long claws. He missed and I scored a direct hit across the back of the offending paw in the process, making him recoil instinctively.

Which gave me the perfect opportunity to stab him in the shoulder with the blade, using it as an anchor-point to swing my bodyweight directly behind his shoulders. With a quick flick of my wrists, my sneaky bracelet became a garrote, and I looped the metal wire around his thick throat in a tight choke, abandoning my dagger in his shoulder. I spun my wrists, crossing the wire for maximum control and then yanked back. Now I had reins for my pony-bear.

He tried to roar through his constricted windpipe, claws raking at his throat, but neither the thick pads of his paws nor his claws could find purchase as I choked him. I yanked back even harder, arching my back so that my weight pulled him off balance. I dug my feet into the fat of his back, arms straining as I tensed for the crash, anticipating he would try to use my body to break his fall.

He did try, but I danced across his back so that I wasn't in the way. He hit like a meteor, snow rippling around us in a wave. He scrabbled in the muddy snow, claws raking and digging for purchase, but he only managed to compact the snow into little barriers. He snarled and huffed desperately, but the lack of oxygen was affecting his muscles, weakening him.

I waited a few more seconds, letting him keep his honor for as long as he chose.

"Peace," he rasped like a whisper of wind, muscles going completely slack.

I let out a breath of relief and released one end of the wire. It whipped back into my bracelet with a hiss like a school janitor's key ring.

I hopped off him and took a few steps, shaking the soreness from my arms. Choking out a half-ton Grizzly was no walk in the park. The clearing was utterly silent.

Then a rasping wheeze emanated from the downed bear, which slowly turned into a rattling chuckle, his injuries repairing on the spot. After a few moments, his bellows of laughter thundered across the snow, echoing off the trees and nearby rocks.

Claire rushed over to him, studying his throat, thumbing back his eyes, and checking on the brief slashes from my blade. She shot me a look over his quivering form as she yanked my dagger out from his shoulder, not finding the situation as funny as Kenai did. Because as a veterinarian for the Kansas City Zoo, she was the person who healed wounds, not inflicted them. She ignored the smirk plastered on my face. It wasn't that she was offended by my win, but that Claire always considered consequences, and knowing my level of lethality, she always wanted me to use the lowest level of violence at my disposal. She didn't understand that her philosophy would get me killed in the real world.

Someday, it might get her killed, too. Because she wasn't just a veterinarian any longer. She was also a shifter-bear, and that was one of the reasons we were all out here. To help her get used to that, and to make peace with her first kill – a true son of a bitch named Yuri – the bear who had turned her against her will several months ago.

Kenai gently shoved her away, shifting back to his human form. A large, tanned naked man stood from the ground, his back easily four feet across and rippling with muscles. And back hair. A whole lot of back hair. His human form was even as hairy as a bear. No wonder he was never cold. He turned to face me, his dark beard extended down his neck and under his ears to connect with his jaw-length hair like a helmet. He dipped his head, his pale gray eyes twinkling through the curtains of his dark bangs. "Damn, girl," he finally chuckled, shaking his head.

"What does it feel like to have your ass kicked by a *hormonal little girl?*" I teased, using his statement from the night before.

He grinned. "Better than I imagined," he admitted with an easy shrug.

Then he bowed his head again, lowering his eyes this time. Part of me instinctively waited for a second attack, even though I knew better. Bears were ridiculously noble. To a fault, even. He lifted up his palms in surrender, walking away. "Callie wins."

I saw money change hands. The losers of the bet didn't look angry, just thoughtful. I had impressed them.

I made sure I didn't trip as I made my way over to Claire.

2

C laire aimed her laser eyes at me as I approached, and I didn't
bother to hide my grin. "Don't look so pleased with yourself. Bears
don't value arrogant pride," she admonished.

"Good thing I'm not a bear," I whispered back, earning a brief flicker of
amusement before she let out a resigned sigh.

"You're impossible," she muttered under her breath, but she squeezed my
hand as we made our way back towards Starlight and Armor. Beckett stood
beside them wearing his Arctic coat with the fur-lined hood pulled up. He
was shaking his head absently, blue eyes distant as if rehashing the bout. I
locked eyes with him and then Claire. "You two ready?" I asked.

Their faces grew stony – not with anger, but with focus. They both
nodded. I turned to Starlight. He was black and tan and if you didn't notice
the gray hairs on his muzzle, you might mistake him for a cub. But his eyes
were deep, wise, and ancient. Sometimes they were playful and deliriously
naïve, as if everything was some big cosmic joke. He was a strange little old
bear. "You're sure this is a good idea? Beckett is a Regular, and Claire is still
learning control. I don't want an accident. They're both testing out this
brave new world."

Starlight glanced at Armor, the Alpha of the Kansas City bears. He
studied both for a long moment, considering all the factors in silence. He
finally nodded. Starlight turned back to me. "They're ready. I encourage

8

both to go easy on each other. This isn't about winning. This is about learning. Sparring. The journey, not the destination. Both will grow and change with time, so there is nothing to prove here, only abilities to test and hone." He locked eyes with them. "Sparring is like staring into a mirror, revealing your own strengths and weaknesses. It will show you what you are capable of doing... and what you are capable of dealing with." He winked.

The two contenders nodded, lowering their eyes as they considered his words.

I appraised them. "This still seems like a bad idea. Why don't you let them beat on one of your more experienced warriors?" *Someone who won't lose their shit at first signs of pain.*

Armor considered it, but then shook his head, deciding to actually speak this time. "No. Starlight is correct. Punching a bag teaches you to punch, not to fight. Vital difference. They both know how hard they can hit something. This is about teaching them to anticipate the unknown, to adapt and evolve on the spot. It is as much mental as it is physical." He scratched his snout, thinking. "No. *More* mental than physical." Beckett looked thoughtful, but I was distracted as Armor shot me an intense look. "Like how you beat a grizzly ten times your size."

I nodded, knowing he was right. Roland had taught me much the same. He just hadn't had another student for me to train with, so had enrolled me in his accelerated program. Against him. Sink or swim. Get beat down. Get back up. Again. Again. Again.

Most students couldn't handle that approach well, and the mentor would need to back down at some point or the student would break. The goal of a successful mentor was to find that line where the student wanted to give up, let them fail on the other side of it, and then back up a few steps. Right before that uncomfortable line was the ideal point to teach the student, redefining their sense of *normal*. As their comfort increased, their mentor brought them closer and closer to that line until pretty soon they were past their original breaking point. The student would look back at the previously impossible milestone they had overcome and realize that their mentor might actually know a thing or two. Trust had been earned.

That was the punching bag stage.

Next came the *real* training.

Armor settled his warning glare on Claire and Beckett. "No injury, no emotion. This is about control more than anything. You two are allies in this. Like sex, your goal is to learn more about each other."

I blinked into the silence.

"Just without the whole sex thing," I elaborated, in case that was unclear.

Claire blushed furiously. "Thanks, Callie. I might have just raped him by accident without that piece of advice."

"Feel free..." Beckett offered with a sly grin, eyeing Claire, making her blush even darker.

I found myself glaring at Beckett, but quickly masked it. Why did I care about a comment like that? Beckett and I weren't dating. And I was used to his brash comments, by now. He was always trying to get a rise out of me. He liked poking... well, no pun intended... the bear.

Without further ado, Beckett began taking his coat and shirt off, as if we weren't in the middle of Alaska standing in ten inches of snow. "What are you doing?" I hissed.

He ignored me, taking off his pants and boots until he stood in only his boxers. Claire's stunned look had turned into a smoldering appraisal of his muscled frame. Starlight suddenly held up a hand in front of my face, stopping me before I could interrupt them, sensing the wild look in my eyes. He looked interested at the unexpected development.

I glared at the tiny bear, but he simply winked at me. "Your human is more clever than he lets on..." he said softly, loud enough for only me to hear. He patted an empty space on the log for me to sit beside him. I sighed, obeying with a huff of air.

Claire was studying Beckett like a fresh kabob, and I realized I actually was jealous.

Armor cleared his throat as the two squared off. The other bears suddenly focused back on the make-shift ring, eating berries and whatnot, watching the spectacle as if it was nothing out of the ordinary, but I could tell by the gleam in their eyes that it truly was unique. A Regular against a bear. Kenai was mumbling to a few bears off to the side, smiling as he shook his head at me, good-natured in his loss. Which was just... abnormal. At least to me.

This was my second night here, and their Zen attitude was beginning to get under my skin.

Beckett – the only real human in attendance – had chosen to come with me, taking a day off work to go 'camping' for a long weekend. But his true goal was to test himself and get better acclimated to the supernatural community.

And the bears thought the best introduction was to toss him in the ring with Claire, the newest, most unstable bear here – the one they had needed to take out of the city in case she lost control of her new shifter abilities. Granted, that had been about four months ago, but still. Where Beckett would enter the ring ready to do anything to win, Claire wouldn't know when to stop. Although I agreed with Armor's thoughts on sparring, this was the worst setup imaginable. But he was the Alpha here, and I couldn't keep Beckett on apron strings if he didn't want to be. I'd hoped that my bout with Kenai would signal the end of sparring for the day, especially after the long night of drinking we'd had.

But that wasn't the case.

And to prove how good their judgment was, one of them had just stripped naked.

3

Beckett had a hatchet in either hand as he stared down my best friend, a tiny hundred-pound blonde girl. Claire licked her lips absently, studying her adversary with a look that didn't belong here in a sparring match. She looked hungry for a fresh hunk of man meat, which was currently on full display in a pair of light boxers. The Kansas City homicide detective looked entirely unaffected by the encounter, as if this were a totally normal happenstance for him. I dialed back my anger, which was out of check for some reason I didn't want to admit. Beckett was well-experienced in the gym, judging by the slabs of muscle over his torso, especially his chiseled abs. His hair had grown longer since I first met him, and I had to admit that right now he looked delicious. Just needing some of that edible body-paint to show a girl a good time.

Claire shot a look at Armor who grunted as if he'd been waiting for it. Claire slowly began removing her clothes, staring at Beckett the whole while. He didn't leer, but something about the intensity of his gaze affected her. When she was down to panties and bra, she turned to shed the rest of her clothing. Then she shifted into her Polar Bear form, a giant ten-foot tall monster before turning back to her opponent. Beckett didn't even bat an eye.

He began spinning the hatchets in his palms, as if born with them as he approached in a crouch. Claire studied him on two feet, looking uncertain.

Not with fear that he could win, but with the fear that she might go too far, like an adult suddenly in the ring with a toddler. Beckett advanced as if his life depended on it, grinning darkly as he came within striking distance. Claire's shoulders tightened as she fell down to all fours, hiding her vulnerabilities. Beckett struck like a snake with his hatchets.

He slashed her shoulder and she lashed out with her opposite paw to bat him away, but he was suddenly spinning the opposite direction, striking her swiping paw with the back of his other hatchet, eliciting a sharp growl of pain as the flat of his hatchet struck bone.

Then his other hatchet bit into her foreleg, and she groaned in pain, her weight faltering as she struggled to dance back. Beckett didn't give her the chance, though, suddenly sprinting after her as if anticipating it. He struck the same leg twice in quick succession, but suddenly slipped in the snow, falling on his ass.

Claire's jaws opened wide in both pain, anger, and triumph.

Beckett pelted her with a fistful of snow right in the teeth and tried to kick himself free.

She snorted the snow out of her nose and shook her head. Her jaws flashed out like a snake and clamped down on his thigh. I shouted in alarm, not able to see clearly. The crowd of bears was silent. I sidestepped very slowly, trying to assess the damage. "Claire, release. You wo—"

"No. She didn't," Beckett said, sounding amused.

Then I saw it. Beckett had one hatchet resting against her throat and the other above her eyes, easily able to kill her. And her teeth hadn't pierced his flesh. I had feared that her beast had taken control and that she had just turned Beckett into an amputee. But...

"Tie!" Armor bellowed, sounding amused, and proud. "Back down. The match is over."

Claire was staring up at Beckett, blood painting her fur in several places from his strikes. She noticed how close her snout was to his magic stick and suddenly released, shuffling back a few steps, panting. Beckett grinned at her as he climbed to his feet. He kept that smile going for a few long seconds and then spun, hurling his hatchets with full force. The bears freaked the fuck out for a minute as the hatchets spun through the air. Then they struck a tree, burying within an inch of each other into the trunk, disgorging a heavy pile of snow from the branches.

Right beside Kenai.

He blinked at them, slowly turned his head to stare at Beckett for about five seconds, and then showed him his teeth. Beckett dipped his head before jogging back to his clothes. He did his best to look casual, but I could tell he was eager to get his clothes back on. Once his coat was in place, he finally walked back up to Claire, who was still watching him in her bear form.

She dipped her head, and then loped off into the woods by herself.

Beckett turned to me, his smile faltering.

I met his eyes, and honestly didn't know how I felt. Was I proud of him? Hell yeah. Was I upset that Claire was apparently ashamed? Hell yeah. So...

I gave him a weak smile, scooped up Claire's clothes, and then took off after her.

Sisters before Misters.

Claire Bear needed a hug.

4

I walked away from the sounds of more bears gearing up to spar, pushing through the snow-laden branches to follow Claire's tracks. I found a large polar bear sitting on a rock overlooking a snow-swept valley far below, watching a herd of elk.

Claire's shoulders were tight, and I wondered if she was hungry, or if she was just staring through the herd in a daze, rehashing the match. Claire had always had a thing for animals, an affinity. It was why she had become a veterinarian. But now she was a shifter, and part of her craved the hunt.

She shifted slightly, letting me know she had heard or sensed me. Without a word, she scooted over on her rock, making room. I sat down beside her, but didn't speak, watching the animals below instead. Part of me wanted to nestle up against her thick fur, but I wisely chose not to. Sometimes simply being near your friend when she was frustrated was enough. Advice was not always... advisable.

I knew she was probably embarrassed to suffer a draw in her matchup with a human. Here she was, a big, badass polar bear, and a naked dude without powers had gotten the better of her.

Or she was having issues with her new powers – being a shifter bear. Angry at her loss, and suddenly battling a craving for fresh blood. Like the elk down below.

Or she was angry, and trying to bottle that up like any proper woman did.

Really, it could be any number of things, and until she decided to say something I was simply there for her comfort, to do whatever I could to fix what was bothering her. She saw the clothes in my lap, shook her fur violently, and suddenly a naked babe grabbed them out of my hands.

"I need to have sex. Hard, violent, angry sex," she muttered, wiggling into her clothes.

Oh. Well that was definitely going above and beyond the standard best friend duties.

I glanced at her, feeling a slow smile tugging at my cheeks, wondering if she was just trying to ease the tension. She turned to look at me and I almost flinched back at the intensity I saw burning in her eyes.

"No, Callie. I *really* need sex," she growled as she tugged on her boots.

I tried not to burst out laughing at her vehemence. "I'm sure you could have a line waiting for you if you put up a sign that said *this blonde needs a good pounding* or something outside your cave..." I said lightly, hoping to crack the tension. "Kenai would probably slap your ass to kingdom come—"

"What about Beckett?" she asked, looking up as if she hadn't been listening to me.

And a little fire of my own roared to life deep inside me. I instantly squashed it down, careful to keep my face from flushing red. He wasn't mine. But I suddenly knew that Beckett had played a very clever card when sparring with Claire. Armor had reminded them that sparring was more mental than it was physical. I had wondered why he had stripped down before the match. There had literally been no reason to do so, and every reason not to do so.

I wondered if he was as clever as he thought he was, or if he had been playing another game of some kind.

"Well, I'm not his pimp," I said, sharper than I intended.

Claire sighed. "Sorry, Callie. I don't mean to poach. I literally just want to get this out of my system. Several times. Hard times. Angry, violent, no holds-barr—"

"Jesus, Claire! I get it, you freaking masochist," I cried out, holding up my hands and shaking my head clear of the image of her and Beckett bumping uglies. This time she did blush, as if hearing her words for the first time. Then she thought about it harder and shrugged.

"What's a girl got to do to get some pole around here?" she finally muttered, and then shot me a playful look out of the corner of her eye.

I heard a commotion behind us as a branch dislodged some snow. Beckett appeared, waving at us. "I'll have you two know that I'm an excellent sounding board. I can literally talk about the first thing that pops up without hesitation," he said, smiling lightly.

I burst out laughing. He had no idea what he had walked into and how perfect his line was.

Claire grumbled hungrily. "This rock is cold, and that conversation would go better if I was sitting on his lap," she whispered to me, grinning. She watched the innocent man approach. "Or I could sit on his face. I really don't care at this point," she added, eyes growing darker.

I smacked her arm and she flinched, snapping out of it. Beckett noticed the whispers and stopped, frowning from a dozen feet away. "Do you two need some girl time?" he asked warily. "I just wanted to congratulate you, Claire. We all know in a real fight you would have repeatedly slammed my head into the back of a woodpile as you bore down on me," he admitted.

Claire's body shifted subconsciously, her hips rocking at the mental image as she turned to fully face him. "Mommy want..." she whispered under her breath, soft enough that only I could hear. I carefully reached over to scoop up a handful of snow.

Then I reached behind her to shove it down the back of her pants. She squealed, jumping to her feet and cursing at me. "What the *hell*, Callie?!" she snapped, dancing up and down, trying to shake the snow out of her underwear. This made Beckett pay very close attention, realizing he had stumbled onto something he didn't fully understand. His analytical eyes studied the effects of gravity on Claire's chest as she hopped up and down.

"Leave, now. We'll talk to you soon, Beckett," I said, shooting him a glare.

He turned to me, puzzled. "I know how hard it can—"

"You have no idea how much that is not helping right now," I all but shouted, pointing a finger for him to leave.

Claire had stopped jumping and actually licked her lips at him, taking a step forward.

"Now!" I shouted at Beckett.

He turned and ran at the tone in my voice. "I'm at your disposal!" he called out.

Claire had taken another step, eyes only for her fleeing prey. I blindsided her, tackling her to the ground where we rolled in the snow. I did my best to dump as much of it down her coat and pants as I could. She shrieked angrily, struggling to bat my hands away while trying to scoop out the snow touching her skin. After a few seconds she began to laugh, and was shoving as much snow as she could down my own clothes until we were both giggling as we rolled around in the snow. Then I had her straddled, sitting on her hips with snow in either fist, grinning down at her. "Say mercy," I warned.

Instead, she bucked her hips, much stronger than I had expected, lifting me into the air. With shifter strength, she latched onto my jacket and flung me six feet through the air before I fell through a snowdrift, instantly buried.

I shrieked at the sudden cold, thrashing wildly to get out of the drift and finally came to my feet scowling at Claire for good measure. She was brushing off snow and giggling.

Once we were both composed, I flung a ball of fire at the rock we had been sitting on, letting the flames wash over it, melting the snow in seconds. I heard faint whispers and cocked my head, trying to place it. Was it just the wind howling through the trees? It faded, so I dismissed it. I let the fire burn until the melted water was gone and the rock had warmed up. Then I cut it off.

Claire walked over to it, placing a careful hand on it. She grunted satisfactorily and then sat down, squirming as if to get the maximum ass to warm stone ratio. Then she slapped the space beside her.

"Just for the record, I'm not going to bone you, Claire," I said, joining her.

She rolled her eyes, but I could tell the topic was still on her mind. Good god. Had it been that long or was this a bear thing?

I let that silent question sit there, knowing she had to sense it. She finally sighed. "Everything is just so primal now. On the tip of my mind. If I want something, I *really* want it. And sparring always gets my blood hot. Especially with him taking his damned clothes off beforehand. He did it on purpose, didn't he?" she asked softly, sounding as if the idea had only just come to her.

I shrugged, considering how to respond. "If he did, he's very clever. But I don't think he was trying to seduce you. I'm betting it was just something to make you pause. Giving your opponent a random variable to factor in, something that doesn't make sense. It's a great tactic when sparring. Or in anything, really. They get so annoyed with the subtle question that they aren't focused on the matter at hand." I shrugged.

The silence stretched a little longer. "Can I sex the detective? I'll be gentle. Well, kind of."

I didn't dare turn to her, trying to keep my own flash of anger out of view. Because I had no justification for being angry. Beckett wasn't my plaything. If he wanted to slap ass with Claire, that was between them. But... I realized it bothered me. Very much.

But on a personal level, not with concern over one of them casually using the other.

I had never spoken to Beckett romantically, so it wasn't fair for me to insert myself into the equation. If he wanted to shag Claire, that was ultimately up to him. "Like I said, I'm not his pimp. You'd have to check with him," I said through gritted teeth. Because I wasn't going to put myself in the middle of two friends, especially when I had no right to think Beckett and I were anything other than friends. Work friends.

It still sucked.

Claire must have noticed. "If he's yours, just say the word. I don't fancy any of the bears. Not really. And I want something more normal. Something where I won't feel like such a rookie. If I do anything with the bears, all I can think about is like I'm some kind of charity, and that I'm an apprentice to the ways of their world. I want to take something of my own. Run a man to exhaustion, and see that look of wonder in his eyes. Not feel like I was banging my college professor and learning something he was already very familiar with." She kicked at the snow.

I let out a long sigh. "That's between you two. He's not mine. But I do have to work with him, so if you're just looking for fun..."

Claire nodded, not turning to me.

I muttered dark things in my mind. I should have just left the bastard back in Kansas City.

T he night sky was clear, showing us a beautiful view of the Northern Lights. I tried to use them to clear my head. They looked like ribbons of magic, making me smile. I finally turned back to my best friend, feeling more composed.

I cleared my throat. "You did well today. It must be hard trying to figure out your new limits."

Claire chuckled. "Understatement. Trying to figure out how to *control* myself is the issue. I know how to kill. It's like I've known it all along. But sparring with a human? That sucked. I felt like I was going to kill him by accident." She muttered again, under her breath. "And that hesitation cost me the fight."

I nodded. "That's the hardest part of any new power. Control. Learning to destroy things is much easier than learning precision. Being able to destroy everything around you doesn't make you a good person to have in a fight. Unless it's a war where everyone around you is a bad guy."

"I'll get better," she finally said.

I smiled. "You kicked Yuri's ass. Hardcore."

A ghost of a frown crossed her pale features. "Yeah, but I almost didn't. He had more endurance. Almost got you killed."

I squeezed her thigh. "But it didn't."

She nodded, smiling to herself. "Yeah. You're right. Not sure why I'm so grouchy. Just frustrating trying to figure all this stuff out." She paused, leaning back on her palms as she kicked her feet at the snow again. "I turned in my notice at the zoo," she said softly.

I flinched. I knew the obvious reasons why she might do so, but had expected her to fight it harder. Being around animals as a shifter could get difficult if she became hungry. And killing a tiger or something was probably a felony of some kind. But I had assumed the other bears had normal jobs, and that Claire might get to keep hers after she gained more control.

"Did Armor make you quit?" I asked warily, not sure if I was overstepping myself. He was her Alpha now, and maybe he held that kind of control.

Claire snorted. "No. He argued with me about it. Kept telling me it would get easier with time... But I know it will just be another razor blade for me to juggle. Always making sure I'm not going to freak out one day and lose it." I nodded, not wanting to offer comment. This had to be her decision, but it hurt my heart to know she was giving up something so important to her.

All because I had gotten her involved way over her head and she'd been attacked by an asshole of a shifter bear. Sure, she had gotten her ultimate revenge, but the cat was already out of the bag, so to speak.

"Starlight offered me a job as the Cave's doctor. Made my decision much easier. Basically, it's like I was recruited by some high-tech research lab, learning about new species and how to take care of them. It will also help me understand my own changes a little better. He said that if I get comfortable with it, I can even consult for other types of shifters in town."

I frowned. "But don't shifters heal pretty fast already?"

Claire shrugged. "From simple injuries, sure. But silver wounds, punctured lungs, severe traumas. Sometimes they need immediate assistance before their body has time to start the healing process. Imagine a lung filling with blood while their body heals the tear. They'll drown while their body seals it up. Someone needs to drain that." I shivered at the thought. "Also, Starlight says it's not a far jump from becoming a Shaman, like him. Medicine Man of the pack. Or Medicine Chick, I guess."

"What does that mean?" I asked, leaning forward. I had been curious about Starlight.

I had recently come to learn how woefully ignorant I was when it came to other flavors of supernatural, or Freaks, as the conspiracy theorists called us. I didn't even know all the main groups in town. But they all knew of me. So, my new task was to learn and socialize.

It seemed that a lot of supernatural beings were suddenly *very* interested in Missouri. None of them knew why, but they all seemed to be making their way here. As if compelled. I wanted to crack that nut, or at least learn as much as I could about my incoming neighbors. Because like it or not, I kind of worked for the Vatican, and I was beginning to learn that they thought they knew much more than they really did. In a time of turmoil, it would behoove us – me – to have better relations with the various Freaks in my city.

Like Nate Temple had been doing in St. Louis.

Claire cleared her throat. "Bears are pretty... homegrown," she finally said, attempting to describe it in simple terms. Seeing my frown, she furrowed her brows and shook her head. "They are very reclusive and spiritual. They have all sorts of rituals they do in the privacy of their pack. Think Native Americans. They don't necessarily worship a god or anything, but they are very in tune with nature and those around them. They spend a lot of time with each other, and even if not blood, we're all one family. At least in Armor's Cave, anyway. Most bears are sages and hermits, wandering the woods to... well, find themselves. But Armor and his crew found themselves in Kansas City, and realized a bunch of other bears had done the same. Pretty soon they got locked into politics and were fighting for their own slice of Kansas City. Not for power, but for a safe haven. A place for other bears to have the chance to try out their new concept."

I nodded. I had always thought bears were loners. Armor's Cave was something of an anomaly. Sometimes you'd find a group of two or three bears together, but eventually they would disband and go their own ways. Armor, Kona, and Starlight had formed a loose family of sorts with more than two dozen bears. And it had lasted for a few years now.

"But what about the Medicine Man thing?"

Claire smiled. "I'll show you."

And she grabbed my hand, leading me back to the bears.

❧ 6 ❧

Claire pressed through the woods, veering off the main path I had taken to find her, and not bothering to warn me about each branch she shoved out of her way. I either got slapped by the rebounding branches or suffered the airstrikes of dislodged snow. Either way, Claire kept on tugging me like a toddler's blankie.

We reached the edge of the clearing that housed the bears and I let out a sigh of relief. The bears sat around a large fire, watching a roasting elk as it hung on a spit. Some remained in bear form, napping or wrestling, while those in human form toasted with their thermoses and chatted back and forth, warming their hands by the fire. Beckett was sitting beside Kona. She had been out hunting earlier, but had obviously returned with an elk. She was Armor's head of security or something, and although we had started off on a rough patch, we'd had a lot of fun last night. The two were talking absently, but seeing us, Beckett made his goodbyes and headed our way.

Claire saw and waited, eyeing him like a piece of meat. His steps slowed as he saw her look, assuming he had done something wrong. "Am I still in trouble?" he asked, smiling crookedly.

"I wouldn't mind giving him a spank—" Claire began.

I squeezed her hand and she cut off, chuckling under her breath. "You're fine. Claire was just going to show us something," I said, grabbing his hand

and pulling him after me as Claire suddenly did the same, tugging me in a new direction, but still back into the merciless woods.

It wasn't a territorial hand holding, even though Beckett grinned at the contact of flesh on flesh, even squeezing my hand affectionately. I didn't blush. I promise. The heat from the massive fire had hit me, and it just felt nice to slap flesh to flesh.

Okay.

Stop it, Callie, I chided myself.

"Where are we going?" Beckett asked. "Because it looks like you two are leading me to a secluded cabin..."

Claire missed a step but I kicked her foot, forcing her to press on. "Claire wanted to show us something," I said, glancing over my shoulder at him and shrugging.

He smiled good naturedly. "I'll try anything once, I guess."

I smirked, shaking my head at his playful grin. *Flesh on flesh*, I reminded myself.

"Promise?" Claire asked under her breath before halting and releasing my hand. Then she grinned and jumped between two tall firs, disappearing from view. I blinked. I hadn't thought there was enough room between them for her to fit.

We shared a look, shrugged, and jumped after her, covering our faces from the spiky branches. We landed in a clearing I hadn't known existed and a quaint, single story log cabin stood before us. I glanced back to see that the hut was surrounded by a ring of fir trees, blocking it off from the main area where we had been sparring. Invisible unless you knew to look for it.

Claire was already up the stairs and waiting by a wide wooden door – much too big of a door for such a small cabin. Unless bears had built it, of course. What was she about to show us? She held the door open, motioning for us to enter ahead of her. She curled her lips in an entirely inappropriate grin at Beckett as he walked by. "What's your safe-word?" she asked him, leaning close as she bit her lip.

He blinked, and then smiled. "Teddy bear?" he said, and Claire froze. I burst out laughing, but the sound was cutoff as I began coughing at the thick clouds of smoke in the room. I momentarily began to panic as my eyes adjusted, but then I realized the building wasn't on fire.

And we weren't alone.

Starlight sat before a small fire, sprawled out on one of a dozen pillows surrounding the pit. He looked up at us with lidded eyes, nodding slowly. "Puff, puff, pass?" he asked, holding out a pipe. I coughed at him, sensing Claire and Beckett step up beside me. He chuckled at my blank look, and then patted a pillow beside him. What the hell? He was a stoner?

We joined him, Beckett and I sharing blank looks. "You're smoking pot in here?" Beckett asked, waving away more smoke and not looking pleased. He was a cop after all and needed to go back to work Monday.

Starlight shook his head, and handed the pipe to Claire, who set it beside her without taking a puff. She stripped off her clothes until she was entirely naked. Then she began to fold them very meticulously into a neat pile, which she set beside her. Then she crossed her legs and closed her eyes, facing the fire. The smoke around her abruptly shifted, leaving her in a cocoon of clear air. My jaw dropped in disbelief as I watched the smoke outside of the cocoon eddy and swirl. Starlight murmured approvingly, nodding twice, but didn't say anything to her.

Instead, he turned to us and spun his paws in a circle, urging us to hurry up.

I glanced at Beckett, who looked just as confused. "I don't get it..." I said.

Starlight cocked his head playfully. "Clothing. Remove it. No ties to the world. Come clean to this place. Did Claire not explain?"

"Definitely not," I said, shivering instinctively at the thought of taking my clothes off in a strange hut with drugs, a bear, my best friend, and a cop. *Goldilocks Gone Wild.* I realized the room was much warmer than I thought, and that I actually had loosed my coat already. I shot Claire another look, but her eyes were still closed. Her breasts were misted with sweat now, and the hair above her ears was damp with perspiration. I blinked away the smoke and realized Beckett was waiting for me to make up my mind.

"Why don't you catch us up," Beckett said, studying the tiny bear. His eyes might have drifted to Claire, and he might have even licked his lips at her glistening display. Either that or he was licking away the sweat that was trickling down his nose and upper lip. I wiped my own forehead, staring down at my wet palm. What the hell? I was sweating, too?

Starlight sighed. "Bears are very spiritual. We take after the Native Americans in a way, and try to become one with the land around us in order to balance our human form with the emotional urges of our beast," he said, waving both paws at his own bear form.

I nodded. "Why haven't I ever seen you in human form?" I asked.

He stared at me but didn't answer my question. "We spend a considerable amount of time getting to know ourselves, searching inward to find our totem. That essential part of ourselves that is neither beast nor man. This ritual shows you this raw self, among other things. This is a form of Peyote. It is not addictive, and is only used on these pilgrimages, not on a regular basis. This is a privilege. Each bear does this only several times per year. It shows us our past. Eventually, with understanding of the self, it can show present and even futures. Unlocking your subconscious mind, connecting dots you may otherwise not see."

I nodded, leaning forward eagerly. "This shows you your past?" My heart raced. I would give anything to see even one glimpse of either parent. They had abandoned me on the steps of Abundant Angel Catholic Church to keep me safe from... something. Possibly demons. My mother had been a wizard named Constance, but I didn't know my Nephilim father's name.

Starlight nodded. "How we came to be. Well, not how we became shifters, but certain memories of those first shifters. It's not a science, so everyone sees it differently."

Beckett coughed, waving away a tendril. "Out of respect, I would like to accept, but I'm a policeman. I must weigh the consequences." Starlight nodded respectfully. "Is this illegal?"

The impish bear shrugged. "We don't have a permit because it's not even known to your police. It is all natural, and has been used by our kind for generations. You're free to leave," he offered. "But I ask that you not take this away from our people. It is not recreational."

Beckett nodded, looking torn. Not judgmental, but conflicted.

"What will it do to us? We're not bears..." I said, staring at Claire. She was entirely slick with sweat now, the water dripping off her breasts to splash onto her thighs. She breathed deeply, but still didn't open her eyes. Starlight made a strange purring sound as he glanced at her.

As graceful as an angel, she blindly reached for the pipe and took a large draw. I found myself leaning forward, waiting for her to start *tripping balls* or whatever people called *getting high* these days.

She breathed out a thick cloud of smoke, and it struck her small cocoon of protection, swirling around her as if she was in the center of a vortex. Then she did this again, two more times, entirely filling her small cocoon so that I almost couldn't make her out anymore. She was... hotboxing with magic. Hardcore. Then she set the pipe down, and began to hum to herself.

There were no words in her melody, but it was gripping. Alien. The tune swept me up, carrying my mind far away. The tone spoke of family, of holding a newborn close to your breasts and feeding them for the first time – even though I didn't know what that felt like from personal experience, I *did* feel it in her song. Then it shifted to loving frustration in trying to rationalize with a toddler, fear as they scraped their knees for the first time, encouragement for them to get back up and try again, pain, more pain, smiles, pain...

And the heartaches continued as the child continued to progress through life, learning the harsh lessons involved with growing up – scraping a knee, surviving bullying, losing fights, arguing with friends, failure, success. Life.

Then the song shifted to loving sadness – of that loved one leaving the home, setting out on their own for a new life unsupported by family. A life of danger, fighting, challenging death, fear, coldness, loneliness. I felt my heart ripping, and realized tears were falling down my cheeks. I briefly saw through the smoke that Claire was sobbing as well, but her lips formed a smile, as if knowing what was on the other side of this pain.

Then it came to me. The offspring coming back with a child of their own, bringing the newborn back to me to hold, their lover in tow. They had survived. Won at life. Returned.

And my heart exploded, too big for my chest to contain. I wept in silent sobs.

I found myself panting as the song faded. Claire was rocking back and forth on her rear, the cocoon gone, but her eyes still closed. When she opened them, her eyes were distant, glazed, but deliriously happy. Euphoric.

Beckett cleared his throat, vocal chords raw. I glanced at him to find his eyes bloodshot, and not from the smoke in the room. I finally turned to Starlight. "What happens if we try it?"

He studied me thoughtfully. "Only one way to find out, Heaven Walker."

I ignored the title with barely a shiver. I'd heard it before in a demon-possessed house. Without looking, I held out my hand for the pipe. "You don't have to do this, Beckett."

I heard a rustling, and realized he was taking off his clothes, folding them as neatly as he could, trying to replicate Claire's focused attention when she had done it. I blushed, realizing that we were all going to get naked and try a hallucinogen. And that I had forgotten that part of the ritual, asking for the pipe before meditating and getting down to my skin.

I withdrew my hand, let out a deep breath, and began to undress.

What happens in Alaska stays in Alaska.

If Roland could see me now, I would be in a confessional booth for a millennium.

7

S tarlight waited until we were naked, our folded clothes set to the side, and then motioned us closer to the fire. Beckett scooted up beside me, his hairy legs brushing my own damp flesh, but I didn't glance down to measure his... dedication to our crime.

With a curled lip, I focused my thoughts, relaxing my mind, remembering Claire had seemed to meditate. I knew how to do that. I'd spent years training with Roland on just that. I wondered how Beckett would fare here, but that was up to him.

"I will be your guide," Starlight murmured from directly beside me. I flinched, not realizing he had moved. I saw Claire murmuring similar words to Beckett. She definitely assessed him as he closed his eyes. I bit back the flash of anger, but was relieved to see Claire look guilty for a moment, shaking her head as she forced herself to focus on the spiritual task at hand. She began whispering into his ear, slowly circling him, massaging his shoulders – not inappropriately – but as Roland had once shown me. Helping me to relax and clear my mind. Sometimes physical touch helped still your racing thoughts, giving you something else to focus on. Smell, taste, and whispered mantras also helped. She used her soft voice and the touch of her fingers to ease Beckett into meditation.

Starlight murmured in my ears, barely a whisper, almost as if I was listening to myself.

"You can use the pipe or you can have a diluted tea if you prefer. Either has the same results, but the drink will wear off sooner. The choice is yours, but if you have trouble quieting your mind, I recommend the drink," he whispered.

"I'm fine," I said, breathing deeply. His claws began tracing my upper back, making me shiver. They paused on the shoulder blades, as if noticing something. I heard faint whispers and wondered if it was a result of the second-hand smoke. It reminded me of the wind I had heard with Claire while overlooking the valley, but this was louder, more insistent. Not wind, definitely voices. I dismissed them, sensing Starlight's claws still resting on my scars.

He knew what they were from. He had seen them. Where I had temporarily sprouted wings during a fight with a demon. I wasn't sure if it was a Nephilim thing – since my biological father had been a Nephilim – or if it was related to the Angel's blood I had accidentally come into contact with.

The wings had also come with the ability to use a silver form of magic that I didn't fully understand, but using it had attracted an Angel named Angel who lived in Kansas City. He'd sent one of his Nephilim to let me know that I had passed some kind of test and that I was now ready to talk to him. Since I had just killed a Demon all by myself, I hadn't felt charitable and had booted the Nephilim out of the Church. Literally.

I hadn't bothered to take them up on their offer, but I had been practicing with Roland. Turns out that forcing wings out of my back wasn't easy. I was getting better at using the silver magic – whatever it was – but it drained me faster than my wizard's magic. The one major difference was that it seemed to function on *need*.

Which was why I'd had a hard time sprouting wings. I could do it, but it drained me quickly. I had even shown off for the bears last night – after a few drinks. But it was hard to find a legitimate need for wings. Plenty of *wants*, but not *needs*. For now, when push came to shove, I banked on being a wizard, not a Heavenly mutt on an Angel's leash.

Starlight continued dragging his claws down my back, as light as possible, not scratching me, but tracing unseen designs across my entire back.

I felt tension slip away, even though I hadn't known I carried any. Then again, it could be the last of the cold leaving my bones. Still, where his fingers touched, my skin felt hot, like he was tracing warm wax on my body.

My ears began to grow fiery hot as I realized that the relaxing sensation was eliciting a very different response from my lady bits. Then I heard Beckett moan in pleasure beside me, almost as if surprised to feel the calming effects of meditation for the first time. Which lit me up like a firecracker, but soon I didn't have time to be jealous. Each erogenous zone of my body suddenly felt dipped in molten oil. Not painful, but as hot as they could get while still causing pleasure. Genitals, ears, hip bones, nipples, the tip of my tongue, my lips, and the arches of my feet.

Before I could grow concerned at this rapid progression, Starlight murmured into my ears. "This is entirely normal, do not worry. You will remain in full faculty of your actions. Your senses are simply heightened from the smoke in the room. It won't have the ultimate effect unless directly inhaled from the ritual pipe, but for your body to react so strongly so soon means you are in very firm control of your body, no stranger to introspection..."

I mumbled agreement. My tongue felt thick. "Meditation is one of my main disciplines. For over a decade..."

Without warning, Starlight was suddenly cupping my breasts. For some reason, I didn't flinch, but relaxed further, almost pressing into his touch, my mouth opening slightly. The warm pads of his paws were surprisingly soft and his fur almost tickled. His claws felt like ice-cubes in comparison, and each frozen tip pressed different points of my breasts as he gently squeezed. I shuddered and almost had an accident – an entirely pleasant one, because my eyes were still closed, and the loss of one sense had heightened all the others.

Good fucking god. What was this stuff, and why wasn't it illegal?

I didn't even find it weird that a bear was fondling my breasts, because there was nothing sexual in his motions – it wasn't his fault how my body chose to respond.

He relaxed his hold but his claws maintained contact, arcing around my breast in icy lines against my molten, sweat-slicked skin. They skated laterally until they rested above the sides of my rib cage, pausing. Then they slid down, causing me to shiver before his paws gently squeezed my sides just above the hip bones.

I was panting, but my mind felt like it was drifting away on dandelion fluff. Then I felt the pipe touch my lips and my mouth opened further instinctively, teeth clamping down on the stem. I took an inhale.

"Hold," he rumbled in a low tone from directly in front of me. I held the smoke in as he withdrew the pipe and I heard him place it beside me.

His paws gently gripped my upper thigh, the claws gripping almost the entire perimeter of my flesh as he placed his furry forehead against my own. "Exhale..." he breathed.

I did, and my fucking soul left my body.

I may or may not have climaxed. Sue me.

❧ 8 ☙

Wind whipped past me as I stood on a cloud above Kansas City. I wore white robes, stained crimson at the hem, and my feet were scarred and calloused, used to being bare. The city below me was on fire, and the only buildings that remained standing had giant, glowing runes carved into their sides. Winged shapes flew through the skies around me, too fast for me to get a clear look other than to say they were humanoid. All I could see for certain was their wings. Some were made of formed smoke, others of fire, others of ice, some of liquid, shifting metal, and some of nothing specific at all. My vision distorted as I tried to identify them clearly, as if I was looking through multiple prisms of crystals stacked on top of each other, an optical illusion. But for every type of wing in the sky, there were two different variations.

Take the wings of fire, for example.

Some were bright and gleaming – silvers and golds, reds and oranges – in other words, *light*.

But some of those burning wings seemed stained by shadow, as if someone had tossed smoke into their substance, or black tar. They were still fire, the same colors of flame as the *light* ones, but they were *dark*.

Angels and Fallen Angels? Something else?

The light and dark fought, slamming into each other, cutting wings to send their opponents wheeling down to the ground, where hundreds of dark, grotesque monsters or light, majestic beasts – some as large as small buildings, and others merely seething swarms of normal sized creatures – devoured the free meals. Or continued fighting their opposites. Light beasts versus dark monsters. Again, specific details were distorted, but the light and dark aspect was clear.

Most of those falling from the skies were the light Angels.

Which probably wasn't great.

A sharp crackle of power caught my attention, and I glanced down at my fist to see a bar of light gripped in my scarred knuckles. A spear of pure light. I pointed it absently, inspecting the haft, and bolts of white lightning exploded from the tip, striking a dozen dark Angels simultaneously.

Several of the light Angels that had fallen to the ground instantly overwhelmed their attackers, rather than being devoured, decimating the monsters in their immediate vicinity.

I glanced from them to the spear, and then I thrust it out again, a small smile creeping over my face. More lightning shot forth, slamming into yet more of the dark Angels now fluttering towards me as if seeing me for the first time. As one, their black, stained faces locked onto mine – not clear enough to make out features, but more like a smeared oil painting. Some kind of disguise? Then they flew at me, screaming loud enough for me to jolt physically.

I was suddenly in a different place.

A dark, murky alley, and Abundant Angel Catholic Church rose before me. Arthur, our new janitor-slash-security guard lay sprawled on the ground, stabbed to death with a crucifix that the murderer had left behind.

The church itself was smoking. Not on fire, but as if the stone itself was hot to the touch, creating smoke as soon as air touched it. A large cross was buried into the earth just to the right of the steps beside the statue of the angel that had been there as long as I had known the place.

The cross was made of smoldering coals and held together by red, crackling chains of darkness. No flame licked the air, but the cross of embers was barely being held together by the magical chain. Each time it threatened to crumble, the chains flared darker, shifting to hold it together at all cost.

Roland knelt before it, muttering in a dried, rasping breath, praying to God in Latin over and over again, as if he had been doing it for days without rest, food, or water.

As if he was the only one holding the cross together.

The chains were his. The last of his power.

"Roland!" I shouted in disbelief, unable to move my body.

His head flinched, and he turned briefly, making me gasp. He was crying blood and had no eyes. He recognized my voice though, and burst out crying and laughing.

"Save me..." he rasped, and then he fell face-first to the ground, and the cross began crumbling as his magical chains evaporated.

I flung out my hand, desperate to maintain whatever he had been working on, and the world flashed black.

I found myself back in a familiar office. The demon – Johnathan – had been working on a project before I had killed him, and his sister, Amira, had tried to pick it back up before I killed her as well. The room was covered in soot, now, because when I had last been here it had burst into flame. But one thing was glowing on the wall.

Well, three things.

WHY MISSOURI?

NATE TEMPLE?

CALLIE PENROSE?

These three lines of words were glowing with green, greasy fire. As I looked closer, I realized they were carved into the stone, and the green fire was actually from the other side of the wall – revealing the hellish pits of an entirely different place beyond.

I pressed my face against one of the wider cracks and saw a throne made of smoke. A great hulking figure lounged, his wings flaring behind his back. His head swiveled, locking directly onto me. I scrambled back with a shout, but green fire obliterated the wall, showering me with gravel, stone and crumbling mortar.

Then I was falling and the green fire enveloped me.

Whispers carried me on the winds of time, and I wept as I listened to their stories of the Fallen Kingdom of Man.

9

My eyes shot open and I panted desperately. I was back in the hut. Claire was sitting beside Beckett, who was smiling as he spoke to her, looking entirely relaxed. A paw squeezed my thigh and I glanced down, following it to see Starlight frowning at me oddly – as if a smile had just begun to falter.

"Callie?" he asked softly. "Are you okay?" He was staring at me as if wondering why I was panting.

I tried to catch my breath. "How long have I been out?" I whispered hoarsely, trying to recall what I had seen. My mind abruptly seared with pain and I felt something slam down between me and the memory, like a mental portcullis in a castle. *No...* a voice purred inside me. *Not yet...*

I groaned as the pain receded, stars flashing in my vision. It hurt so much I didn't even worry myself about the voice.

Starlight hesitated. "Not even five minutes. You were fine until you just opened your eyes, panting as if you had just sprinted a mile. What happened?" he whispered, seeing the fear in my eyes.

"I... don't know. I saw... things," I shivered, struggling to batter down the wall in my mind, but it was futile. What the hell? "Horrible, horrible things," I whispered. That was all I remembered. That whatever I had seen was beyond bad.

He suddenly wrapped me up in a tight hug, and I felt myself latch onto him like a lifeline, sobbing and shivering. What had I seen? The past? Present? Future?

"Was it real?" I whispered, grabbing fistfuls of his fur and holding him close. Even though I didn't remember anything, I needed to know if it was real in case that mental barrier ever came down. I needed to know that I could stop whatever it was that had shaken me so badly.

When he didn't answer, I pulled back to look at him. He was comically small compared to the other bears. Almost as if he was a young cub. But I was pretty sure he was much older than any of the other bears because he had gray hair on his muzzle. He had a deep resiliency about him, too, whether it was his aura, wisdom, or some deep inner strength, I wasn't sure. I remembered that I had once seen him do a form of magic, but had never questioned him about it. And Claire had called him a Shaman. A Medicine Man. "What are you, Starlight? Can you do magic?"

He smiled crookedly, unsure which question to answer or if answering a naked girl tripping on shifter peyote was borrowing trouble. "I don't know if it's real, Callie. I've seen events that never came true, but also those that have. I've also seen things from the past that I have no way of verifying..." He studied me. "What did you see? The past? Future?"

I shrugged helplessly. "I have no idea, but it was terrible." I felt anger creeping over me. "What the hell, Starlight? I thought this was supposed to be fun?"

He grimaced. "It usually is, but it depends on the user. I don't think I've ever seen anyone walk away scared or afraid. Some angry, but that was later explained as not being happy about a particular thing they saw – their lover with another bear, for example. Or not pleased about their past or something. Nothing like..." he waved a paw at me.

Then he glanced at Beckett, jerking his snout for me to look. Beckett had a smile on his face, crying softly as he mumbled to himself, eyes still closed. I studied him. Claire was sitting very attentively beside him, watching, waiting, ready to do anything that he may need. She didn't even seem to notice I was awake, so intent on the detective.

I turned back to Starlight, relieved that he was okay. "What the hell is wrong with me?"

He placed a palm on my thigh and then reached behind him to withdraw a canteen of water. He handed it over and I guzzled it. It was still cold, despite the warmth of the room. I drank all of it, not even considering if it had also been intended for Beckett.

"Nothing is wrong with you, Callie. But unless I know what you saw, I cannot offer any aid."

I nodded absently, but even if I could have remembered it I was pretty much convinced I didn't want to share details about it with Starlight. Not because I didn't trust him, but because I didn't want to give him a front row seat to my inner psyche.

"Have you always spoken Latin?" he asked in a low tone, not wanting to disturb Beckett.

I shot a look at him, ready to shake my head, but then I remembered that I'd had a few out-of-body experiences where I had done just that. "A little," I admitted. "But I can't consciously do it. A few times I've muttered things in my sleep or dreams that people have asked me about, but I don't remember it."

He tapped a long claw against his snout, considering.

"You didn't answer my question. What are you?"

He let out a resigned sigh. "I was a wizard, once. A long, long time ago. I chose this life when it became more... bearable than my own." Then he must have heard his words, because he chuckled. "Bearable. Wow." He shook his head, looking embarrassed. "I experienced some things in my later years that made me lose faith in the Academy, so I found a witch to help me become a bear. I didn't fancy having one attack me, hoping for the change to take me as I bled out in the middle of the woods. It was either let the witch try to do it or kill myself. Luckily, she was able to do it. In a fit of cosmic irony, I found that I still retained some of my magic, but that I couldn't ever shift back to my human form. I was a wizard bear. Not really a shifter, and not really a wizard. But both at the same time."

My mouth was hanging open. "You're not really a shifter, then?"

"Who knows these things? I sure as hell don't. I went through the same problems, but I can't hop back and forth like they do. I ran into Armor not long after and have stuck with him since. In search of inner peace, we traveled the world looking for totems. Something to ground us in reality, neither of us happy with the first life we had been given, and wanting to make this one better. Armor did this by seeking out those like us, the lepers, the outcasts, those who wanted a new life. I focused on old lore, merging my knowledge of magic with any lore on bears I could get my hands on. At some point, they named me Shaman. Medicine Man. Crock of shit, if you ask me," he grunted.

I laughed in surprise. "In the land of the blind, the one-eyed man is king."

He grunted. "I am no king, Callie. Not even close."

"What's your name? Who were you? How long—"

He held up a paw. "I left it behind for a reason, Callie. Respect it, please." There wasn't a hint of kindness in his eyes, so I nodded obediently.

"I'm sorry. I didn't think about that," I admitted sheepishly. "I didn't mean any disrespect. I just don't know much about the Academy. Nate doesn't seem to like them either…"

Starlight grunted. "I should like to meet this Nate Temple someday…" he said, eyes distant.

I shrugged. "I can arrange that."

"Please." He turned to Claire, smiling softly. I followed his gaze, smiling at my best friend.

"Do you really think she can become a Shaman? She was never a wizard."

Starlight didn't immediately respond. "Being a Shaman is not being a wizard. It is a gift granted only to a few bears that I've ever heard of. But there is something different about her…"

"She's special…" I agreed, smiling at her.

Beckett's eyes shot open. "Goddamn!" he whispered. "That was amazing."

I scowled for good measure, but hid it when he looked at me. His eyes latched onto my nakedness and widened. He averted his gaze to turn to Claire, but she was naked and even closer. She didn't seem to notice the panic in his eyes, so focused on her role as spirit guide. She leaned over him and gripped his shoulders, whispering to him in soft tones I couldn't make out. He looked down at himself and saw that he was also naked, and very much excited about his current situation, making his face blush almost purple now. He slapped his hands over his goods, marginally relieved, and finally looked back to me. Well, his eyes were about a foot above my head, as if not wanting to risk his peripheral vision catching a peek at my naked flesh.

"Wasn't that great, Callie?"

I scooped up my clothes with a sigh, but before I could begin tugging them on, Starlight handed me a towel. I mumbled thanks and dried off before getting dressed. I took my time about it, amused at Beckett's furtive glances when he thought I wasn't looking.

When I finished, I looked up to find Claire also clothed and escorting Beckett from the hut with one arm over his shoulder, speaking softly to him about his... well, his trip, I guessed.

I nodded to Starlight. "Thank you..." I whispered, not sure if I meant it. "I think Beckett and I need to leave." He sighed, placing a paw on my shoulder for comfort. I had planned on leaving tomorrow, but the thought of spending one more day here terrified me. I needed to see Roland. Now. Maybe he could help me remember what had scared me so badly.

And if we could change it.

❧ 10 ❧

I approached the fire to find Claire and Beckett joking with Kenai. Several bears dozed nearby while others prowled the perimeter, alert for any danger. Beckett, despite appearing engrossed in the conversation, tracked me with his eyes. I jerked my chin and he didn't even hesitate before standing and offering quick goodbyes to the two bears. Kenai shook his hand, but Claire stood to give him a very... familiar hug. Then she followed Beckett over to me. I could see the confusion on his face as he neared, wondering why she had hugged him goodbye and then followed him. I rolled my eyes. Like randomly catching up with an old friend in a grocery store, saying goodbye, and then realizing that you had parked beside each other.

Claire was trying to avoid my anger, thinking it would bother me if they hugged in front of me. I almost snapped out that we weren't in grade school any longer, but thought better of it.

She meant well.

They reached me and then stood in silence, bringing their icky awkwardness with them. I let out a deep breath, realizing I hadn't shared my experience in the hut, and that I hadn't asked Beckett about his. But we had time for that later. Right now, I needed to see Roland.

"I need to go back. Something has come up," I lied.

Beckett nodded. "I'd rather hitch a ride with you than try walking back or living with these guys for the next few months. They don't seem in a rush to do... well, anything."

Claire shot him a playful punch in the arm. Then she resumed her awkward shift from foot to foot, sensing the dark cloud around me but not wanting to pry in case she was at fault. I held out my arms and she almost let out a sob as she barreled into me. I smiled, inhaling the scent of her hair as I hugged her back. "Take care of yourself and try not to kill them. It will only make more work for you as their medic," I said.

She stepped back, wiping her nose quickly. "I'm sure we'll be back soon. I can't wait to be back in the land of the toilet paper," she said, face serious.

Beckett coughed, smart enough not to comment. Without further ado, I opened a Gateway back to my apartment in Kansas City, not wanting to appear anywhere public out of thin air. The ring of sparks caused some grunts from the nearby bears, but I stepped through without acknowledging them. Beckett followed and we waved one last time to Claire before I closed it.

I breathed in the familiar scent of candles. Home. I turned to Beckett, feeling slightly uncomfortable. I wasn't mad at him because he hadn't done anything wrong. But I wished he hadn't seemed so open to Claire's flirtations. My rationality was locked in the basement.

But that didn't matter. I had the prerogative and natural right as a woman to not have to explain myself – even to myself.

I was angry. Fact. But not at him or Claire. Fact. At... myself, I guessed.

Beckett must have sensed something on my face. "You okay?" he asked, taking a step closer. I could smell his natural scent. It was clean, but sharper from the sweat in the hut. We also reeked of shifter peyote.

I nodded quickly. "I'm fine. Just..." I struggled for an excuse. "The drugs messed with me more than I thought. Just want to check up on some things and then sleep it off."

He nodded, not seeming to buy it, but not challenging it either. "Okay. If you need anything, I'm here." He waited a few seconds for me to change my mind, but I just stood there. The brief image of him ripping my coat and shirt off entered my mind and I almost squeaked.

Not knowing what else to do, I ushered him to the door. He watched me as he left, sensing the tension in the air. "Look, Callie," he began after stepping into the hallway. "You said something came up. If you need any help, please call me."

I nodded stiffly, trying not to slam the door in his face or jump his bones in the hall. What the hell was wrong with me? "Thanks, but I'll be fine."

The door clicked closed and I leaned against it, breathing heavily in order to calm myself. Beckett wasn't mine. I hadn't made any advances on him. It hadn't ever really crossed my mind. He was a good catch, but I hadn't considered him as dating material. I had promised to someday help him find his wife's killer for crying out loud. Subconsciously, that must have put him in the dreaded friend zone.

We had spent a lot of time around each other lately since I'd been trying to catch him up to speed on my world – a crash course in the supernatural. We flirted occasionally, but it was more for fun than anything else. Because I knew he was a widower and had loved his wife like fire.

But all our time together had done something to me, and I had apparently been too close to realize what I was feeling for him. Even now, I wasn't sure I wanted anything more.

But seeing Claire suddenly take an animalistic interest in him, and then serving as his naked spirit guide had bothered me greatly.

But the other thing that bothered me about it all was that a part of me was smitten with a man in St. Louis. Nate Temple.

Now that was a grenade waiting to go off, if our last meetings were any warning. I had kept him at bay, wanting to learn more about myself, my past, my powers, and he'd had plenty on his plate when we first met. But now? It seemed like he was almost in vacation mode, and I couldn't blame him. We'd grabbed dinner recently to catch up and I had been too stunned to eat. Killing a god, having two almost immortal Makers chasing him down, learning that his own past had been a carefully crafted lie – and that his own loved ones had been behind that lie...

Well, you could say he had deserved a little rest and relaxation.

Now, rest and relaxation for Nate wasn't the typical vacation for most. I'd heard that he was still kicking ass – just in a less world-ending way.

I realized I was smiling and muttered under my breath, walking away from the door.

Nate was hot as shit. Powerful as all hell, and although a perfect gentleman when he wanted to be, he was a renegade, a rebel, and I enjoyed that. He was the best kind of crazy – loyal and dependable when the war was on. Calm and lazy as a cat when it wasn't. But did I want that kind of chaos? Especially with our similar powerbase? Him as a Horseman in training and me as... well, whatever I was. In summary, I didn't trust myself around him. Like gasoline and a match.

Beckett, on the other hand, was also handsome as hell, smart, clever, and almost too rational to feel fear. Well, he had *mastered* fear. If something scared him, he quickly found a way to overcome that fear. Not letting it control him. Like finding out about the magical world. He'd accepted the facts with an open mind, and then asked what he needed to know. Unflappable. He was dependable in the other kind of way – steadfast, loyal, and trustworthy. Without the chaos factor. In fact, you could say Beckett Killian was the long-term kind of dating option, where Nate was the bad boy who may or not be able to be housebroken.

And both men had dark relationships in their past. Nate's ex had faced too much power too quickly and had been taken advantage of by those who promised to keep her safe, starting a war.

Beckett's wife had been killed, and now that he was aware of my world – monsters and magic – he was pretty confident that she had been murdered by something from my side of the fence. He hadn't yet wanted to talk about it, but I had promised to help him look into it at some point.

I wondered why he hadn't asked me about it yet. It had been months since I had killed the second demon in town, so he'd had ample time. Maybe...

He was having fun with me, seeing me as more than a friend, and hadn't wanted to bring his murdered wife between us...

I realized I was smiling and slapped my cheeks lightly. I decided to shower later. Now was time to see if Roland could help me remember my vision quest. Girl stuff could wait.

I readied myself to Shadow Walk to Abundant Angel Catholic Church, but a sudden knock at my apartment door made me flinch, almost jumping out of my skin.

I peered through the peephole of my apartment door, expecting Beckett. I stepped back, frowning. Then I checked again. Yep. They were real.

I glanced in the direction of my weapons room, seriously weighing the pros and cons of murdering a few impatient Nephilim. I'd only met one of them before, a black guy with dreads named Alyksandre – I had actually booted him out of the church months ago. The other guy didn't look important in his own right. I spotted an old bag of sliced bread on the counter and a devilish grin split my cheeks. I grabbed it and returned to the door, opening it a crack.

Alyksandre smiled pleasantly. "Callie, we need to—"

"Shoo," I hissed, tossing the bag at him. Then I slammed the door, checking the peephole. He stared down at the bag, his mouth still open. His lips thinned and he rapped on the door again.

"Hilarious. Tossing bread at *pigeons*. Ha. Ha. Ha. Can you please just open the door?"

With a tortured sigh, I complied, flashing him my best glare and ignoring his pal.

"I really, *really* don't have the time or patience for this sh—"

The hallway flashed with blindingly white light as they grabbed me.

❦ 11 ❦

I found myself in a greasy spoon diner across the table from an Angel and two thugs. Well, I assumed it was an Angel, with my having just been abducted by the two Nephilim sitting on either side of him like guard dogs. I had only met Alyksandre up to now, but his pal looked like a real hard ass – pale hair pulled back in a tail and the sides shaved. Stubble covered his cheeks, and his eyes were flecks of greenish blue. His knuckles were scarred and although he looked tough, he also looked green.

The place smelled of coffee, cigarettes, and pancakes. Yum.

The man between the two Nephilim was tall with a long, narrow face and triple-cleft chin. His wavy blonde hair brushed the top of his black trench coat. Underneath he wore a tee with a picture of Jesus on it. The caption below the picture made me cough: *I never said that – Jesus.*

The man wore sunglasses.

I glanced out the wall of windows beside me before turning back to him. I placed my head in my palms. It was either that or begin thumping my head against the cheap stained table between us. Patrons had actually used the table itself to extinguish their cigarettes over the years, so I didn't want to touch it with my head. No head thumping, then.

"You must be Angel the Angel," I finally mumbled, looking back up at him.

He gave me a slow nod, not finding the absurdity in the chosen name. "How did you know?"

"My first hint was the two Nephilim that just abducted me. But the real kicker is that only an Angel named Angel would be the kind of douche to wear sunglasses at night."

"It's a disguise. What is a douche?" Alyksandre's eyes tightened with anxiety, but Angel didn't notice, cocking his head at me.

I lowered my head to one palm, propping my elbow on the table as I muttered to myself. "I can't do this... I can't do this..." I casually held out my other hand to the side and began snapping my fingers in an irregular rhythm, fast and then slow. Double. Pause. Single snap.

"You haven't even heard why I summoned you here." he said, frowning. "What is it you think you can't do?" In my peripheral vision, the three sets of eyes took in my snapping fingers, and I could see their jaws beginning to clench in both thinly veiled annoyance and curiosity.

"I meant that I can't deal with *you* right now," I said, forehead still in my palm. "Mommy needs some wine, and the naked toddler keeps riding his invisible dinosaur around the kitchen screaming *Old McDonald Had a Farm* as loud as possible." *Snap. Snap. Snap*, I continued.

They were silent so I looked back up. The three of them stared at me as if I was drunk.

I smiled back, still snapping erratically as I lowered my other hand below the table, concentrating. This next part was dicey. "That look. That's exactly what I feel right now. You have no idea what my statement meant so you have no idea how to respond. That's how I feel around you guys."

Angel stared at me for a few minutes, eyes actually twitching at the snapping sound now. He hadn't noticed the magic under the table, too distracted by the constant snapping of my fingers. He leaned forward. "You belong with us, working for me, not the Vatican. You have been marked, you have our blood."

"Not going to happen. We just met." I felt like sweat was popping out on my forehead as I concentrated below the table, stretching. "And I already don't like your HR Department."

"Would you stop that?" he hissed.

"Why?" I asked, sounding bored. *Stretch...*

"Why are you doing it?" he asked, grinding his teeth at each snap of my fingers.

I shrugged. "Keeps me grounded." It was an effort to talk, I was concentrating so hard under the table. I *needed* this. Badly.

"You are going to work for us. Where you belong," he commanded.

"Nah," I said lazily, forcing a yawn. I was going to pass out soon. My vision was already tunneling as I worked beneath the table. *Almost there...*

"It wasn't a question," he snarled. The smell of burnt plastic filled the air, the table melting underneath his fingertips.

I stopped snapping my fingers, a slow smile stretching over my face as I finished my spell. I was almost ready to pass out, but I kept the exhaustion from my voice. "Ah, that's better. Now, here's how this is going to work. I will make my own decisions. Or the silver blade beneath the table will impale you. One wrong move and you die. Right here, right now. In this shitty diner."

All three froze, wanting to scoot back but respecting my resolve. Angel flicked his eyes down at his lap and saw the silver blade I had extended right up to his stomach, almost touching him. Using my Heavenly magic had been a gamble, but that's why I had been snapping my fingers. A distraction. I knew he wasn't very familiar with my world, thanks to talking with Nate, and would be bothered by the erratic clicking of my fingers to the point he might overlook my magic.

It had worked. Angel was watching me very intensely, his eyes seeming to spark. He looked... surprised. Hooray.

"I'm leaving. Try to stop me and we all die here," I warned.

The two Nephilim just stared at me, furious. Angel gave a subtle jerk of his chin. "One week."

"Whatever," I muttered.

"You have heard the Whispers..." he added. I froze, something about the way he had said it made my skin crawl. He didn't move, but the look of surprise was turning into a hungry, anticipatory smirk. I could tell he was already calculating how to use my ability to his benefit. From the sudden flinch of his Nephilim, I realized this Whisper business was news to them, too.

"I hear whispers all the time..." I waved a hand, trying not to squirm.

He shook his head. "Not like this. They will aid you, but they come with a price. Free will doesn't always lead down a good path."

"What are you talking about?"

His eyes flicked down to the silver blade again. "They helped you. You listened to them. Fed them. They are of Heaven. The power of Angels." He leaned forward, careful not to impale himself. "Both light and dark Angels. Be very, very careful with what they tell you, Miss Penrose." Then he leaned back again, smiling smugly. "I think we're going to have a lot of excitement soon. In about one week, to be exact. I can't wait."

"What do you know of my father?" my voice sounded like a sword leaving a sheath.

His grin grew anticipatory. "When do you start working for me?"

I kept my face blank, but I almost shoved the blade into his gut. I glanced at the two Nephilim beside him, making sure they understood what had just happened. Extortion from an Angel. "Be careful who you choose to follow." Their faces slackened, realizing they had been placed in a very awkward situation. Acknowledge me and piss off their boss, or defend their boss and admit they were okay with his tactics.

Angel's eyes sparked, but he didn't speak. The two Nephilim looked like they would rather be anywhere else but here.

I'd had enough. Before they could change their minds, or before I rationalized killing the lot of them, I Shadow Walked out of the diner, stumbling as I landed. Then I let out a relieved breath as I studied the familiar walls of the training room beneath Abundant Angel Catholic Church. Whispers? What the hell was he talking about? Was that what I had heard in Alaska? Something to do with my silver powers? I thought it had been the wind, or my imagination.

I'd been practicing my new power for a little while now, but the whispers were entirely new. I hadn't ever heard them before tonight. What did that mean? I shook my head, muttering angrily.

I had to admit that I was stunned by the Angel. Deliberately withholding information from me to get me to work for him? An agent of Heaven using *extortion*? What the hell kind of world did I live in? At least he had made my answer easy enough, not that I had any intention of working for him before the meeting, but at least I had no guilt about it now.

I didn't have time for Angel's strong-arm shit. Especially when he hadn't bothered to help me fight a demon several months ago. Actions spoke louder than words, and I had never done well with authority. I wasn't going to have a serious discussion with this particular Angel until I had met the one in St. Louis, Eae, the Demon Thwarter. Nate said he vouched for him, and that he would give me the unvarnished truth. I would ask him about these Whispers. I wasn't about to make a deal without knowing everything at stake.

I didn't want to work for the Nephilim. I didn't want to work for anyone.

But it looked like I needed to have a meeting with Eae sooner rather than later, because the Angel in Kansas City seemed entirely too interested in me, and pretty soon I would be forced into a decision – and its consequences.

I was understandably proud that I had managed to use my new magic for something productive. Making a silver sword right under his nose. Had I heard any Whispers? I couldn't recall, so shrugged it off. Later.

12

P art of me considered my casual use of magic. Rather than jogging or driving places lately, I had relied more and more on my magical means of travel.

Gateways could be opened between two locations, creating a flaming, sparking doorway through nothingness – ripping a hole in reality to connect two geographical places that typically didn't touch. Imagine an ant needing to get from one end of a string to the other. Gateways were akin to pulling the two ends of the string together like a bridge rather than the ant walking the whole length of it.

The other option was Shadow Walking – where I imagined a place in my mind and instead of connecting that place to my current location, I ripped my own body to that new location.

Sounds horrifyingly dangerous, but apparently it wasn't.

But Roland liked to give me crap about being lazy as often as possible. *Power corrupts, idle hands are the Devil's workshop, blah, blah, blah.*

I rolled my eyes at the imagined response from my mentor. "Two feet have carried me this far in life, and relying too much on easy solutions taints the soul," I said in my best impersonation.

"I don't sound like that, Callie," a voice growled from a dark corner of the training room. I flinched, jumping back two steps to find my mentor staring at me, his eyes reflecting the candle light beside him. He'd been meditating.

The Vatican Shepherd unfolded from his crouch, rubbed his hands together, and then walked my way. I blinked at him, remembering the time. "The Early Bird Special keeps getting earlier and earlier," I mused.

He rolled his eyes with a patient sigh. "I'm not that old, Callie. Not yet."

"Well, what the hell are you doing up? I had this whole plan to dump holy water on you while you slept..." I complained.

"I thought you were in Alaska? Make too many jokes with Armor and he chased you out?"

I grunted, sobering up. "No. But I do need to talk to you about something..." This wasn't going to be fun. Not just what I had seen but forgotten in the vision, but telling him that I had taken drugs. It almost felt like admitting it to my dad.

I let it all out in a rush. "I smoked some shifter reefer and saw something so scary that I forgot it all. Or my mind locked it away. And I just threatened an Angel after he abducted me. Have you ever heard of the Whispers?"

He blinked at me. He opened his mouth and then closed it. Then he shook his head, muttering as he ran his hand across his scalp, which was buzzed close to the skin. He looked as if I had just shit on his already shitty day. "I... need my coffee. But first I need to show you something." He turned his back on me and began walking from the training room towards the utility room behind it. He shifted a loose brick on the wall and a keypad slid out. He placed a thumb on it and the entire wall shifted back, revealing a rickety service elevator. I stared at him, frowning at his unexpected reaction, but finally followed. This couldn't be good.

He blindly reached out to snatch up a thermos from a side table, and began guzzling it as he stepped into the elevator, holding it open for me with his other hand. He lowered the thermos as I joined him, wiped his mouth and cleared his throat. I didn't smell any scotch in the air, but he had tossed back the thermos as if it was last call before a tour in Iraq. I noticed that his eyes were bloodshot and frowned. Was he drunk or just exhausted?

He leaned forward and typed in a code, concealing it from my view because he knew me so well. I averted my eyes innocently, troubled by his demeanor. I'd never seen him use a code on the elevator before. Was he taking me to one of the restricted levels? One of the levels so secret that even after over ten years training with him I hadn't been allowed to see? Was that where he stored his Manna from Heaven, his Biblical Brew?

Coupled with his bloodshot eyes and his sudden caffeine addiction, I felt a very uneasy sensation in the pit of my stomach. Did his choice to let me finally see these floors have anything to do with what I'd told him? Maybe one of the floors was a rehab clinic where he was going to detox me with holy water, washing out the sin from my system.

Like that would be possible.

He'd need a helluva lot of holy water to do the trick.

I watched the stone wall ahead of us as the cage-like elevator descended, counting the doors we passed by. We passed three levels, and I had no idea what they contained. We stopped one floor above the dungeon – the lowest floor I was aware of – and my arms pebbled with anticipation as Roland heaved the door up, the metal squeaking and shuddering like an old storage unit. This was going to be super cool. I just knew it.

I followed him into a stone hallway, wondering what amazing sights I was about to witness.

My excitement began to die after five minutes of walking through a stone hallway. We finally exited the cramped tunnel and I gasped in astonishment, staring up at a vast stone cavern. Hundreds of doors hung on chains from the ceiling, all different colors and styles – some of stone, wood, glass, metal, and made in just as many patterns. Each was entirely unique. Some looked to belong to castles, some to homes, even one that was just a curtain of beads. Some of the doors spun in lazy rotations from their individual chains, others were entirely still. There were no torches, but the cavern had an ambient glow to it. Either that or I just couldn't see the recessed lighting. But I was pretty sure it was magic because this place didn't look remotely modern. Well, other than some of the more expensive doors.

I turned to find Roland studying me. "You needed to see this place," he said in a low tone, almost sounding regretful.

I frowned. "Why now?" I asked uncertainly.

He tapped his lip absently, eyes a million miles away. He finally let out a deep breath. "A Shepherd was murdered in Rome."

I gasped, one hand instinctively rushing to my chest. "What?" Shepherds were badasses of the highest order. They trained for dozens of years – in their faith, their magic, and their bodies. They were the supernatural military arm of the Vatican Church, hunting monsters, demons, and anything else that God wasn't a fan of. Or, more accurately, that the Pope and his Cardinals weren't a fan of.

He nodded grimly. "I only just heard. It's why I was awake. Planning my trip to Rome."

"Well, let's fucking go! Let's Shadow Walk!" I said anxiously, mind racing at the thought of what or who could take down a Shepherd. They weren't invincible, but they were tough to kill. Extremely tough. Let's just say that only a dozen Shepherds were required to take care of the entire world. The more I thought about it, the more I wanted to go. I had good reasons to skip town right now. Angel wouldn't be pleased at my exit.

Roland was shaking his head. "Shadow Walking is not permitted. At least not into the Vatican. Sure, we could arrive outside of town and then travel in, but it's frowned upon."

I blinked incredulously. "Well, I'm not too concerned about making a few old men frown," I argued. "One of your friends was just *killed*. We need to find out what's going on, right?"

Roland nodded at my last question, but held up a hand, stalling me. "The trip to Rome is considered a penance. One must travel there in contemplation, accepting the gravitas of the situation. It's why we don't Shadow Walk or make a Gateway. Also, the wards prevent direct entry – to keep the Vatican safe from attack."

"Well, consider my gravitas full. I think we can bend a few rules under the circumstances."

He sighed wearily, not completely convinced. "Perhaps."

I studied him. He wasn't telling me everything. And he had chosen to show me this strange room when he could have simply explained everything upstairs. I glanced back at all the doors hanging above us like bird cages. "What are these, Roland? And if time is of the essence, why are we here rather than getting on a plane or whatever ridiculousness you were planning?"

He cleared his throat. "You needed to see this," he said, holding out his hand. "For the day that I may not be here any longer. You need—"

I plugged my ears. "Nope. Not listening to that nonsense. One, because you aren't dying. Two, because I don't want to be a Shepherd. I'm not like you. I don't follow rules well. You know this, Roland. I don't know how many times I have to explain it. Our motives are different, even if our means align. I don't want monsters running amok, but I'm not doing it so that God can sleep better at night. And I'm especially not doing it for the Vatican. Have you forgotten that one of them betrayed us?" I said icily. "Almost getting us both killed." Another thought hit me. "Wait, the dead Shepherd..." he winced at my callousness, and I felt momentarily guilty before pressing on. "Do you think he was betrayed like we were? That there might be another mole?"

Roland... hesitated. I sucked in a breath of disbelief. He saw the look on my face and began shaking his head urgently. "I am not ruling it out, but after the last mole, they went through rigid security checks on all personnel. I don't see how..."

"Never discount the foolhardiness of a bureaucracy," I said angrily.

His shoulders tensed instinctively, but he finally sighed. "I'm considering that avenue, don't worry. But none of my compatriots will hear it." He turned back to the doors. "Regardless of your beliefs, Callie, you are a Shepherd in training. Unorthodox, sure, but you're tied to the Church whether you want it or not. They don't let go easily."

"We'll see about that," I muttered.

Roland rounded on me, actually taking a step closer. "Grow up, girl," he warned, face reddening. That made me slow down. Not his anger, but that there might actually be some truth to his words. Me being stubborn wasn't helping anything. He was trying to show me something important to him. We could debate semantics later.

"Fine, old man. But if I need to grow up, you need to bring your ass to the modern age. Taking a horse and buggy to Rome won't help anyone. Just because something has always been done a certain way doesn't mean it should continue. The demons and bad guys know this. I think the Shepherds should stop reminiscing and wake the fuck up."

Roland didn't like that one bit.

13

His hand instinctively went to the sword on his hip. He was panting, glaring at me with barely restrained rage. An instinctive reaction to attacking his cause. I squared my shoulders and returned his glare. He finally released the hilt and let out a breath. Not apologizing, but backing down. "You... are right," he finally admitted. I nodded neutrally, not wanting to press him further. I had stated my case. The rest was up to him. If the Shepherds didn't evolve, they weren't going to last long. Which was probably why he constantly peppered me to join. New blood. A different perspective. The Shepherds needed fresh ideas.

I was especially leery of their interest since they were apparently down one man, now.

But that wasn't going to happen. Just like with Angel, I wouldn't be backed into a corner.

"So, the doors..." I offered, changing the topic, my mind racing with plans. I had never been to the Vatican, and wasn't sure how I felt about going. Especially under these circumstances.

He nodded. "They are doorways to other places, countries, and realms. Some accessible, most not. Over time, we have lost the ability to use many." He pointed at one particular door, which was a charred mass of carbon. "Others had a welcoming committee on the other side," he added drily.

I blinked, taking in the hundreds of doors. Then I frowned at him.

"Well, which one do we need, and why am I just now hearing about them? Shouldn't we be hurrying?"

"I just told you why. They're unpredictable." He had ignored my last question. Why?

"And you just have a bunch of entrances to other places hanging around beneath Kansas City..." I said, hoping he caught my tone.

"We have many such repositories in the world. At the other ends of the doors."

I felt an instinctive shiver, suddenly realizing why the floor had been locked up from me. If we could use the doors, so could others, giving them a back entrance into our compound. I rounded on Roland to find him watching me. He nodded, reading my panic. "Exactly right." He extended a hand up high to reveal several doors wrapped in glowing, golden chains, prevented from opening. They were so high up I hadn't noticed them. Then he pointed at the floor, where large runes were carved into the stone. I frowned, walking closer to inspect them. They looked like Enochian script – the language of Angels. Powerful stuff. "For the most part, these keep us safe. Also, the hallway has wards to prevent unadmitted access. I had to get approval for you to use it, otherwise you would still be sobbing on the floor near the elevator."

I blinked, surprised. "Oh..." I scanned the doors and realized quite a few of them were chained up, although not as heavily as others. A few even sported glowing golden locks. Looking closer, I saw that golden crosses adorned the chains and locks. "Why are you showing me now?"

"Because we will be using them shortly. To get to the Vatican. There is a trial, and a hearing."

I frowned. "A trial and a hearing? They already caught the murderer?" Was that why we hadn't left yet?

He looked entirely uncomfortable for a few moments. "The two wolves we saved from the rapists. Jasmine and Tiffany. They were found at the scene." He met my eyes warily, but my mind was reeling. The two rape victims had killed a Shepherd? "But the hearing is for you..."

My brain fizzled, overloaded by his last statement. I held up my hands, taking a step back, forgetting all about the wolves. "No, Roland. I'm not going to the Vatican to be questioned. I don't work for them."

Roland began ticking off fingers, not looking pleased with himself, but simply stating the facts. "You have lived, trained, and studied with me for over a decade, accepting the Vatican's resources and paychecks. By default – common law, if you will – you are an extension of the church, and therefore fall under their jurisdiction. Whether you want to become a Shepherd or not. You *owe* them a hearing."

My vision throbbed both in fear and anger. "On *what*? I haven't done anything wrong!"

He blinked. "It's not a trial, Callie. It's a *hearing*. They want to meet you. And likely to ask about the Spear of Longinus..." he said carefully.

I grimaced. "Well... that's not good. Do they know about it?"

Roland looked very torn at that, but didn't hesitate as he shook his head. "They do not." He was internally bothered that he hadn't told his superiors the full truth. A mole had sold us out to the demons, and he hadn't wanted to risk them learning about it. But it was still a lie, and Roland was not big on deceit, especially to the Vatican.

The Spear of Longinus – the blade that had pierced Jesus Christ's side during the crucifixion.

It all started when a demon named Johnathan decided that he would use the three broken pieces of the Spear – that should have been locked up in the Vatican – to lure me out of hiding. My birth parents had pissed him off at some point, and he had spent twenty years searching for yours truly, unbeknownst to me. I had beaten him, but the Spear had disappeared. His pal, Amira, had come at me with a vengeance after that. In some alternate dimension – or a dream – I had met her, and she had pointed down at my hand, which held the three pieces of the Spear, reforged into one whole again. It was still damaged, weakened by rings of darkness where the pieces connected, but I was holding it like it belonged to me.

When I woke, the Spear was gone. I had killed her, but was nowhere closer to accessing the Spear again. It was locked away inside me. Roland and I had tried numerous times, in numerous ways, to call it forth, but had so far been unsuccessful.

"They are wondering where Amira could have hidden it if she took it after Johnathan's death, and why we haven't found it yet, since you killed her."

"So, it *is* a trial..." I spat. "I find the timing particularly coincidental," I said in a flat tone.

He shook his head. "An inquiry. A hearing."

"You can church it up as much as you want, but slapping lipstick on a pig doesn't make it a whore."

He blinked, and then as if forced, he burst out laughing. The unexpected sound echoed around us and I realized I was smiling. He had needed that. A genuine laugh. "We'll need to work on your delivery before we address Mass," he finally said, wiping a tear from his eyes.

I sighed. "This is going to suck, isn't it?" He nodded. "What about the two wolves?" I asked, remembering his other news. "Do you really think they killed him? Why would they do that? The Shepherds were helping them recover from their trauma."

He looked concerned. "They were found injured beside the body. As if there had been a fight. We leave in a few hours," he said, eyeing the doors warily.

I felt my stomach drop out and splat onto the floor. "Well, shit."

"Shit, indeed," Roland agreed, still looking concerned about the two women in Italy. He was practically a veteran sailor with his newfound gift of cursing. This wasn't good.

But if we were leaving tomorrow morning, we had another problem, and it was obvious that Roland had completely forgotten about it in his fear for the girls.

We had an appointment with Haven, Master Vampire of Kansas City tomorrow night.

14

Without another word, he led me back towards the elevator. I took one last glance at the suspended doors before the tunnel swallowed us back up. I tried to sense the wards Roland had mentioned, but felt nothing. I wondered how I had been granted access without Roland doing any magic on me. Then I stumbled. Did... the Vatican have some essence of myself – hair, blood, nail clippings? I eyed the large man's back as I thought. It made sense. In a very creepy, Big Brother kind of way.

I scanned the walls, not trying to sense the wards reacting to me but just feeling out the wards in general – maybe spot a marking carved into the stone. But I saw nothing. Whispers called out to me and I spun. Roland paused, frowning at the alarm on my face. "What's wrong?" he asked.

I stared at him, listening as the sounds faded. I suppressed a shiver and shook my head. I hadn't been able to make anything out. Just faint whispering sounds. I didn't want to add more to Roland's plate, so let it go, but inside I was terrified.

What the hell was happening to me?

"So, the Vatican has a piece of me," I said out loud, my voice echoing in the tunnel.

Roland grunted. "Yes."

I wanted to kick him in the kidneys but knew it wouldn't do any good. It was over and done with anyway. "Anyone else you've given my DNA to that I should know about?" I snarled.

"By the way, they're called the Conclave. They guide the Shepherds, and you can trust them."

"Except when you can't," I fired back. The Conclave... it sounded both religious and ominous. Why hadn't he shared that name with me before? I wasn't very excited about all these revelations. It signified that I was getting closer to their secrets, tied to them with invisible strings. Closer to becoming one of them.

Roland didn't have a response to my comment, remembering all too well the traitor who had sold us out to the demons. The man had blown himself up rather than turning himself in. That was dedication for you.

I followed Roland into the elevator and stared ahead at the passing doors as he brought us back up to the training area. He exited and approached the wall where my dragon-chain weapon hung all by itself. He smirked at me over his shoulder and then touched part of the trim on the floor. The wall swung up on silent hinges, revealing a small room behind it, complete with a few chairs, a fireplace, and a well-stocked bar. He set his thermos on a table.

I blinked at Roland. "No wonder you fought me so hard on using this wall for my weapon!" I hissed, following him into the room. He flicked on two lamps, poured two drinks that smelled like cognac, and then handed one to me before sitting down with a tired sigh. I inspected the unique, bell-shaped glass – a snifter – and took a whiff. Definitely cognac.

I sat in the other chair and touched glasses with him before taking a sip. As I did, Roland casually flicked his wrist at the cold fireplace which suddenly flared to life as if it had been burning for hours, filling the room with a soothing heat that was not conducive to staying awake.

"So, Whispers, drugs, visions, and the Angel..." Roland said, leaning back with his eyes closed. "Start wherever seems to make the most sense since it all sounds terrible." I glanced over to see him smirking to himself, resigned to hear about my failures.

I took another drink and then began to talk. He particularly enjoyed the sparring, but before long he was sitting up, head cocked as he listened in rapt attention. At one point, he even held up a hand for me to pause so he could grab more liquor from the bar. He took a sip straight from the decanter and then filled my snifter to the brim before settling back into his chair, hugging the crystal bottle like a security blanket. He drank often, muttering under his breath as he shook his head – both in disbelief and concern. Especially about my forgotten visions.

First cursing, now alcoholism. This wasn't good. Roland was in the badlands.

Once finished, I took a shaky breath and tried to mask my fear by taking a long drink. It burned on the way down, but I also felt something loosen in my neck, some unknown tension.

Roland was now staring into the fire, seeming to argue with himself. He glanced back, not directly at me, but over his shoulder. "Starlight used to be a wizard... I never knew that."

I turned to him. "After all that, you focus on the teddy bear?"

He shrugged. "Easiest one first. How about this?" he said, leaning forward as he pinned me to my seat with a glare. "You got high, and then saw things that scared you so badly that you mentally locked them away," he said.

I scowled at him. "I was in a spiritual place. It's an ancient rite of pass—"

"You were stoned, Callie. Let's not bandy words. I'm not discrediting your story, but I do want you to be honest with yourself. You were literally high when you had these... *visions*. Sometimes people have very bad experiences on drugs, and their minds can only take so much."

He didn't sound angry, he sounded... academic. I still wanted to throttle him. I knew it hadn't just been a bad trip. I had seen something. Something important. "You want to tell Starlight that his spiritual hut is just a stoner's lodge? Let me know. I can call him right now, but I'd really rather see you tell him in person." I frowned. "In fact, I can take you straight to the bears. We can get them all together so you can call them junkies..."

Roland grumbled in frustration until he saw the smile on my cheeks.

"I'm being serious, Callie. You have to admit the possibility that you just had a bad experience. You said Beckett was fine..." he added, not sounding pleased that the detective hadn't grabbed me by the hair to drag me out of the hut. "My only advice on the visions is to let them simmer on the back burner. If they were important, they'll come back to you." He took a swig of his drink, smiling crookedly. "But good little boys and girls don't do drugs. We're Catholic. We drink," he said, wiping his mouth with his sleeve.

I laughed. The image of Roland drinking from the bottle while judging me. "Shifter weed, the gateway drug," I sighed. "Kids these days, right? With their dang-fangled electronic telephones and whatnot. Back in my day, I had to *really* want to call someone, or track down a pigeon—"

"Hilarious," Roland interrupted. "I'm dying laughing over here. Seriously." His voice had all the emotion of a slab of stone.

I sighed. "You can at least try to lighten up. The Vatican wants to question me about giving a demon the Holy Waterboarding treatment without permission, shifter reefer ruined my life, I just threatened an Angel, I'm hearing whispers in my head—"

He looked suddenly alert, recalling my brief explanation. "Whispers... And you couldn't understand them? What did they sound like? Was it English or something else?"

I tried to recall, but finally grunted. "They sounded like goddamned whispers, Roland. I couldn't make anything out clearly, but the Angel seemed pretty interested in them."

He tapped his lips in frustration. "I've never heard of them," he admitted. "But you used your silver magic on an Angel? And he didn't notice? That's impressive. I'm even more surprised he didn't flay you alive for refusing to work for him. He's an Angel, Callie..."

"I've told you over and over again that I have a problem working for groups of people in general. Anytime you're working for a group, the mission statement can change and become political. This applies to both the Vatican and the Angels. You know this. I'm not taking a stab at God or Christianity, I'm saying I don't want to work for anyone I haven't personally met."

He scowled back at me, but finally conceded my point. "But Nephilim and an *Angel!*"

I shrugged. "Allegedly. Let's be clear about something. They have literally done nothing to help me before. The only Nephilim I can say that tried to help me was Gabriel – who was murdered before my eyes by Johnathan, and I can't even say he was a big help, because he lied about who he was. And what if he didn't actually work for Angel the Angel?" I added. "Because so far, their track record is less than stellar." Roland sighed, nodding his agreement, but likely ready to chime in with *Free Will* this, or *Free Will* that. I wasn't having any of it. I was judging on actions, not titles. "I'm more interested in finding out what they know about my father, not their quest for good will and peace on earth. If they don't share, we're done. Even if they do share, I may still walk away. I'm not looking for a Sunday School lesson."

Roland stared at me, both angry and... agreeable, I realized with a frown.

"That... is very logical." He met my eyes, looking concerned. "And if you're wrong, that is very... stupid. They don't suffer disrespect lightly. Especially not twice."

"I don't suffer *fools*, Roland. Or those who would use me for their ends. They haven't helped me. Not once. For such a supreme group of noble fuckers, their virtues are sorely lacking."

Roland grimaced at my choice of words, but he couldn't argue my point.

I met his eyes, trying to let him know I was finished talking about it. He finally relented.

I cleared my throat in relief. "Now, tell me about the murder. Was he a friend? And what were the wolves doing with him?"

Roland's eyes grew very far away, the silence in our small room seeming hollow enough to shatter at anything louder than a breath. "Constantine. He was... my mentor."

"Fucking hell..." I muttered.

❧ 15 ❧

H e was so lost in thought that he didn't even admonish me, which was saying a lot. He could almost do that in his sleep by now. "I'm sorry, Roland..." he nodded absently, staring into the flames. I waited for him to speak, and when he didn't, I pressed. "You don't really think the girls did this, do you? Jasmine and Tiffany?" He shook his head angrily. "How much do you know?" The cynical part of me had reared her head. If Roland had found this out from the Vatican, did he even know the truth or had they fed him a lie? Was there another traitor? What if it was an inside job to frame the wolves and make Roland look bad? He had said they cleaned house, but cockroaches could hide anywhere, and the better they were at hiding, the more dangerous they were. Hell, the last one hadn't been particularly crafty, but he had sure taken a page from suicide bombers, willing to risk dozens of lives rather than be caught.

Roland spoke very softly. "After I left to come back here, Constantine took them under his wing as a personal favor. He went on patrol in the city, letting them tag along with him for practice, much as you and I did in the beginning." I smiled nostalgically. Werewolf Shepherds? Cool. "They were late bloomers, and although they hadn't had any accidents, they still needed to be supervised for safety. They had been doing very well – able to shift at will, control their anger, and scent like they were born to it..." he said, smiling proudly. I stared at him. That was big. Shifting at will? This early?

That was impressive. "They had found a new purpose in life, deciding to use their curse for good, rather than fall into depression. Surprisingly, they don't hate men, which is very rare. They consider this a new shot at life. To make sure what happened to them never happens to anyone else." His voice had taken on a dark edge, as if remembering the night we had saved them.

We had found them chained to the wall in a bakery's storage room. The thug werewolves had infected them and raped them. Repeatedly. The noble, calm Shepherd before me had killed them in the most brutally efficient manner I had ever seen. An execution.

It had been a short, sweet symphony of carnage set to the tempo of a sunrise.

Roland took a calming breath. "I didn't want this life for them, and neither did they, but I'll take it over the alternatives. It's not like I can bring them back from the dead. Who they were before doesn't matter anymore. To the world at large, especially your friend Beckett, they died. Their choice, not mine."

I clicked my teeth shut at the last statement. "Beckett could—"

Roland shot a red-rimmed eye at me. He shook his head very slowly. "No. They asked this of me, and I will see their wishes fulfilled. The two women we found in the bakery are dead. Two wolves rose from the ashes, and they want to do some good in the world. They can't do that if anyone discovers they survived. Swear it."

I nodded, but Roland didn't lower his glare until I lifted my hands in surrender. He finally muttered under his breath and turned back to the fire. I wondered if the church was trying to indoctrinate them into becoming Shepherds. Or Initiates like me. Shepherds in training. The Junior Varsity God Squad. "What happened next?" I asked.

Roland was shaking his head. "It doesn't make any sense..." he growled, sounding pissed off. "I know them. They wouldn't have laid a finger on Constantine. He was like a father to them..."

"Roland..."

He finally tensed his shoulders, voice bitter. "I wasn't *allowed* to talk to them. They're imprisoned." I tried to maintain my steady breathing so as not to set him off. They had survived rape and kidnapping, only to be turned into werewolves against their will – to be used as baby-makers to build a new pack. Then, they had found a way to turn that curse into something good – at least as far as Roland had been told. But... now they were accused of killing the one man who had taken them in? It didn't make any sense. Roland and I had saved them from a life of slavery. If anything, the church should be their best friend. They had no motive.

"What happened?" I repeated.

The room was silent as Roland considered his response. "It happened last week, but the Conclave waited to tell me until tonight," he snarled. "The girls were found naked, injured, and unconscious beside Constantine's body. His throat had been slit. No surveillance, but they have witnesses," he whispered. Crap. It looked exactly like the wolves had killed him and taken a victory nap.

Roland saw my face, and his eyes lit with an inner fire. "That is why I must go to the Vatican. Even if you weren't requested as well, I would still go, to vouch for them and get to the bottom of this disaster. I know them, Callie. I can read young women. They didn't do this. The witnesses are wrong."

I nodded, mind racing. I was more objective about the subject than Roland because I hadn't spent as much time around them. They hadn't had time to latch onto me, but I had heard how devoted they had become to Roland. Perhaps they had shifted and been startled to see someone other than Roland beside them. A man. Self-defense, in an odd, twisted way. But... that didn't track with their supposed records.

I stood and walked over to Roland, placing a hand on his shoulder. His muscles were rigid beneath my hand, showing me how worked up he was. He was genuinely concerned for these girls. Protective. But did that make him biased? Was his heart or his mind in charge?

"If you trust them, Roland, I believe you. But word of advice. If you go around telling people you are a good judge of character, and they meet me, they'll call you the worst liar in the world."

He stiffened, glancing up at me with wet eyes. A surprised laugh coughed up from his stomach, despite his best efforts. "Thank you, Callie," he whispered. "Maybe I can reschedule your hearing for a few weeks after I get this taken care of. I'd hate for your performance to ruin my chances at proving their innocence," he said, eyes twinkling with amusement.

I rolled my eyes. "Men. See a new piece of candy and forget all about their previous commitments. Always trading up for the newest model..." I muttered, feigning anger.

He shrugged. "It's the way it's always been done, and I would hate to change that." He winked at me.

"We'll figure this out together. But if we're leaving tomorrow, we have a few things to take care of." He frowned, and then his eyes widened.

"I almost forgot. The vampire meeting is tomorrow!" he all but hissed. "When do we meet them? Have you scoped the place out? Made sure we're covered in case it's a trap of some ki—"

"We're good to go. Tomorrow at midnight. For lunch," I added drily, using Haven's words.

Roland rolled his eyes. "Vampires," he spat. "Hilarious at the jokes." He tapped his lips, thinking. "Let's go right now. Rome is seven hours ahead of us, so I would rather leave early. But if we cancel on Haven that slippery bastard will put us off for weeks. At least we can say we did something useful before we left." He snapped his fingers and the fire went out. His eyes caught the light from the other room, looking downright sinister. "And it would be nice if Haven decided to upset me right now. I've got some things I need to work out. Some Free Will to exercise..."

I smiled, shaking my head, realizing I was going to get no chance for sleep tonight. Also, Roland had cursed again. He was well and truly on the highway to Hell.

We had been trying to schedule a meeting with the Master Vampire of Kansas City for months now. Haven wanted to show us that he had his people in line, and I wanted to get more familiar with the various factions in town. I had no reason to suspect Haven of doing anything wrong, but that meant it was the perfect time to go scope his operations out.

So that if he ever did do something wrong, I knew exactly where to find him and all his little vampires. So I could kill them all with less effort.

"Let's go see the vampires," I said sweetly. "Unannounced should be fun."

Roland replied by cocking a pistol and following me from the training room.

We drove up to Haven's mansion about an hour later, around three in the morning, not wanting to Shadow Walk there and start an all-out war. Seeing my truck pull up to the gates was alarming enough, judging by the stunned looks on the guards' faces.

"We weren't expecting you until tomorrow," one guard said. I didn't recognize him.

"It's three in the morning. That counts."

The guard beside him leaned in to whisper something into his ear. The speaking guard nodded, and then flashed me a fake smile. "I will call in to see if he's available."

I leaned out the window. "We're here for a pleasant, previously agreed-upon meeting, but that can always change. For your sake, and his, I surely hope you can reach him. Good help is so hard to find these days. And I'm bitchy when tired."

His shoulders stiffened at my subtle hint that he wouldn't survive if I didn't get the answer I wanted, but his fellow guard placed a hand on his shoulder. I recognized him as one of the guards I had met at a gala when Haven first came to town. Looked like he had been demoted, but still had some credibility if the lead guard here was listening to his advice. His warning.

The lead guard finally departed with a nod to place a call on a cell phone.

Roland was leaning out the other window, inhaling deeply. "Did you know these woods are famous? Used to make the best spears for miles from these trees. Stakes, spears, even the beams for the local church." He shrugged, pretending not to notice the tightened look in the guard's eyes. "What I hear, anyway." He leaned closer and took another sniff. "You're human."

The guard nodded. He wasn't as talkative as the last time I had seen him.

I took the time to study our surroundings. I had been here before with Nate Temple, under cover of darkness, to steal back one of the stolen pieces of the Spear of Longinus. It had been a setup, and the vampires had attacked, forcing us to kill a lot of them before escaping with our prize. The previous Master Vampire − Simon − hadn't survived.

Now the Spear was inside me, and we didn't know how to summon it.

And we had no one to ask about it, because asking would only get me locked up for poking and prodding by the Conclave. After all, the Spear was theirs, and if the Spear was locked up inside me, that must make me belong to them as well. At least that's how I thought it would play out. And Roland had agreed.

In short order, the gates began to open, and the guards let me through, their faces decidedly pale. I smiled at them, waving before I continued on to the house.

Not having to sneak around this time, I was able to appreciate the house much better. I had known it was nice, but whereas before I had been lurking and searching for sentries and guards, now I was walking through the front door. Different Masters had different customs. The King is dead. Long live the King.

Master Haven was in charge now, and although he had been a friend of Simon's, he had understood my position in killing him. Simon had been working with a demon, leaving me little choice. So, this meeting was to set some ground rules, have a good time, and put each other at ease. Roland must have missed that memo because he looked ready to bite off vampire ears.

I clucked my tongue and he glanced at me. "There is literally no point to this meeting if you're going to pick a fight. They're already our enemies, by default. This is to see if we can be... if not allies, at least pleasant neighbors."

"If they step out of line—"

"I'll be the first to pull the trigger. But they haven't. And neither will the local Shepherd. Especially if you want the Conclave to consider your defense tomorrow... Starting a war before we leave won't help."

He flinched as if struck, eyes widening in disbelief. "That's low, Callie."

"It got your attention, right? Now, play nice until they give you a reason to do otherwise. You're too high-strung right now. Let me handle this."

He grunted agreement, but didn't sound happy about it.

We parked on a large circular drive and climbed out. Haven was standing at the top of the stairs, smiling at us. He was a tall, pale man, very handsome, and his eyes danced with cunning. I had first met him a few months ago, thinking he was an enemy, but he had been angling to turn on Amira just like I had. Or so he had said. She'd backed him into a corner, and he was fresh in his new position of power of an already weakened coven of vampires.

But... he'd had every opportunity to kill, maim, or torture Beckett after kidnapping the detective for Amira. Instead, Haven had given Beckett the keys to his own handcuffs, injected him with some Holy Water, and then handed Beckett over to Amira, giving us a wild card for our final confrontation. Then the Master Vampire had surrounded the area with snipers, men ready to take down Amira at the first chance.

Without that action of giving Beckett the keys to his handcuffs, I wouldn't have survived and either Amira would have won, or Haven's snipers would have taken her out and he would have been the hero of the city.

So... I didn't quite trust him, but his actions had spoken pretty loudly, so far.

He had earned a sliver of trust, despite Roland's deeply-ingrained prejudices. The Shepherd was simply too old school. He couldn't comprehend that the world was changing, and that both the humans and the monsters were adapting, using social media, politics, and any number of paths to victory. Hell, Dorian Gray had even helped us take her out.

However, Roland had an image of Count Dracula sitting in Transylvania stuck in his head, and his instinctive response was to storm the keep to kill the vampire on his throne.

But nowadays, those in charge were typically business savvy investors, had a bevy of lawyers, and were typically above reproach, untouchable by the mundane or *Regular* police.

Like a supernatural Mafia. At least that's how Kansas City seemed to operate.

And I had realized very quickly that all those mafia families knew about me – the Woman in White, as they called me – and I knew nothing about who occupied my city. When I had invaded Johnathan's office, I had seen that the city was divided up into five sections, like territories. The bears controlled one, the vampires with Haven had one, and the wolves had controlled one – but they had fled town a long time ago.

Which meant there were two more factions in town, and I had no idea who – or what – they were. Were the Nephilim crew one of the mafia families? I knew my Church wasn't, because it had been drawn outside the territory lines on the map I had seen.

But Haven might be in bed with these mystery families, and to be a good cop, to keep people safe in my city, I needed to know the players before someone snuck up on me and killed me in my sleep.

I smiled at Haven, motioning to the Shepherd. "Roland Haviar, Vatican Shepherd of Kansas City. Stacks of titles and accomplishments that you wouldn't pay attention to if I told you, so we'll just say he's got the Silver Star in kicking bloodsucker ass."

Haven blinked, staring at Roland, and then burst out laughing. Roland – already pissed at my introduction – did not like being the butt of vampire laughter. Before he could do anything stupid, Haven stepped forward, and gave a very formal bow, still struggling with his laughter.

"My apologies, Mr. Haviar. I wasn't laughing at you. I was laughing at the unorthodox way Miss Penrose decides to do things – and at the most unexpected of times. I imagine it's quite infuriating to train her," he said, standing as he smiled politely at Roland.

Roland was now in an uncomfortable situation.

He could either accept the apology, and agree with the vampire – which was against every fiber of his being – and basically team up with the vampire in mocking me, even though it was likely something he wholeheartedly agreed with. Or, he could take offense and we would throw down. Either way he would be doing something wrong.

He simply nodded. I smiled back, hiding my small exhalation of breath. I hadn't expected him to get so bent out of shape, although I hadn't really considered this a formal meeting, since I had already met Haven once and spoken with him on the phone a few times.

I had made a miscalculation, and Roland would make me pay for it later. Because the Shepherd was on his last nerve, too focused on the girls in Italy.

"I am a lot to handle," I said, smiling at Haven. It was very obvious that my reply could be taken multiple ways, and Roland's lips curled in a very faint smile. "But I meant well. Roland is like a father to me. A father that taught me such tough love that even two demons couldn't slow me down." I shrugged.

Haven's forehead creased in contemplation of that. I was beginning to realize that Haven would be a lot of fun to talk with in the years to come. If I didn't have to kill him, of course.

"Roland, this is Haven something or other. The King Fanger. The Grand Bloodsucker. The—"

"Master Vampire of Kansas City," he interrupted, rolling his eyes in mock frustration, showing Roland that he shared the Shepherd's pain. He extended a hand. "Haven Frost," he said, smiling politely. "And the other esteemed titles Callie mentioned," he said with a faint smirk.

Roland grunted in agreement before he thought about it, scowled momentarily at the vampire, and then shook his hand.

Haven leaned back, nodded at the two of us, and then said, "Pleased to have you. No vampire weapons will be permitted beyond the door." I shot Roland a look, and he grunted.

"You have my word," he said gruffly. He wasn't happy about it, though.

"Then you may enter my home." Then he hesitated, glancing over his shoulder at us with a guilty smile. "Whoops. Force of habit. You two don't need permission to enter buildings, do you?" he chuckled, referring to how vampires needed invitations to cross thresholds. It was one of their weaknesses. Something about a home – the magical energy that built up in a home after a group of people lived there long enough, experienced enough there, had been kept safe there – built up a magical protection against them. Vampires couldn't cross them without permission.

I batted my eyelashes at Haven. "I've always thought it's better to beg forgiveness than ask permission," I said, pointing a thumb at Roland. "But forgiveness is kind of his bread and butter. I think he uses it as an excuse for a lot of things."

Roland played along. "I never ask permission either. But I always grant forgiveness."

Haven turned all the way around. "*Ask* forgiveness, you mean."

Roland smiled, miming pulling the hammer back on an imaginary finger pistol as he clicked his teeth and winked. "That, too."

I clapped. "This is going to be fun."

"You were more fun alone, Callie," Haven said before turning back to the open door and striding inside.

I turned to Roland and he shrugged. "Just because I played along doesn't mean I'm happy with you right now," I warned. "We're here to potentially make an ally, or at least not make him a personal enemy. Let's stop pressing buttons, shall we? It's immature."

He sputtered in argument as I turned my back on him and followed Haven inside. I pretended not to hear as he grumbled under his breath about me starting the button pressing.

He had a point, but mine was not confrontational. Mine was a social lubricant, breaking tension. Roland's was passive aggressive. Threatening. Mine was sly. Show them up front that I was snarky and mouthy, so that when I acted sincere, they bought it.

Whether I was actually being sincere would never cross their minds, since they knew I had a penchant for speaking before thinking. But with Roland ratcheting the tension back up, he wasn't helping. He was making things a lot worse.

"Just follow my lead," I hissed over my shoulder. "Trust me."

Roland sighed wearily. "I will, but we are going to have a long talk later."

I entered the living room, mentally considering the next few minutes.

I had made sure to leave my weapons in the truck. We'd given him our word. There was always the chance that if Roland couldn't calm the hell down, he might decide to whip out his manliness wang on the table to make a point to Haven.

Ironically, men simply couldn't understand the long game. Such emotional, frivolous creatures. A lot could be solved by them just keeping their hammer of justice in their pants.

❧ 17 ❧

oland nodded at Haven, smiling politely. "Women can be overly emotional at times, yes. They often make things harder than they need to be."

I gritted my teeth, scowling at the both of them. It was astounding how quickly they had shifted from mortal enemies to long-lost friends. I wondered if Roland was just trying to be agreeable with Haven, like I had asked him to be. If he actually meant this drivel, I was going to carve out his ears and stake them to a Bible.

With Haven's fangs.

"Alright, boys. That kind of talk isn't good for your health," I warned, plastering on a thin smile. They chuckled, lifting their palms at each other as if I had just proven their point.

But Haven dipped his head politely in my direction, smiling playfully.

Haven had taken us on a tour of the property, showing us every single door, floor and room. Then, asking if we were satisfied with our inspection, we had agreed and had assumed we were heading back inside the mansion for a few refreshments and idle talk. But an elegant Maybach had pulled up beside us. The driver got out and held the door open for us to enter with Haven behind the wheel. Roland and I had grown uneasy, but after the guard had left us, Haven told us he had one more thing to show us, in honor of full disclosure.

He had taken us to a nearby cave on the edges of the large property. Inside the cave – which had ceilings thirty feet high – he had parked the car and taken us on a tour through the majority of it. Recessed lighting had been built into the rock, and the central corridor was fifty feet wide in most places. He had shown us refrigeration units filled with blood bags – and, to Roland's surprise – all the requisite paperwork showing that it had been legally obtained. They were also individually warded so that they resembled transparent intravenous fluid, not blood. Haven had waved a hand over one, murmuring a spell, and presto! Blood. They did it to prevent awkward questions in transit. No smell. And it didn't look like blood. Roland hadn't looked pleased.

On the other hand, Roland *had* been impressed by Haven's transparency. By the end of the tour I caught him studying Haven when the vampire wasn't looking – likely realizing that his old methods of dealing with vampires might very well be out of date. My words hadn't meant crap, but a Maybach, invisible blood bags, and a tour of Haven's Batcave had done the trick. Men!

We were now back in the mansion, and the two were joking around like teenaged boys after summer break. I never would have connected the new Roland with the one from an hour ago.

Haven held out a hand, indicating the chairs near the fire, motioning us to relocate. Before I could move, Haven was already walking past me. I remained perfectly still as he did, my shoulders relaxed, even though I sensed Roland was suddenly very alert, reminded of what Haven really was beneath the calm, friendly demeanor. I didn't want Haven to see I feared him. The whole point of this was to establish trust.

As he passed, he stopped, leaning in close to my neck. He reached out with long pale fingers, and removed a loose strand of hair from the side of my neck, careful to not touch me in the process. He held it up for me to see, and then dropped it in my palm with a smile before continuing on to one of the leather couches. I pocketed it without a word.

I let out a small breath and flashed Roland a tight look, reminding him to back down. He let out a barely concealed sigh and tried to sit beside me on the couch, as if to protect me. Right before I sat down, I suddenly stood again, shooting him an accusing look to let him know I didn't need his help.

Then I sniffed and walked over to a third chair.

Haven watched me with amusement, but Roland simply looked frustrated. He was too used to protecting me, but now it was time for him to cut that shit out. If everyone saw me as his little helper, I wasn't going to be of much use in Kansas City. And I was finished standing in someone else's shadow. Because I had done pretty damned well on my own. Against two demons, no less.

Haven's eyes sparkled briefly, too quickly for Roland to notice. The Shepherd finally seemed to get my point and folded his arms with a patient sigh. Perfect. I needed Haven to see us as associates, not a two-on-one Holy Tag Team sitting directly across from him. Also, sitting apart from Roland forced Haven to split his attention between both of us, a psychological ploy I had read about – while at the same time masking my action as simply being annoyed with Roland.

Roland had picked up on it quickly. Or he really was annoyed. Either emotion worked. Haven would see the wedge between us, and realize that my fresh blood – no pun intended – might be just the thing to change an old Shepherd's opinions. And that this meeting might just be worth his time after all.

I glanced around the richly furnished room. The last time I had seen it a swarm of vampires had flooded up from the nearby basement door in an attempt to kill me. I made sure I kept the door in my peripheral vision. "Where are all the other vampires?" I asked. We had spoken to a handful while touring the property, but had seen fewer than I had expected. Now that we were secluded, I felt we were private enough to ask without offering offense.

Haven grinned. "Hearing of your unannounced arrival, they may have found more urgent matters to attend. Quite suddenly. Some might even have called it a scurry."

I flashed a proud smile at him and he grinned, shrugging. "Vampires scurrying..." I mused.

Haven cleared his throat. "Have I not entertained you in good faith, even with your early arrival? Shown you areas of my property that I very easily could have concealed?"

I shot a look at Roland that very easily translated to *I told you so*. He let out a sigh, as if having to refute the existence of God, and finally nodded. "To say I'm pleasantly surprised would be the biggest understatement ever," he admitted with a guilty shrug.

Haven nodded in gratitude, lifting his glass of blood to signify a toast.

We matched him and were sipping our pricey scotch when he spoke again. "Then why have you broken your word during our truce? Our peace talk?" he asked in a soft yet firm tone.

I coughed on my drink, ready to argue with Haven. But I realized he wasn't staring at me. And a very disgusting sensation wriggled inside my stomach as I turned to look at Roland. What had he done?

His face was guilty as hell. He set his drink down very slowly. "Old habits..." he admitted.

Then it hit me. We had given Haven our word that we wouldn't bring vampire weapons on the tour. He... had lied. I wanted to punch him in the face. Everything had been going so well!

"You lied to me," Haven murmured. Oh, that voice was so soft.

"Perhaps it explains your hospitality," Roland argued, eyes defensive.

I slapped the table with my palm, glaring at Roland in disbelief. "What the *Hell?!*" I shouted. Because breaking a promise was not good. It was so *not good*, that I considered fleeing on the spot. We were in deep shit now. Roland had likely assumed he could get away with it. It wasn't as dangerous as breaking Guest-Right, because he hadn't directly harmed the Master of Kansas City. Roland might have instantly lost a chunk of his power if *that* had happened. But he – a Shepherd – had broken a direct promise during a peace talk. That was a declaration of war. I wondered how Haven had even figured it out, and what Roland had brought. Not that it mattered.

Roland very carefully reached into his coat and I suddenly heard the sound of a rifle cocking from the hallway. Roland hesitated, eyes turning to flecks of stone at the sound, but he continued until he set a round glass bottle of clear liquid on the table. Such a small thing to signal the start of a war. Roland stood very slowly, holding up his arms. "You may search me if you wish. I brought only enough to guarantee a distraction if we needed to flee. A backdoor, if you will."

A guard slipped into the room and patted Roland down, which did not make him happy. Hell, I would have been perfectly fine if the guard drop-kicked him in the groin as a new pat-down procedure. The guard found nothing, scooped up the holy water, glanced at Haven with a nod, and then departed.

Haven didn't look angry. He looked... weary. He glanced at me and then turned back to Roland. "You lied to me. Against your own partner's wishes.

Your partner, I might add, is the one responsible for earning this meeting in the first place – based on my trust in her word."

Roland looked both angry and guilty, the two emotions warring for dominance. An old anger based on decades of habits in dealing with vampires his way. Apologizing to one was anathema. Guilt at seeing his old methods turned against him. And also guilt at betraying my confidence.

I sighed, calculating, wondering what we could do. What Haven would do.

Haven cleared his throat. "A breach such as this should typically be reported to your superiors, the Conclave. And to mine... the Sanguine Council."

Roland's face blanched, and my heart stilled. That could cause a war. Very literally.

Haven held up a finger. "As the rules dictate, your life or power will be forfeit. My position as new Master of this city is not strong enough for me to overlook such a slight. It would cause my coven to rebel, and nobody wants that... I cannot brush this under the table. We had a truce, you gave me your word, and then entered my home, conscious of your deceit." Roland must have assumed that a promise to a vampire was not a real promise at all. He should have known better. Concern with Italy had pushed him over the edge to make such a stupid decision.

Haven's eyes looked troubled. The next words out of his mouth would change everything, but I could sense his hesitation. He wasn't telling us everything. I replayed the situation. Haven's manner had been beyond reproach. I wasn't sure when he had become aware of Roland's lie, but he had continued the tour with the utmost sincerity. The perfect host. Then he'd even sat to converse with us over drinks. He had played this well. So why was he hesitating?

His face showed no excitement at the prospect of killing Roland. He liked his position as Master of Kansas City, and likely sensed the shit-storm coming our way. It wouldn't turn out well for anyone, even though he hadn't done anything wrong. War rarely harmed only one side.

"I may have another solution..." he said softly, as if the idea had only just come to him.

"What is it?" I asked through gritted teeth. I knew it wouldn't be appealing, but anything was better than a war. Especially since we would be heading to the Vatican tomorrow for my hearing – to feed them a steaming pile of lies about the Spear that they wouldn't like one bit. Then we were going to politely pick apart their investigation of Constantine's murder.

Now this.

Haven tapped his lips, thinking. "I must insist on a walk," he said cryptically. Almost imperceptibly, his eyes flickered to the corner ceiling. I hid my look by taking a sip of my drink and noticed a camera. I didn't react. Haven was being watched? Spied on? By whom?

I nodded before Roland could speak. "That sounds wise. Let our heads cool," I said, standing, and shooting a very dark look at Roland before he could argue. The Shepherd nodded once and then climbed to his feet. Haven called for a vehicle as we made our way to the entrance. Within moments, the Maybach was back, idling before us. Haven spoke softly to the vampire valet – who glared at us with pure hatred before nodding. I noticed that the number of guards around the house had increased. Haven spoke loud enough for all to hear. "They have already made one fatal offense. I am safe with them, because killing me would only make things infinitely worse for them." No one responded, but I could sense that the guards looked a little less murder-y. It would have to do. Everyone knew about our deceit. Shit. This would spread like wildfire.

I wondered what the hell was going on as I climbed into the front seat of the car, letting Roland climb into the back to think about what he'd done wrong. I was furious. I had set up everything so neatly – and in one fell swoop, his closed-mindedness and emotional instability after the murder in Italy had ruined all of it.

Haven drove in silence, lost in thought. Something about his posture made it very clear that conversation was not welcome, and after seeing the camera in the office, and the way the valet had glared at us, I considered the fact that even the car might not be safe. What kind of operation was this if the Master Vampire wasn't in full control of his own property and coven?

Haven pulled up to a hill after a few minutes. A weathered statue of an angel overlooked a sprawling field with distant human-shaped targets. I stepped on a few shell casings as I climbed out of the car. This must be where the guards practiced their marksmanship. Either that, or Haven had taken us to his execution block. But studying his profile as he turned his back on us and approached the statue, I sensed no threat or danger. More... wariness and frustration.

He finally turned to find Roland and I before him, waiting.
"Your own people are spying on you..." I said neutrally.
His eyes flashed crimson and he gave me a tight nod.

Haven sighed, his eyes returning to normal. "I apologize for the subterfuge. With the two previous Masters of the city dying in such a short span of time, the Sanguine Council has decided to keep a close eye on matters. I intend to make that observation short-lived. I don't like being watched. I am the Master of Kansas City," he growled territorially, eyes flashing crimson again. He let out a breath, and then stared at us, his crimson irises fading. "You broke your word. You know the potential ramifications of that, correct? My due rights…"

Roland gritted his teeth, nodding. Not angry at Haven, but at himself. This was going to eat him alive. He would rather sacrifice himself quickly than tarnish his name or bear the shame.

"If I don't kill you for your transgression, the Sanguine Council will go to war with the Shepherds," Haven continued. "If I *do* kill you for your transgression, the *Shepherds* will likely go to war with the Sanguine Council. We both know that a war will very likely destroy us all."

We nodded in unison.

"What do you propose?" Roland asked in a hoarse growl. Not with fear, but with the look of a man walking to the chopping block. Resolved. "If my death will satisfy your Sanguine Council, I can write a letter to the Conclave, telling them I voluntarily chose my punishment. They won't be happy, but they won't go to war over it."

I grunted. A piece of paper wasn't exactly bulletproof. It might not be enough to stop a war. I couldn't make myself look at him. My hands were shaking with anger. If Roland hadn't been so riled up about events in Italy, he never would have made a mistake like this. He was barely keeping it together, and it had brought him to this moment.

Haven nodded at the gesture. "But life is such a precious thing... What if you could keep it? In a manner of speaking."

Roland stiffened. I spoke up. "He should probably say *thank fucking god*, if he has any sense left in him," I growled, glaring at him. Roland didn't notice.

Haven smiled – at my words, not at the situation. He waited until Roland met his eyes, confirming he had his full attention. Then he took a breath. "You could become a vampire."

The Shepherd's face paled, and then flashed to murder. He even took an instinctive step closer to Haven – the words like a slap to the face. I grabbed his arm, jerking him back to me. He began swearing under his breath, cursing himself, shaking his head, and clenching his fists. "No. No way in *hell*!" he hissed.

My anger was replaced by sudden sorrow. To see his world crumbling around him. His entire purpose relegated to becoming that which he had hunted for so long.

But...

Other than death, it really was the only way I could think of to save the situation. In fact, the vampires would probably be pleased as all hell to turn a Shepherd to their fold.

But the Conclave? Oh boy.

And Roland? Trading his life as a man of God, a Shepherd – one of twelve holy warriors that protected the world from... well, vampires, among other supernaturals – to *become* a vampire. That was an impossible price to pay, and I was pretty sure that this option signaled the end of the discussion, even though I wished I could help him see reason.

I frowned suddenly. "I thought Shepherds were immune to vampire venom?"

Roland didn't even acknowledge that I had spoken. Haven turned to me. "A *Master* Vampire may turn a Shepherd."

I blinked. But since Roland hadn't commented, I knew I was hearing the truth. Shit.

I knew that becoming a vampire didn't make one a bad person. I even kind of liked Haven – what little I knew of him. And Nate was friends with a vampire named Alucard. Even though he was a Daywalker now, Nate had become his friend *before* that. It was possible to be a good vampire. Hard, but *possible*. But, Roland was old school. He didn't buy into this new world of grays. It was black and white to him. Vatican good, vampires bad.

Roland would rather die. Period.

He was shaking his head repeatedly. "No. I... cannot."

Haven nodded, expecting the answer, not a hint of victory on his face. He didn't like this anymore than we did. He was literally being forced into the situation. Because Roland had been a stupid idiot, bringing a weapon specifically aimed at harming vampires to a truce meeting – after telling the host that he wouldn't do so.

Haven turned to me, his eyes pleading. I shrugged and then shook my head. "I can't make him do something he's spent his entire life fighting. Not a decision like that," I whispered.

Haven nodded. "Very well." He was silent for a few moments, staring up at the statue. Then he turned to me, looking uncertain. "I have come across some information that could put me in significant danger with the Sanguine Council. Some information that may be of use to you..."

I frowned. Why would he share that? Roland didn't appear to be listening, too lost in his own thoughts. Likely making peace with himself, praying to God for forgiveness. He wouldn't even look at me, his shame was so great. "What is it?" I whispered, not really caring.

"Your wolves in Rome are innocent," he said in a soft tone. "I saw them in a video."

Roland's head whipped up as if he had been punched in the jaw, and he was suddenly holding Haven a pace off the ground by the front of his shirt. Haven let him. Not because he was scared, but because... this was obviously very important to the vampire. I knew Haven could have easily dodged Roland, not shared the information, even killed him outright –because that was already a foregone conclusion. So... he must consider this piece of news very, very important. To him and us. Why? He had said *your wolves* as if he knew exactly who they really were. Which wasn't surprising. He had been in the center of the mess with the demon, and knew of the wolves abducting young women. If he had seen them in a video, it would be easy to connect them with the faces that had been plastered on the local news channel for weeks as missing persons.

I felt a surge of excitement. He had a video of the murder. No wonder he was being cagey. Was this an olive branch? Or something else? A negotiation tool... but that wasn't necessarily a bad thing. "Roland, put him down. Now," I warned. "The situation is already bad enough."

Roland was shaking as he lowered him to the ground. He didn't back away, remaining inches from Haven's face as he panted, eyes on fire as he waited for Haven to explain. "I'm already a dead man. Speak or I will end you. If your Sanguine Council had *anything* to do with this, no power will save you from the wrath of God," he said in a low tone. It sounded suspiciously like Roland was justified in speaking for God on the matter. A Hall Pass from Heaven.

Haven met that glare with a straight face. Not backing down and not scared. Accepting it with the respect of a worthy adversary. I could honestly say that I had never met anyone quite like Haven. He very easily could have taunted us, laughing as he butchered Roland in front of me, and if I didn't want a war, there wouldn't have been a thing I could do about it.

"I have various connections overseas, having spent the majority of my life there – over two hundred years, to be precise. These are personal, not official, connections," he elaborated. We watched, motionless. "One of these private contacts sent me a video. Of a murder in Rome. Two of the missing Kansas City girls from several months ago seemed to be alive and well in Italy."

"Be very, very careful, vampire," Roland warned.

I felt like a piece of glass. Roland was seconds from murder. Information was all that kept Haven safe from Roland's rage, consequences be damned. Haven had connected the dots, but *what* dots? Was the Sanguine Council involved in the murder?

"Master Vampires receive daily updates from the Sanguine Council regarding current events that may impact our business," Haven explained. "You could say that news of a murdered Shepherd caught my attention, and you would be right. But what *really* caught my attention was the fact that I received a video of a murder caught on tape *before* the Sanguine Council told me about the Shepherd. When I first saw the video, I simply stored it away as an unfortunate turn of luck for the two girls. But after the Sanguine Council made the news public, I did some digging and knew that everyone was wrong. The Sanguine Council informed us to be very careful around the Shepherds in the coming weeks. Because the Shepherds had no evidence other than the two wolves found at the scene." We blinked at him, incredulous. Haven nodded. "The Sanguine Council doesn't know about this recording. The Vatican doesn't know about the recording." He let out a sigh. "Well, my contact suffered a car accident two days later. His recording equipment was missing from his shop. So, someone knows something."

I held up a hand, interrupting Roland with a sharp look. He quivered, but backed down. He knew he was too close to this. He practically stood on the balls of his feet, though, ready to intercede if he didn't like my direction. Someone had taken the surveillance equipment. Shit.

"Why would you share this with us?" I asked, but I was pretty sure I knew.

"I'm not pleased with how the Sanguines have treated me of late..." he said in a cold tone.

I began pacing, forcing my exhausted mind to work. Someone knew, or at least suspected the video. Otherwise, why kill Haven's contact and steal the equipment? "You're confident that your own people aren't behind it?"

Haven shrugged. "I highly doubt it. If they were, they would have told us about it in the briefing – given us a carefully rehearsed script. They're pretty open about this sort of thing." He met my eyes. "I believe someone at the Vatican framed your girls. And the Conclave bought it."

I blinked in disbelief. "Someone at the Vatican framed the wolves for killing a Shepherd? Why would they do that? Was the Shepherd dirty?"

Roland growled at me. "He was as far from bad as one could be. He was the best of us..." He turned back to Haven, absolutely no emotion on his face. "Who. Killed. Constantine?"

Haven frowned. "I don't know. I swear it. The killer wore a scarf to conceal his face, but the scarf had a cross on it. Someone – or a small group – has infiltrated your Conclave. The highest form of treachery. A Judas Iscariot. It's the only thing that makes sense."

Roland grunted, not entirely buying Haven's answer, but knowing that the two wolves were now in very real danger. Roland had sent them there to learn their powers with people he trusted. And someone had betrayed that trust.

All too quickly, I saw the situation in perfect clarity.

If he wanted to help me save the girls, he would have to become what he hated. Because if I went to Italy by myself, they would slam the door in my face. I was just Roland's disciple.

"Roland," I said in a soft tone. He slowed, taking a few seconds to stare at the stone angel before us. Then he turned to face me, as if I was a firing squad. The utter desolation in his eyes shattered my heart. Especially with what I was about to say. "We need to save them, and I can't do it alone," I whispered. He nodded stiffly, our eyes locked in a silent conversation.

And there is only one way for me to leave this property... his eyes said.

I nodded, a tear falling down my cheek. *It's the only way to save them. And to make the traitor pay. To bring them to justice. To follow your life's purpose, you must betray your life's purpose...* I tried to convey with my eyes, my vision now entirely distorted with tears.

Roland turned to Haven who had his hands clasped before him, waiting with a blank face.

"I accept your offer. May God forgive me..." he added the last in a haunted whisper.

❧ 19 ❧

I cleared my throat, trying to wall off my emotions as I wiped the tears from my eyes. Big girls don't cry. "How would this work? I take it we can't leave until he's a vampire?" Haven nodded sadly. "You have to bite him before we leave..."

Haven nodded again. "To prevent a war, yes. I need to bite him in front of three vampire witnesses to verify that the truth gets out to the Sanguine Council. Otherwise, war."

I knew he was likely overjoyed to know that Roland was going to join his side, but at the same time, part of him didn't like the method. Then again, I knew Haven was a schemer.

This could all be some elaborate trick. Turn a bad situation into a win. It was his style.

"Don't take this the wrong way, but I need you to prove your statement. Roland would gladly die for his reputation. The only reason he's considering otherwise is to prove the wolves' innocence." I waited for his nod before continuing. "And if I ever find out that you somehow set this up on purpose, I will *gladly* risk war to balance the scales," I warned. "I'm not as pious as Roland." I didn't see how it could be possible to be a setup, but the threat needed to be said.

Haven nodded, face serious. Then he pulled out his phone. "This is a burner phone. I use several to keep in contact with my informants. The

Sanguine Council does not have access to it, or I would be dead right now. We all would be. They don't want to get involved with the Conclave, and information like I'm about to show you would start war no matter what anyone wanted."

He held out the phone to me and Roland approached on leaden feet, as if shackled.

A grainy black and white video began to play, and I watched in breathless horror as I saw an older man walking down a dark alley with two familiar women. The wolves we had saved. They were apparently joking back and forth, the two women dancing around him playfully. Like a rich John and his two paid escorts for the evening.

A figure in black with a lighter scarf over his lower face and down his chest darted into the picture, swifter than possible and kicked one of the wolves in the chest. She flew into a dumpster, before collapsing to the ground. The figure had already punched the other wolf in the face and body three times, dropping her to her ass on the pavement. They stumbled to their feet, their clothes exploding like confetti as they shifted into their wolf forms, the pain instantly igniting their instincts.

A ball of fire erupted in the Shepherd's hands and flew at the attacker, hitting him directly in the chest despite his crossed hands before him. But...

The fire flew right through him, erupting out the other side and crashing into a building. The dark figure froze for a moment as if surprised. Then he darted in closer to the Shepherd, and sliced his throat savagely with what looked like his bare hands, decapitating him in an instant before the Shepherd had time to react to his failed magic.

The assassin made short work of the wolves, as if he were fighting toddlers, leaving them unconscious on the ground beside the dead Shepherd. I caught a flash of the cross on the scarf concealing his face before he slipped out of the frame.

The video cut off and Haven slowly lowered it.

"The Conclave mentioned witnesses," Roland said, eyes thoughtful.

Haven shrugged. "That could help." Roland's grimace let him know it didn't. "I... see."

"Do you recognize the scarf?" I asked Roland instead. These 'witnesses' hadn't stopped the Conclave from condemning the wolves, which smelled fishy. Someone was definitely playing a game with the Conclave. Haven was right.

He scratched his cheek before finally shrugging. "Italy is full of religious factions wearing modified crosses. I can list two dozen groups that don crucifixes of some kind, but nothing stands out. It's not clear enough to see details of what kind of cross he or she wore."

"What the hell kind of man is immune to magic?" I whispered out loud.

I looked up to see tears streaking down Roland's face, his eyes a million miles away.

"I do not know what he is, or how he did it, or who he is working with. But you just saw one of your most legendary Shepherds and two werewolves taken out in less than a minute with what seemed like no effort on the assassin's part." Haven let that sink in, his voice neutral, as if not wanting to provoke Roland into anger. "That is what you face in Rome. What the wolves face. Well, I have no doubt they will face a different execution, but my point remains. Someone very powerful is playing a very dangerous game in one of the Holiest houses in the world."

I nodded numbly, realizing that things had just gotten a whole lot worse. "We have to try, Roland. If they took out your mentor, the others don't stand a chance. Who knows what their ultimate plan is..." I realized the futility of the situation. We were going to be surrounded by the strongest of the strong, and one of them was secretly a traitor. Everything we did would be observed – both by Shepherds just doing their jobs, and by a killer hiding in plain sight. I didn't stand a chance on my own. I couldn't just waltz in treating everyone like a criminal or they would lock me up. I had to have Roland.

Roland nodded stiffly, eyes lifting to Haven. He grimaced in disgust, but it was likely a result of knowing that very soon he would be just like Haven. A blood-sucking vampire. "How would this work?" he rasped.

"I will bite you in front of three witnesses and Callie. We will record it for proof. We will all need to say something to the effect of agreeing with the terms. Especially you, Roland. Then we send it off to our superiors." He sensed our trepidation, but held up a hand. "The recording is mandatory to cover ourselves. Word will spread regardless, and we would all benefit from transparency, so that no one gets trigger happy later." I growled to myself. He was right. If he was being watched, we had to be very careful. We might not even get a chance to try if the Conclave learned of this development too soon. "I'll try to keep a lid on it as long as possible, but word will travel fast. The good thing about my people is that immortality has made them somewhat lazy. Well, not as concerned with urgency," he clarified.

I frowned. "Then why don't we wait to turn Roland until after we save the wolves and find the real killer?" I asked, hoping against hope.

Haven and Roland were both shaking their heads. The Shepherd answered first. "If he waits, you can guarantee his Sanguine Council spies will rediscover their sense of urgency. Also, if we fail and I die without making up for my transgression with Haven, there will be war when the Sanguine Council demands payment. Especially when I would have also wronged the Vatican at that point by not immediately telling them. You can bet that if the real killer is in a position of power that he will make sure to agree with the Sanguine Council's demands for blood. To further shatter the Conclave." His eyes grew distant. "I wouldn't be surprised if that isn't the killer's long-term plan. To sow seeds of confusion. Discord. One Shepherd murdered by werewolves, another turned to a vampire and 'attacking' the Vatican..." he shook his head in disgust. "I need to be turned. Now. And we need to get to the Vatican immediately, before they hear what I've done. We need to not only find the murderer, but find him before anyone hears about me turning cloak, or our game will be up before we know it. At *best*, they will lock us up in a cell."

I punched a fist into my palm. "Before you argue, I'm going," I warned him. Roland didn't even bother to argue, so wrapped up in his concern for the wolves. But he did smile.

"New vampires are uncontrollable! Bloodlust rules them. They will know something is wrong. Not even counting the fact that as a vampire, I'm going to have one hell of a time spending a few days in the Vatican, surrounded by Holy objects," he pressed.

Haven cleared his throat. "I can help with that. I have an amulet that will both mask your powers and help with the Holy objects issue. But beware as your body begins to change. You end up flashing fangs or running too fast in front of the wrong person, and your gig will be up," he warned. "We can provide you with enough of our untraceable blood bags that you never get hungry. You will need to drink even when you don't feel thirsty. These blood bags will curb some of the effects for a time. But it will be temporary. You will need to feast on living blood at some point within the first few days. Or the body will reject the gifts and you will die. Or you will lose control. Staying... hydrated will prolong that first real shift," he said, emphasizing *real*. "This will simply trick the body into thinking it's okay, slowing down the need for fresh blood." He held up a finger in warning. "But I must reiterate. You will have to murder someone. Soon. Within days. And drink their blood. Or you will turn savage and there will be no saving you. The monster will erase all that is Roland."

"Monster," Roland muttered angrily, beginning to pace.

"Once you've taken your first life, you can continue with the donated blood if you prefer. Or hunt animals. But the first time is different. Your monster will force your body to take a life and devour the blood. After that is up to you. Tricking it with blood bags will only last so long, and I must remind you that you will need to drink even when you don't feel thirsty."

I nodded, watching Roland as he shook his head. I knew who he had in mind for his first kill as a vampire. The killer. He approached the statue of the weeping angel, and knelt before her. The angel stared down at him with a sad smile as he began to pray. I motioned for Haven to join me beside the car, leaving Roland in peace – for perhaps the last time – with his ties to Heaven.

"Why would you help us?" I asked him. "You're sending your new vampire to his death."

He shrugged, leaning back against the car as he studied Roland. "Don't get me wrong, part of me is ecstatic about turning him. I won't lie. Proving to him that I am not a monster will benefit both of us in the long run. Aiding him in his cause to fight evil is also in my best interest. Him dying only days after I turn him will look very bad to my superiors, and I can imagine it won't sit well with the Conclave. I'm ensuring he will kill someone – and remain a vampire – by giving him a target." I nodded slowly. If we survived. I couldn't even be mad at Haven. Roland had brought this on himself.

He could always accept execution.

At least this way gave him a chance at life. And vengeance.

"I am at great risk here..." Haven said softly, still watching the Shepherd praying to the angel statue. "Every Master Vampire in the world was commanded to not interfere in this murder. All too easily, this crime could be pinned on us. Cooperation has the penalty of death."

"Nothing ventured, nothing gained," I said sadly.

Haven nodded. "Yes. But the only other option to us is for him to die, which would mean the murderer gets away without facing justice. And I gain nothing," he admitted with a shrug.

I nodded, unable to prevent the tears streaming down my cheeks as I watched Roland speak to his God for the last time. He finally climbed to his feet, a broken man. He placed a hand on the Angel's wing for support. He stood motionless for almost a minute before turning to face us.

His face was a mask of vengeance, resolution, retribution.

"Let's do this. We leave for Rome immediately after." He glanced at Haven. "Stall as long as you can or all this is for nothing and war will come. To prevent a war, we must risk a war..." he said softly.

Haven nodded. "I think I can help with that," he said with a mischievous twinkle in his eyes. "I have a plan, but we better hurry."

❧ 20 ❧

The three vampires watched with obvious anticipation after we each stated our names, titles, and agreement in the turning of Roland Haviar to a vampire for his betrayal of trust with the Master Vampire of Kansas City. A guard stood nearby, recording it on Haven's phone.

Roland stared straight ahead, face expressionless, arm outstretched, because he refused to be bitten on the neck.

Haven approached him confidently, nodded his head at Roland, and then his head darted out to Roland's forearm and bit down hard. I flinched, my heart ripping in half, but I didn't cry on the outside. On the inside, I was a ship lost at sea. Whispers drifted on the winds of my mind, salivating at the scene before me, sounding both anticipatory and haunted. I walled them away with a nervous breath. I would figure out my own shit later.

Roland's eyes tightened in pain, but he withstood it like a statue – penance – the price of his failure, and the cost to do the right thing. Haven lifted his fangs and then raised his own arm. He bit into his wrist and blood immediately splattered on the drive. He locked eyes with Roland and then extended his arm forward. Roland didn't flinch as he took the wrist and drank his Master's blood. I knew inside he was a raging tempest of fury, but his fear for the wolves outweighed his disgust. Also, someone had betrayed the Conclave, and that wouldn't sit well with Roland. He never averted his eyes from Haven, the two staring at each other in a battle of wills. Haven finally nodded.

Roland flung the hand aside and took a deep breath, his eyes flashing crimson. Then he doubled over in pain, clutching at his chest. I gasped in alarm as Roland tore off his shirt, twitching and spasming as if he was being struck with a whip right before my eyes.

He was suddenly bare from the chest up, and I watched in horror as his skin tugged and jerked, pulsing with crimson light. Then I realized what was happening.

Roland's torso had been liberally scarred with religious text, passages, and scripture. I had never learned why – if it had something to do with being a Shepherd, or some personal choice of his – but that was all changing now. I watched as his flesh healed perfectly smooth, all scars and religious tattoos disappearing in a wash of agony.

Roland grunted and hissed for a good minute as the last of the scars faded from view. Then he took a deep breath and stared at Haven. The Master Vampire looked stunned, apparently not having known about the tattoos, and even more surprised to see Roland's ability to withstand such obvious torture.

"I was forged by the fires of Heaven," Roland finally whispered. "Hell will never break me." These words seemed to hurt him, because he flinched as he spoke. Then I remembered. Vampires had problems talking about God. Yet more physical pain for him to bear, but it had been worth it to him. Another crack of the metaphorical whip.

Haven nodded very slowly, deep respect replacing his surprise. He reached into his pocket absently as he spoke. "Welcome to my fold, Roland Haviar, and Happy Birthday."

I heard the guard muttering to himself and glanced over a shoulder. He was frowning down at the phone angrily.

Haven cleared his throat and the guard looked up to see a very furious vampire staring at him. "What is wrong, soldier?" he asked in an icy tone.

The guard stammered under that glare. "I-I'm not sure, Master Haven. The phone glitched out and won't turn back on," he said, jabbing the screen repeatedly.

Master Haven was on him in a blink, snatching the phone from his hands. He studied the screen, trying to get it working. Then, with a curse, he casually swept his other hand back, slicing the guard's throat. The guard fell to his knees, a look of surprise on his already dead face. Haven snapped his fingers and the three vampires flinched eagerly, ready to dive into the free meal.

"Stop!" Roland roared. The three vampires spun in surprise, faces suddenly challenging. Roland casually walked closer to the now dead guard and knelt before him. I held my breath, knowing this was all part of the plan, but still horrified by it. Roland cocked his head, smiling at the three vampires. "The new kid is hungry," he said.

Then his fangs flashed out and he dove into the guard's neck, drinking greedily. I ignored the slurping sounds – both disgusted at the act itself, but even more so that I was watching my mentor do the one thing he abhorred most in the world.

But Haven's plan was quite clever. He'd turned on a small device in his pocket that fried the phone in the guard's hand, eliminating the video, and hopefully buying us more time. But we couldn't have anyone get suspicious about that, so we had needed a show. Haven had told us that he was confident that this specific guard was one of his watchers, so had wanted to find a way to dispose of him anyway. And him failing with such a momentous recording was grounds for that. This was an historic event... the willful turning of a Shepherd.

If Roland hadn't wanted to take a drink, the vampires might have started gossiping, questioning the ritual. Roland got to reaffirm his legend as a new vampire, eliminating any doubt for the witnesses. So that when we left in a few minutes, none would think anything amiss. A guard had screwed up the recording and had paid with his life. But they had witnessed the brand-new Shepherd Vampire take his first drink.

Which was about as momentous as an event could get, something they could tell their friends for years, centuries even.

Roland had sounded emotionless as he agreed to the plan, taking his penance more gracefully than I ever could have. But that was just Roland. If turning himself into a monster let him save some lives... well, that was the only acceptable answer. No use whining about it.

Roland finally stood, his neck awash in blood. He held out his hand to the fallen guard as he glanced at the vampires. "I left plenty for you three." He tried to take a few steps, but his body began twitching and shaking as the blood hit him.

I waited nervously. This was the part I hadn't been sure about. We couldn't risk Roland actually killing someone and turning all the way. If we did, the Vatican would recognize his change in an instant. As it was right now, we hopefully had a few days before all the changes solidified in him. But we had to make sure the guard was dead before Roland drank.

Which was a hell of a guess.

Roland finally straightened with a sigh. Then he flashed a grin at Haven. "That... felt nice," he finally said. His eyes still looked understandably troubled, so the other vampires wouldn't think his change too drastic, but they all remembered their first drink as a vampire, and chuckled good naturedly. They approached, patted him on the back, and then quickly scooped up the soldier, carrying him inside.

Roland wouldn't look at me as Haven approached him. The Master of Kansas City discreetly slipped his new vampire a golden drachma on a thick golden chain. I felt a faint humming in the air and casually swept the area for threats. I didn't see any danger, so dismissed it as nerves. Or a resonance from the Whispers. I heard Haven murmur under his breath as he gave Roland a congratulatory hug, "I'll have the blood bags waiting for you at the angel statue in one hour. Just do your magic travel thing to get it without being detected." Then he held out a hand towards Roland, speaking loud enough for several nearby guards to hear. I spotted a few vampires at some of the windows in the mansion, watching excitedly. "I'm excited to see you after your trip home. Make it quick, though. Too long near mortals will be... difficult for you until you master your new abilities." Which was an easy explanation for our sudden departure.

Roland nodded sadly. "I want to see them one last time before..."

Haven nodded, not needing Roland to finish. "You'll find a new family here with me, but I understand. Say your goodbyes. I'll see you soon."

And then we climbed into my truck and left.

21

We sat in the training room, clearing our heads. Roland had barely spoken a dozen words since leaving Haven. I had so many questions. Could he still use his magic? What was our plan? How were we going to get to Rome? The Doors? Did he have anyone he trusted there? Did he have any idea where we would begin our search? What could I expect at my hearing? Would the Conclave or other Shepherds already know about Roland's change? What would we do when they ultimately found out? Because at some point, they would find out, and all hell would break loose when they learned we had chosen not to forewarn them.

Basically, we were both going to be fugitives soon, no matter what happened. We might have time to save the girls first, or not. The end was already determined for Roland. We were just watching the clock, hoping to do some good before the buzzer sounded.

The conclusion wouldn't be a sunny day in paradise.

Well, Roland would never have a sunny day in paradise, now. No sun at all, actually.

Roland checked the duffel full of blood bags Haven had left us. I had picked them up without issue, thankful that none of his people had seen me or else all sorts of problems would have resulted. The blood bags were concealed under a false bottom in the duffel bag. The Master vampire had also left some magical sunscreen with a note that told us it would give

Roland a few hours of protection, enough time to seek shelter and hide his affliction.

Hopefully Haven could keep his vampires from getting word to the Sanguine Council about Roland becoming a vampire. At least the recording of his turning had been destroyed. Now we just had to race word of mouth as the vampires bragged about turning a Shepherd. Roland had taken the video of the murder and hidden it in the church, not daring to take it with us.

I was also acutely aware that Haven had put himself at great risk. Granted, he got Roland in exchange, but he was still playing a very dangerous game with his own people. If they found out what he was doing – lying to his Council – he would be punished, as would Roland. And then the Conclave would find out, and doubly murder us.

"Embrace the suck," I said out loud like a mantra. "Embrace the suck."

Roland grunted. "Vampire jokes already?" he said in a low tone, emotionless.

I winced, not having considered that. "No. I didn't even think about that," I said honestly. *Stupid idiot*, I chided myself.

"I kind of liked it. Embrace the suck," he repeated. Then I heard a faint chuckle. I looked up at him to see his shoulders shaking slightly.

"You okay, Roland?" I asked nervously. We couldn't afford to have him falling to pieces.

His laughter cut off abruptly, filling the room with silence. My heart broke. Poor Roland.

"I'm... sorry, Callie. I let you down," he whispered, almost too low for me to hear.

"No, Roland. Don't apologize. That's the beauty of paying the piper. You don't have to apologize after payment, otherwise what's the point?" I said, sniffling slightly.

"You can't even look at me."

I gasped, jumping to my feet to stare at him directly. "Roland!" I shouted.

He slowly turned to look at me, face devoid of any life. Embracing the suck.

"That's not what I'm doing," I argued. "I couldn't care less about you being a vampire. I don't judge others on what they *are*. I judge others on what they *do*. And what you did is sacrifice everything you hold most dear to help your friends. Two living friends, and one friend who was murdered in cold blood. That was the most selfless act I have ever seen," I said, voice shaking with anger, pain, and sadness. "I can't look at you because right now, all I can see is the loss in your eyes. I know how much this cost you, and it hurts me to see you in pain."

He took a deep breath, and the ghost of a smile crossed his lips. "I'm sorry for looking so pitiful. I just..." he trailed off, eyes growing distant. "Everything that made me who I was... all I ever stood for... I just traded it in to become exactly what I've hunted for so long," he said. He no longer sounded sad, just... cold. A statement of fact.

"This doesn't change the man inside, Roland. That's up to you. It changes a lot of things, but not your core. Consider it a shitty haircut that won't go away," I teased, smiling hopefully.

He smiled crookedly.

"Except... I'll have to kill at least one person," he said tiredly.

I bared my teeth in a feral smile. "Then let's make sure that person deserves it..."

He blinked at me, as if the idea hadn't registered before now, which was surprising. It had been the first thing I thought of. A very wolfish grin split his cheeks. "That... sounds quite agreeable, Callie." I saw the flush of purpose suddenly fill his body as he found a way to make his curse the tool for his vengeance.

"Damned right," I said. "We'll kill him with your shitty haircut." Roland burst out laughing and I let out a sigh of relief. Baby steps. Keep his humanity in check. The golden necklace Haven had given him hung outside his shirt – a Greek Drachma. Haven's amulet. "How's that holding up?" I asked. We were in Abundant Angel Catholic Church, but I had yet to see him recoil in pain being so near to religious paraphernalia.

He glanced down, thumbing it thoughtfully. "No issue whatsoever. I think I'm going to keep it, no matter what Haven says," he added in a threatening tone. I shrugged.

"Sounds fair to me. We can be very convincing."

He smiled faintly. "I hope his sunscreen works."

"It's not a perfect solution. You can't just hang out in the sun all day, but he said it will give you a few hours without harm. Enough to find shade." I stared directly into his eyes, thinking of what else we might need. I had asked him about the scars on his body, the ones that had disappeared. He had looked disturbed, but told me to focus on the task at hand. We had enough on our plate already. On that note, he also encouraged me to stay guarded when in Rome – not to share anything about the Whispers, Angels, my new powers, or my vision quest.

We were all set.

"Let's find this son of a bitch, Roland. He betrayed everything and everyone. Either the Conclave is fully aware and corrupt from within, or they have no idea. This person must have some serious clout if they've been able to frame the wolves so easily."

Roland's lips thinned. He had caught me up on the Conclave and how they operated. I had always thought the Pope ran things, but apparently not. The Pope was aware and supportive of our group, but we were independent. Kind of like how a new U.S. President was briefed on all the secret departments behind the scenes when he first took office. The Pope had veto power, but otherwise left us alone. He had the rest of the world to look after. He let a group of seven wizard Cardinals run the Shepherds, and they called themselves the Conclave.

It wasn't a requirement for them to be ex-Shepherds – because many Shepherds didn't make it to retirement age. They also weren't required to be wizards, but the current members were.

"We're walking into a den of vipers. If they are truly innocent, they won't like us stomping all over their investigation. And the killer will do whatever causes the most chaos. Basically, we will be watched, and we will be watching them. Anything too overt and they will get suspicious. We need to be very, very careful with how we approach any questions," he said. Then he took me in with a regretful sigh. "Which means you probably won't become a Shepherd, after all."

I shrugged. "We're doing the right thing. That's all I need," I said. I didn't say *win, win*.

But I definitely thought it.

"It's going to be tough keeping your secret. You'll have to stay calm." He nodded, his eyes reflecting the same advice, to keep my own secrets close. He was right. The Conclave finding out I had Angel blood wouldn't be beneficial. I straightened the backpack on my shoulders. "You ready to go vamp out in the church of all churches?" I asked him, trying not to fidget with the thrill of danger looming before us.

A devilish grin split his cheeks, revealing his fangs. He held up a palm, and a red ball of fire popped into existence above his palm. I didn't clap in glee to see that he still had magic, but I definitely felt a huge wave of relief. The color made sense, but at the same time it made me leery. Would his tainted magic cause suspicion?

"I've still got some of my old tricks," he chuckled darkly. "Let's put them to use."

He flung his hand out and a Gateway appeared. We both froze.

The Gateway didn't resemble the typical doorway of sparks. Instead it was a rippling oval of crimson-hued liquid, like blood. Although vertical, it looked like we were peering at a distant apartment through a pond. We shared a very thoughtful look before I extended my foot through the rippling Gateway. Other than a small shiver on contact, nothing was different. I wanted Roland to see me trusting him completely. This new magic was just one of the things we both had to get used to. But it didn't hurt to bring up a good point. I smiled back at him encouragingly.

"It tickles," I said with a shrug. "But let's limit your use of magic in the Vatican. Just in case..." Then I stepped all the way through, having faith in my mentor's magic.

22

I studied the room of the apartment, ready for an attack. Everything was dusty, but nothing leapt out to kill me. I glanced down at my hands, fearing to see myself covered in blood or something from Roland's strange Gateway. But I was perfectly fine. His vampire powers were having unique effects on his magic, but I was simply glad to see that he still *had* magic.

Roland had chosen to use a Gateway to get to Rome – to a safe house he owned under a false name, not tied to the Vatican. We had briefly considered using one of the Doors to travel here, but after careful deliberation had decided against it. Who knew what would happen to a vampire that went through a door taking us to the Vatican? Also, using the doors might alert everyone to our early arrival, and we didn't yet know who we could trust, or who the traitor – or traitors – were.

Since my hearing wasn't until tomorrow, we had a full day to do some investigating into the murder, hopefully enough time to solve it before anyone was even aware of our presence. Not that I had any idea of where to begin since I had never been to Rome before.

I watched Roland step through his Gateway. He looked thoughtful as he studied it for a moment. Seeing no ill effects, he released it, the apartment falling to silence. He shrugged at my look. "No magic is probably a good idea..." he said. Then he opened his duffel bag and took out a pile of the bags. He rolled back a rug, lifted a board in the floor that looked like all the others, and stuffed the blood bags inside. He looked up at me and shrugged. "Just in case," he said, returning everything to normal. He zipped up the bag and hefted it over his shoulder, popping on some suave sunglasses, making him look like a distinguished badass in his casual blue suit and white shirt. I'd tried getting him to add some ruffles as tribute to his new powers. He had glared.

"Let's grab some food and get a feel for the streets," I said, shouldering my own backpack and readjusting my blue scarf. I wore navy capris pants and gold sequined flats. My blue and white striped top was concealed by my white jacket, and my own oversized sunglasses and red lipstick made us look like either celebrities or the worst kind of tourists. Our clothes would attract moderate attention and then we'd be dismissed for what we obviously appeared to be.

Hiding in plain sight.

Roland grunted his agreement and we exited the apartment. We had left our phones and wallets behind in Kansas City, not wanting to have any identification on us. Because showing up in Italy without a passport would be a bad idea. If we were swept up by the local police, we could always use magic to get home before they dug too deeply into our background. We would pick up some burner phones and use cash. Like terrorists. I reminded myself to give Claire my temporary number. It was a standing rule between us. Always have a method of communication.

We walked down a flight of stairs and were soon on ground level near a large fountain and a bunch of tourists. The late morning sun shone down on us and I instinctively shot a look at Roland, making sure he wasn't a pile of ash. He lifted his face to the sky, a faint smile tugging his cheeks. Phew. A man spontaneously combusting on the street would have attracted unwanted attention. And I didn't have time to baby Roland's sunburn with vamploevera.

I took a deep breath, inhaling all that was Rome, which was a mistake. It didn't smell as pretty as the pictures made it look, but the architecture was astonishing. Even the normal shops and businesses had an eclectic feel to them. But we weren't here to sightsee. We had a job to do, and limited time to do it. I followed Roland to a small electronics store, and twenty minutes later we had new phones in case of an emergency. I shot Claire a text, telling her I was out of town and this was my temporary number. Then we headed to a small restaurant with an outdoor seating area several blocks from the apartment. We ordered some espresso since we hadn't gotten any sleep, and a large tray of meats and cheeses. As an afterthought, Roland chuckled and asked for a bottle of Brunello, shrugging at the waiter. "We're on vacation, right?"

The waiter gave us a practiced smile and soon returned with our drinks and food.

I shook my head at Roland, smirking. "Red wine? Nice touch. We're definitely tourists in his eyes." I wasn't against his consumption of alcohol or anything, but I was surprised to see him doing so much of it lately. I was pretty sure the waiter had already pegged us as tourists, but it never hurt to reaffirm assumptions when trying to conceal your true purposes.

He shrugged, sipping his wine. I heard a faint *clink* as his fangs clicked the glass. I stilled, hoping he hadn't broken it. He looked angry, using his hand to wipe his stubble absently, but really checking his fangs.

"You're going to need to work on that," I said under my breath. Then, "This is really good, baby." I giggled loud enough for those nearby to acknowledge the ignorant Americans with a weary grunt.

He nodded. "Much better than back home, honey." He took another cautious sip, and then leaned forward over the meat tray, inspecting the options. "I got a whiff of the woman behind me and they just popped out," he murmured, barely louder than breathing. He was very carefully masking his frustration and embarrassment, but I knew him too well.

I placed a hand on his, smiling up at him adoringly. "You can do this," I encouraged.

He nodded, plucking up a piece of meat. He stuck it in his mouth and I saw his lips immediately clamp shut, as if trying to prevent himself from spitting it out. He forced himself to swallow, taking another sip of wine to wash it down.

I studied him. Could he not eat regular food anymore? That could be a problem if others caught on that he never ate. He waved a hand absently. "It's not terrible. I'm just not as hungry as I thought, but this wine is quite good." Translation – I can eat, but I don't enjoy it.

I nodded. "More for me." I casually glanced around us, pretending to take in all the sights. I could see the top of the Vatican from here, but it was still a good distance away. Tourists with cameras flocked near the fountain, taking pictures of a horde of pigeons. None of the other diners were very close, definitely not close enough to overhear if we spoke softly.

"We should pick up a Bloody Mary next. I've had a craving for them ever since that one you ordered on the plane." Roland nodded hungrily, and I hid the small shiver that went down my spine. That sounded good to him. But not the drink, just the fact that he could mix it with blood.

The steady flow of tourists walking by the small metal gate by our table was constant, and most of them seemed to be American, which was good for us. As much as being in a crowd of strangers didn't feel great when I didn't know who we could trust, it was also the best place to hide. One man stopped to take a picture of the fountain, shifting his camera to get the perfect backdrop. I watched him waddle away after a few clicks. I let out a nervous breath.

I noticed a man studying me from across the street. He flinched when I saw him. Then he extinguished his cigarette on the sidewalk, scowling. He entered a butcher shop and I saw him tie on an apron through the window. A butcher, not a spy. I needed to get a grip. Glaring at everyone who looked at me would be bad for my sanity.

I leaned closer to Roland, an excited smile plastered on my face as if anxious to get to the sightseeing. "Where to next?" I asked him.

"How about the Vatican?" a new voice said. We both tensed like startled deer as we saw a man peel out of a nearby crowd. He wore jeans and a light gray sweater. I had seen him pause to take a few pictures, but had dismissed him as harmless. He was facing us from only a few feet away on the opposite side of the small fence surrounding the outdoor seating area, and I realized I was gripping the butter knife in my palm under the table.

Roland's lips ticked up into a smile – but I could see the hidden tension in his shoulders. He knew this man, but that didn't necessarily mean anything. It also didn't bode well that he had found us less than thirty minutes after our arriving in Rome. Or less than thirty minutes since he'd had enough time to stalk us and hide in a crowd outside our restaurant.

Roland shook his head in surprised excitement. The man returned the look, not approaching at first. His smile seemed genuine, and he didn't move until Roland stood from his chair to reach out a hand. And... it felt like a respectful motion. The man giving Roland a moment to digest the surprise before he locked grips with Roland in a big hug, patting him on the back. He was a very handsome middle-aged man with thick dark hair and pearly white teeth. His nose was slightly crooked and I could see the scars on his knuckles.

This man was no stranger to danger. And as I looked closer, I saw the haunted look in his eyes. The look of a man who had lost a friend.

Still, I wasn't comfortable with this development.

Someone had just conveniently found us after we snuck into the city. I was more upset that out of all the people I had profiled in the crowd as suspicious, he hadn't been one of them. Was he that good, or was I simply off my game?

I realized he was staring at me, and that I was glaring at him. He smiled at me, eyes flicking to the knife under the table as if he could see it. "You were correct, Roland. She does look like a handful. In the best way possible, of course. You must be Callie Penrose," he said, extending his hand. "I'm Windsor Hart."

Not recognizing the name, and not wanting to earn his suspicion, I glared at Roland, setting the knife down. "What the hell did you tell him about me? A handful?" I asked, folding my arms.

The man coughed, muffling his laughter, and Roland sagged his shoulders in defeat, flashing Windsor a desperate look.

I finally extended my hand and shook his professionally. "Windsor. A pleasure." A Shepherd.

He smiled again, and I had to restrain myself from batting my eyelashes. He reminded me of an English aristocrat – genteel and sophisticated. I turned to Roland. "Any more of your old pals you're planning to surprise me with?" I asked him, tapping my foot.

Roland looked thoughtful, turning to Windsor. "That's actually a good point. We only just arrived. How did you find us so fast?" he asked, cocking his head curiously. I mimicked him, putting on a show for Windsor, acting as if the thought had just come to my attention.

"Wait, you just happened to find us? He didn't tell you to surprise me? Because he knows I hate surprises, so I just thought he was pulling one over on me," I said, frowning at Windsor.

His smile faded and he shrugged, glancing to make sure no one else was listening. "The city is warded. Any Gateways or significant magical surge produces a Flare on our systems. Then they send a Shepherd to investigate. Especially after..." he trailed off, shooting Roland a miserable look. I could tell that Windsor had also been close to Constantine. Either that, or he just felt terribly bad for Roland's loss.

I waited. Had he sensed anything off about Roland's magic? He didn't appear concerned. Curious at our arrival, but nothing else. We were still safe.

Roland nodded at the answer to his question. "That's new," he said. Then he took a deep breath, letting it out slowly as he acknowledged the reference to Constantine. "Terrible news," he grumbled. "I still can't believe the wolves were in on it. I never would have left them here if I had any suspicion they were a threat," he said. "I would have kept them in Kansas City or warned you to keep an eye out. Did they show any signs of violence before..." he trailed off.

Windsor shook his head. "Nothing. Constantine couldn't speak highly enough of their progression. He spent every minute he could with those girls, treating them like his own daughters. But I guess every monster is just waiting to lash out." Roland didn't even blink, but I sensed his breath stopping. Windsor didn't notice. "But we've found no other explanation. His throat was slashed with claws about the same size as a wolf, and we found them all together, obviously after a fight. If there had been a third party, they wouldn't have spared the wolves."

His voice sounded angry, but reserved.

I nodded at his assessment. "Have you spoken to them?" I asked.

Windsor shook his head fiercely. "No one is allowed to talk to them. Except the Conclave."

I frowned. "I presume they're locked up, right? Not a danger to anyone from behind a cell. Why wouldn't you question them? They saw everything!" I said hotly, not bothering to hide my anger. After all, they needed to be convinced that I was firmly embedded on their side, which meant I needed to show I could be coldly logical as well. It was a fine line, though. Because we didn't want anyone thinking we were interested in the *girls* – only the *situation*. Outraged that one of our own had been murdered. I let out a breath, trying to look embarrassed at the hard set to his jaw. "I'm sorry. I just feel terrible that I helped catch them, and that it ultimately led to this. A confession might be in order."

Windsor nodded, calming down. "We have time to discuss this later. For now, let's talk of lighter things." He winked at Roland. "I like her," he said, elbowing his friend.

Roland grunted. "We'll see about that. She's like alcohol. Fun at first sip, but the longer you spend time around her, the worse your hangover will be."

I glared at him, then at Windsor when he unsuccessfully tried to conceal his surprised laughter. Roland looked positively pleased. I had a lot of things I would have normally replied with, but since we were on Holy turf, and I didn't know Windsor well, I didn't want to step too far out of line. We might need a favor from him before long. Or he might be the killer. We just didn't know. Still, Roland had described me as a handful, so I couldn't appear meek.

"I am too refined to dignify that with a response, miscreant." I leaned closer to Windsor, whispering conspiratorially, loud enough for Roland to hear. "But I am *thinking* of several."

Windsor studied me curiously, as if trying to get a read on me. To categorize me. He seemed... different somehow. As if social interaction wasn't necessarily his strong suit. He could manage it, but he wasn't as quick on his toes in the wit department. More like an accountant. Again, I was reminded of the stereotypical stuffy Englishman. He quickly shifted back to business. "We expected you via the Doors," he said, watching our response.

Roland shot him a guilty smile. "I was hoping to show her a bit of the city before we got immersed with Constantine's murder and her hearing. I had hoped our arrival would be less... official. These American bumpkins know nothing of beauty or sophistication."

I punched the sweet spot on his arm, not trying to hold back. He grunted, shaking it off. Then he arched a brow at Windsor as if I had just proven his point. We couldn't afford them getting suspicious about our choice of travel. "I really don't care, but the old man seemed intent to show off the city. I would have rather gone straight to the big house," I admitted, pointing up at the top of St. Peter's Basilica in the distance.

Windsor watched us like a science experiment before finally shrugging. "No rest for the wicked, I guess." Then he smiled. "To be honest, I almost fell over when I realized the magic signature in the city was you. We never know what we're walking into when we get a flare. I watched from a distance, just to be sure," he admitted. Then he smiled. "Seems like the world does throw pleasant surprises every now and then. If you're finished with your meal, I can drive you to the Vatican," he said, extending a hand for my bag. I had to fight myself from recoiling.

"I can manage," I said, smiling at his offer.

He shrugged, as if to say he was just doing his job.

Roland sighed as if disappointed that he had to forego his planned relaxation, but resolved to get to the work ahead. "We're finished," he said, glancing at the table with a shrug. "Embrace the suck, right Callie? Isn't that your new mantra?"

I grinned delightedly. "You *can* teach an old dog new tricks!" I said, winking at Windsor. He was watching us as if not quite sure what to make of us. Stoic Roland and mouthy me. Maybe he didn't know what to do with a less grumpy version of Roland. He looked amused that old-school Roland had been paired with his polar opposite for a student. He did discreetly study Roland's hip suit, his curiosity obvious. If he knew Roland, he knew *style* was not part of his vocabulary. All in all, it was apparent to Windsor that I had changed the Roland he knew. Maybe that would work in our favor, attributing any changes in Roland to my influence.

Windsor had no idea how severe those changes were. The old dog had new tricks, alright.

And we were both hoping those new tricks wouldn't end up biting us in the ass.

We followed Windsor to his car, the two of them chatting idly as I studied the beauty of Rome. Roland shot a concerned look over his shoulder as if asking if I was ready.

"Embrace the suck," I said determinedly, as if speaking to myself. Windsor glanced back, shaking his head in amusement.

Roland was very careful with his duffel bag as we climbed into a small car that resembled a toy in my opinion. Because anyone who realized his bag was full of IV bags might have to be dealt with before they could blab about it.

And we didn't prefer to start off our trip to Rome by killing a vigilant Shepherd, security guard, or Priest.

But we would if we had to.

24

I had asked Roland about the Vatican after he survived a bombing there a few months ago while trying to track down a mole. The mole had decided explodey exits were fun, and had tried to destroy all evidence of himself and anything he was working on. It had worked, for the most part. Except Roland had survived.

Regardless, that instance made me realize that although spending a lot of time with Roland, I hadn't been familiar with exactly what went on in Rome. I had questions. How many Shepherds did they have stationed here in Vatican City? Shepherds were nomads, traveling the world as they saw fit, but the Conclave had to keep a few here on a permanent basis, right? How did their command structure work? Were all the Shepherds equal? Did they report to someone in particular, or just the Conclave?

How aware was the Conclave of the world at large? Did the Shepherds get to choose their missions as they saw fit or were they sent out with orders?

Roland hadn't been very forthcoming, so since I had Windsor trapped behind the wheel, I interrogated him. Windsor frowned in the rearview mirror, glancing over at Roland thoughtfully, as if wondering why I didn't already know the answers.

Roland sighed wearily. "I wanted her to focus her attention on more important things, saving the bureaucracy for her first visit here." Then he closed his eyes and leaned back into his seat.

Windsor nodded, and then, like a nerd asked about his first Sci-Fi Convention, he got a case of explosive oral diarrhea, eager to answer everything I could ask. I sensed that he saw this as a way to not only impress me, but also Roland. It was obvious he looked up to the older Shepherd.

Apparently, once you became a Shepherd you were allowed to wander the world, but were expected to stay in regular communication with the Conclave – or at least a specific member within the Conclave. If they ever had need of a Shepherd they would reach out, find the nearest one, and send them out to investigate. Other than that, the current Shepherds were pretty seasoned, and didn't need much guidance. On the other hand, if a Shepherd was new, they were kind of kept on a tighter leash, which made sense.

It was also encouraged for the Shepherds to find a student at some point, like Roland had with me. I had lucked out, though, because students were typically required to get a degree in theology or a related discipline. Either that or spend time working through the ranks of the Catholic Church, much like a priest. This took time. A decade or more of apprenticeship. They remained students until there was an opening for a replacement Shepherd or found a job working with the Office of the Conclave, helping with the behind-the-scenes work, fielding requests for assistance with exorcisms and monster sightings all over the world. It seemed I was the only student worth more than a casual grunt, and I was surprised to hear I had the most seniority.

Great.

Another fun tidbit was that after one mistake, the student could have their memories wiped to protect the Conclave's secrets from getting out. I struggled not to panic at that.

To go through all that training and then have it wiped away? I had been horrified. But Windsor had reassured me that these individuals were placed into strong careers that more than made up for their forgotten memories, or that they typically were fast-tracked into the Catholic church hierarchy to become priests. No other students were currently at the Vatican, and Windsor hadn't picked one yet, either.

Only four other Shepherds had made it in from out of town for the trial. When I'd asked how many Shepherds the Conclave kept in Rome, Windsor had simply smiled. "You'll see."

I sat in silence, fully understanding that I was a viable candidate for their memory wipe protocol. Roland had never told me. As I watched the buildings fly by, Windsor changed topics.

"It's actually good that you showed up early. An acquaintance of yours has requested to address the Conclave." He was smiling at me in the rearview mirror.

My blood chilled, but I kept my face neutral. "Oh?" I asked with a frown.

He nodded, eyes oddly animated at mention of this acquaintance. "Nate Temple from St. Louis. He said that he knew you personally, and that if we knew what was good for us, that we would let him speak to our..." his eyes flashed with amusement, "book club."

I bit my tongue. "Did he now..." I mused, smirking enough to mirror Windsor's amusement and nothing more. "I would hardly say we were close. I met him less than a year ago. But..." I locked eyes with Windsor, "it might be wise to give him a bit of excess rope, if you will. He's a very powerful wizard, and you know how those billionaire trust-funders get if you don't make them feel special." I winked at him.

His smile cracked, and I realized I may have just offended him. Was he a trust-fund kid, too?

Roland actually went into a coughing fit, waking from his pretend nap. I slapped him on the back. "You hear that, Rollie? Your pal Nate is here. That should be fun," I hooted, winking at Windsor's curious look, letting him see my sarcasm.

He seemed to choose his next words carefully. "I think I'm going to like you, Callie. Anyone that can add that many gray hairs to Roland's head is okay in my book." I nodded as I turned back to the window, watching as the Vatican drew closer.

What the hell was Nate doing here? I thought he was relaxing, taking a break.

Not demanding an audience with the fucking Vatican. And dragging my name into it.

The Swiss Guard manning one of the side entrances to the Vatican recognized both Roland and Windsor in the front seat of the car, but gave me very critical looks. They didn't say anything outright, but their eyes warned me to watch my ass. I smiled at them, feigning innocence, but they recognized a fellow soldier when they saw one. Their eyes pierced the façade of my outfit, and they knew I was just as dangerous as the two men in front of the car, I was just in disguise.

I took this as a compliment.

Judging by the way they spoke to Windsor, I wasn't sure if they were aware of his real duty as a Shepherd – that he was the guard against monsters while these two got to handle the simple things like guns and knives. They didn't search our bags, thank God. Whoever they thought we were, we ranked high enough to avoid that.

When I asked about it, Windsor had smiled. "On paper, we are the Ministry of Outreach. We help developing nations learn about God." Roland chuckled. "In all sorts of vague ways. We have wide powers and are granted our privacy, since working with other nations can become political. We also need guards, because strange lands can be dangerous..." He winked. I smiled back, nodding. That would explain why the Swiss Guards weren't concerned about priests who walked like soldiers living in Vatican City.

I tried not to let my eyes fall out of my skull at the beautiful architecture and history surrounding me, but I wasn't too reserved, because acting like the doe-eyed apprentice might give me a little more wiggle-room to sniff out the murderer.

So, I ogled everything. It's hard to say this without being judged a cynic, but from a business standpoint, it was kind of incredible how effective the Christian marketing department had been throughout history. Stunning, as a matter of fact.

Starting as such a small force, and growing to one of the top belief systems on the planet in the blink of two-thousand years. Some might say this was proof of God, but from a purely historical standpoint, or even anthropological, it was hard to see it through the same lens. Christianity had swept into new countries like a flood, and as was often the case, adopted facets of the existing religions, washing them into their own system to drown out the competition.

When politicians did it, they called it *spin*.

Rather than enter one of the more iconic buildings typically advertised on postcards – and I'll admit I couldn't have guessed the names of even two out of ten of those – we approached a smaller, but still elaborate building separate from the rest. Not a storage shed, exactly, but relative to the other structures? A storage shed.

"Holy Shed!" I exclaimed, pointing at the wide two-story building surrounded by groomed shrubbery and bushes. It was artfully crafted with twin columns leading to a covered entrance. Ornate wrought iron grates decorated the windows on both floors, and carved stonework decorated the roof. Like I said, it was still beautiful. Just not a junior Sistine Chapel.

Windsor looked as if he had just seen me twist the Pope's nipples, but Roland growled in a familiar manner. "We don't curse here, Callie," he reminded me.

"I didn't curse. In comparison to the other buildings, this is a storage shed. A Holy Shed."

Roland let out a very tired sigh and continued forward. "Welcome to the Conclave," he said over his shoulder. Windsor stared at me for a long second, not quite knowing how to respond before turning to follow Roland. The crimson was fading from his cheeks, but it still stood out. I shrugged and followed. Uptight bunch. For the first time, I noticed two hard-looking men standing at the entrance, staring open-mouthed at Roland. They wore jeans and matching, dark gray pea coats. They had obviously expected us to arrive via the Doors, and hadn't considered that Windsor's response call to a Flare in the city would net him such a big fish.

I saw their shoulders subconsciously straighten, as if trying to show the older Shepherd how much they had grown since last Christmas. He hid it well, but I could sense the hesitation in his stride. He feared them sensing his new... gifts. I'd lived with him for over a decade, and knew all his tells. Probably better than anyone but his old mentor, Constantine – just like he knew mine. Sure, these Shepherds might know secrets that Roland would never share with me, but I knew the *man*. The human. The psyche of Roland Haviar, Shepherd for—

Well, once-Shepherd. Now vampire Roland Haviar. Shepherd-pire.

I felt a phantom trickle of sweat roll down my spine at the chance they would sense his new changes despite the protective amulet tucked beneath his shirt. I shrugged my pack uneasily.

Roland bellowed at the two. "Crispin! Fabrizio! Where are your diapers?" he teased.

They rolled their eyes in unison. "You're closer to diapers than we are, old man!" the smaller one, Crispin, teased. But he had glanced behind him to make sure that no priests were around before saying it.

I clapped my hands, laughing. The return banter had not only been funny, but had put me at ease. We were close enough for them to sense Roland if they had been able to. Crispin making an old man joke? The call of my people. Maybe they weren't all as stuffy as Windsor.

At my outburst, the two Shepherds appraised me curiously, Crispin grinning in obvious appreciation. Not inappropriately leering, but a clean, wholesome look of admiration. I actually blushed, surprising myself as I took in the handsome blonde. Because even though he had a baby-face, his eyes were anything but innocent. They were playful, daring, and bold. Again, nothing creepy. Just a glimpse into his personality. He was the first to enter and the last to leave kind of guy. He smiled at me. "Crispin Voigt," he introduced himself, dipping his head. Then he hesitated, his shoulders straightening as he glanced at Roland. "First Shepherd..."

He obviously felt uneasy saying this to Roland, and there could only be one reason why. But Roland only smiled. "You will make Constantine proud." It wasn't quite a compliment, and not quite a warning. A little of both.

Crispin nodded. "If I can't, I'll step down," he promised. This seemed to satisfy Roland.

I turned to find Fabrizio staring at me, not looking impressed. He was bald and squat. His entire frame could be described as thick, and it wouldn't have been offensive. He was just solid. But he did have a belly, and even though I could tell it wouldn't hinder him, it was surprising to see on a Shepherd. This close, I noticed an emblem on his lapel – a white crucifix and a lightning bolt side by side. Crispin had the same emblem on his coat.

"Is it bring your daughter to work day?" he asked drily.

"Did you really meditate under a tree for seven days?" I asked without blinking, shrugging my backpack from my shoulders. I very dramatically tossed it to the side.

26

Roland grinned excitedly.

Fabrizio's forehead furrowed and I saw his fists flex at his side. At first, I took his response as anger, but I quickly realized that – even better – he hadn't understood my reference. I leaned closer to Windsor, knowing he was already socially awkward, whispering loudly. "Buddha joke. I find it's funnier when you have to explain it after," I said before leaning back again.

His face flushed purple in an instant, and Roland took a very exaggerated step out of the way.

Windsor blinked at that, wondering why Roland would step aside to allow Fabrizio easy access to beat his student bloody rather than defend me from the seasoned Shepherd.

But Windsor just didn't understand. Roland was stepping out of *my* way before he became collateral damage while I ruined Buddha's day. If I was up for it. I had enough anger to fuel my confidence, though. I hoped.

Fabrizio was apparently smarter than the other Shepherds, because his eyes darted to Roland's feet, picking up on the placement and recognizing the subtle shift that signified Roland's opinion – I was the greater threat. His eyes darted to Roland's face, looking momentarily stunned. Then he turned back to me, the color fading as a slow smile split his plump cheeks.

"Well," he said, as if wanting to rectify the older Shepherd's silent opinion.

I held out my hands and curtsied, never lowering my eyes from his.

Then he burst out laughing. "The stories about you must have *some* truth to them."

He stomped towards me, not aggressively, but purposely. I waited until he was directly in front of me – within my bubble – where he stopped. He held out his arms. "Can I have a hug?"

I blinked, wondering if this was some sort of trick, but his face was devoid of any of the telltale tremors that might indicate his readiness to throw down. He looked entirely relaxed.

"I love hugs," I said with a wide smile. I opened my arms and leaned my head towards his right shoulder in the universal hug gesture. Which meant I had a perfect view of his instep. I saw the subtle shift of his right foot and reacted instantly.

I gripped the sleeve of his shirt with my left hand as I stepped forward with my right foot, placing it beside his instep. I twisted my entire body as I lunged, my right arm wrapping around the left side of his significant waist. I slammed my hips below his belt near his upper thighs as I dipped down into a slight squat. Despite his massive size advantage, the sudden power of my hip striking below his center of gravity rocked his balance minutely.

This left me in a very odd-looking position – my ass pressed against his groin and my body huddled low as his upper body loomed over me. All he had to do was fall forward to squash me to death with a Pillsbury Doughboy giggle for good measure.

At least that's what it looked like. But I wasn't a victim here.

I was a fulcrum. I suddenly heard Whispers cackling in my mind, and idly wondered why. This wasn't magic, just hand-to-hand combat. I ignored them.

I exploded up, straightening my legs as I jerked his shoulder forward and spun his body over my back in the hip toss motion Roland had made me perfect so long ago. Knowing the size disadvantages that I would face over the years, he had focused on these types of movements before all else. Before I even looked at a blade or a weapon.

His legs flew straight up over his head as I slammed him down before me. Rather than ride him down to the ground, I released him. His shoulders hit first as he flipped upside down, followed by his legs slamming into the earth, his own weight and size used against him.

His breath left his body in a rush and he wheezed for a few moments, staring up at me in disbelief. It wasn't that he didn't know the move, but that he had likely forgotten it decades ago, never having to use it because he never encountered someone bigger than him.

He finally emitted a low, belly laugh, shaking his head in wonder. Soon he was belting out, the basso sound echoing off the nearby building. I held out a hand, offering to help him up.

He stared at it. "Now *that* was a hip toss, girlie!"

I scowled back at him. "Call me *girlie* again and I'll show you the second move I learned ten years ago, Fabio." His eyes instinctively darkened and I knew I had scored a direct hit. "We can continue the trip down memory lane until my name penetrates your thick skull. Callie Penrose."

He chuckled even harder, holding his hands out in an *I surrender* gesture. I nodded and then pulled him to his feet, not as graceful as I would have liked, because he hadn't helped as much as he could have, a subtle ego boost to ease his damaged pride.

Crispin was shaking his head, grinning from ear-to-ear. Windsor looked at a loss for words.

It wasn't that these men didn't know how to fight, it was that arrogance – as it usually did – had convinced them to underestimate me. They were used to being the big kids on the block, their title scaring monsters into hiding. They had forgotten what it was like to be hungry, needing to prove oneself on a regular basis.

And hungry people usually won.

Fabrizio scooped up my backpack, handing it to me before he wrapped a beefy arm around my shoulders, jostling me playfully as he grinned at the others. "Everyone, I would like you to meet my new best friend, Girlie Penflower." He instantly jumped back a step, dodging my elbow to his ribs with a chuckle. "But *you* can't call her that. Everyone else must call her Callie Penrose," he told them in mock seriousness.

I found myself smiling back at him. Then I shrugged. "I'll allow it, Buddha." He liked that better than Fabio, so I stuck with it.

He chuckled and then spit in his palm, extending it my way. "Fabrizio Donati." I did the same and we slapped skin, doing the testosterone shuffle that was common between two warriors.

Roland cleared his throat, striding up to Crispin. "As fun as it is to watch my student beat up the boys, I'm fairly used to it by now. Windsor made it sound like there was some urgency..."

Crispin nodded, placing an arm around Roland's shoulders in welcome. "You must mean Master Temple requesting an audience. Windsor texted us to wait for him, but didn't tell us why. Master Temple said he knew you, Callie."

I rolled my eyes at their mention of Nate, but on a distant level I was curious why Windsor hadn't warned these two ahead of time. For fun? Or some other reason? "You'll find that like most boys, Nate exaggerates." My familiarity with his name confirmed that I did know him, but that I wasn't pleased to be judged by this act. I needed to establish distance between Nate and I. Because I knew one thing.

If Nate Temple was here, the Conclave was about to have a very bad day. Nate was as tactful as a bull in a china shop, and if he wanted an audience, it couldn't be good. For the Shepherds.

The three Shepherds smiled, anticipating a lover's spat from my tone.

"Girlie, you can come back to Rome anytime. This might be the most fun we've had in years." Crispin and Windsor nodded their agreement, but I could tell that they were more reserved than Fabrizio. Sure, they could all joke around with each other, but I saw their game faces slowly shifting into place.

I glanced at Fabrizio. "Let's just hope that my next trip won't be for a funeral."

His face tightened, realizing how his words may have sounded. He made the cross over his chest and then strode ahead of me, wrapping Roland in a big hug. Roland rolled his eyes but hugged back. Then Fabrizio grasped the doors with Crispin. Roland and Windsor stepped up beside me as they opened the doors and we entered the mouth of the Holy Shed.

Before I left, I was determined to make that name stick.

27

We entered the building to find ourselves in what felt like a large museum. Gilded columns rose up to the ceiling twenty feet above our heads, creating what felt like an open hallway leading to two sets of doors at the end of the building. Hallways branched off on either side of us, but we marched forward, our footsteps echoing. I saw two more hard-looking men waiting at the door, but they didn't look as playful. They looked more like Roland. Like they had read the Old Testament a dozen times more than entirely necessary.

I wisely didn't ask them to confirm this.

Without a word – although they did dip their heads respectfully at Roland – they opened the doors for us. I heard Fabrizio and Crispin speak a few words to them before following us inside. This room felt more like a courtroom mixed with a church. But that could have just been because seven old men were seated in a row at the end of the large room, like Supreme Court Justices. They all wore robes in different designs and colors, but all seemed somewhat uniform at the same time. Did that mean this wasn't their only obligation? Saving the world from monsters was just a hobby of theirs? Or was it to help them blend in with the other members of the Church? The men themselves varied in about every way imaginable, other than the fact that they were all balding or had thin patches of white hair. One was black, another was Asian, but the rest were old white dudes.

Other than the sense of raw power radiating from them, like an electric fence of magic, they were entirely unremarkable. But they all had the same pin as the Shepherds and a milky white film over their eyes.

I frowned, then shot Roland a sharp glance. He nodded very slowly.

I turned back to them, trying to hide my shock. Then I realized it wasn't necessary to hide my emotion. The entire Conclave was blind. Literally. And they were searching for a murderer.

Sweet, baby Jesus.

It was obvious that we had interrupted them, because the Conclave looked on the verge of shouting. The source of their ire was obvious. I studied the two much younger men standing before them, where a lawyer would state his case to the judge and jury.

Nate Temple was handsome, and even staring down seven powerful wizards, an easy sense of authority rolled over his shoulders like a cape. His hair looked darker than when I had last seen him, but I knew it shifted from lighter to darker with the seasons. He claimed to be a dirty blonde – and maybe at one point he had been – but his hair had always leaned more towards brown in my opinion.

His pal was Alucard Morningstar. He was a Daywalker Master Vampire, but had no ties to the vampire nation as far as I knew. He stood before the Conclave, shoulders erect, and face blank. He had long dark hair, and reminded me of a romance novel cover model. He also spoke with a faint Southern drawl, which flat did me in.

A vampire was standing on Vatican grounds with seven angry wizards and a handful of warrior priests. I almost flinched to see that he was clutching a Bible. Roland's shoulders shook, and I prayed he wouldn't do anything stupid. Inwardly, my mind raced. Alucard was unique, a Daywalker, but did this mean that he also had an amulet, or had he found a way to handle religious items? Hope shone in Roland's eyes.

I regained control, thinking furiously. Neither looked properly humbled before the Conclave.

The old men looked pious, official, and highly annoyed at this strange pair before them. Even blind, their disdain was impressive, as if they could somehow sense Nate's arrogance.

The man sitting in the center of the line of wizards opened his mouth to speak, but cut off abruptly as Nate turned his back on them to smile at me. Maybe they weren't *entirely* blind.

"Hey, Callie. Imagine seeing you here." Nate's green eyes sparkled playfully.

I couldn't help but smile back, even though I wasn't pleased to see him here in the middle of my mess, making it messier. "Hey, Nate." I turned to Alucard with a warm smile. "Good to see you, too, Alucard. You let him drag you into this?" I asked, smiling.

He flashed me a grin, nodding in resignation. "As usual. Never been here before."

I didn't let anything show, but alarm bells were going off in my head. I could sense that Roland was unnaturally still. He knew Alucard was a vampire.

As if on cue, Alucard casually sniffed the air. It was so subtle that only Roland and I noticed it. Did he sense Roland? Or was it something else? Maybe he sensed the murderer nearby? Blood still on his hands or something? Or an increased pulse somewhere, which could mean anything.

But it brought everything back into stark clarity. One of the Shepherds had been murdered, and it was highly likely that someone in this room knew the truth – possibly one of the other Shepherds. After all, they worked for the Conclave, and if the Conclave gave one of them a command to kill their fellow Shepherd, what trumped that?

Was faith or loyalty more important to these men?

I realized I was standing in a crowd of wolves, and that the blind sheep on the dais were calling the shots. I didn't let anything show on my face as I turned back to Nate. "What are you doing here?" I asked casually, but my eyes warned him to flee.

The center man in the Conclave coughed loudly. He was taller and thinner than his cohorts. "We can handle this from here, Miss Penrose," he said with a commanding glare. His crosshairs were slightly above and to the left of my face. I forced myself not to laugh.

Nate ignored him and Alucard let out a suffering sigh, as if making peace with his life up to this point. "I already told you. I wanted to introduce you to Alucard. He's my friendly neighborhood vampire pal. This *monster* is better than most *humans* I know." The threat in his voice was crystal clear as he indicated the Bible in Alucard's hands. The other Shepherds took notice for the first time and their jaws dropped in disbelief.

But why had Nate found it necessary to make a trip for that? My pulse quickened as he continued to watch me, eyes trying to comfort me for some reason. "My second course of action is to make a hefty donation to your book club," he said with an easy shrug. "Like I told you in the beginning, Roland takes exceptional care of Kansas City." His eyes included my efforts, but he was smart enough not to mention that here. "I want to offer aid to his cause. But I want his opinion on where my donation should go," he added, staring straight at Roland.

Roland locked eyes with Nate, silently wondering what game the billionaire was playing. I briefly wondered why Nate hadn't just offered the donation to Roland in Kansas City, but as I thought about it I found myself nodding proudly. Doing it here, in front of Roland's bosses would offer a compliment that couldn't be ignored. Handing the money directly to Roland might have raised suspicions from the Conclave, but appearing here to treat it like an award?

At any other time, I would have called it a stroke of genius. But right now? He had just drawn a big assed bullseye on our backs. At a time when we were trying to remain incognito. *Damn it, Nate...* I thought to myself.

The other Shepherds were staring at Roland, frowning. Then their eyes shifted to Crispin, but he was looking to the Conclave, reading their faces. The Conclave was grumbling to themselves, but Nate wasn't paying attention to them. Well, they probably didn't even see his attention.

This was the most ridiculous thing I had ever witnessed. A blind Conclave?

Roland finally dipped his head at Nate in gratitude, and then pointed at Crispin. "He leads us. I trust his judgment, but I will offer my advice." Nate finally turned to Crispin and gave him a friendly nod, the matter settled in his eyes. The Conclave hadn't even noticed the exchange.

He let out an annoyed breath as the Conclave began to mutter louder behind him. He shot me a weary look as if having to deal with a toddler throwing a fit before finally glancing over his shoulder at them. "It's my condition, and if you have a problem with that, I can take my money elsewhere. Are the Palmarians still a thing? Speaking of, isn't the Antipope visiting today?"

You could have heard a pin drop. Alucard raked his fingers through his hair, looking like he had decided to use the Bible as a weapon if it could help him escape. I glanced at Roland, hoping for some insight into whatever the hell Nate was talking about, but he merely looked uncomfortable, back to discreetly studying the vampire out of the corner of his eye.

"That will not be necessary, Master Temple," the taller Conclave member said, looking like he was chewing tinfoil with a mouth full of cavities. "Of course, you may speak with the Shepherds and get their input on where your... donation will be best utilized." His heavy eyebrows settled directly on Nate, as if he wasn't blind at all. Huh. "But you should know you cannot buy your way into Heaven." Nate blinked at him.

Then he burst out laughing, doubling over as he slapped his knees. He did this for a good ten seconds before taking a deep breath and standing back up, wiping his eyes. "I'm not here to buy a bus ticket, but where I'm from people usually say *thank you*, and I return that courtesy with *you're welcome*." The tall wizard did not look pleased at this, but Nate waved a hand dismissively, turning back to the Shepherds instead, much to the Conclave's outrage. He raised his voice over their shouting. "What am I doing talking to them?" he said, smiling politely at the Shepherds, who looked about as uncomfortable – and untrusting – as it was possible to look. "I find that bureaucrats are very good at spending money... in all the wrong places." He winked.

Nate turned to collect his bag and saw Alucard standing very still. Nate glanced back at the Shepherds, a menacing glint flickering in his eyes. "Oh, and he's with me. If even *one* of you so much as *thinks* about harming him, I'll murder *all* of you." In a blink, the menace was gone and he gave them an easy shrug. "Fair warning," he said with a friendly laugh.

Then he scooped up his satchel – the one I had given him from Darling and Dear, I noticed with a pleased grin – and strode up to me. The Shepherds around me were as still as statues. Before I could extend my hand for a professional handshake, he wrapped me up in a hug and was detaching himself before I could slap him. He wrapped his arm around Roland's shoulders like they were old pals, and was guiding him from the room before Roland could argue.

Not knowing what else to do, I shot a look at Alucard who merely sighed in agreement before setting down the Bible. He held out his elbow to lead me from the room.

"We are not finished here!" The taller Conclave member roared.

I glanced over my shoulder, readjusting my pack, to find the seven wizards staring in our direction. Nate and Roland had already left the room. Not knowing what else to do, and doubting they could see me anyway, I shrugged with an innocent smile. "I'm just escorting a generous benefactor and his guest. As I understand it, you didn't need to talk to me until tomorrow, and since this meeting is apparently over... I'd rather not have one of those Pomeranians find Nate Temple in the hallway."

Fabrizio burst out laughing. "Pomeranians!" he hooted, and the other Shepherds battled smiles of their own, not in any effort to further infuriate the Conclave, but at my comment.

I shrugged, embarrassed. "Whatever they're called," I amended, frowning. "I better follow my mentor. He gets worried if he can't find me," I winked at Crispin. He nodded tersely, not finding fault in me, but knowing he was about to get his ass reamed by the Conclave.

I led Alucard from the room. "You better tell me what the hell you two are really doing here, because you walked right into a den of vipers," I hissed to the vampire under my breath.

He grunted. "You don't know the half of it..."

Which sent a very real blast of fear down my spine as the doors closed behind us.

28

I found Nate talking to Roland outside the building. The two men saw us and waved us over eagerly, which was surprising to me. Roland getting along with Nate?

I squared my shoulders and scowled at the billionaire wizard. "What are you doing here, Nate? We've got some serious shit going down right now, and your arrival just made it worse."

Nate frowned, but he did look suddenly guilty. "I'm not here about you. I just name dropped you to get my foot in the door." He glanced at Roland. "I really am making a donation, and I really do think it's better to get input from you and the other Shepherds rather than the Conclave." His frown grew thoughtful. "Alucard was with me, and I couldn't turn down the opportunity to rattle them with his Bible trick." He jerked his chin at Alucard, cooing in a soft tone. "Who's a good vampire? *You* are! Yes, *you* are!"

Alucard suffered this with a sigh, and Nate finally gave up.

He turned back to us, checking to make sure we were alone. "They need to see that the world is changing. Things aren't always what they seem, and what used to be considered evil might not be as evil as they assume." He pulled out a coin from his pocket, letting us see the meaning of his words before pocketing it.

Roland grunted, but his eyes danced with silent excitement. He had finally found a reason to like Nate. I considered the coin in silence. It was the Horseman of Hope Mask. Nate had been drafted onto the Apocalypse squad as the Fifth Horseman of the Apocalypse. His actions kind of made sense, now. He would need the Shepherds at one point, and it was better to piss them off now and let them get used to the idea of working with monsters rather than them hesitating at the idea when we needed to band together later.

I shivered at the thought. I had enough on my plate as it was. If our mission went tits up here, the Apocalypse wouldn't matter at all to me. We'd be dead.

"What are you two doing here?" He asked as he handed Roland a check.

Roland blinked at the amount, shaking his head. I didn't even want to ask.

"I left the *pay to the order of* line blank," Nate said, shrugging. "Because I don't know how you guys handle the books." Roland nodded dumbly, still staring at the check. He finally put it in his pocket, very carefully, as if it were a bomb.

Alucard was studying Roland again. "Might want to step out of the sun," he said casually.

Nate frowned at Alucard, then rolled his eyes and turned back to me. "Well? What's up?"

But I was studying Roland, who suddenly looked as tight as a coiled spring. He slowly lifted his arms and stepped into the sunlight, spinning in a slow circle. Then he locked eyes with Alucard. "I find the sun agrees with my complexion in my old age."

Alucard's eyes tightened, looking thoughtful as he stared at Roland's skin with a frown, but he finally let it go, sniffing the air again. I let out a sigh of relief. The amulet Haven had given Roland was working, masking his abilities. If that secret came out, Nate would never leave.

I turned to Roland, silently asking him if it was okay to answer Nate's question. After a brief hesitation, he shrugged in response.

Then he turned to Nate. "I'm not going to lie, seeing you put the Conclave in their place was surprisingly satisfying. Callie's a bad influence on me."

Nate's jaw dropped as if he had seen Hell freeze over.

I rolled my eyes and took Nate's arm, forcing the others to follow me as we walked the grounds. I didn't want to stand too near to the buildings in case they had surveillance. "One of the Shepherds was murdered, and two of our friends were framed for it," I said softly, ignoring the whiff of black licorice that always surrounded Nate – some odd kind of cologne. Or he had been gargling absinthe. Either was likely.

He didn't slow, but his face did grow tighter. He didn't speak as he continued walking. I could hear Alucard and Roland speaking softly to one another behind us, but since I didn't hear hissing, I assumed the two weren't about to kill each other. If they decided to fight, every single warrior for a hundred yards would pound them with bullets, seeing two vampires go head to head, or worse yet, the Shepherds seeing one of their own attacked by a vampire.

"What's up with Roland? He seems different," Nate murmured, not turning to look at me.

I opened my mouth, truly wanting to tell him because I trusted Nate. Even though he was brash, bold and dangerous, he was unbelievably loyal and would never betray me.

On purpose.

But it wasn't my secret to share.

"It's complicated. You can ask him if you want, but I know he's very concerned about the dead Shepherd. He was Roland's mentor," I added meaningfully.

Nate grunted, but I wasn't sure which comment had elicited the response. "You think it was an inside job. Why? And you must be onto something if Roland agrees," he added.

I nodded. "He was the first to suspect it."

Nate arched a brow at me in surprise. "Shit. Do you have any leads? Proof? Evidence?"

I shook my head. "It's why we're here." Then I sighed. "Well, not the only reason. Apparently, they have a hearing scheduled for me tomorrow. About my recent exploits."

Nate skidded to a stop, spinning me to face him, his face a thunderhead. "I don't like that word. Especially not after what you just told me..."

I locked eyes with him. "I'm a big girl, Nate. And I have a Roland."

He glanced back at the two men, eyes scheming. I pinched his arm and he flinched turning back to me. "We've got it, but I appreciate your concern. Now, who was the other party you mentioned? The Palmer-something."

He blinked at me. "You haven't heard of the Palmarians?" Seeing my blank look, he shook his head. "How do I know something about religion that you don't?" he said under his breath. Then he cleared his throat, preparing to lecture.

"I'm pretty sure they're defunct, now, but they caused quite a stir for a time. I just said it to ruffle their feathers," he admitted. Of course he had. "They were a schism of the traditional Catholic Church. In the late 1970's there was a major disagreement and a group of Bishops broke off from the Vatican, declaring the sitting Pope excommunicated. Over time, they elected their own Popes and constantly refuted the legitimacy of the Vatican. That's their side," he winked. "People on your side called him the Antipope. The Palmarians were much more… conservative in their beliefs, and weren't fans of the *open-mindedness* of the Vatican." He leaned closer. "Suffice it to say, they weren't friends. Neither considered the other legitimate, and it was a highly contested argument in certain circles." He finally let out a breath, waving his hand dismissively. "Basically, they were a big media spotlight that didn't do anyone any good. A lot of questionable activity surrounded them, too. I don't know what happened to them, or if they are even still around, but their actions gave rise to numerous other factions. A similar Bishop is here, now, visiting the Vatican. I've heard him referred to as the new Antipope. Bishop Anthony Gregory Gutierrez. I only said it to make them see reason in my donation," he admitted.

I shook my head in amazement. I remembered hearing something about an Anti-Pope years back, but it had sounded like some far-fetched conspiracy theory, so I had never looked into it. "The Palmarians had a real church with priests, buildings, and everything?" I asked, incredulous. Why hadn't Roland ever told me about that?

Nate shrugged. "Not sure how much power they had or anything, but I know they were a thorn in the Vatican's side. This new Antipope isn't a Palmarian, but he may as well be."

Roland strolled up to us, clearing his throat. "Let's get out of here and grab some food. We were rudely interrupted earlier." Nate nodded. Was that a hint that Roland was thirsty? "Oh, and Temple? Don't use your magic in town. They have some kind of tracking device. A Shepherd paid us a visit less than thirty minutes after we got here."

Nate frowned. "That sounds… useful," he said, his eyes growing distant, likely wondering what he had to do to steal it from the Church. Then he shot a curious look at Roland, wondering why the Shepherd had opted to share an inside secret. The two weren't exactly friends.

I pinched his arm again. "No stealing from the Church, Nate. I mean it." He looked suddenly guilty, as if the thought had entered his mind. I rolled my eyes. Incorrigible. "Do you have time for lunch before you leave? We have enough on our plate without having to worry about them finding out about your white whips or that coin."

Nate nodded, not looking concerned, but knowing I was probably right. "We fly out in about two hours. I've got a meeting back home I can't miss," he said, eyes intently sweeping the grounds out of habit, checking for dangers.

"Good," I said, hiding my relief. Nate wasn't sticking around.

He approached one of the Swiss Guards. "Mind pulling my car around?" he asked to the man's back. He was obviously on break. The guard instantly looked offended at being interrupted, but when he turned and saw who it was his eyes grew hungry, likely realizing he was being offered a few seconds to drive a stupidly expensive car.

"Of course, Master Temple." He scurried away as if the Pope was on fire.

Nate nudged me in the ribs. "Watch this."

A few minutes later, the car pulled up – a gleaming silver Bentley of some kind. I couldn't even afford the magazines that advertised such vehicles. It glistened in the sun like liquid silver, and a small part of me purred – that Angelic power I had been practicing with, which had a silver hue. When used, my vision changed to a world of silver, and let me see a few seconds into the future. It also gave me some kind of Holy armor, which had saved my life when fighting a demon. Oh, and freaking *wings*, can't forget the wings.

I flinched when I realized I was listening to Whispers in my mind, almost understanding them this time. Nate was studying me critically. "Sorry. Nice car," I complimented, kicking myself as the Whispers faded like smoke.

The Swiss Guard climbed out, shaking his head with a grin that was definitely not standard issue. "I'm sure I felt a ticking in the suspension. We should probably have the mechanic—"

Alucard snorted. "Nice try."

The guard let out a long sigh. "Worth a shot. Have fun out there, and try not to sin. They frown on that kind of thing here," he said with a wink.

He had no idea.

29

We sat in a casual restaurant with a pleasant view of the streets – much like the one we had visited earlier today when Windsor had found us – and were sipping coffee after our meal as the early afternoon breeze kept the air fresh, but not too cold. Our bags sat beside the table.

Nate's rental car – or, hell, maybe he had bought it just for his short trip – had been stunning. It wasn't until I sat inside a Bentley that I really understood the difference between it and my truck. Like entirely different worlds. From the outside, they were easy to dismiss as expensive shells over the same clunker I drove, but once inside? Wow.

The leather had felt soft enough that it may have still covered a living body. The wooden trim had been hand-carved from a single tree in some foreign magical kingdom, and sitting inside gave me the natural feeling that I was wealthier than everyone else in the world. Like the air-conditioner had infected me with arrogance and elitism. That being said, it was pleasant, reminding me of just how different Nate and I were. He had been born into this world where having piles of money was normal. But what I appreciated about these wake-up calls was that he never flaunted it as a weapon. Sure, he showed it off, but always in ways that were more like a gift to his friends. Not showing off the car as his, but happy to share a very fun, unique experience with them. But it was hard to see it that way sometimes. It was easy to let jealousy take control, and remaining objective was hard while surrounded by a million dollars' worth of car. I somehow managed. First world problems.

After dinner, Roland had taken several sips from his personal thermos – having tucked it into his duffel bag back home – his eyes twinkling at Alucard's response, which was fun to watch. Alucard's eyes had practically bugged out of his skull and he looked on the verge of a conniption. I kept Nate distracted, asking him about St. Louis and his recent drama since I had seen him last, as Roland pulled Alucard aside for a private talk a few tables away. My mentor shot me a look, as if imploring me to trust him, but it wasn't like I could have stopped him.

If Roland wanted to tell Alucard he was a member of the blood-sucking club, that was really up to him. And to be honest, it was probably better to tell Alucard outright before he started digging into it on his own, asking questions.

Finished catching me up, Nate shot Roland and Alucard a wary look. "What's up with Roland? And why does Alucard care? Is it the Bible thing?" he asked, scratching his jaw.

I shrugged. "I find it's better not to ask. Probably a good guess, though," I said, latching onto his idea. "Maybe he's trying to convert the vampire to Christianity," I added, grinning playfully.

Nate studied me. "Except you know he's not," he said firmly. For a moment, my heart froze, staring into those green eyes and wondering if he would ask me outright. I didn't want to lie to Nate. He finally grinned, shrugging unconcernedly. "If you don't want to tell me, that's fine. Everyone needs their secrets, and I imagine Roland has a wagonload. I would never ask you to betray him. But I do expect you to let me know if it's something I could help with. There's a fine line between respecting privacy and the land of *Keeping the Secret Gets Him Killed*."

I nodded in agreement, glancing back at Roland. I could tell Nate was dying to know, but that he was sincere about not being upset with me for keeping Roland's secret.

"You're heading back to St. Louis?" I asked, changing the subject.

Nate waved a hand as he took a sip of his wine. "Meetings. Boring, but necessary." He set his glass down and leaned in closer to me. "You sure you don't need any help here? You made it sound pretty serious." We hadn't talked about me, because I knew if I mentioned anything he would find a reason to stick around. I had doggedly kept the discussion focused on him.

But because it was Nate, the word *hearing* had been enough to keep him on the scent. I debated, swirling my glass. Not because I was considering asking him for help, but because he was right. It was serious. "We've got it. Kind of an in-house problem."

He nodded, leaning back in his chair as he mimed dusting off his hands. "My part is finished. If you do end up needing me, you know I'll be there."

I nodded, smiling at him. "Thanks, Nate."

Roland led Alucard back to the table, having to guide him back with a supporting hand. Alucard looked like he had been punched repeatedly in the groin. I could tell from the look on his face that he didn't intend to blab, but Nate cleared up the situation very easily.

"None of my business, Roland. I won't pry. But like I told Callie, I'm here if you need me." Then he lifted his glass in cheers. Alucard looked as if a huge weight had just been lifted from his shoulders, realizing he wouldn't have to lie to his friend. Roland studied Nate for a moment, as if debating to spill the truth.

He lifted his glass instead. "Thank you," the Shepherd-pire said.

Nate shrugged it off, hefting his glass higher. "To the Vatican," he smiled. "May she survive the wrath of Missouri." Roland's eyes twinkled in amusement, which was rare for him.

We finished off our drinks and stood from the table. We walked outside to find a sleek SUV idling beside Nate's car. A logo on the side showed a plane taking off. The passenger window lowered to reveal a man in a suit, waving at Nate.

I frowned, but caught the keys Nate tossed my way as he climbed into the SUV. "He works for the private airport. I texted him earlier to give us a ride," he admitted with an easy shrug. "I'll call the rental company and have them pick your car up in..." he studied me thoughtfully, "a few days?" he asked.

I grinned, nodding. "This means a lot to Roland."

Alucard burst out laughing as Roland scowled. "Callie doesn't have an international driver's license," Roland blurted, darting towards the driver's side and shoving me out of the way. Nate sighed, shooting me a compassionate look. He waved his goodbyes and I turned to glare at Roland, even though he wasn't looking as he climbed into the seat. I took a step and—

"I hate to see you leave," Nate shouted out, making me spin. "But I *love* to see you walk away!" The SUV pulled out, the engine revving. I heard

Alucard burst out laughing before their windows rolled up. I glared at the fleeing car, fighting the smirk that threatened to break free.

Roland was busy fidgeting with the seat adjustments, ignoring my disappointment. He cheered as he finally got adjusted properly and hit the *Start* button. Since I was close enough, the car purred to life with a throaty rumble. He held out a hand, grinning triumphantly. I threw the keys at him and stormed over to the passenger front door. Then I had another thought.

I climbed into the back instead. "Take me to the Vatican, Driver," I said pompously, turning to stare out the window as if he was beneath me.

He grumbled unhappily. "Nate is rubbing off on you."

I glanced at the peasant, sniffing in distaste. "There goes your tip."

Roland responded by pressing down hard on the pedal, and as we tore through the streets, I was soon grinning from ear-to-ear.

It seemed money *could* buy happiness.

"We have work to do, Callie, and I may need you to be the objective one. I grew up with these people, and the victim was my mentor. I'll have trouble not taking this personally." He rubbed his amulet between a thumb and finger. "Especially with my new appetite..."

I nodded. "We don't know who we can trust. Someone is behind it, and to get the jump on such an experienced Shepherd," I met his eyes, "it's got to be someone who knows the organization well. Someone close... Someone very dangerous. We need to be careful with our questions."

He nodded, his lips curling back at the betrayal.

"You didn't tell me the Conclave was blind," I complained.

He glanced at me. "I thought that was apparent from their sloppy investigation." I blinked. Was that... a joke? He didn't give me time to applaud. "They aren't as blind as you think..."

And with that cryptic comment, I shivered. His fangs glistened in the rearview mirror, and I wondered if we were making a terrible mistake.

30

We sat at a table in a private room of the Holy Shed. I had been informed that it was officially named after their pretend Ministry of Outreach, but that the Shepherds simply called it the Conclave. I told them I liked Holy Shed better, but was outvoted. Fabrizio agreed with me.

The room was plain, but the furniture was of good quality. And without seven blind wizards angrily staring in my general direction, I felt infinitely more relaxed.

The Holy Trinity, as I had dubbed them – Crispin, Fabrizio, and Windsor – had been alerted the moment we returned and had walked us back to the Holy Shed to discuss Nate's donation. They had changed into a uniform of sorts, almost like black military fatigues with a small white cross on each shoulder. I'd never seen Roland wear anything like it. I eyed our bags discreetly, sitting near Roland's feet. We needed to get them somewhere safe. Even though the blood bags were spelled from detection, it would raise questions we didn't want to answer if anyone saw Roland carrying around IV bags. Good thing they were hidden.

But it still made me nervous. I was mildly annoyed we hadn't been offered rooms yet.

We needed to start digging for information, but we had to be careful about it. It would be strange if we didn't ask about the murder, but it would attract unwanted attention if we seemed too interested in the murder. It was a fine line, and before *that* we needed to earn a little trust. Camaraderie. Get a feel for everyone here. Check schedules, alibis, friends, and anything else that might lead to a lie.

Because there had to be a pile of lies to keep the truth of a murder so secret. And as much as I wished it were different, I couldn't just show them the video of the murder – the proof that it wasn't the two werewolves – because that would lead them to learn about Haven, and subsequently, that Roland was now a vampire. We might also end up showing it to the wrong person. The killer. Who had taken the time to destroy the surveillance equipment and murder the store owner in a freak car accident.

If we showed anyone that video without sharing where we had gotten it, Roland had been adamant that we would be tossed in a jail cell until we revealed our source. Because the Conclave were supposedly rigid in verifying every single detail.

They had done a real bang-up job verifying details so far.

Revealing the video could also alert the killer into running, where he might prepare to strike again from an unknown location. Perhaps on a bigger scale. We needed to catch him and gauge the level of corruption within the Vatican's walls. Make sure he was working alone. That he hadn't been sanctioned by the Conclave itself.

To this effect, Roland had casually asked after security, wondering if the Vatican had undergone any upgrades like the magic Flares they could track in the city. Windsor had been all too eager to share, rattling off a bunch of comments about wards around certain areas, but nothing overly alarming.

It was a relief to learn that they didn't have any wards against certain flavors of supernatural, like vampires, because they often held meetings with various supernatural dignitaries, and it wouldn't be productive to incinerate guests during a talk. Roland was safe from that, at least.

They also informed us that the Shepherds in town had been temporarily assigned to various parts of the Vatican. Crispin, Fabrizio, and Windsor – being the permanent locals – managed the area around the Conclave building. With the recent murder, they were taking no chances, so even though it was overkill, they shared the task of guarding this area. Four other Shepherds visiting for the trial were patrolling other sections of the Vatican. We hadn't seen them because we hadn't left this area yet.

I had already coaxed the three Shepherds into sharing stories of their youth, about the trouble the four of them had gotten into as students, or on their first hunts. Even Roland had seemed to relax into a state I wasn't familiar with – he was easygoing and nostalgic.

It was time to shift gears. "What do you think the Shepherds should use Temple's donation on, Crispin?" I asked.

He leaned back in his chair, studying Roland and me. Then, with a smirk, he pointed a finger at Roland. "What about some fancy bling like Roland? Or did his lady love buy it for him?" he said, teasing me. Fabrizio grinned, leaning forward.

I bit back my immediate response, and then reconsidered. It just might help. Either that, or Roland was going to kill me. Worth a shot. "You might be used to older men hooking up with younger disciples around here, but it's frowned upon in Kansas City," I said.

Crispin groaned and Fabrizio burst out laughing. Windsor looked anxious, as if unsure whether he should laugh or remain professional. Crispin finally sighed, shooting a desperate look at Roland, who merely sighed. "I've tried and tried. There is no domesticating her."

"Damned right, there's not," I said hotly, sending Fabrizio into another fit of laughter.

"She *has* to be Italian," he wheezed between breaths, slapping Windsor's arm, who was struggling to remain neutral, hiding his smile from Crispin. "It's the only explanation."

Crispin finally turned back to me. "Just be careful how free you are with your tongue around some of the others. They're not as... open-minded, believe it or not," he said sarcastically, smiling enough for me to see that he hadn't taken offense. I could sense him struggling under his new duties – wanting to be the hardcore, straight-faced leader while having fun with his old pals.

"Back to my bling," Roland muttered, unsnapping the clasp on the chain and taking a risk. I held my breath, hoping this was worth it. They needed to see the amulet as nothing special. And although wizards couldn't sense vampires, there was still the risk that this could go horribly wrong. At least we knew there were no spells preventing vampires from this building.

Roland tossed the amulet to Crispin who caught it easily before inspecting it. I held my breath, waiting for the world to end – for Roland to vamp out and kill everyone. But nothing happened. As I stared at it, I realized I could sense it in a way. Like turning an ear towards an electric fence. The sensation faded as I turned my ears slightly away. I remembered a similar sensation when Haven had given it to Roland. A faint... vibration to the air. An almost unnoticeable hum of power. And it was definitely the amulet, not anyone in the room. No one else seemed to notice it. I wondered if it had something to do with my silver magic – or the Whispers. But they were silent.

The important thing was that no one else noticed anything.

The coin itself wasn't inherently special – it had been spelled after the fact, not made with magic. Just a Greek drachma with Athena on one side and an owl on the other – although it was gold rather than silver, which was unique.

Crispin grunted dismissively. "Not my style," he said, preparing to toss it back to Roland.

Fabrizio leaned forward eagerly. "Let me see it. We Italians value our bling."

I smiled. Fabrizio was growing on me. He was the prankster of the group. Still hard and determined, but like the fun-loving Uncle. The guy not afraid to laugh as he got his hands dirty.

Windsor reminded me of middle-management – attempting to straddle the line between authority and a fun coworker. He frequently studied Crispin and Fabrizio out of the corner of his eyes, as if watching his role models to find his place in life. The weird part about that was that they were all pretty much equals. Well, they had started around the same time.

Crispin was obviously in charge as First Shepherd, and was more reserved and serious than the others, but to be honest, he made Roland look like a grouchy old man. Crispin desired to deserve the respect of his new title. He looked like he could be a harsh taskmaster, but also knew how to unwind when necessary.

In order of their fun factor, it was Fabrizio, Crispin, and then Windsor.

Crispin tossed the amulet to Fabrizio, and I began to grow uneasy. Roland needed to put the damned thing back on. Show and Tell was over, before something went wr—

Fabrizio caught the amulet, and it zapped him clear out of his chair.

To be fair, the amount of power discharged by the amulet hadn't actually zapped Fabrizio out of his chair – the surprise of being zapped *at all* made him jump back and trip over his own chair, like a horse slapped on the flank. "What in tarnation!" Fabrizio shouted, scrambling to his feet and glaring at the amulet, which was now resting on the table, totally inert.

⚝ 31 ⚝

R oland burst out laughing, slapping the table as he roared. I grinned, playing along with him, hoping my face wasn't sweating with anxiety.

Fabrizio shot a look at Crispin, who looked very concerned.

Roland waved a hand. "It bites sometimes. Did I forget to mention that?"

Crispin frowned at him. "Why didn't it bite me?" Roland shrugged, still laughing.

"Is no one going to comment on the fact that Buddha just said *tarnation?*" I asked in disbelief.

Fabrizio shot me a warning look and placed a finger over his lips. *The adults are talking, sweetie,* the motion said. I rolled my eyes. He smirked, and something in the brown depths of his eyes twinkled in amusement. He liked my sass. Good to know. I would use that against him.

Roland masked his concern with humor. I saw that he realized his plan to make them dismiss his amulet as nothing special was about to backfire.

It had worked about as well as a plan to use unsupervised candles for illumination in a pillow factory. I wondered why it had zapped Fabrizio and not Crispin. What did that mean? Did it mean Fabrizio had something to hide? Or did it mean that Crispin did? These same thoughts were going through everyone's head.

"Where did you get it?" Fabrizio asked, sucking his fingers as he plopped back into his chair.

Roland shrugged easily, scooping it back up without an ounce of concern in his eyes. "Some fanger. He didn't need it anymore." Roland's face clouded over and he let out a sigh after a few seconds. "I almost punched my ticket that day, so now I wear it as a reminder to be vigilant," he said softly. The others nodded solemnly, knowing all too well the dangers in their line of work.

I glanced over to see that Windsor was very quiet. Since he seemed to be so introspective, he was likely still bothered by the fact that it had only zapped Fabrizio and not Crispin. It made me nervous as well. Was that a sign that we needed to be careful around one of them? Which one? Or maybe Windsor knew exactly what it meant.

Part of me wanted to stand and give Roland a round of applause for his quick thinking. He had played it off effortlessly – at least in their eyes. Was that the vampire part of him shining through? Seducing a victim into seeing him as a trusted friend? If so, maybe this vampire thing wouldn't be so bad. It might make the old man more tolerable.

If we weren't discovered and jailed, or killed before we found the murderer.

"Well, keep your trophies to yourself from now on," Fabrizio chuckled.

Crispin cleared his throat, literally tapping the edge of the check from Nate onto the table with a steady sound. Roland had handed it over to him without a word earlier. "I think we should put it into the armory fund," he said, changing the topic with one last furtive look at Roland's amulet. "Weapons always need replacing. And I know a few of the Shepherds could use raises." Fabrizio and Windsor perked up at that. "But not in Rome. We live in a palace compared to the others." He glanced at Roland, ignoring their grumbled protests. "What about Kansas City? Need anything there, or are you good? We have you to thank for this in the first place, after all."

Roland waved a hand after thinking for a few minutes. "Some precious metal for an updating of our protective circles in the prison, but our weapons are fine. Maybe a few new punching bags..." he rattled off a few more things, and I found myself nodding in agreement. Then I considered the fact that Roland wouldn't be a Shepherd in a few days, and I had to force myself not to cry. It was just so unfair.

I did notice that Roland hadn't listed any vampire hunting weapons, which was enough to curb my sadness.

The men discussed back and forth about several Shepherds across the globe, and who had deserved special commendation. I found myself growing sleepy, bored at the mundane operational side of the business, but it was nice to see Crispin letting the men offer input.

He would do well as First Shepherd.

I had heard Crispin quietly complaining to Roland on the way here. He didn't like the promotion, and hated being relegated behind a desk most days. He had sounded sincere, and judging by the overly-analytical tick to his eyes now, I could see the truth of that in action. He doubted himself, second-guessing every decision. Otherwise I would have suspected him of killing Roland's old mentor – the previous First Shepherd – to get the job.

I wasn't ruling anyone out yet, but his frustration seemed genuine. He would rather switch places with Fabrizio, but I sensed that Fabrizio would hate the responsibility even more. Maybe Windsor would like it since he was so introspective. I sighed at the problem before us, wondering how we were supposed to find a killer in the middle of this mess.

Because according to them, they already had the killers in custody, and no one was allowed to talk to them.

Crispin glanced down as his phone chirped. He read the screen and then sighed, looking annoyed. "Duty calls," he said, climbing to his feet.

The other two Roman Shepherds arched a brow at Crispin, but then suddenly frowned as their own phones chimed. They read it and looked up to find Crispin nodding. "Meeting," the two said in unison, climbing to their feet and wistfully eyeing their half-full wine glasses.

Roland began climbing to his feet, but Crispin waved him off. "You're a guest. For today, at least. Tomorrow, you're on duty like the rest of us. We will live vicariously through you," he said, smiling and jerking his thumb at the half-empty bottle of wine.

Roland didn't argue, kicking his boots up onto the table to rub it in. I shrugged and reached for the bottle, topping off my glass as I muttered under my breath, but loud enough for all to hear. "Tarnation, tarnation, tarnation."

"Easy, Girlie," Fabrizio growled in mock warning.

Once they left, we sat in silence for a time. I tried not to fidget with impatience. Then, Roland climbed to his feet and placed his ear against the door. He turned back to me. "We're alone."

I unloaded on him. "What the hell is up with the amulet?" I hissed.

He thumbed it thoughtfully, finally raising his eyes. "How am I supposed to know? They did seem to buy my story, though, and it wasn't a lie," he added proudly.

I grunted. That was true. "Windsor looked entirely too thoughtful for my taste." I didn't bother telling him about being able to sense the amulet. It would just distract him.

Roland had explained their leadership structure to me on the drive back in the car. Crispin was obviously First Shepherd, the top of the chain. Fabrizio was next, and then Windsor, but they didn't have fancy titles. It was just known that these were the top three. They were all stationed in Rome, responsible for different territories around the city. Needless to say, the Vatican was their home base, kind of like Roland in Kansas City.

Four other Shepherds from across the world had made the trip to Rome, but the rest were out on missions and couldn't make it back for the trial. Which was understandable. They couldn't be expected to drop everything and head back to Rome, leaving a feral wolf or demon-possession to simmer for a few days.

When in Rome, everyone deferred to Crispin, Fabrizio, and Windsor, in that order.

We hadn't been able to dig too deeply, but Roland had managed to indirectly bring up the night of the murder as we made our way over here to discuss Master Temple's donation.

Crispin had been out hunting vampires, and had even brought back a decapitated head as proof to the Conclave. The offending kiss had been a thorn in their sides for some time.

Windsor had been performing an exorcism out of town.

And Fabrizio had been on his weekly date with his long-time girlfriend – a standing tradition.

Roland would verify this later, but they all seemed to have rock-solid alibis. Maybe the killer was one of the Conclave wizards?

No other Shepherds had been in town. "What about the Conclave?" I asked Roland.

"That's my next step. I'll verify the Shepherds' alibis, and then check on the Conclave."

I frowned. "And how are you going to do that without them noticing?"

He smiled. "I have contacts in unlikely places within these walls. Those who would have no benefit from his death." He saw my doubtful look. "I'll be careful. Verify from different sources, only confirming if I have multiple people agree on the same point."

I didn't need to tell him how to do his job, but I was concerned. Because Roland considered everyone here a friend. He had known them for years.

Still...

Someone had to be the traitor, which meant that someone he trusted was a killer, and we couldn't let them know what we were up to.

"Go take a walk. Get used to the grounds. Familiarize yourself with the battlefield. I'll drop off our bags in our rooms and do some sleuthing. Rekindle old flames." I blinked at him in surprise and he chuckled. "Figuratively speaking," he corrected.

"Make sure you get a lot of fluids," I said meaningfully. "We don't want you to get dehydrated."

He kicked the bag lightly, looking disgusted at his dependency, but he also looked.... Well, thirsty. He finally nodded gruffly.

There was a knock at the door, and we instantly tensed. Shit. Had someone heard us?

32

Windsor stared at us, breathing heavy as if he had jogged back here. Roland grew instantly alert, coupled with the fear that he had overheard our conversation.

"What is it?" I asked, shoulders tensing.

"I was sent back to tell you that the Conclave wishes to speak with you."

"My hearing is tomorrow..." I replied, cocking my head. Roland didn't look pleased.

Windsor's face took on an anxious tone, as if agitated that delivering the message was delaying something important, not that he was annoyed with me personally. "It's not your hearing. They just want to talk to you." His eyes drifted to Roland. "In private. Now. I've got to go. Please hurry to the same room you first met them or we will all suffer for it. They're not in the greatest of moods after Temple's visit."

I nodded. "Okay." With a dip of his head and a sigh of relief, he turned and jogged down the hall to catch up to his own meeting since he had been called back to deliver my summons.

I arched a brow at Roland who grunted, but finally shrugged. "It's not a hearing, so you should be fine. Want me to wait outside?" he asked.

I shook my head after a brief hesitation. Was I nervous? Hell yes. But I could handle a meeting. Roland needed to do his sleuthing. "No. We don't have the luxury of time. You have more important things to do. And if they're meeting with me, you'll have fewer eyes watching you," I added, smiling. "Get a big drink before you go. We can't risk you..."

He nodded grimly, clutching our bags in one hand. "I'm going to find some rooms for us since no one has offered to help. I'll see you soon." He shot me an encouraging look, patting his phone in his pocket, and then whisked down the hall.

"Godspeed," I muttered sarcastically as I headed to the meeting room. This should be fun. The bureaucratic arm of the Shepherds – better known as a bunch of old, blind wizards who thought they knew best – wanted to meet with me in private. But why? If not my hearing, what else could they want to talk to me about?

Had I done something wrong already? Were they wanting to grill me on my knowledge of Nate Temple? Alucard revealing his Daywalker powers? My breath caught and my steps slowed as another thought hit me. Did... they know about the Angel in Kansas City? About my blood? Had they sensed it on me?

I let out a sigh and pressed on. Only one way to find out. I was pretty sure I would be under guard if I was in trouble. Seeing as how they trusted me enough to walk to the gallows on my own, everything was probably fine.

Probably.

If things went badly, Roland and I would have to flee or risk a war. And as good as we were, if the Conclave pointed a finger at us, we would have seven Shepherds chasing us down. I knew Roland was willing to die to save those girls, but I was inclined to keep my head attached. This would all be so much easier if we could just share the video Haven had shown us. I seriously contemplated calling Haven to ask him to change his mind, or to find a way for him to get the information to the Vatican indirectly. Something.

Even though we had destroyed the evidence of Roland being turned, it was only a matter of time until word reached the Conclave. The vampires would be bragging about a Shepherd turned vampire. I couldn't ask Haven to get involved. It would only lead to the Conclave finding out about Roland sooner. Haven had his own bureaucratic group to worry about – the Sanguine Council – the oldest and most powerful vampires in the world. I shivered at the thought of Roland having to meet them someday. I wondered who was part of the group? Vlad the Impaler? It was surprising how many people from legend and myth were still breathing, so it was entirely possible that some of history's most famous vampires were still pulling strings.

Hell, the infamous vampire hunter, Van Helsing, was pals with Nate.

I approached my destination, staring at the doors with a quizzical eye, attempting to look casual. No guards. Maybe things were going to be alright after all.

I took a calming breath, placed my hands on the door and walked inside with my chin held high. Three wizards sat huddled together at a side table, arguing softly with each other. I was simply glad they weren't sitting on the raised stage. At the sound of the door opening, they looked up to study my approach in silence. They didn't look pleased, but they didn't look angry either. More like this was their default face. Maybe they expected me to grovel.

That wasn't going to happen.

I smiled politely, studying them as I approached the table, wondering if I was supposed to sit in a specific spot or if we were all going to leave to get lattes and makeovers. At a hand gesture from the taller one who had spoken during the meeting with Nate, I sat at their table. They didn't try to sit in a row, overwhelming me with three on one. Instead, they sat equidistant from one another, putting us all on equal footing, so to speak.

I showed them my teeth in a bright smile, trying to connect the names and descriptions Roland had shared with me in the car to their faces. I found myself avoiding their white eyes with a suppressed shudder. "Windsor told me you requested my presence?" I said neutrally, wording it so that it was clear I had not answered a *summons* – that I had voluntarily chosen to answer a *request* instead. Semantics, but I wouldn't have them thinking I was a pushover. Things were going to get worse, soon, and if I acted sweet and weak now, it would be a very noticeable change when shit went downhill and they saw the Supreme Bitch, Callie Penrose, in action.

No, I had to be rough enough around the edges that they formed a preconceived notion in their heads of me being difficult, ornery, and challenging, but not too difficult for them to manage. That way any questionable activity that happened later would match up with their assessment of my personality.

Also, this would put the spotlight on me rather than Roland. I couldn't risk them looking too closely at him. Haven had warned us that it would be dangerous, but that he shouldn't be noticed unless he murdered someone and vamped out. Until then, his amulet should keep him safe from detection.

They dipped their heads politely, but I sensed their annoyance at my choice of words.

"Miss Penrose—"

"Callie," I corrected, smiling as I leaned closer, folding my hands before me on the table.

The taller man's lips thinned at me from across the table. "Callie," he said, trying to reassert control of the conversation. "My name is Daniel. This is Richter," he said, pointing to the balding, liver-spotted man on his right, "and this is Christopher," he said, pointing to the lean black man on his left. "We wanted to discuss—"

"My pleasure. But where are the rest of you?" I asked, furrowing my brow.

Daniel let out a breath. "They are otherwise occupied. Now—"

"Please don't take this the wrong way. I only ask because it's highly improbable that all seven of the Conclave are... visually impaired," I scrounged up the politically correct name. "It caught me off guard. Before I start answering your questions, I would have the answer. Please."

Richter smiled. "The price of leadership," he admitted in the raspy tone of a lifelong smoker. "And we can use our magic to see well enough." A cold sliver of fear went down my spine as I forced out a nod. Did that mean they could sense magical auras? I almost ran screaming from the room, thinking they knew exactly what was happening, that Roland and I were not just wizards. After a few breaths, I realized they would have brought it up if they knew.

"Thank you."

Daniel spoke back up. "The reason we... *requested* your presence was to get to know you a little better. Of course, Roland sends in his reports, but face-to-face is always best."

I nodded, eyes distant. Sensing he was finished speaking, I refocused on him, drifting to the other two after a moment of speculation. "I hope everything is okay."

The three of them stared back at me with different variations of confusion.

I waved a hand at the raised stage. "The other Conclave members. The Shepherds all received a message to leave, and then Windsor was sent back – almost like it was urgent – to ask me to meet with the Conclave. But... not all the Conclave is here. I assume only the Conclave has the authority to request Crispin's attendance to a meeting with the other Shepherds. Which means part of the Conclave is *there*, and part of the Conclave is *here*. With me." I said all this absently, as if commenting on the weather. Then I turned back to Daniel with a frown. "Either that or the other Conclave members weren't as interested in getting to know me." I waited, not hostile, just observing. I even let my eyes study the room for a second, admiring several pieces of art.

When I glanced back, they were studying me with their milky eyes. Richter was the only one smiling. Christopher looked impressed. Daniel looked stern. "You are... very observant," he finally said.

I shrugged. "Roland's a very good mentor."

Something about that comment finally broke his façade, and he smiled. "How... refreshing," he mused, leaning back in his chair. "You are correct, of course. The Shepherds are meeting with the other Conclave members on a matter of... security. Making sure everything is in order with... recent events."

I leaned forward. "Curious..." I said, not smiling, but staring at him very intently.

His smile faltered under my blank stare. "Pardon?" he finally asked.

I leaned back, shrugging lightly. "Roland is a Shepherd, yet he was not called to the meeting."

Richter cleared his throat. "The meeting was for a local matter. Crispin, Windsor and Fabrizio reside here. And Roland arrived a day early, so he's not on the schedule. Until tomorrow."

I nodded, tapping my lips. "That's a relief." At his curious look, I turned back to him. "That the other Conclave members are otherwise occupied rather than simply not interested in me," I explained, letting a smile slip out. "I hope everything is okay with security?" I was sure to look properly concerned, as if considering the situation like a student of Roland's would. Or should.

They paused before they nodded, risking glances at each other. "Many guests have arrived recently, and we are not known for our love of change," Daniel finally admitted with a guilty smile. Christopher snorted at the quip. "We are just verifying everything is in order."

I acknowledged Daniel's lame attempt at a joke with a shy smile and shake of my head, my long hair brushing my shoulders. "Okay. What can I help you with?"

Daniel finally leaned back again, interlocking his fingers as he studied me. "You have scored very well on Roland's aptitude tests. His reports are nothing short of glowing, although your attitude can sometimes get in the way," he said with an amused smile. I was going to kill the stupid Shepherd-pire. My attitude? He had mentioned that in a report? "But attitudes can be good. They offer fresh perspective, and the Shepherds need as much of that as we can stomach. Lest we get set in our ways."

I nodded, smiling guiltily. "I agree."

"It seems Missouri has seen a lot of action in recent years. Kansas City and St. Louis, specifically. Then, wonder of wonders, a St. Louis resident appears, Nate Temple, to make a donation to our cause the same day you arrive. An acquaintance of yours."

I rolled my eyes indelicately. "Acquaintance – although accurate – may be stretching it. We met less than a year ago, but haven't spent much time around each other."

They didn't respond, simply watched me.

"But regarding your other question, Missouri has been very busy lately…" I had to be careful here. Perhaps they knew more than I did. But there was always the chance that it was the other way around, and I didn't want to spill my guts out. That would look bad on Roland, making them wonder why he hadn't informed them himself.

Christopher leaned forward, his forehead wrinkling into three grooves above his stark, white eyes. Faint dark freckles peppered his chocolate brown cheeks. "We were able to speak to Master Temple in private before you arrived," he mused. "The Daywalker was a surprise, reading scripture from the Bible…" he shook his head in wonder. "Let's just say that he caught our attention. We weren't happy with his delivery, as you could see. Old men like us have little tolerance for rude behavior." His eyes flashed brighter for a moment. "But we've had time to cool our heads. A little," he said, chin subtly shifting to indicate Daniel.

Daniel cleared his throat. "Yes. We have. Master Temple confirmed that Missouri was a bubbling cauldron. We proposed opening a church in St. Louis, or more accurately, stationing a Shepherd there on a more permanent basis." Daniel met my eyes, and I saw a faint glint of hardness in those milky depths. "Master Temple… laughed." I grimaced, realizing I was nodding as if expecting it. I noticed the other two men frowning at me and I shrugged.

"Master Temple is not… the most diplomatic person."

They frowned, as if suddenly doubting my earlier description of our relationship. I rolled my eyes at them. "You seem very suspicious of me for some reason, and I don't think I like it," I said in a very frosty tone. "You met with him for ten minutes and came to the same conclusion about him. That he's not one to bite his tongue. Should I suddenly assume that you have known him for decades?" I arched an inquisitive eyebrow at them and watched as their frowns evaporated and they gave me polite nods.

Daniel cleared his throat. "Accept my apologies. We don't doubt you, we just... we're not used to such tactics, as Christopher explained."

"Here there be monsters..." I murmured under my breath.

"Dragons..." he corrected, looking startled at my reference.

I shrugged. "Mine sounds better."

"Speaking of Dragons, it seems Master Temple is also familiar with the Obsidian Son... the Dragon King, if you will. He lives in St. Louis as well. Master Temple helped put him into power, if rumors are true."

"I heard the same," I said honestly.

They waited for me to say more. And kept on waiting. I treated it like a staring contest, determined to win. "We seem to be straying far from topic," Daniel finally said. "The point is, we mentioned a Shepherd in St. Louis, and Master Temple's secondary response – after laughter – was that you and Roland had Missouri... *on lock*. I presume that is a compliment?"

I couldn't help it. I laughed. "Yes, I believe it was meant as a compliment." In fact, it was a big compliment from Nate. I couldn't let the three wizards see how much it meant to me, but it was like a professional basketball player acknowledging a good shot I had made during a street pickup game. Nate was deadly, a nightmare to bad guys. For him to say I had Missouri under control was huge. It also didn't slip my mind that Nate could have been angling for the Conclave to insert me into St. Louis as their local Shepherd.

But that wasn't happening. Firstly, because I wasn't going to be a Shepherd. Not after Roland's secret got out.

Secondly, I wasn't moving to St. Louis. Although it was a clever move on Nate's part.

Daniel watched me again, studying my face. "Yet you hardly know him..." he reminded me.

I didn't hesitate. "Word gets around about what we've accomplished in Kansas City."

Christopher nodded, looking interested. "Indeed, it does."

Richter piped up. "I'm going to meet my Maker before these two get around to it, so let me cut to the chase," he said in a rasping breath, a no-nonsense kind of guy. My favorite. I was used to cantankerous men after working with Roland, but I knew this man had things to teach Roland in that regard.

He took a sip of water and leveled his gnarly eyebrows my way, staring at me with those milky eyes. "We are considering promoting you to Shepherd, Miss Penrose."

My heart stopped.

33

I t kicked in after a few seconds as I struggled for words. "Call—" I attempted to correct him.

He snapped his fingers. "Silence, or I'll devolve to calling you *little girl*," he warned, faint amusement in his threat.

I smiled, nodding as I closed my lips. He was fun. But this was bad.

"We wanted to meet you in private before we made our decision. You seem capable, of that there is no doubt," he said respectfully, a hundred unasked questions darting in the depths of those ancient eyes. "But there is something you are hiding, and we must have obedience in our flock." I didn't react, simply studying the three men before me. I could understand why they thought that, and wasn't offended by it. I had a lot of personal secrets, concerns, and even frustrations with these guys. I also knew that after our trip, I had zero chances of becoming a Shepherd. Instead, I would be a traitor.

But...

What held me up was something in his eyes. I studied the other two and saw the same thing. They seemed to be concerned about something else entirely, and it wasn't me. Something to do with their argument before I arrived? The other Conclave meeting with the Shepherds? They had shot glances back and forth this whole time, silently reminding each other to consider whatever it was. Maybe it was the recent murder. Or Roland. Had

they already discovered his lie and decided to probe me to see if I was innocent? Was that the real reason he hadn't been invited to either meeting? I
began to grow very, very uneasy, but kept my face respectfully neutral.

Underneath all of this, I was also a bit angry. Because I had told Roland
repeatedly that I didn't want to be a Shepherd. Had he not told them?

Then I thought about that, and remembered how they wiped memories
of those who messed up in their training. Or... maybe also initiates who
refused the call to promotion. Was that why Roland had persisted so
intently for me to join him as a Shepherd? Knowing it was a one-way street?
That I joined or had my brain scrambled?

I took a deep breath, and lowered my eyes, speaking softly but clearly.
"I'm sure you are aware of my... unique circumstances. Being left on the
steps of Abundant Angel as a child." I heard them murmur softly, sounding
like sympathetic prayers. "As a rule, I play my cards close to the chest.
Roland has helped me open up, but it's still a weakness of mine. And coming
to the Vatican for the first time, meeting the other Shepherds, you..." I
trailed off, not sounding scared, but respectful. "I am understandably tense."

Richter rasped out through his aged vocal cords, doing his best to sound
pleasant, but not succeeding. "If you can't trust men of God, who can you
trust... Callie?"

I looked up, smiling sheepishly. *Who indeed?* I thought to myself, not
letting the question show on my face. Instead, I nodded guiltily. "I'll work
on it."

Daniel clapped his hands softly. "Well, we are short a Shepherd, and if
Missouri is as busy as we hear, we need another soldier on the ground. She
has my vote." The other two grunted their agreement, and my smile almost
shattered from fear. Before I could decide what to do, Daniel continued. "Of
course, we will have to discuss with the others, first. Once they're finished
with the Shepherds. Until then, keep your nose clean. We have a few urgent
matters to attend, but we wish to move your... hearing," he said the word
disgustedly, as if annoyed by it, "to tonight since you're a day earlier than
anticipated. But first, we must discuss and pray on the idea."

I nodded woodenly, mind racing. "Not that I'm not honored, but are
there no other students available for the promotion?" I asked, trying not to
sound unappreciative.

Christopher sniffed disgustedly. "None with more than five years under
their belts. They can't even be let off apron strings yet. Glorified choir boys,

with only a few beginning their martial arts studies." I forced a fake smile at that.

But inside I was shaking. Roland and I needed to hurry our asses up. Or I might just be the first Shepherd hired and executed in the same day.

The Angel in Kansas City had also offered me a job of sorts. So, now I had two Heavenly armies wanting me on the payroll.

And I didn't want to work for either. It wasn't that I had a problem with God. It was that I liked to meet my boss, and have more discretion in my duties. Even then, I wasn't a fan of rank and file jobs. Being a good little soldier. I worked alone, or with a small group. *Blindly obedient* was not on my resume. I needed to save the wolves before one of these two groups swooped me up as a fresh recruit.

Nephilim or Shepherd. Heaven or Vatican.

With nothing else to discuss, the three wizards dismissed me, seeming eager to leave out the side door – but not before giving me a polite, encouraging wave goodbye. I returned the gesture before I walked away, trying to appear calm. Not afraid, but not excited. Meaning, I tried not to collapse to the ground in terror.

I left the room and saw no Shepherds in sight. Understandable, since they were meeting with the other Conclave members. Still, I had hoped to see a few here and there. Or at least some of the visiting Shepherds' students. Then again, Christopher had made it sound like the other students in training were derelicts – only five years under their belts. Picking a student was a big deal, and it took Shepherds a long time to find someone worth their time – what with them being busy smiting monsters all day.

Rather than going in search of the rooms Roland had found for us, I decided I needed to walk off some of my energy. Otherwise I would sit in the room throwing knives at a bust of Mary Magdalene or something. I was still in the clothes I had arrived in, totally out of place as I saw Sisters, Cardinals, Bishops, and other official people wandering about in close conversation or peaceful contemplation of the religious book in their hands. I saw several teenagers running around as if chased by a demon, only to realize they were probably clerks for the various departments.

The Vatican wasn't just a church. It was a mega-corporation. Global. With dozens of departments, representatives, churches, legal issues, and public opinions to appease.

Not even considering the secret Conclave and Shepherds.

I spotted Roland walking down a sidewalk in calm, measured strides, as if having somewhere important to be, and that it was best not to disturb him. He spotted me, and although no reaction showed on his face, he subtly shifted course so that we would cross paths as if by coincidence.

He slipped up beside me with a dip of his head, and soon we were walking the same direction, as if by chance, to any watchful eyes. Nothing to see here.

I caught Roland up to date on my meeting, speaking softly under my breath, keeping a polite smile on my face so as not to look suspicious. Roland did the same, nodding absently, pointing out random things as if giving me a tour, but his eyes...

They flashed crimson twice while I spoke.

"Everyone is acting weird lately. The Shepherds suddenly called to a meeting, only half of the Conclave meeting me for a recruitment speech, and then urgently leaving..." I sighed, shaking my head. "Think it's something in the communion?" I asked, hoping to get a rise out of him.

It definitely did.

His face turned horrified, likely considering it a viable threat. I placed a palm on his arm to let him know it was a joke and his fangs flashed out. He hid them, looking suddenly embarrassed. "That never happens," he quickly blurted. Then, hearing how *that* sounded, he blushed crimson.

I winked at him. "I hear it happens to the best of men."

He groaned.

"Maybe it's because of the approaching full moon," I offered, searching for anything even remotely explanatory.

Roland rolled his eyes. "Nice redirect," he complimented. "But I doubt it. None of the Shepherds are werewolves."

"How many Shepherds are vampires?"

He looked sick for a moment. "None." He jerked his hand clear of mine. "I did some digging and came up with nothing. Like we heard, Crispin, Windsor, and Fabrizio are clean. Their alibis checked out. Worse, I can't find anything suspicious about the Conclave. They were all seen in Mass together by independent sources, and before you ask, none of them left."

I muttered darkly under my breath. "I guess that leaves Constantine's office," I offered. He shot me a saddened look, nodding.

"My thoughts as well, as distasteful as it is."

"The Shepherds won't like us snooping around."

"That's just too bad," he said, altering our course. "This way."

After a few minutes of silence, I forced myself to speak casually. "Thanks for letting the Conclave know my interests in working for them. It really helped to be unaware of the job offer. I think it was the blank look of horror that really pushed them over the edge, making them realize I was perfect for the job. That's some hardcore reverse psychology skills you have, Roland—"

"I'm sorry, Callie. I never told them you weren't interested, for obvious reasons," he interrupted, reminding me what refusal meant. The brain scrambling.

I was still pissed about it. "You had to see this coming," I muttered. "Bringing me here, you had to know something would happen."

He met me with a harsh glare. "I had other things on my mind..." he hissed between clenched teeth. I nodded, still angry, but realizing my anger was unjustified compared to what he had on his plate. That he was a vampire on borrowed time, standing in the center of the Vatican and about to be fired, killed, or burned at the stake by his friends when they found out.

"This is the second job offer I don't want," I said, kicking a small pebble. "Angel minion, or Vatican minion." A nearby Sister scowled at me, and I averted my eyes sheepishly.

It was like magic, the ability for a Sister to make a person wince in guilt.

Roland found that entirely too funny, so I punched him in the ribs.

34

We had arrived at Constantine's office twenty minutes ago after a nervous clerk had let us in, not having anyone higher in the pecking order to turn to, and terrified of the menace radiating from Roland. I had winked at him, smiling wide, before placing an arm around his gangly shoulders, letting him know we wanted to pay our respects to Roland's mentor. To make sure his stuff was well taken care of, and that we had no intention of taking anything. He could even watch us if he wanted to do so.

Imagining his boss finding us all in the room at the same time terrified him into trusting us.

He had unlocked the door and scurried back to his small cubby in the empty bullpen, since all the other Shepherds were on patrol. He fidgeted at his desk, shuffling papers in quiet desperation of discovery. I had estimated that we had fifteen minutes before someone came to yell at us, but twenty had gone by already. We found nothing helpful.

"Maybe he was working on a case that went too deep?" I repeated. Roland growled at the desk, shoving a drawer closed with more force than necessary. I closed my own side table drawer and we both turned to the last piece of furniture in the room. One of three filing cabinets. We had searched the other two, and after spending a lot of time and finding nothing remotely mysterious, we had decided to check the more personal areas in the room –

desk, side tables, bookshelves, and loose stacks of paperwork by an armchair – before circling back.

Roland's hand touched the handle and began to pull the first drawer open. I heard excited conversation from the room beyond and immediately let a sad mask wash over my features, as if on the verge of tears at having to search through a departed friend's office, but resolved to the task at hand. We both turned. Roland's stormy glare somehow fit the situation at hand as well. Anger at the loss of a friend.

A stork of a man entered the room, his face beet-red as his body quivered with indignation. He began hooting and hollering at us in a constant stream of sounds that didn't even sound like words. Just pure, unfiltered outrage. Either that or he was speaking in Tongues. Or cursing us with ancient magic. Roland held up his hands in a calming gesture.

I simply stared back, impressed at the man's ability to say so much without taking a breath.

Roland approached him, speaking in a soothing tone. "My name is Roland, a Shepherd from Kansas City. I was Constantine's student, and wanted to make sure his personal effects were—"

The stork of a Bishop began slapping Roland's chest in fury, ordering him to leave, that he was trespassing, and numerous other heinous crimes. My ears actually throbbed at the shrieking as Roland unsuccessfully tried to calm him down.

As if things weren't bad enough, Fabrizio and Crispin suddenly burst into the room, faces ready to kill. "What's going on?" Crispin demanded, eyes shooting from us to Bishop Stork.

The red-faced cretin leveled a shaking arm at us. "They were snooping through his office—"

"There you are!" I blurted excitedly, smiling at Crispin as if relieved.

Roland sighed, also looking relieved to have a fellow Shepherd in the room. "We were checking for clues, something that maybe only I might recognize," he admitted, frowning at the huffing bishop.

The Shepherds turned to me as if we had never met, eyes menacing at our trespass. Everyone needed to calm the fuck down. I nodded instead of unleashing my temper. "I've helped on a few homicide investigations in Kansas City, and wanted to see if any of it had rubbed off."

Their faces didn't change, and the stork began to voice his opinion again, but Fabrizio held up a hand, silencing him. Then he turned back to us as

Crispin seemed to scan us and the office for stolen items. "This should have gone through the proper channels. Let's go."

Roland's face turned into a storm cloud again, both angry at the curt dismissal and that our search had been fruitless.

"You were all *gone!*" I argued. "We couldn't find the *proper channels.*" They didn't flinch, continuing to glare. Roland muttered under his breath and left the room, the Shepherds following him like prison guards, leaving me behind with Bishop Stork. He had his finger pointed out the door, commanding me to leave. I took a threatening step towards him and he actually squeaked in surprise. I altered course to stomp past him. "We were only trying to help," I seethed.

I could have sworn I caught him sticking his tongue out at me, still shaking with the adrenaline coursing through his veins. He looked old, as if made of dried paper over thin bones, and I considered that this might be the most excitable moment of his life, and that he was past the age where he could handle such things safely.

I spotted the young man who had let us in. He looked on the verge of a panic attack. But why? Did he know something? Was he hiding something? Or was he terrified of the fallout he was about to receive from Bishop Stork? Maybe he wasn't guilty, but it sure looked like he knew something. "We're only trying to help," I said, in a much softer tone, frowning sadly.

He just stared through me, his eyes far away. I heard Bishop Stork shout something at him, and the clerk jolted before clumsily scurrying over to the bishop, passing me without a word.

I sighed, chasing after the others as they stepped through the outer doors. I wondered why Crispin and Fabrizio had seemed so angry with us. I could understand them not wanting us to snoop around, and being defensive of an enraged bishop, but it had seemed more personal. Like they suddenly distrusted us. Like we were suddenly enemies. Which was the exact opposite of how we had last seen them before their meeting.

I slipped through the door leading outside to find Crispin glaring at Roland, who stared back blankly. Not yielding, but not challenging either. Crispin looked up at me, eyes flashing from head to toe as if checking to see if I had stolen something in the brief span of time I had been unsupervised. Anyone else giving me a look like that would have had a blade shoved against their throat or a mouthful of loose teeth, but I knew we were on thin ice here. We needed freedom of movement to clear the girls from the murder, and we needed to do that quickly – before Roland was forced to kill someone and drink their blood.

Crispin cleared his throat. "You are to be escorted from now on," he said.

"Why?" Roland demanded, taking a threatening step forward without even realizing it.

Crispin didn't flinch. "Conclave orders. I do as I'm told." But he did look somewhat annoyed by the statement, as if he wasn't in agreement with it. Despite his personal opinion, he would do as commanded.

"Like a good little boy," I said without thinking, face devoid of any emotion.

Crispin lost all signs of sympathy for our situation at those five words. He glared at me, but Roland cleared his throat in warning. Then Crispin reconsidered me with an appraising glance, seeming to remember how easily I had dispatched Fabrizio. He backed down.

"Things are crazy lately," Fabrizio said in a neutral, peaceful tone, sensing the tension. "And everyone is on edge. We're just trying to keep everyone safe. No one wants another murder." He looked like he wanted to say more, but clamped his mouth shut at a look from Crispin.

I frowned at them in confusion. "I was just offered a *job* and now I'm under *escort*? Change your mind much?" I spat incredulously.

"We're just doing our jobs, Callie..." Crispin finally admitted, slowly reverting back to his original sympathy, forgiving my snide comment. He didn't look happy at this turn of events. In fact, he looked downright pissed off. But Roland had told me how loyal Crispin was. He would do his duty. Right now, that sense of duty was conflicted. Trusted friend or Conclave?

I was also aware that neither of them seemed surprised to hear I had been offered a job. Potentially. Was that the reason for their meeting with the other Conclave members? To perhaps quiz them on me? Get their opinion? And maybe that was why Roland hadn't been invited, since he was my mentor and would be biased. Perhaps he would have his own meeting with them about me. Maybe I could convince him to tell them how terrible I was.

Regardless, secrets were bubbling to the surface in the House of Truth.

"Fine," I eventually said, folding my arms. They nodded tersely, and motioned for us to join them on a retreat from the scene of our break-in. Soon, we were silently walking back down the path. We didn't have time for silence, and I wanted to offer an explanation since we had been caught red-handed. I chose my words carefully, phrased in terms they would subconsciously agree with.

"Tell us about the suspects," I said to Crispin. "Did they exhibit any signs of stress before the murder? Anger? Depression? Fear? Instability? Anything to hint at murder?"

Crispin shook his head, looking troubled. Not bothered by my questions, but as if he had asked himself the same things a million times already and wasn't pleased by the answers. "No. They had everything they could have wanted. Like I said, Constantine took them out often and treated them like his own daughters. They were excelling at an incredible pace."

I nodded. "What about the two witnesses?"

Fabrizio piped up this time. "They are under observation."

"Why?" I asked, frowning.

"In case they were turned."

"Did they have any scratches or bite marks?" I asked. Fabrizio shook his head. I frowned again, wanting to throttle someone. "Then why are you concerned with them turning into werewolves?" His face grew stony, not appreciating my tone.

"Maybe because the wolves are murderers and attacked Constantine," Crispin said in a low tone of warning. "Covering our bases."

I turned to him. "What real evidence do you have that the wolves killed Constantine? Because I know homicide detectives. Good ones. And they have three things they always look for," I said, holding up a finger with each word, "Means, motive, and opportunity."

Roland grunted his agreement. "If they're guilty, I'll be the first to line up as executioner," he said, with a resolved stare. They looked relieved to see him finally agreeing with them. Then he held up a finger. "But all I've heard is that they loved Constantine, liked their new home, never hurt anyone, and were beaten up at the scene of the crime where Constantine's throat was slashed. Did it look like Constantine used magic on them to defend himself? Burned skin? Anything?" Their faces grew harder, as if making up for their momentary relief in finding him on their side. "And these witnesses... Were they attacked? Where were they in relation to Constantine's body? What did they see? Are they aware of magic? Werewolves?" The silence was deafening. "What is so compelling that you can ignore all these inconsistencies?" he asked in a softer tone, as if begging to understand. He didn't shout, didn't sound angry, and he didn't sound condescending. Basically, it was the most professional statement he could have made.

"Yeah," I argued, folding my arms across my chest to back him up like a good minion.

Roland let out a sigh of frustration, clearly wishing I had kept my trap shut.

"We're just trying to help," I said. "We don't like this anymore than you do. Consider the fact that the victim was his mentor," I said, pointing a thumb at Roland, "and that he brought the wolves here in the first place," I added. "We feel a measure of responsibility in this."

Crispin latched onto that like a shark. "Exactly."

Roland frowned, as did I.

Fabrizio glanced back at us. "He means that Roland is biased. Not objective."

I blinked incredulously at the large man. "You're saying that we're not objective... but we just asked every objective question available. And you can't seem to answer them—"

Crispin waved a hand, cutting me off. "Enough of this. It is not your concern."

"If we could just speak with the witnesses. These surviv—"

Crispin rounded on me, apparently losing his patience. "You will not speak to the witnesses. None of us will. They are not aware of magic, or werewolves, or anything. Letting them see that could put the Vatican in a very awkward position. They saw a murder. Were banged up as they fled, and that's that."

"How were they banged—"

"Enough!" Fabrizio shouted, losing his temper as we pressed his boss. I met his eyes, breathing heavily, not backing down. "You are not a Shepherd, Callie. Not yet. But even if you were," he said, glancing meaningfully at Roland, "it is not your position to question, only to obey. We scanned the witnesses, tested them. They are entirely Regular. The scene only had traces of wizard and werewolf. Nothing else. That is why we removed them from the suspect pool." He began ticking off fingers as he continued. "No Regular could have gotten close enough to knock out two wolves and slice Constantine's throat. And before you ask, we questioned them for hours, dug up full dossiers on them. No military training. No martial arts. No secrets. One is a baker and one is a waiter. They live in cheap homes, no family, no mysterious savings account with surprising balances. Literally," he said, drawing the word out, "nothing suspicious."

I let the silence stretch for a few moments. "A good assassin is always set up in a similar way. False backgrounds, no loose ends in his history, modest life, nothing suspicious. They could still be highly trained killers. Even if they're only Regulars," I said in a last-ditch effort.

Fabrizio turned to me with a patronizing smile. "I walked into the interrogation room and tossed a bloody sword onto the table, wiping off my hands before I told him I was here to ask him questions about the murder. He pissed himself. On the spot. The other one passed out when Windsor tried to hardball him in a similar fashion."

Roland muttered darkly.

I swore.

35

hat would be a level of commitment and skill that most successful assassins might not manage. They were typically arrogant. Sure, they could act innocent when necessary, but to pass out and piss yourself? Maybe the Shepherds were right.

But that didn't mean the wolves were guilty.

We had seen the goddamned video.

"What were they wearing?" I asked. At Fabrizio's growl, I held up a hand. "Last question and then I'll drop it. I promise."

He sighed, raking a hand through his hair, and I saw Crispin smirking out of the corner of his mouth. Not at the topic, but amused by his fellow Shepherd's exasperation.

"Khakis and a blue windbreaker over a white tee. The other had light gray slacks and a white dress shirt, his attire for the restaurant he works at."

I nodded, but inside I wanted to curse. The killer had been wearing uniform dark clothing. Sure, they could have changed clothes, any successful killer would have, but there was always the chance they could have overlooked it and worn black. The problem was that we were looking for proof of something unexplainable, and questions of *what if* couldn't enter the equation yet. Those came later when you were trying to wrap up loose ends on your prime suspects' actions.

Which meant Roland and I needed to focus on the wolves. Find something – anything – that revealed it was impossible for them to have done it. And just our luck, the Shepherds were now very aware of our interest – not that it had been a secret before – because Roland was tied to it whether he wanted to be or not. He'd brought the alleged killers here.

But now we had been caught snooping, and had managed to impart a suspicion of incompetence on Roland's brothers, which wasn't going to make our job easier. The conversation had needed to happen eventually, though.

"Thank you. We just... don't understand how it can be possible. If we had any suspicions they were a threat, we wouldn't have brought them here. And Constantine was experienced, so it seemed unlikely he would overlook them as a threat since he spent so much time with them."

"I want to appease my conscience. Or find the mistake in judgment I made," Roland said.

The two Shepherds nodded in understanding, their anger slowly defrosting. "We understand, Roland," Crispin said, placing an arm on his shoulder. "This hurt all of us. But have a little faith. We didn't blindly suspect them because they were wolves. Fabrizio checked the surrounding buildings for surveillance and found nothing. We worked with the police. This was our ultimate conclusion, even though I'll admit it isn't foolproof. Still, the world needs to see us act decisively. And in unison," he added.

"Even if it's the wrong suspect, the world needs to see that the Shepherds will respond," Roland growled unhappily, fully aware of both sides of the situation.

Instead of arguing, since I had promised I was finished pestering them, I nodded sadly. "Where to next, Roland?"

Just then, Crispin glanced down as his phone chirped. He read it, let out an annoyed sigh, and then placed a call. He turned away from us as he spoke, and I felt anxiety building up in my shoulders. Why hide his phone call? He hung up and pulled Fabrizio aside to speak in a low tone. I arched a brow at Roland, wondering if he had enhanced vampire hearing yet, but he grunted to tell me he didn't. They turned back to us and Crispin sighed. "Duty calls. Windsor will replace me and then you four can be on your way. Wherever that is," he added. Which was interesting. Crispin was First Shepherd, so likely had dozens of other jobs to perform, not considering his new task as our babysitter. But more interesting was the fact that we had the freedom to go where we pleased... under supervision. Like house arrest.

Windsor finally jogged into view, nodded at Crispin, and then stepped up beside Fabrizio. Crispin left, and the two Shepherds waited, holding out their hands to let us know we could lead and they would follow. Their smiles were polite, fixed, and I could tell that something big was definitely going on behind the scenes.

I shrugged and started walking, Roland joining me. With our guards, we could no longer talk freely. And we were about to have a helluva a time finding evidence to prove that the wolves were innocent.

WE HAD WALKED THE GROUNDS FOR ABOUT THIRTY MINUTES, ROLAND pointing out various buildings, statues, and other familiar places to him from his childhood. I even caught Fabrizio and Windsor loosening up, smiling at their own memories of the places Roland pointed out, but they didn't speak. It was comforting to see the happiness in Roland's eyes. To see him as a younger man, not the hard-ass Shepherd of Kansas City.

Roland had casually asked Fabrizio and Windsor about our new supervision requirement, not sounding annoyed, but thoughtful. "Is it because we searched Constantine's office?"

"Everyone is being guarded at present," Windsor said in an official tone.

Roland frowned at that, because these two obviously weren't being guarded. Windsor had replaced Crispin, and neither of them had guards accompanying them as they did.

"Why do we need a guard but not you guys?" I asked Windsor. I pointed a thumb at Roland. "It can't be because you're Shepherds... or this conversation is going to get very uncomfortable."

Windsor wouldn't meet Roland's eyes. "He brought the wolves to the Vatican..."

"Ah, I get it," I said, letting my flat tone speak volumes.

Roland didn't immediately comment. He just shook his head in disappointment – at the truth of Windsor's comment and the guilt of knowing as much as it hurt to not have their trust, he technically didn't deserve it because he was hiding a set of new fangs from them.

"I'm going to go get some rest," he finally said. "I'll talk to you soon. All this searching for knives in my back is exhausting..." he added before turning to a building backed up against the Holy Shed. Now I knew where our rooms were! Windsor looked both hurt and angry, but didn't reply.

Fabrizio nodded at Windsor and then followed Roland like a good guard dog.

I looked at Windsor, waiting for a reaction. He looked torn as he watched Fabrizio jog up to Roland. Both frustrated and angry, but determined. What the hell was going on here? When he turned back to me, those emotions were gone.

"With friends like these..." I said sweetly.

He held out a hand and I sighed. We were near the Holy Shed, so I decided to do a little more walking, rather than follow Roland to our rooms. Considering Windsor and I were all alone, and that he might be the killer, I chose to take my walk indoors instead. As I neared the entrance, I saw that the two buildings did in fact look connected.

I walked inside the Holy Shed, the same entrance where I had first met Fabrizio and Crispin. The familiar hall stretched before me and I took my time, studying the various religious paintings, decorations and artifacts as I walked, thinking over the afternoon's events.

I didn't walk to the door where I had met the Conclave, but down a side hall instead. Reaching the end of the hall, I decided I was ready to head back to my room and change clothes or talk with Roland or something. Strategize or just take a nap. I rounded another hallway, guessing that it led to the other building, and almost bumped into an older man. A younger, blond-haired man shadowing him suddenly looked much more alert, as if I had attempted to attack the octogenarian. The younger man was dressed in a suit, and looked like he knew what he was doing, maybe only a few years older than me. But he looked hard, as if those extra years had been the equivalent of a decade of war.

I quickly stepped back, sensing the lethal grace of a fighter. He studied me with a harsh face, not angry, but that alert quality found in competent bodyguards.

Windsor cleared his throat. "Easy. There is no danger, here," he said to the guard, who seemed much less concerned than he should have been at the presence of a Shepherd. He recognized a fellow fighter, but didn't look particularly impressed.

I turned back to the older man. "I'm sorry. I wasn't paying attention," I admitted.

He chuckled softly, waving a hand to dismiss my apology. He wore traditional robes with a wide collar, not unlike the other bishops, cardinals, and priests I had seen. But instead of a vibrant color, his were cream. He was a short, squat man, probably in his early sixties, although I wasn't that great of a judge once someone got past their fifties. He looked healthy and somewhat fit, with sparkling blue eyes and a thin dusting of white hair. He didn't look familiar, and his darker skin tone made me think he was Hispanic.

He smiled at me, cocking his head as he absently scratched at his arm. "Do I know you from somewhere?" he asked.

"I sure hope not," I said with a tired sigh. I just wanted to sit down for a minute. In private.

He smiled in amusement, chuckling lightly.

"You okay?" I asked, noticing he was still rubbing his arm lightly and didn't intend to leave.

He looked suddenly embarrassed, lowering his arm. "Old men get scratches and can't recall how," he admitted with a resigned shrug. "But enough about me. I meant that you dress... differently from most women I've seen here. Like a visiting celebrity on a private tour," he added, inspecting Windsor, who was dressed in his sleek black outfit.

I laughed at that. I glanced at Windsor and was satisfied to see him flinch. His face tightened, no doubt imagining what I would say, and knowing he wouldn't be happy about it. I took it as a warning not to mention we were part of the Conclave – that this old man knew nothing about us.

"Must keep the womenfolk safe," I said, reaching back to pat Windsor's shoulders like a good little bodyguard. His eyes threatened murder but his face remained neutral. Payback was a bitch. Treat me like a duty and get treated like a detail. "You know how much trouble we can get into when left unsupervised." He flashed a grin, amused at the comment but smart enough not to answer. I eyed his own guard, and my smile faltered at a sudden realization.

Windsor's warning look. This man had a bodyguard. "Wait, you're the..." I didn't quite know what to officially call him.

He was smiling, interested in hearing me finish the comment, but I clamped my lips shut. I was in enough trouble as it was, and realized I had just walked into a civil war.

He finally shrugged. "My name is Anthony Gregory Gutierrez." He didn't give a title, and I could tell it bothered him. He was the man who stood against the current pope. The one who thought he was the one true Pope.

The Antipope. *Shit. Shit. Shit.* Maybe he saw a kindred spirit in me, a person not tied to the cookie cutter version of the church. But that being said, wasn't he against the Vatican because he thought they were too lax? Wouldn't that make me an abomination?

"The... Antipope," he clarified, watching me with a humorless smile.

I winced, not quite sure how to respond to that. *Oh, I've heard all about you!* probably wouldn't fly. And what the hell was he doing just walking around the Conclave? Had he slipped through because Roland and I were keeping the Shepherds busy with personal guard duty?

"Callie Penrose," I said, extending my hand lamely. Windsor groaned behind me. Too late, I realized Anthony was just staring at my hand. What the hell? Was I supposed to fucking curtsy or something? I realized I had reached the point in the day when a girl only wants one thing...

To just fuck off to somewhere else. Anywhere but where I was. It happened to all of us.

Anthony smiled up at me. "A breath of fresh air... Walk with me," he said, after accepting my hand in a limp shake, as if unfamiliar with the motion. He glanced at Windsor and then his own guard. "I'm sure our guards can give us some privacy..."

The two nodded at us, then at each other, before politely walking a dozen paces away down the hall, the best place to keep their eyes on us and any approaching threats. After scanning the hall, they finally turned to each other, speaking softly. Neither looked happy, but they at least attempted small talk.

I turned back to Anthony. This was going to be interesting.

✸ 36 ✸

nthony had started off conversationally, speaking of the weather, the historic buildings, and the surprising number of polite people he had encountered on his visit, but I had felt him angling the conversation to the most important topic on his mind – his faith. I had let him, listening to him vent about the numerous disagreements he had with Vatican City.

At first, it felt nice to sort of have an ally, at least someone who shared my current feelings – even though his were seeded in fertile ground with ancient, stubborn roots and mine were only weeds rooted in recent frustrations and a murder mystery. I couldn't have cared less about theological debates concerning which practices were considered sinful and which were not. I wasn't very familiar with the traditional arm of the Catholic church anyway, so had no idea what they told the masses. I was one of the enforcers. Whether or not the Pope denounced gay marriage didn't really change the fact that monsters needed to be killed.

To put it simply, did I have an opinion on social issues? Yep. Sure as hell did.

Was that opinion more important than the fact that monsters attacked innocent people every day and that my focus was better spent on saving lives? Nope. Sure as hell wasn't.

Personally, morality arguments usually lit my fuse quickly. It was one reason I wasn't a fan of organized groups, and why I would make a terrible Shepherd. I had no tolerance for historical biases and no patience for blind zealotry. If a proclamation had a caveat, I disregarded it.

If you condone – insert activity – then you are going to Hell. Caveat? Bye, Felicia.

It was a very simple philosophy.

Also, if I noticed guilt used as a weapon to sway opinion, I disregarded the argument.

Roland had called me a venomous cynic, but he had smiled as he said it. Then he had spent a long time explaining to me that Shepherds served a higher purpose, and that we didn't have to believe everything the Vatican preached.

Granted, most Shepherds were advocates for the Church, and did believe everything the Vatican stood for, but it was by no means a requirement.

My eyes had begun to glaze over as Anthony vomited his version of the Holy Spirit all over my cherub-like cheeks. He didn't like the direction the Vatican was heading, and thought it needed a reset button. Him. Because *blah, blah, blaaaaahhhh...* I had almost fallen asleep on my feet when he said something that revived me.

"Christians have lost their way," he said with a tired sigh.

I almost shouted *Amen*, but didn't want to put another quarter in the anti-Vatican machine.

My lack of interest must have shown on my face because he sighed. "My apologies. It's hard being here, but we must attempt to work together at times. Even if it is in debate," Anthony said. Then he waved a hand. "What brings you here, Miss Penrose?"

I blinked, not having really envisioned *what to say if I run into the Antipope.* "Visiting a friend," I finally said.

Anthony nodded, eyes casually checking on our guards. Then he shook his head with a frown. "I have heard troubling news, but no one seems inclined to speak of it. To need guards inside a House of God..." he muttered, sounding offended. He must have thought I had provided my own guard, or had been provided one. Either way meant the Pope was incompetent in his opinion.

"Just trying to keep everyone safe, I guess."

Anthony pondered that. "I have heard a man of the cloth was recently murdered. Who would do such a thing? And why does no one say anything? All I see is… duck lips everywhere."

I almost snorted. "I think you mean tight-lipped," I said, trying not to embarrass him. He was too busy considering that to notice my sudden anxiety. If he hadn't caught me off guard with his mistaken *selfie* reference, I might have instantly grabbed him by the shoulders to demand where he had heard about Constantine. It hadn't happened on Vatican soil, so how had he connected that to the church?

He finally grumbled indelicately. "Not enough transparency these days. We need to open our ledgers and get back to basics. God is not a business. He is *all*. We're becoming too political." He studied me thoughtfully. "Is it like that where you are from?"

I blinked at him, and then realized he was referring to my American accent. "Missouri is awesome," I said, remembering that funny YouTube video poking fun at my state.

"I've heard disturbing things about St. Louis and Kansas City in recent months."

Well, wasn't Anthony just the gossip queen of Rome? Where the hell had he heard *that*? But I shrugged offhandedly. "Big cities have big problems."

He grunted affirmatively. "I've considered opening a church in St. Louis… How well do you know a Master Nate Temple? I hear he is also visiting the Vatican today." I almost flinched. For the love of god, how did I get out of here? I could tell how hungry Anthony was for information – or possibly Temple's donation check, if his sources were as good as they sounded. With his level of knowledge, he had to be getting information from somewhere he really shouldn't be digging, only confirming my beliefs that something was wrong in the Vatican. Was he aware of the Conclave? Monsters? But I didn't want to lie, either. He was the freaking junior pope.

"He left earlier. I actually had lunch with him before he got on his plane. We've only met a few times, though. I actually didn't know he was going to be here today," I admitted. All facts.

Anthony sighed, realizing my well of information was dry. He opened his mouth to speak when a flash of movement caught my eye. Two Cardinals slowed to a stop at the other end of the hall, spotting Anthony. As if they had been searching for him. The Antipope turned at my attention and saw them. His bodyguard gave him a slow nod, and Anthony growled, sounding annoyed. "It seems I have been summoned…" he said in a dark tone, not sounding pleased about it. "That's the problem with being treated like a criminal rather than a guest."

I grunted. I knew exactly what he was talking about. "Nice meeting you," I said instead. And then he left. Windsor peeled away to make his way back to me, looking as if he wanted to demand a full synopsis of our conversation. Loud boot steps made me turn away from him.

Roland entered the hall just as Anthony, his guard, and the two Cardinals left behind me. He came from the area I had assumed led to our rooms. He looked mildly relieved to see me. Like one rock had been removed from the mountain of rocks still pressing down onto his shoulders. Probably because Fabrizio was hot on his heels, chubby cheeks flushed.

I was very relieved to see Roland, guards or not. No more lone walks for me. Maybe I really did need a guard, because my luck was obviously gone. Running into the freaking Antipope...

Roland read my face, sensing something was wrong, and likely realizing that it had something to do with the group of Cardinals who had just left, but not wanting to ask about it in front of the Shepherds. I heard Windsor picking up his pace behind me, likely sensing Roland's mood.

"There you are, Callie," Roland said, striding closer. He ignored Windsor and Fabrizio entirely, as if they didn't exist, stopping beside me. "I have something to discuss with you." Then, he leaned in close to whisper in my ear, wrapping an arm around me as if pulling me in for a hug to mask his words. "That bishop from Constantine's office had a clerk drop off a file in my room. All the evidence they have. I need your eyes." Then he pulled back, assessing me. "You look like you've run into a ghost," he said.

Rolling with his deceit, I shrugged. "I met his Holiness, the Antipope. Fun times. I probably need a guard or something." As one, we both turned to deliver blank stares at Windsor and Fabrizio. They returned the look without comment.

"Let's head back to our rooms. I need a drink... to pray," I amended, rolling my eyes.

Fabrizio's lip quirked up instinctively, but he quickly killed it. What was wrong with everyone? Why were things so different than they had been only a few hours ago?

The moment things had changed was either during the meeting with the Conclave and the Shepherds, or when they had caught us snooping.

I was very curious about Roland's whispered message, though. He looked both excited and wary. Why had Bishop Stork changed his mind? He had been furious with us. Or had it all been a show? Maybe he really did know something and had just been scared to share it. He'd used a clerk to deliver the file, which meant he didn't want to be seen with us. And after shouting at us, he had the perfect alibi. The clerk had seemed terrified when I last saw him.

"Let's do it."

Roland turned to lead me back to our rooms. Fabrizio and Windsor followed behind us in silence. Well, Fabrizio walked with heavy strides, but they didn't speak. Not even to each other, although I was confident that Windsor would tell him all about my conversation with Anthony.

As we walked, another thing hit me. Even though I was under guard, Windsor hadn't tried to stop me from speaking with Anthony. Was that because I wasn't personally in trouble, or that he hadn't wanted Anthony to get suspicious about what really went down in the Holy Shed?

I'd have to ask Roland.

We were making our way upstairs when Crispin spotted us, entering the building from a front door. He looked physically and mentally drained, as if he had just survived something too terrible to share. Roland's utter lack of sympathy upon seeing his plight even gave me pause. This didn't deter Crispin as he jogged past Fabrizio and Windsor to catch up to me.

His face was flushed from his short run as he strode at my hip. "The Conclave has requested your presence in two hours."

I nodded, remembering Daniel telling me that they had moved up my hearing. Roland was just ahead of us, opening one of a dozen doors lining the hallway on either side of us. "Thanks, Crispin. We'll just be in Roland's room. Pick me up when ready?"

Crispin didn't miss a beat. "I'm afraid I was told to wait here for you. And I have updates to pass on to Fabrizio and Windsor." His voice was clipped and he wouldn't meet my eyes.

Roland motioned me inside. "Well, have fun watching the door."

I followed Roland into the room, and smiled as he slammed it in their faces behind me.

37

I yawned, stretching out my back. Roland had made a pot of coffee from a dated unit found in his rooms. Surprisingly, Roland, the man who usually avoided excess in all things, did some serious damage on the black tar caffeine. I studied him as he paced back and forth. His skin looked pale and I could tell he was more agitated than normal. Was he frustrated at all the secrecy, or was he thirsty for more blood?

We had read the delivered file front to back several times over, and it was almost time for me to head out for my meeting with the Conclave. "Someone here knows something," Roland muttered for the fifth time. "Why are they suddenly treating us like criminals? Something must have happened in that meeting. It's like everyone is under duress and won't talk to outsiders."

I shrugged. We'd had this talk a few times already. I'd told him that the three Conclave members I met with had been surprisingly pleasant after puffing their chests for a few minutes.

No matter how obscurely we manipulated the file, we hadn't found a smoking gun. No active cases Constantine was working on. Nothing we didn't already know about the murder. It seemed Constantine had devoted his entire time to the wolves' training. We found circumstantial evidence that implied the wolves *could* have done it, but nothing that solidly incriminated them. A lot of *potentially, possibly, could be,* and other suggestive language.

"And you burned the note from Bishop Vincente, right?" The first page of the file had been a hastily scrawled note from the stork-like bishop stating that he didn't want to get involved, but that he wanted to help in any way he could, out of his love for Father Constantine. "I'd hate for him to get in trouble for helping us. I wonder who he's scared of..." Roland nodded absently.

I knew he didn't want Bishop Vincente to take the fall, but he was too wrapped up in the big picture. This had hit him on a deeply personal level. He considered this place home, and the people here his family. This was the ultimate betrayal. To know that one of the people he trusted – a person walking around as a man of God – was purposely framing the girls for the murder he had committed. Or that the Conclave was just picking someone to take the fall rather than leave it as a cold case – for political reasons. The world needed to see action. Someone needed to pay, or it would be open season on Shepherds.

It was possible that the murder hadn't been committed by an insider – which just meant the Conclave was incompetent to solve it and had decided to find a scapegoat instead. Sacrificing two innocent wolves to save face with the supernatural world.

Whichever way the cookie crumbled, something was very wrong in Vatican City – the Conclave was broken. We needed to get to the bottom of it to save two innocent lives – no matter who stood in our way. Before Roland turned into—

"I just drank the last of the bags," he whispered, as if reading my thoughts.

I shivered. That wasn't good. "What have you been doing with the empties?" I whispered back, aware of the Shepherds outside our door, keeping guard. I knew he had more stashed at the apartment, but we would have to leave the Vatican to get those.

He pointed at the juncture between wall and floor. I stared where he had indicated but could see nothing amiss. He must have pried back the trim. Clever. "I feel full, but I don't know how much longer I have—"

Someone knocked on the door and we both jumped. "Time for your meeting, Callie," Crispin's voice called through the door. Roland rushed to hide the file under the covers of his bed, using the pillows to hide any telltale bulge, and straightening the sheets. Not wanting to arouse suspicion, I reached out to slowly open the door. All three Shepherds waited before me, and they looked as if they were ready for a funeral. I seriously reconsidered that something was wrong with the air or the food, because everyone seemed to be worse the longer they were here.

I hadn't eaten here, but I had sipped wine with the Shepherds. Roland had pretty much been on his liquid diet of blood, so it was entirely possible that my bizarre hypothesis was right.

Fabrizio was discreetly trying to look over my shoulder to see what we had been up to, but at that moment, Roland walked out of the bathroom adjusting his belt as if he had just finished using the toilet. Then a different idea hit me, making me blush. Maybe Roland and I had just finished a very private Black Mass.

Roland strolled up to the door beside me and stared down the three Shepherds. "I want to visit the crime scene," he said. "Either you can take me there, or you can chase me there," he said casually. He leaned closer to Windsor, as if to kiss him on the neck, and my sense of alarm immediately jumped through the roof. Was he going to fucking bite him? Sweet baby Jesus.

"Unless I'm under arrest?" he whispered. My sense of alarm dropped, but my heart was still hammering wildly against my ribcage. Windsor leaned away, obviously uncomfortable.

Crispin didn't seem to care at all. "Suit yourself."

I spun on Roland. "You're not going with me?" I asked, skin pebbling. He hadn't told me that I would face the Conclave alone.

"Hearings are for you, the Conclave, and Shepherd escorts," Roland said, as if quoting a passage. I snapped my fingers as if to nominate him, but he cut me off. "Mentors are not permitted. They will question me separately if necessary." Windsor nodded succinctly, as if he had just compared the answer with the Shepherd Manifesto and found no errors.

Roland leaned towards Windsor again, his voice a low purr. "And it is a *hearing*, not a *trial*, correct? I'd like to be razor-sharp on that point," he added, grinning like a shark as he met the eyes of each Shepherd – daring them to challenge him. His mixed metaphor hit home, judging by their grim nods. I was feeling decidedly less optimistic about this meeting for some reason.

Windsor made a cross over his heart. "In the Lord's name, I swear." They each did the same, and whatever Roland saw in their eyes was good enough to grant them a reprieve from violence.

He turned to me with a pleased grin. "Good news. They can't kill you. Or else I can slaughter them in disgustingly creative ways before sending their souls to Hell," he laughed cheerfully.

The Shepherds shifted uncertainly, as if not quite sure what to make of this new Roland, and reconsidering how loose a leash they had given him so far. He must have been fairly close on the consequences for failure, because they didn't correct him.

"Gee, thanks," I told him. Then I turned to the others. "Which one of you Holy Hitmen is my escort for the confusing walk downstairs? I'd hate to get lost." They all frowned at my tone, but Fabrizio stepped forward. "That would be me, Miss Penrose." I blinked. No Girlie Penflower this time? It looked like Fabrizio grew silent when angry.

"Lunchbox is with me," I said. "Thank the Good Lord." My sarcasm oozed like honey.

Roland roared with laughter. Was he drunk or was his body that desperate for blood?

After a quick glance at Crispin, Windsor straightened his shoulders. "I'll take Roland to the crime scene." Roland rolled his eyes, as if allowing a bureaucrat to state the obvious to maintain a semblance of authority – taking credit for something he had no business taking credit for.

Crispin cleared his throat, raking a hand through his hair, looking on the edge of his patience. "Since we've been *ordered* to watch over you," he emphasized the word, reminding us that none of this was his choice, "our regular duties have been piling up all day. Now, I have yet *another* distasteful task to perform before returning to being your dutiful babysitter." He took a step closer to Roland, letting my mentor see the conflux of emotions warring over his face. I couldn't quite describe what was going on there. Because I didn't think Shepherds were used to sharing their feelings. He seemed to be having a hard time of it. But he was trying very hard to look... human? Instead, it just looked like his brain was constipated with conflicted emotional buildup.

Now that I was directly focused on it, and it wasn't aimed at me, I realized that all the Shepherds shared the same manic look. Frayed. Raw. What would cause that?

"Understand that as much as you despise this situation," Crispin continued, "I despise it even *more*. I trust you with my *life*, Roland. But when duty calls I will not run away..." he finally whispered in a ragged hiss. Was he threatening Roland or trying to prove we were on the same side? Because his words could be taken so many different ways. What the hell other jobs did he have that were so stressful. And what made Shepherds cry?

I gasped. "You're not going to execute the wolves!" I shouted, gripping him by the lapel.

Fabrizio suddenly held a ball of crackling flame in his open palm, and Windsor had a hand on a dagger at his belt. Roland was utterly motionless, his lips a thin pale line. Crispin blinked down at me, as if I had spoken a foreign language. "What? No. Their trial is tomorrow. We don't execute in secret," he hissed, sounding offended.

My heart slowly returned to normal and I saw Roland back down as I released Crispin. "You just made it sound... ominous," I clarified. The other Shepherds let out shaky breaths as their weapons disappeared, flame and dagger gone in a blink.

"Distasteful, not immoral. Things have been... odd lately." He saw our sudden spark of interest and held up a hand. "I will not speak of it. I may reconsider after your hearing." I saw a glimmer of hope in Roland's eyes, as if seeing a hint of his old friend for the first time in years. Not fully, but a glimpse. He looked satisfied at the development. A chance to find out what all the secrecy was about.

But that didn't make me feel better. He had said *after* my hearing, but that should have no impact on whatever he was referring to. Rather than dwelling on that, I straightened my shoulders, anticipating my meeting, and wanting to make a good impression on the Conclave, so that maybe Crispin would extend a little trust our way again.

Roland shot me an encouraging smile. "Embrace the suck, Callie. You've got this."

I smiled. "Be careful out there," I warned, silently reminding him that he couldn't kill anyone or our game was up. He nodded with a grimace and left. Windsor and Crispin followed him down the stairs.

I glanced at Fabrizio and sniffed self-importantly. "Take me to the Conclave, Lunchbox."

I ignored the startled look on his face before he turned to lead me to our meeting.

Small victories were all I had left to me.

38

I stared at the seven blind wizards before me. I was speechless. This meeting hadn't been what I had anticipated. Not at all. And I had only been here a few minutes, long enough for them to officially call the hearing to order and to state their names and titles. Then they had said that the scope of the hearing had changed, and that they had something to discuss with me instead. I had assumed that meant I was about to be raked over the coals about my private investigation into Constantine's murder.

Then they had dropped the Hail Mary of all truth bombs. I was still reeling, trying to reboot my brain. Fabrizio stood off to the side, close enough to react to any sudden outbursts I might consider, but distant enough not to smother me.

"Someone robbed the fucking Vatican?" I blurted, incredulous.

I forgot that cursing wasn't welcome here, but it was an instinctive reaction on my part. That had been the first thing they told me after their introductions. They had been robbed while we spoke with Nate and Alucard in this very room. Then they had apologized for any inconvenience I may have suffered, but that they had been searching for the thief, and had wanted to keep tabs on everyone's movements.

Daniel nodded in answer to my crude question, face not as friendly as it had been hours ago.

And a very sickening fear bloomed in my mind like a poisonous flower as

I considered recent events. The abrupt attitude change of our previously friendly Shepherd friends. Them guarding our door, escorting us every-where. Their anger at finding us in Constantine's office.

"Wait," I said, shaking my head in an effort to shake off my suspicion. "Do you think *I* robbed you?" I almost laughed at the absurdity of the silent accusation. "Check my rooms!"

The door clicked closed behind me and I turned to see Crispin standing there, hands clasped behind his back as he dipped his head at the Conclave. His eyes lifted to mine. "I just did."

I waited, part of me wanting to murder him for even suspecting me, but another part distantly understood his suspicion. I was a stranger.

So why didn't he look relieved? Apologetic? I hadn't even *seen* my room yet.

With a flash of anger, I recalled the distasteful duty he had mentioned. Now I knew what it had been – searching our rooms. He met my eyes, unflinching. Then he began to lecture in a clinical tone. "We all sat in this very room during the window of the theft – which occurred on the opposite end of Vatican City in an obscure Conclave storage building that only we knew about. The only people not present were the four visiting Shepherds, who were patrolling this building. We checked the surveillance feeds, and confirmed none of them left their posts. Not even for a minute. No magic was used during the theft, but surveillance of the inner vault revealed that the item simply vanished from sight between one second and the next. Our magical detection system picked up nothing. At all."

My eyes widened. No magic sensed, but the item was on video disap-pearing out of thin air?

Crispin continued. "With nothing to go on, we were forced to resort to more... clandestine and archaic methods. We were called to a meeting where we were informed of the theft, and then we randomly assigned trios to search each other's private rooms." His eyes glinted. "Since we had forgotten to give you rooms, we saved yours for last. I'll admit, your bags gave me pause. But they were clean," he admitted without a sliver of shame. I hid my shiver, thanking fortune that they hadn't chosen to search Roland's bag earlier. The blood bags were already gone when Crispin checked them. I realized he had stopped speaking, and looked up at him.

I spun my hand in a rolling motion, encouraging him to get to the point and clear my name. "The tension is killing me," I said harshly.

Crispin clenched his teeth, the first sign of emotion I had seen since his report. He pulled his hands from behind his back to reveal the file we had just been reading in Roland's room. Even though that didn't have anything to do with the theft, it definitely didn't look good. We had been ordered to leave the investigation alone. Repeatedly.

I had a moral conundrum on my hands. Did I come clean and put Bishop Vincente in danger or remain silent? Because the bishop had obviously wanted his name kept out of it. Did that mean he suspected the identity of the killer and was scared? Or was he just covering his ass?

Deep down, I knew that if I had to bring up the bishop's involvement to earn some breathing room to exonerate the girls of a murder charge, I was perfectly fine with that. But only as a last resort. I wished Roland were here. He knew the players involved better than I did.

"Explain," Richter demanded in a dry rasp from behind me. Crispin gave me a moment to come clean, but when I said nothing he simply strode past me. He set the file on the raised desk for the Conclave to pass around at will. Startled, angry gasps filled the courtroom as they passed pages back and forth, listening as Crispin explained finding it in Roland's rooms.

Finished, Crispin turned to pin me with a harsh glare. I turned to see Fabrizio staring at me like he had never seen me before. They both looked betrayed, but we hadn't betrayed anyone. They found a file. Big deal. We'd just been trying to help find the real killer! Unless... that's why they were upset. Because one or both were the killers and weren't happy at our poking.

I'd officially bought a home in Paranoia, Land of the Crazies.

The seductive Whispers began to echo through my mind, and I realized I was dangerously close to lighting the room on fire, and unfurling my Angel wings to scare the living hell out of these judgmental assholes. I took a deep breath, and the Whispers faded away.

"Although this has nothing to do with the theft, you were told to leave the investigation alone," Daniel hissed.

I'd had enough of the accusations. I was finished keeping secrets for people. These bastards were beyond paranoid, and seemed intent to accuse based on convenience, not fact. I had seen it with the wolves, and had now experienced it firsthand. Enough.

"That file was delivered to us by Bishop Vincente," I snapped back at him.

I really shouldn't have been surprised to find that this comment only seemed to somehow make matters worse. My words echoed off the walls as nine pairs of eyes skewered me with varying looks of hatred and outright murder – like one hive mind considering killing me in cold blood. Fabrizio was panting, a hand on his dagger. What had just happened?

Daniel attempted to loom over the desk, but sat back down with a haunted grunt, as if his knees had given out. He settled for staring at me as if I had just admitted to torturing baby seals.

"Bishop Vincente died of heart failure... fifteen minutes after your alter-cation with him." I staggered, my mind going blank for a few seconds, trying to wrap my head around his words. Roland had received the file an hour or so after the time of death? "He *definitely* didn't deliver this file to you. Unless he did it from his grave," Daniel rasped.

I saw that Fabrizio was actually crying. Not weeping, but his face looked like a statue streaked with tears. I suddenly understood the looks I had seen on the three Shepherds' faces outside of Roland's room. Heartache at losing a man of the cloth, knowing that if they hadn't been forced to guard us, they might have been there to save him, to get him help.

I shook my head, trying to make sense of it all. "Well, it was actually his assistant," I said, realizing – too late – how lame it sounded. Then I remem-bered that Roland had burned the only evidence that could prove my claim. The note from Bishop Vincente. I wanted to scream.

"He had no assistant. He *was* an assistant," one of the other Conclave members snarled. "If you're referring to the young clerk who let you into Constantine's office, he was interrogated within minutes of your departure and then escorted from Vatican City for his failure."

I grasped at the first thing that came to mind, needing to make sense of something. Anything. "Heart failure?" I asked very softly, reining in my emotions.

"Overstressed. Perhaps related to finding two strangers ransacking his dead friend's office without permission," Fabrizio growled. "He went into cardiac arrest as his clerk was escorted from the property." My fury was a mushroom cloud, the reins burned away.

"*Ransacking?* Oh, that's *rich*. You and Crispin walked us out. Are you saying I managed to conceal a file that size," I pointed at the desk, "wearing this?" I waved a hand at my outfit.

Fabrizio just glared at me.

"Just to be clear, what exactly am I being accused of? The theft?

Murdering Bishop Vincente? All of the above?" I let my words rattle off the walls. They were silent. The best answer.

The two Shepherds looked ready to lock me up or kill me outright. One of the Conclave members spoke. "This is not a trial, you are not being accused. We are asking uncomfortable questions," he said calmly, his milky white eyes warning me to get a hold of myself.

I nodded stiffly, taking a deep breath. At least one of them seemed rational. I remembered he had been introduced as Stephen.

He nodded his appreciation before continuing. "Windsor verified you never left his sight, but Fabrizio said that Roland went to his rooms for a short time, and then left with some sense of urgency." Even though he tried to mask it, emotion began to taint his voice as he continued. "While you were meeting with the *Antipope*. As soon as Fabrizio arrived with Roland, the Antipope had other matters to attend. Convenient. Almost like a handoff. Then Roland whispers in your ear and you lock yourselves up in his room with that file. Claiming it was delivered by a dead man!" He actually slapped the table with his palm, the wood singing from the contact magic coursing under his skin. So much for calm.

I shook my head in wonder. Then, I began to laugh. It wasn't even a conscious choice. It was just how my brain decided to cope with the lunacy.

My only other option was to kill everyone in the room, but aside from abrupt onset mental retardation, they hadn't done anything wrong. Well, someone had, but I couldn't kill nine people for the successful scheme of one person. And it was blatantly apparent that he was succeeding.

Because the only two people who seemed to give a damn, risking Roland's life by coming here in the first place, were either being framed, or judged by blind imbeciles.

"I'm going to break down the fallacy in your logic exactly one time, so dust off your hearing aids," I said in a deadened voice. "How did I manage to give the Antipope that file before I went to read over it with Roland?" Silence. I smiled brightly, snapping my fingers at a thought. "Oh, that's right. I must have secretly made copies while Bishop Vincente was screaming at us to leave – in the thirty seconds it took for Crispin and Fabrizio to evacuate us from the building – and while Bishop Vincente was staring at me. Then, like we already discussed, I managed to discreetly conceal not one, but *two* very large files as I took a leisurely walk under the watchful eyes of these two strapping Shepherds." I took a breath, winking at Fabrizio. "While under the supervision of at least one Shepherd at all times, I managed to somehow deliver one of the stolen files to Roland and another to the Antipope. You caught me," I said, flashing my teeth. "But you missed the part where I sexually molested the Easter Bunny."

The silence was deafening.

I shot Crispin a disappointed look. "How incompetent can you be to let me get away with all of that right under your nose? First Shepherd... Constantine would be disgusted. Or maybe, just maybe, your accusation is flawed and you owe me an *apology*. I'll wait for it. Take your time." I began tapping my foot, folding my arms across my chest.

I watched his face darken and idly wondered if Roland was having as much fun as I was.

39

I waited until one of the Conclave members opened his mouth to speak before overriding him. "And just to clarify, the Antipope left to meet with two of *your* cardinals. They were waiting for him before Roland even arrived. Ask Windsor. Or, hell, ask the Antipope and his guard."

Then I took two slow, aggressive steps forward, ignoring Crispin and Fabrizio as they rushed to defend the Conclave. "But don't you *ever* fucking accuse me of a crime without solid evidence." A new thought hit me as my F-bomb ignited a vortex of stunned silence in the room, even a few crosses drawn over the chests for good measure. "Maybe you should ask what urgent matters Crispin had to attend to after he kicked us out of Constantine's office," I said, slowly turning to face him.

He glared back at me and I knew I had him. Or he was still pissed about my last comment. Or the Easter Bunny thing. "I had to go check Windsor and Fabrizio's rooms for evidence of the theft." His shoulders bristled.

"Right," I rolled my eyes.

He pulled out his phone and flicked through it for a few seconds. "Here are the time-stamped pictures. Their rooms are nowhere near Constantine's office or this building. Anyone here can do the math and see that I had no time to go anywhere near his office and make it back to you when I did." He met my eyes, and then shifted to the Conclave. "If anyone doubts me, shackle me now," he offered, setting down the phone and holding out his wrists.

Daniel shot Crispin a thankful look, waving at him to lower his hands before turning back to me. "For your information, Miss Penrose, he speaks the truth. I was *with* him," he admitted. "I do appreciate your attempt to keep my name out of it, though, First Shepherd," he told Crispin.

Fabrizio spoke clearly, taking no offense at the thought of his rooms being searched. "I checked Crispin and Windsor's rooms as well. With..." he averted his eyes, not wanting to reveal his accomplice, "a different Conclave member."

Daniel dipped his head in acknowledgment before turning back to me, taking a calming breath. "Even our rooms were searched. Other than Crispin's sprint to meet up with me, and Windsor's sprint to replace him with you and Fabrizio, we remained in groups at all times. In an attempt to eliminate the chance of the thief concealing his crime. No one was allowed near their own rooms during this search." I opened my mouth, but he cut me off. "And before you belabor the obvious, two randomly paired Conclave Members waited around the corner for Windsor after he told you to meet with me. They escorted him to the meeting. In record time, I might add," he shot an amused look at two of the older gentlemen on the council. "Windsor was never out of their sight."

Daniel gave me a moment to digest it all before proceeding. "We chose Crispin to search Roland's room last, out of respect. It seems we have only succeeded in turning on each other. Unjustly, and for that, I apologize." It sounded like he was having his teeth pulled, but he had said it. "Despite our best efforts, we are very aware that someone within these walls has betrayed us," he admitted tiredly. I knew this was as much of an apology as I was going to get, so let it go. "And if you're going to ask who supervised Christopher, Richter and myself after our meeting with you, the answer is no one." He shrugged. "We share the same alibi, as flimsy as that is. But within ten minutes of leaving you, we were back with the rest of the Conclave and Shepherds."

Nods all around, vouching for them.

"Oh," I expelled a breath, unable to find a hole in the story. Which meant all this shouting had been for nothing. We still didn't know who killed Constantine, another man had died, and now we had a theft on our hands. No one here had been a part of the theft. Unless Daniel had just admitted it with his weak alibi. Then again, nothing criminal had happened during that brief period of time. The theft was already over by that point, and they had an alibi for the theft.

We all did.

My own magic was dangerously close to the surface, ready to destroy something though. I took a deep breath and turned to Crispin. "I'm sorry."

He nodded stiffly. "Me, too."

I forced my mind to go through the chronology, searching for anything. "Still, I shredded your accusation of my involvement in less than a minute. Just consider how wise it would be to *use* me rather than *accuse* me... You asked *us* to come here. I definitely didn't want to visit," I said, struggling for composure. "And to suspect Roland? In either the theft or the murder?" I blew a very unflattering sound from my lips.

"Roland was Constantine's student, and he led his killers through our door," Richter rasped. Christopher instantly reached out to catch him as he stumbled in his effort to stand, rubbing his back and murmuring in his ear.

The rest of the room grew silent as a tomb. "As we mentioned earlier, Miss Penrose, we had been considering a promotion for you. But I think we should let our tempers cool before we broach that topic again," Daniel said in a tight voice. His tone made me acutely aware that any future conversation – if there was one – would be very brief.

And that it would probably be to inform me they were about to wipe my mind and send me packing in a Sister's habit. Good thing Roland and I would be on the run long before that.

On the up side, at least I wouldn't be a Shepherd.

If we escaped, that was. In all likelihood, this mission would lead to our doom. Our only real chance at success would be to break the girls out of their prison cell and run as far and fast as we could manage. Because to find Constantine's killer, we had to now work around an entire organization who didn't trust us. Even if we saved the wolves, Roland was on borrowed time, having only the blood bags from the apartment for sustenance. Pretty soon someone would tick him off at the wrong moment and he would rip the offending vocal cords right out of someone's neck. I shivered, imagining Roland having to hear any of what I had just gone through.

It would have broken him, turning him into a vampire in an instant.

"You are dismissed," Daniel said, meeting my cold glare. "We... apologize for jumping to conclusions. We will keep the file, and will continue our investigation into exactly what happened here today."

I tried one last time. "Why won't you just let us help find the real killer?"

"Because we already found them, and their trial is tomorrow," Daniel said. "The witnesses will put everything into perspective. They positively identified the wolves. Well, the girls, since they don't know that werewolves exist."

I gave it up, knowing it was fruitless. Of course the witnesses had identified them. Roland and I needed to come up with an exit strategy. Because we had come here thinking to deal with rational men, but instead, found a raging ocean of paranoia and incompetence.

I realized we hadn't discussed the theft in detail. What had been stolen? Something big if it had created this clusterfuck. But I knew I wasn't going to get any answers right now. I was lucky to be dismissed rather than have my head detached.

One thing I was certain of, was that the real killer might just be the cleverest son of a bitch to ever fall out of a vagina. He had probably even convinced his mother it was an immaculate conception...

40

I had spoken with Roland on the phone, giving him the very broad strokes of my hearing with the Conclave. Telling him the whole truth with every raw detail might have sent him over the edge. He had returned to tell me he had found nothing useful at the crime scene. Then he had informed the three Shepherds that he wanted to talk with them in private. I had told him how stupid his idea was, and that because it made no rational sense, maybe it did make sense in this crazy place.

"Make sure you come back to my room after you murder them so I can help you hide the bodies. We'll probably have to leave quickly," I said, tapping my lip as if planning.

Roland grunted, not finding it funny. But I hadn't been joking. Not really. Well, maybe a little.

The truth was that I was beyond caring. I had no sympathy left for them. I had entered that critical stage in a woman's life – that place when emotion starved to death and the only two options left to fill that void was to become a serial killer or to take a long, hot shower.

I spent three minutes, exactly, debating these two options.

The shower won, but it was a close thing. I even doodled a *pros and* cons list while Roland paced, his thoughts absorbed with his upcoming meeting with the Shepherds. I read the list one last time, verifying that the shower had, in fact, won. Then I signed it, my pen stabbing through the paper at the end, and tossed the paper on the bed in case the Conclave needed evidence later. They'd probably miss it and accuse the janitor anyway. Incompetent bastards. For good measure, I hurled the pen across the room.

Roland looked up at me, saw the paper, and walked over. He grinned from ear-to-ear as he read over it, and his fangs even popped out. When he looked back up, I just shrugged tiredly.

He tossed the paper back on the bed and sat beside me. "I need to look into their eyes when I speak to them, Callie. They will be more open with me if you're not around. I know their vices and virtues. They can't claim piety around me. We were students together. It will be four brothers hashing it out. Maybe I can find a discrepancy somewhere."

Since I wasn't entirely concerned if he decided to kill them, I simply nodded. "Okay. See you later." I stood and walked into the bathroom, turning on the shower. I stripped down, clipped my hair into a bun, and stepped inside, closing the door behind me.

I shuddered in relief as the hot water splashed my chest, and I let out a sigh of relaxation. Finally, something enjoyable from this hellish trip. I turned to face the glass so the shower could hit my back and hopefully wash away the last of the homicidal particles that threatened to smother me. I closed my eyes, lathering up with a bar of soap and sucking in deep, calming breaths of the steamy air as the hot water brought peace and prosperity to my soul—

"I've accepted my bloodlust," a voice said from directly opposite the clear glass door.

I shrieked in alarm, slamming into the back wall and dropping the bar of soap onto my toes. "Damnit, Roland!" I snapped, hopping on one foot and panting as I tried to wash the soap from my eyes while covering my naughty bits as best as possible.

"My eyes are closed, Callie. Good lord," he said in a patronizing tone. I cleared my eyes enough to see his silhouette facing me through the clear glass. He did have a hand over his eyes.

"Congratulations. You learned the vampire creep skillset. Now, get the hell out of here and go kill those stupid friends of yours," I cursed.

"I will not kill them, Callie. They are my brothers," he said sternly.

"What are you still doing here? *Git!*"

"I was trying to tell you that I've accepted what will happen to me," he said, sounding frustrated that I wasn't taking him seriously. He stood facing me, eyes still covered.

"This isn't a suicide message, right? That you're accepting your fate and are willing to sacrifice yourself rather than remain an abomination?" I asked warily.

He hesitated. "No. I very much value this life of mine. I will continue to do good with it. I'm just trying to tell you that I am at peace—"

"Great. No suicide means you can get the hell out of here. Now. We'll have an *I'm Fanging Out Party* with Nate and Alucard in a few days. I'll make sure he brings his unicorn. Cool? Great. Buh-bye."

I heard him muttering that unicorns didn't exist as he finally stomped away, closing the door.

What the hell? Just waltzing into my bathroom while I showered? Maybe the creep factor was another symptom of vampirism. Because Roland used to be allergic to boobies. I teased him endlessly about female nudity, and it had never gotten old. But here he was, wanting to have a girl talk while I showered, trying to *not* think about murdering things.

I sighed, taking a calming breath. Then I peeped over the door, verifying he had actually left this time. Confident I was safe, I tried to enjoy the rest of my shower, letting my mind wander.

The Conclave had been robbed while we were all in a meeting with Nate and Alucard.

So, none of us was the thief.

The Conclave hadn't told me what was stolen or if it was somehow dangerous.

In looking for the thief, the Conclave had checked everyone's rooms for evidence of the crime, even though we all had the same alibi. Unsurprisingly, we had all checked out.

At least on the theft.

But they had found their file on Constantine's murder in Roland's room – the file delivered to Roland by Bishop Vincente. Only later did we find out this file was sent after he had died. I had accused Crispin, but he had proof – backed by Daniel – that he hadn't had time to go back to kill the bishop, obtain the file, and then secretly deliver it to us, so he was clear.

Which begged the question. Who had really sent it?

Had Bishop Vincente really died from heart failure, or had he been cleverly murdered?

Because someone had sent us that file, and my bet was Vincente's death was related.

Regardless, finding that file in Roland's rooms had looked highly suspicious. Especially when we couldn't back up the source. Because Roland had burned the note from Bishop Vincente. If it hadn't been a fake note to begin with. There was no way to check now, though.

All in all, we had made absolutely no progress on Constantine's murder.

We'd spent two hours with a useless file that contained zero real evidence.

All other efforts to dig up information on Constantine or the murder had proven worthless, and we had been blacklisted from speaking with the two witnesses. I knew beyond a shadow of a doubt that we had exactly zero chances in speaking with the girls, either. If the Shepherds wouldn't let us talk to the witnesses, they sure as hell weren't going to let us talk to the murder suspects. Because the Conclave thought we were biased.

Unless Roland could mindfuck the Shepherds into letting us talk with them, using his fledgling vampire skills. But that could backfire easily, and then his secret would be outed.

I climbed out of the shower and toweled off. I hadn't spotted a hair dryer in my bathroom, so had decided not to wash my hair. It was clean, anyway. Somewhat. And with the *Desperate Bishops of Vatican City* reality TV show I found myself living, I wasn't really in the mood to pick up a hunk of man-meat for the night.

As a fundamental law of the universe, celibacy wasn't sexy.

Even if I did somehow discover the man of my dreams in priest's robes, I had exactly zero chance of turning the pious zero to a hero. Unless I wanted to break his faith and paint a scarlet letter on my forehead. Home-wrecking the House of God. Go big or go home, right?

I realized I was slaphappy, and spending entirely too much mental energy attacking everything the Vatican stood for. I let out a calming breath as I dried off, and admitted to myself that I was being irrational. The men I had considered most holy and just in the world, had failed to meet my expectations. Not only had they failed my expectations as men of the cloth, but as human beings. Then they'd had the audacity to accuse me of crimes I would never commit.

I no longer considered the warrior priests as untouchable. Instead, I found myself in a city of incompetent hypocrites who were supposed to be the last line of defense between monsters and humans. And I found them wanting. In essence, I had been let down.

Still, it wasn't fair for me to doggedly mock their faith. Even if it was only in my head.

I couldn't blame God for their shortcomings. I tugged on some tight black pants with a black tank top. Then I threw on a white dress shirt over it, buttoning it high enough so that my glorious love devils didn't give instant heart attacks to any of the old men within leering distance. Then I did up one more button to be safe, even though it made me feel nerdy. I tied my hair back in a ponytail and tugged on my Darling and Dear boots. I focused on them, watching as they abruptly shifted into almost knee high, black leather boots. Not that I needed it, but these boots had the ability to sense demons.

And with the glorious chase we were being led on, it actually might make sense to learn a demon was just playing games with us.

I locked the door behind me on the way out, surprised no one was waiting for me. The three Shepherds must still be talking to Roland. I had almost expected to find the three Shepherds decapitated with their blood drained and their heads neatly arranged before my door with a note from Roland announcing it was time for us to leave, and did I need help with my bag?

Maybe I needed some caffeine. It had been a day and a half since I had last slept.

"Where do you find drugs in Vatican City?" I murmured to myself. I heard someone gasp down the hall and turned to flash them an innocent smile.

An older woman winced in a failed attempt to smile, and then fled down another hall.

Oh well.

41

My burner phone rang, startling the hell out of me. It had completely slipped my mind. I frowned down at it for a second and then answered. "Hello?"

"Callie!" Claire's voice rang out. Whenever one of us was heading out of town we always made sure to give the other a way to get in contact, whether it was the address, name of the hotel and room number, or a phone number.

"Claire," I replied lamely, too surprised to think straight as I wondered why she was calling from the middle of Alaska – where I hadn't even thought she had cell service.

"I came back to town early. What's up with the foreign number? Where are you?" She paused, and her breathing got heavier as if she was speaking directly into the microphone. "Are you on a romantic adventure with a certain billionaire?" she purred.

"I wish..." I wondered where to even begin to lie about my trip. Then I realized how my answer had sounded. "I *meant*," I said, ignoring her outburst of delighted giggles, "I'm on a job, and it's sucking hard. Nothing to do with Nate. I'm with Roland." I had to be very careful here. So much had happened, and I didn't want to give her too many details or she would be on the first flight here.

"Boo. No fun."

"Why did you come home early?"

"I needed a break from all the nature stuff. The bears are *heavy*, Callie. Spiritually speaking. Well, literally, too, I guess. I needed to get away. And I thought we could use some long overdue girl time," she pouted. "Watching crap movies and devouring popcorn." She sounded disappointed that her vision of reality didn't align with the universe.

"Soon," I agreed. I hoped I wasn't lying. It did sound nice. But Roland and I might be on the run soon. And we would hopefully have two were-wolves to babysit.

Realizing this was the only means of girl time, Claire decided to unload her life story on me, and I couldn't exactly tell her that I was about to walk into a room where Roland might have killed his coworkers. "Kenai didn't want me to leave, and thought it would be hilarious to steal my credit card and keys, telling me I could use his room at the Cave instead of my own house. Of course, he told me this over the phone... *after* I had already landed in Kansas City."

I laughed. Such a tiny problem to have, although I was wise enough not to tell her that. "And what did you do to deserve that?"

She grew quiet for a few seconds. "Nothing."

I burst out laughing at her obvious lie. "You can crash at my place," I said, reading between the lines about her motive for calling me, and not making her ask me for help outright. "My purse is on the table, and you know where my spare key is." Luckily for her, people in Kansas City rarely asked for ID when offered a credit card.

"Thank you," she said, sounding relieved. "Wait, why don't you have your wallet?"

"I didn't need my wallet, so I left it." I hoped she didn't dig into that, because it was flimsy as hell, even though it was true. Roland had made us leave all that behind, knowing what we might be getting into in Rome and not wanting authorities to discover who we were if we were caught. To keep our friends' safe. Still, the mystery was enough to make Claire drool, and I waited, trying to come up with a story.

But she didn't bite. "I'll pay you back when the bank opens on Monday and use my ID to get some cash. Don't worry. I'll just order some food. Maybe pick up some beer."

"How are you getting back from the airport without a wallet?"

It took her a few seconds to reply. "Beckett said he could pick me up."

I bit back my instinctive growl, having forgotten all about that fiasco.

But he wasn't my property. And he was just picking her up from the airport. Nothing scandalous.

"I didn't want to ask him for money on top of a ride," she admitted guiltily.

"Okay," I said, hiding a deep breath. Her words gave me a very unpleasant image of Claire riding Beckett, and my vision was darkening, even though she hadn't implied any such thing. "I need to jump off. Roland's glaring at me," I lied.

"Be safe!" she said before I hung up, panting as I stared down at my phone. Jealousy threatened to turn me into a monster, and I didn't know why. Beckett wasn't mine. I wasn't even sure how I felt about him. Well, part of me was telling me exactly how I felt about him, whether I wanted to acknowledge it or not. I mentally shoved that part of me into a six-foot-deep grave, poured gasoline on the corpse, and tossed a match at it as I stomped down the hall.

Fabrizio and Crispin were waiting for me as I turned the corner into a new hall. Crispin approached me as one would a wild deer in a parking lot.

"We just finished speaking with Roland," he said, looking as if he had barely survived.

"I hope he didn't go easy on you," I muttered, surprised I didn't see a black eye at least. I did notice a red mark on his cheek, but it was minimal. He'd been hit with something recently.

Crispin abruptly grasped my hands, eyes pleading. I was so surprised, I let him. "I said I was sorry, Callie. Someone close to us betrayed us, and we still don't know who. The two of you show up a day early and begin digging into things that are painful to us. Would you have done any differently?" he asked, sounding both angry and ashamed, as if he was repeating his conversation with Roland.

I considered him thoughtfully, and realized that he had a point. I would have burned something to the ground to find a traitor. Hell, that's what I was trying to do now, and I was getting dangerously close to disregarding innocent bystanders. I sighed, shaking my head. "Let's go see the old grouch. I have questions."

He let out a sigh of relief and guided me towards Fabrizio, who looked like he was ready to defend himself. No longer directly threatening, but wary as all hell. And... guilt also flickered in his eyes. "Hey, Meatball," I said, by way of greeting, eyeing his cut lip. Again, nothing serious, but it was present. Roland hadn't gone easy on them.

He blinked. "Meatball?" he asked, his cut lip curling slightly at the beginning of a smile.

I nodded, face serious. "You're big, Italian, and you keep me safe from healthy food."

Fabrizio roared with laughter, and it sounded like he had needed it. A pressure valve releasing built up steam. "I'll take it," he said, still laughing as he opened the door.

I went in first, followed by the two Shepherds. The room looked disturbed, but not demolished. A broken chair sat in the corner, pointedly ignored by each man in the room. Two paintings hung askew, and water dripped from a side table. I leaned to the side to find a broken vase and a dozen flowers littering the floor in a big puddle. They'd exchanged love taps, at least.

Roland sat in a chair, his feet propped up and hands tucked behind his head. Windsor sat across from him, shoulders relaxed. His face was still introspective, but it looked calmer, as if he too felt much better after their... talk. He shot me a slow nod, as if gauging my temper, and I noticed a cut on his forehead. Nothing major, but enough to signify Roland's displeasure. I was impressed that the blood hadn't sent him over the edge. I dipped my head at Roland, who looked like a lion after a hearty meal. I pointedly assessed the room before turning back to him. "You didn't have to kill anyone," I said. He might have forgiven the Shepherds, but they weren't entirely clear in my book. A few wild punches weren't going to earn back my complete trust.

A person had one shot to earn my trust. If they blew it, they had a long uphill battle before them. Fabrizio had escaped the brunt of my wrath by being jolly and mouthy. He'd also been the first to challenge me in a fight. Despite the very real rage I had recently seen in his eyes, I had reasons to both trust and distrust him. For example, Roland's amulet had zapped the shit out of him on contact.

Crispin was staggering under the weight of his new responsibility as First Shepherd, and I could tell he was hating every minute of it. Especially after such a monumental failure in falsely accusing us. The frustration in his eyes, and his apology, had been genuine, though.

Genuine enough for me to buy it at least, but I knew I wasn't infallible.

He was still on my watch list, but he had been removed from my kill-on-sight list. As had Fabrizio. And Roland's amulet had *not* zapped the shit out of him. They had also both been the first ones to catch us in Constantine's office, in almost record time of Bishop Vincente losing his shit on us. Was that just the Shepherds doing their duty, or had they appeared a little too quickly?

Windsor was a wildcard. He had been the first to find us in Rome. Sure, that had been at Crispin's direction, but his apparent lack of empathy still made me wary. He was typically silent and resolved. He seemed to have no apparent opinion on my existence. Which was different from his character during our first encounter, where he had seemed almost like Roland's younger brother – reserved, but more easygoing. Why the change? Was it because he was back in his professional capacity? Or was he waiting for the right time to reveal his master plan?

All in all, each of the three Shepherds had done things to make me doubt them. They had also given me numerous reasons to trust them. Which meant I was in exactly the same place as the first moment I had set foot in Italy. What a colossal waste of time.

Roland studied me. "We just needed to get a few hugs in and do each other's nails. We're mostly better now," he said, deadpan. I nodded, but silently noted the word *mostly* he had used.

I sat down at the table. The others followed suit. They each looked resigned, as if gearing up for round two. They had succeeded with Roland, but I had been the one in the hearing, subjected to their direct accusations. And a woman never forgets. She may forgive, but she never forgets.

Where men, on the other hand, forget, but never forgive.

"What was stolen?" I asked, deciding not to bandy words. Straight to business.

The Shepherds clammed up. I turned from Windsor to Fabrizio, but they offered me nothing. I finally turned to Crispin, arching one eyebrow.

He sighed. "We aren't permitted to talk about it. Literally. They want exactly zero chance of word getting out. The word ex-communicated was tossed around..." he added.

Wow. That was severe. "Did the mysterious whatsit have any value? Magical or monetary?"

Crispin thought about it, watching as I duplicated Roland, kicking my feet up on the table. Fabrizio did a double-take at my boots, a frown crossing his features. Huh. What did that mean? I had discreetly pointed my boots at each of the men in the room, even Roland, to see if any of them were meat-suits for a demon. But nothing had happened. Did he recognize the brand or did he sense something about them?

Windsor leaned forward, waiting for a nod from Crispin. "Not particularly, but we wonder if it wasn't merely a distraction. That the thief stole something else that we haven't yet discovered. That this might just be a red herring." His eyes were calculating, as if rolling over the inventory in his mind, eager for the challenge of discovering the truth.

"What else is locked away that's dangerous?" I asked, yawning as I spoke.

My yawn had no effect as they clammed up again. Damn. I'd hoped the subtle trick would work. Oftentimes you could trick people into answering a question with a carefully crafted look of boredom, exhaustion, or other subtle sign of weakness.

In fact, one way to find a sociopath or psychopath was to see how they reacted when you yawned. If they didn't yawn back, it might be indicative of a sociopath. If they grew suddenly alert, they might be a psychopath. This wasn't a certainty, but studies had been performed, and it was at least a mildly accurate indicator of disposition towards a certain personality type.

So... none of the Shepherds yawned. They also didn't look suddenly alert.

Well, that wasn't entirely true. I sensed Roland grow instantly still. Which was probably his vampire nature kicking in. A sudden sense of weakened prey. I didn't acknowledge it at all as I switched my feet, crossing them the other way and drawing attention back to me. Not Roland. Just in case the Shepherds were also privy to random pieces of knowledge about human behavior.

Inside my head, I stored the piece of information away. The Shepherds were sociopaths, which wasn't necessarily a bad thing. Being a sociopath just meant you could block off your emotions more easily than others. That you weren't controlled by feelings, sympathy, or empathy. Surgeons, doctors, lawyers, and engineers were all typically sociopaths or had sociopathic tendencies.

Psychopaths typically had zero concern for the general population. If they wanted something, and it didn't directly hurt someone they cared about, they didn't really understand why anyone else cried about the loss of innocent life that had stood between them and their goal. They just took the shiny they had wanted. *What's the big deal? So, a dozen innocent people died. Why is everyone freaking out? Didn't you see this new pretty shiny I got?*

The Shepherds weren't able to share details about the theft. Was it connected to Constantine's murder? Maybe he had gotten wind of the impending theft, and had to be silenced. But if the stolen item didn't have much value... it probably *was* just a red herring. A misdirect. Or it had more value than anyone thought, which spoke of a very intelligent or cunning thief.

One, because they had stolen from the Vatican during broad daylight.

Two, they had risked all the dangers to steal something non-important. Or worse, they had decided to take extra time to stage the scene, and steal *two* somethings. One an obvious theft, another that the Vatican still hadn't figured out. Nighttime theft would have been infinitely easier. But it had disappeared right from under their collective noses.

The Conclave must have had a lot of dangerous items in their vault or they wouldn't have been so concerned. Sure, concerned that someone had succeeded, but they wouldn't have threatened ex-communication over sharing details about a worthless book no one remembered being down there. They wouldn't have minded sharing the scene of the crime.

And the Conclave would only be concerned if it had been something magically dangerous.

The Shepherds weren't being entirely straight with me. Or maybe the Conclave wasn't being entirely straight with them. Circles within circles...

🦁 42 🦁

Roland tapped the table with a finger, catching everyone's attention. "Is it possible that Master Temple stole the item?" he asked. I hated that he voiced this, but it was a good question, and might go a long way into earning back some trust if we were willing to scrutinize our own friends – like these three had been forced to do to us.

Fabrizio shook his head, interlocking his fingers behind his neck as he leaned back in his chair. "He was literally under observation every second he was here. We even had his room under surveillance, not that he used it," he grunted, obviously annoyed that Nate had left so quickly after his arrival. I bet that a lot of people would want to question him about his magic and his name blasting the news seemingly every other week. "He didn't sneak out. We have video of both him and his vampire."

Crispin piped up tiredly. "And he and the Daywalker were in the room with us when the theft occurred." I really wished I would have pestered Nate more about his decision to visit. Surely making a donation to the Conclave and introducing Alucard to the church wasn't important enough to warrant a visit. Nate had no reason to care what the church thought, unless it was about Armageddon, like he had said.

"What did he do while he was here? Other than make his donation and introduce Alucard?"

Windsor scratched his stubble and then folded his arms with a shrug. He had been driving us to the Vatican.

Crispin and Fabrizio cranked their minds, as if searching for anything suspicious. "He said he was flying by on his way home and wanted to introduce himself. We verified his flight plan here. He spent some time hopping from spot to spot in Europe, spending a week in Paris, a month in Egypt, and a few weeks in London before arriving here," Crispin said with a shrug. "It all checked out, even the hotels he had stayed at," he admitted with a guilty shrug, as if not proud of the espionage. "He said he hadn't ever met us in person, and since he wasn't on great terms with the Academy, he figured it was past time to meet us – especially since he was impressed by the Kansas City outfit," he finished with a grin, miming shooting a finger gun at me, directly. I rolled my eyes at the subtle male humor.

Fabrizio piped up after a good chuckle. "As a token of good faith, he offered to introduce us to someone unique and to make a donation to our cause."

"He tried to buy his way in?" I said what they were all thinking, knowing it was never that simple with Nate Temple.

Fabrizio's eyes went distant, as if surprised at the memory. "He said we could still meet Alucard and accept the donation, and then toss him out on his ear if we wanted. He said buying people with money has the unfortunate effect of increasing the price down the road while proportionately decreasing loyalty." He scratched his jaw absently. "Something like that."

Crispin nodded. "Close enough." He turned to me. "Basically, as surprised as we were at the prospect, we were even more surprised by his cavalier attitude. He said he was meeting us halfway, and that the rest was up to us."

I glanced at Roland, who finally shrugged. He knew Nate was sneaky, but the rest sounded like him as well. He was unpredictable in that way, and it did make sense for him to introduce himself to the Vatican in exactly the way they recalled. Not begging. Not buying. Mutual respect. Because we would be on the same side of a war later.

I felt conflicted, because Nate was a Horseman of the Apocalypse, and he hadn't told them.

But he hadn't been left unsupervised. At all, apparently.

Of course, I wasn't pleased to hear about their lack of hospitality, even if

Nate wasn't aware of it. The Conclave had bugged his rooms and spied on his travels. After what I had been through, I shouldn't have been surprised.

But it bothered me on a deeper level. Here I was, standing in Vatican City, according to many, one of the holiest places in the world, and it was as corrupt as anyplace I had ever visited. Governments included. My confidence in their creed was shattered beyond repair, and their job offer now more than mildly disgusted me.

But I was also oddly... relieved? To fear that a group of people were perfectly pious put a lot of pressure on a person to match up. Especially when that person kind of worked for them. Me. It birthed the constant fear that I would never be able to measure up to their holy standards. But hearing and living this... made me realize they were just as human as the rest of us.

Not better. Not worse. The same.

But the part that really concerned me was that they had treated us like criminals after the theft. They had treated Nate like a criminal *before* anything had happened. That meant they had been spying on our lunch as well, even though they hadn't been present. How exactly had they been keeping tabs on Nate? Had they happened to hear Roland step aside with Alucard to talk about vampire puberty?

I shivered in fear at the thought. But among the many accusations we had faced, and how hotly I had argued back with the various members of the organization, no one had brought up that Roland was a vampire. And with as angry as I had made them, surely that would have been their ultimate rebuttal. Or I would have just found Roland staked to his bed, dead as a doornail.

But here he was, alive and well, and no one seemed concerned. Even if it was something they all knew, and were keeping that knowledge a secret, subtle shifts in body position and attention to Roland would have been unavoidable. I would have seen it. They actually treated me with more suspicion than Roland.

So, his secret had to be safe. They never would have entered his private meeting otherwise.

And if they had spied on Nate, I could guarantee they had spied on us as well. And Roland and I had shared very candid conversations when we thought we were in private. They were either blissfully unaware, or incredible poker players, even though Windsor seemed like the only one entirely in charge of his emotional tells.

"Maybe it was the Antipope," I offered, trying to change topics. "He knows a lot more than is good for his health. He's getting information from someone."

Windsor shook his head. "He has been under surveillance, too. But he left earlier today."

Which pretty much confirmed that Roland and I were being watched as well. Or at least had been. "Are *we* still under surveillance?" I asked.

Crispin shook his head. "No. You probably don't believe that, and I don't blame you, but I axed the proposition of spying on you as soon as it was brought up. Other than our mandatory guard duty after the theft, we haven't spied on you. I knew doing so would be a very slippery slope. When all it takes is fear and suspicion – with no evidence – to spy on our very own people, Rome is about to fall. The Conclave's consolation prize was to openly guard you, not in secret, but right where you could see us doing it. But only *after* the theft." Roland studied Crispin over his folded hands, as if searching for a tell. He finally nodded at his old friend. Roland hadn't noticed anything to make him doubt Crispin. Or he would tell me in private and was trying to keep the Shepherds at ease now. "We were just doing as commanded," Crispin said after returning Roland's nod. "I was able to veto spying on you two, since you have ties to us, but not the others. I had to do as I was commanded. Probably used up the last of my good will doing it, too," he complained, but he shot me a wink after a second, silently telling me it was worth it.

Windsor cleared his throat, eyeing Crispin uncertainly, as if wondering why his boss hadn't said something. He took the initiative when it was apparent Crispin wasn't going to speak.

"You must go nowhere near the wolves until the trial. You can be present at the trial, but as a witness only. Unless called upon. That is your only rule... and per the Conclave... your only warning." He didn't look pleased to state this, but he looked less pleased that Crispin had let him look like the bad guy. Fabrizio watched the exchange with a grimace. A thoughtful grimace.

Fabrizio and Crispin both sighed, but nodded their heads.

Roland stood, signaling an end to the conversation. Silence grew as everyone stared at him, myself included. "Constantine was murdered. My mentor..." his voice sounded strained as if dehydrated. "I came here to find the murderer, because everything I know and saw in those two girls screams innocence. They would never harm anything of mine. They might have run, but they wouldn't harm someone I loved. Most importantly, they would have called me the moment that thought crossed their mind. They haven't been here long enough to get involved in politics, and they held no position of power to coerce. When I arrive, I see my brothers holding a flimsy file like a shield, when it wouldn't hold up in any court anywhere in the world. Callie and I try to assist, and we get blocked out." The silence was a physical presence. The other Shepherds didn't even try to argue. "I come home to a House of God. A house divided. And... it breaks my heart." He motioned for me to stand, and I did, my legs shaking at the sorrow in his voice. He turned his back on them, motioning for me to exit the room first. He called out without turning. "I will find the real killer if it's my last act as Shepherd. No matter how deep or high the rot goes."

The door clicked shut behind him and I stared at him for a long moment. Then I held up my hand for a high five. A ghost of a smile crossed his face. And miracle of all miracles, he slapped skin with me. Then he did the explodey thing with his hand. "Like that?" he asked uncertainly.

I didn't have the heart to tell him that high fives didn't explode. Only fist bumps. Everyone knew that.

"Exactly like that." His smile faded as the enormity of our situation became clear. Roland had just given the Shepherds an ultimatum, politely telling them that we would kill anyone – even the Conclave – responsible for Constantine's death.

We walked down the hall with absolutely nothing to go on. "I'm hungry," I said. Then I caught his eye meaningfully. "And you look like you could use a drink."

He nodded, hearing me loud and clear. He indicated the direction of food, and I followed, wondering just what the hell we needed to do next. Whatever it was, we needed to do it fast. Roland was stressed, looked exhausted, and we were fresh out of blood bags for him.

I was very, very glad that Crispin hadn't found the empty bags Roland had hidden behind the trim in our room. If he had, our problems would have ceased to exist, matching our heartbeats.

As it was, we were still in the land of the suck. "Embrace the suck," I murmured.

We were all alone in the hall, and as Roland turned to me, his fangs popped out, eyes shimmering crimson for a millisecond. "Embrace the suck," he snarled.

I realized the motivational phrase was much more impacting coming from a vampire who sucked blood to live, and was devoid of fucks to give.

43

Rather than dine on Vatican food, Roland recommended we head into the city for a light meal. And since Nate had given us a car, we didn't have to rely on help from the Conclave. Which was good. Roland's subtle glances at me made it abundantly clear that we needed to get clear of the city, and that we shouldn't talk at all until we were confident we were out of sight.

Paranoia was alive and well with Roland, and I couldn't blame him. He had just heard firsthand that his fellow Shepherds were well-versed in the art of espionage on any visitor. Roland either doubted his fellow Shepherds when they denied spying on us, or he seriously believed that the Conclave had found a way to do it regardless of Crispin's protests.

Which with any other organization, probably would have been the case. The Conclave ran the Shepherds, and knew what was best for all. Or so they believed. Desperate times called for desperate measures, and with so many things spiraling out of control, it made sense that the Conclave would entertain extreme measures like spying on guests. In less than a week they had experienced the murder of their top Shepherd and a theft from the Vatican vaults.

They would do anything to keep their world safe. Even from itself. Or, under a more cynical scope, they liked their positions of power and would do anything to keep them. Maybe Constantine had pushed them too far and had been permanently put in his place, and that's why they were rushing to convict the werewolves. To close the investigation with a slam dunk.

We had driven through the streets in silence, Roland silently placing a finger over his lips for me to remain silent. I studied him for a second, and then unbuckled my seatbelt with a devilish grin. Roland shot me a panicked look, shaking his head at whatever I was considering.

"I'm so glad we got out of there, *Mentor...*" I said in a seductive purr, licking my lips. Then I giggled playfully and leaned in to kiss his neck. Roland tensed in horror, but the panicked look in his eyes could easily be attributed to not wanting any of his friends to see.

If someone was spying on us – it could be audio or video, so I couldn't just talk the talk. I had to walk the walk. And I was about to give them a show. Maybe it would lead to something. If I saw anyone studying us in disbelief at our secret romantic relationship, we would confirm our fear and know who was spying on us.

I made a big show of kissing his neck, even nipping his skin with my teeth, making him flinch. He growled instinctively, which could also be taken multiple ways if we were being recorded.

"Keep your eyes on the road, Shepherd." I laughed playfully as he squirmed.

"I'll make you pay for this," he growled.

"Like you did two nights ago? Oh, I *pray* that you do. I've been a *naughty girl.*"

Roland was about to die of shame, guilt, apoplexy, or... maybe he would fang out. Shit. Hadn't considered that. As much fun as this was, I needed to hurry it along.

I leaned in closer, nipping his neck again. Let me tell you this, even pretend flirting with Roland was weird as shit. But I had reached that level of desperation where I no longer cared about the opinion of others. When you have a basic assumption of trusting people, you subconsciously admit that they are rational people, not evil at heart, and that some part of you sort of cares what they think of you.

But when you hear those people rationalize their abuse of basic trust – like spying on their guests – and see them constantly stab each other in the backs, you break the illusion and see that they're really viciously flawed, evil, or animalistic vipers.

I no longer cared about their opinions of me. That was the only thing that allowed me to sexually tease Roland as he drove a million-dollar car through the streets of Rome.

Essentially, this wasn't just about not caring about the Vatican. It was about dangling some juicy gossip that would eat them alive from the insides. Knowing of our romantic secret, and not being able to accuse us – because it would give up the fact that they were in fact still spying on us – would torture them. They would despise us for it, yet they couldn't hold us accountable for such dark endeavors if they couldn't admit to knowing about them.

It was a giant middle finger disguised as a jeweled crucifix, and the only way for them to point it out was to admit their own... sin.

This was a chance for payback, and Roland was just going to have to suffer through it as my stage prop.

I inched my hand inside his shirt, grazing over his large chest. He flinched, jerking the wheel instinctively. "Callie..." he snarled in a throaty growl, correcting the vehicle. I laughed huskily and continued exploring his chest, now curious about the lack of the scars that had disappeared after he drank Haven's blood. I had never gotten answers to what the story was behind those scars. Who had carved him up with religious scribbles. The Conclave? Was it part of being a Shepherd?

I'd ask him again later. Instead, I leaned back to his neck, nipped his ear sharply, and breathed into his ear light enough to not be overheard, no matter how good the spying equipment they were using was. "Do we have a tail?" He jolted, sensing the professional, no longer slutty change in my voice. He shook his head almost imperceptibly. "Pull over and threaten to punish me for being such a naughty girl. Get us out of this car. *Now.*"

He floored the car, and then grabbed a handful of my ass to prevent me from sliding back into my seat. I grunted in disbelief, trying to turn it into a sexy squeal.

Or something vaguely erotic. But to be honest, I froze in shock.

Roland swerved back and forth, dodging traffic for about a minute. Then he grunted, gripped my ass tighter, and I felt the car lurch into a spin, tires screeching. We stopped moving and he released my ass long enough to shift the car into park.

Before I could glance out the windshield, his hand was back on my ass, his door was opening, and he was lifting me out of the car. "Time to finish what you started, girl..." he growled loudly. He set me on my feet, shot me an infuriated look and then yanked me after him up three stairs to a large pair of wooden doors. Two young men stared incredulously at us, as if stunned at our coupling. Maybe it was the age gap. Then they glanced behind us at the still idling car, slowly smiling. Roland snarled. "Park the car and open the door. Now!"

They did, faces paling and smiles evaporating.

We were at a hotel of some kind, and it looked pricey. Roland led me to the counter, and I remained in bimbo mode, glancing around me with wide eyes as if ecstatic that the rich older man with me was taking me somewhere so extravagant.

Because everyone around us needed to see what we wanted them to see.

If Crispin had been asked to verify Nate's flight plans – even calling on hotels halfway across the world – they would definitely track down a hotel in their own city.

"Room. Cash. Now," Roland growled at the woman behind the counter.

"Of course, sir. We have several different rooms—"

"A big one. Now. Less talking and more typing. I give big tips," he said, slapping a wad of cash on the counter.

"He sure does," I said, leaning in to wink at her suggestively. Roland let out a groan, but it could have come across to others as a hungry growl.

I turned to stare up at the lights and stonework of the lobby as I heard the woman's fingers desperately clicking on her keyboard. Within moments, Roland had a card in hand and was guiding me to an elevator. I saw a gift shop with swimsuits for sale and jerked my hand free from Roland, rushing back up to the counter.

"Do you have a pool?" I asked her excitedly.

Her eyes smoldered with judgment, but her face was all corporate smile. "Yes, and a hot tub. Down that hall," she said, indicating a glass door with an electric keypad beside it.

She flinched as a shadow fell over her face, and I turned to see Roland behind me. "We'll take two sets of swimsuits," he said, slapping down too much money. "Take care of payment for us. We'll just grab our size." He began to turn away and then hesitated, glancing back at her. "We don't wish to be disturbed. Unless a priest demands access," he added with a lopsided grin.

I let my cheeks flush as I nodded at her, but inside I was dying with laughter at her shocked expression. She had no idea. Roland guided me towards the rack of suits. I picked one hurriedly, not caring what size or color it was. All I cared about was the water. Roland snatched up a random pair of shorts without looking and caught up with me as I was opening the door with the keycard he had slipped me while telling the woman about the priest.

I skipped through the halls in the natural gait of a bimbo – the massive vacuum of air in my head giving me the ability to almost float between steps. I opened a side door marked pool and slipped inside, letting it close before Roland could follow me.

I ducked around a corner as he stormed into the pool area, eyes smoldering as he searched for me. He spun at the last second but was too late as I tackled him into the pool, our new swimsuits falling to the dry concrete above as we struck the surprisingly warm water.

Roland dipped his head under my ass, gripped my thighs, and before I understood what he was doing he exploded out of the water, using his legs and his grip on my thighs to catapult me into the air. I squealed in surprise, but it quickly turned to delight as laughter burst from my lips, ten feet above the water. I tucked my legs, trying to splash him with my cannonball as I landed.

I succeeded, and when I emerged from the pool, I saw Roland laughing and shaking his head at the absurdity of it all. If he hadn't had water streaming down his face, I would have said he was crying with laughter. But since I couldn't tell, I just shrugged, smiling at him.

He looked as if ten years had been given back to him, and he was still smiling as I glided up beside him, resting my head on his shoulders. "Think we're safe?" I asked.

He chuckled. "Yes. The water would have fried anything they put on us. Maybe not permanently, but we'd be safe until they dried out. The car is still a big question mark, though." His lips tightened as if remembering what I had done in the car. "That was quick thinking, Callie. But... did you have to be... so persuasive?"

"It was as much for you as it was for them," I said, grinning at his discomfort. I sighed, leading him from the pool. "Look, things are going to be changing very fast for you soon. Being... what you *are* is the exact opposite of what you *were*. You're going to have to get used to not smiting first and asking questions later." He frowned at that, but finally nodded. "If you don't at least try to fit in, the vampires will gang up on you and take you out.

Many will already have reason to hate you, judging from how many of their kind you've killed over the years. You're going to have to learn how to blend in. I wanted to see how you reacted when surprised."

He shot an amused look at me. "I think you forget that I wasn't always a Shepherd, Callie. I'm sure I'll be able to catch on quickly," he added, rolling his eyes. "Even though it may be distasteful, you have a point."

He squeezed out his clothes and I did the same. Then he tossed our dry swimsuits in the trash and led me out the back door of the hotel. "We don't have much time, and we have a lot to discuss. I didn't think we would have to walk this far, but it will help dry off our clothes faster."

I nodded, bracing for the cold outside.

❧ 44 ❧

It was night time, and although typically cold, an unseasonal warm front had rolled in. It was still chillier than I would have preferred, but better than it could have been. We received many odd looks as we walked down the street, soaked from head to toe.

"You're sure they didn't use magic to track us? To spy on us?" I asked Roland again.

He shook his head. "I would sense it. And if they had, they never would have let us out of their sights. They would have realized we were a vampire and a Nephilim Angel Seductress," he said, smirking at me.

I glared back for good measure, but he had a point. With all the chaos, I had pushed that thought down several times already. The fact that my powers could have made a big impression on the Conclave – whether for good or bad, I didn't know. They could either see me as a pocket Angel to use as they pleased, or accuse me of blasphemy. After all, if they were on good terms with Angels, the Nephilim wouldn't be running around in secret. They would all be teaming up with the Conclave, or more accurately, the Conclave would be allowed to team up with them.

Either way, I could be considered a bargaining chip. And that didn't sit well with me.

As we walked, I noticed there were many fine restaurants open for service in Rome.

Naturally, Roland took me to a dirty food truck. "Hurry. Consider this payback for acting like a floozy in the car."

"Floozy?" I shouted in disbelief. "No one says that anymore!"

"Painted woman, hussy, lady of the evening, strumpet..." he said, grinning. "Any of those still in use?"

An old woman within hearing distance snarled at him and hefted her purse threateningly.

He paled. "That wasn't what it sounded like," he pleaded with her.

I allowed my voice to shake and my shoulders to sag. "I-I've never seen this man..."

The woman's nostrils flared as she stormed after him. He swore, turned, and ran across the street. I shot a thankful look at the woman and bought her a soda as I picked up a meat pie. Then I casually made my way across the street, searching for the angry vamp.

I saw him lurking under an awning, eyes alert for the older woman that had chased him. Satisfied he was safe, he finally unfolded from the shadows and walked up beside me. "Tramp."

I grinned. "That one's still in use!"

He grunted proudly, but was sure to shove me with his elbow right when I tried to take a bite. I let him get away with it. We remained vigilant, knowing that if the Conclave had placed a bug on our car, they would find it parked at a nice hotel, and any further inquiry would let them hear of the flamboyant romantic dalliance we had displayed in the lobby. And that we were likely holed up in our room doing the Devil's Kumbaya and only a priest was allowed to disturb us.

I actually repeated that thought out loud so I could enjoy Roland's laughter.

There was always the chance we had been tailed and just hadn't noticed it.

Or we were both blowing this way out of proportion. Then again, they had admitted to spying on everyone else, so it wasn't much of a stretch. Perhaps admitting those things was intended to lure us into a false sense of confidence.

All it had done was broken our confidence – utterly – in anything tied to the Conclave.

Thirty minutes later, we were back at Roland's apartment. We found no signs of tampering with the lock, and nothing had been disturbed inside.

This had been a growing fear of Roland's – that they would check the apartment.

Roland retrieved his stash of blood and pounded each bag like he was at a frat party with cheap beer. I stared in disbelief and he averted his eyes in shame, lowering the last empty bag. I took two steps closer, holding out my hand with a sad look and he flinched away. I scowled and stormed the rest of the way, jerking him around to face me.

"I wasn't pitying you, Roland. Or judging you. I was surprised to see you were so thirsty. If I had known you were that desperate, I might not have taken things so far in the car."

His eyes flashed crimson, but he blinked it away and took a cautious step back. "It's close, Callie. Very close. I don't know how much longer I can do this. All the stress of the last few hours taxed me. I thought I was going to have to go in there, kill my friends, and rescue you and the girls before I turned into a monster – consequences be damned."

I shook my head sadly as he sat down. "You're not going to become a monster, Roland. Did Haven look like a monster?"

He sniffed angrily. "Haven is a Master Vampire," he snapped.

I let that sink in for a moment, watching as he panted in frustration. Lamenting, or whatever it was that vampires did when depressed. Then it hit him, and his eyes shot up to mine.

I nodded, grinning. "Yep."

He opened his mouth to speak and then closed it, thinking furiously. He finally turned back to me. "I drank blood from a Master Vampire..." he said, sounding astounded that he hadn't considered it before.

Drinking from a Master Vampire didn't guarantee anything, but it sure as hell put Roland on the fast track for becoming stronger than the typical vampire. "And you still have your magic."

He focused, not wanting to risk using it and setting off whatever wards the Shepherds had in place, but trying to feel it deep within himself. A smile split his cheeks as he whispered, "Yes."

"But none of that matters if we die here," I reminded him. He nodded, regaining some of his usual confidence and air of command. We spent the next ten minutes chatting back and forth, going over the details in a clinical manner, but came up with nothing helpful.

One thing we decided was that we couldn't leave town – even if for only a few minutes – to get more blood from Haven. We had the ability to Shadow Walk or make a Gateway anywhere in the world – to simply run. But the wards in Rome would let the Shepherds know in an instant.

And our act would condemn the girls to death and put a price on our heads. Maybe not a price, but at least a big fat question mark. Especially when we didn't return to our usual duties in Kansas City. Because Roland would have issues stepping foot on Holy Ground after becoming a vampire, unless he succeeded in keeping Haven's amulet.

And we estimated that he would have to kill someone and drink their blood within the next twelve hours. We would flee Italy leaving two were-wolves to die for a murder they didn't commit, leave the traitor in power in the Conclave, and leave behind a bloodless body.

Running would make us look like guilty criminals. And it would only be a matter of time before we were hunted down by the full might and power of the Conclave Shepherds.

But our backs were against the wall. The girls had their trial tomorrow, and it wasn't looking like Roland could last that long before needing to kill his first victim and drink their blood.

For the once-Shepherd to murder someone in cold blood.

But even before that, Roland needed more blood to sustain him, or he wouldn't even make it that long. We were running out of time.

"You know what we have to do, right?" I asked. Roland's eyes glinted crimson as he gave me a resigned nod. "We've run out of time. We have to break them out."

"The one place they told you not to go... I don't think I can join you. Being around a wolf right now might bring out my... monster," he said in a restrained growl.

And maybe it would. We just didn't know. Wolves and vampires didn't typically get along well, and a *new* vampire didn't typically get along with *anyone*. Let alone two frightened, imprisoned, new-ish werewolves. It could be a bloodbath. We would never break them out if their inner monsters decided to rely on instinct over a familiar face. The break-out was on me.

To do the one thing I had been warned not to do. But we had nothing to lose. Soon, either the girls would be executed and the traitor would win, or we would manage to save the day. But either way, Roland and I would lose, forced to sever all ties with the Vatican.

We might as well go out with a blast.

Roland had spent twenty minutes going over the details of my target. He was familiar with the building itself, but cautioned that upgrades to security were likely, and he had no way to advise me in that. He gave me the break-down of the security from his time living here, but we both knew it was a long shot thinking that they hadn't upgraded. Technology became outdated after only a few years nowadays. Worst case, I would huff and puff and blow the walls down with my Angel magic, grab the girls, and Shadow Walk on the spot. We could interrogate the wolves in safety, far away from the Vatican, and come back with our evidence.

If we cared to, since we would have severed all ties to them anyway.

As if approving of my plan, I heard the Whispers starting up in the back of my mind. As I found myself listening, and almost understanding them, I walled them off with a shaky breath.

Roland didn't notice, too focused on the last-minute details of the plan.

We left the apartment and I called a local car service to take me back to the hotel. Roland was off to find a late-night butcher and see how difficult it was to find some blood. Even a little would help sustain him. We needed to keep him human as long as possible before he was forced to murder some-one. He had expressed hopes that he could mitigate this crime by drinking the blood from whoever was behind all of this, but we weren't even close to finding that person yet.

Which meant Roland would soon have to kill a stranger, completing his shift to vampire.

If I was able to succeed in my task, we needed Roland as in control as possible when he reunited with the wolves as we fled Italy together. Either that or I would leave Roland behind – per his request – as I took the wolves to safety. Anywhere far away from the Vatican.

Our only hope was that if I succeeded, the wolves might know the true identity of the real killer, and that they had been holding out on telling anyone at the Conclave because it was someone high up, and they knew acknowledging the killer would guarantee their execution.

To put it mildly, the level of loyalty and strength the two girls had shown was astounding. They had chosen to hold their heads high and walk calmly to the gallows.

Or they were hoping for their white knight, Roland Haviar, to save them.

Little did they know he had become a Prince of Blood.

The only human part of him remaining was his honor. At least for now...

I hoped they would settle for a white-haired, irrational wizard with Angel's blood coursing through her veins. I didn't think they'd be picky about their savior.

🦁 45 🦁

I hid behind a statue of a Saint. I didn't bother to check which one it was, but I hoped it was the Patron Saint of Thieves, since I was about to rob the Conclave blind. The night was dark and full of Callie. I wore all black, having tossed on a black jacket from my bag rather than wear the white one. I had considered stealing a Sister's Habit, but that was beyond me. Unless I had to. I also hadn't seen any proof that a Sister could get any closer to the make-shift prison than I could, so had dismissed the option.

A nagging thought kept whispering in my ears, that the theft had to be tied to the murder. The events were too closely linked to be anything else. And if they were connected, the thief was still present. He or she wouldn't leave until the wolves were executed.

I scanned my immediate surroundings and saw no one walking near enough to see me. I had only seen one guard patrolling the building ahead, but there was every chance that a few more stood out front—

My phone rang, scaring the living shit out of me. I answered it in a panic, anything to get the cursed ringing to stop.

"What?" I hissed, eyes flicking up to my surroundings rather than checking the caller's name. The patrolling guard had rounded the corner and was no longer in sight.

"Hey, Callie-Pie!" Claire giggled, followed by a loud hiccup.

Sweet demon nipples. A drunk dial? Now? of all times!

"Callie!" she shouted louder, as if I hadn't heard her. I almost dropped the phone at the drunken shriek – the mating cry of the sorority *woo* girl known to all frat boys worldwide.

"Now isn't a good time—" I hissed, but she interrupted me.

"I j-just—" Loud background noise interrupted her – a man arguing loudly. "Oh, shut up Beckett," she shouted back, followed by another hicca-giggle.

My vision pulsed red. *You've got to be shitting me*, I thought to myself, seriously considering murder when I returned home. She was drunk dialing me after a night out with Beckett?!

She came back on before I could hang up, take out my battery, and stomp on the device. "We had a few drinks and I w-wanted to call an Uber," she managed between more hiccups.

I took a measured breath. "Sure. Whatever. Use my card. I have to *go*," I hissed.

"Luuuuuuuuuurrrvvee you!" she drawled, and I hung up the phone, panting heavily.

Drunk. With Beckett. I didn't' have time for jealousy. Fine. They wanted to get drunk together? Fine. None of my business. Fine.

Just fine.

A distant, rational part of me appreciated that she had called first before using my card for an Uber, but I really wished she hadn't. Because then I could have remained in ignorant bliss, not having to think about her on a date while I risked my life to break some werewolves out of a wizard prison. I wondered why Claire wanted to pay rather than Beckett, but quickly tried to cut off that line of inquiry. I was flamingly unsuccessful.

Neither of them needed money. Hell, I needed money more than either of them, so I knew it must have been an emergency of some kind. They needed my help. To go home drunk together.

I was so distracted, I just stared down at my shadow, not finding anything strange about the two shadows suddenly growing from the shoulders of my shadow on the ground. Something stabbed into my side. I grunted, my mind clearing in an instant at the blinding flash of pain.

I managed to roll away from a second slash of a glinting blade, throwing up my hands defensively. The blade tore through my jacket, slicing my forearm. I hissed, ignoring the blood leaking from my flesh. I crouched in a defensive stance, staring at my adversaries for the first time. They were male, medium build, and wore black long-sleeve shirts, black jeans, and black shoes designed for stealth – not boots. They also wore dirty pale scarves with a red cross on the front hanging down from above their nose to the top of their chests, leaving their eyes and shaggy dark hair visible. Blue eyes and brown eyes. That's the only thing that distinguished them.

No one I had met at the Vatican had similar hair, a distant part of me cursed. Hired muscle.

Then I recognized the scarf, and my stomach lurched. Constantine's killer had worn one.

One of them used my distraction to dart in, swinging both arms in precise, professional swipes. I dodged, danced, and tried to block, but received two slashes on my arms. He danced back as my fingers almost tore out his throat beneath the scarf, and I heard a low laugh.

I needed to hurry before blood loss cost me this fight.

They didn't look like the guard I had seen at the prison only a dozen yards away or I would have thrown my hands up in surrender. And they had introduced themselves by stabbing me and slashing me several times with their daggers. Not very nice of them, and I wasn't the kind of gal who turned the other cheek.

I squared off, and even though I couldn't see their mouths, I knew they were smiling, either in recognition or anticipation of a fun fight. They began to circle me in practiced coordination, proving they were familiar working as a pair. I didn't dare use magic because it would have triggered alarms all over the place, bringing every Shepherd within a mile – where they would find me in black in the one place they had told me not to visit. Hell, the wards on the Vatican might just freeze the three of us in place and we would all be tossed in jail as accomplices.

The only difference between our outfits was their scarves.

One look into their eyes told me they would have no problem becoming martyrs, and that the only words they would utter upon capture would be *she works with us!*

And from our similar clothing, that accusation would stick. I needed to end this silently. They had obviously come for the girls, to finish them off. But why now? The trial was tomorrow morning, and they were basically already proven guilty.

My attackers hadn't resorted to magic either, which meant they were Regulars or knew about the wards. If they had attacked with magic, I would have defended myself with magic. But they hadn't. But the man who had murdered Constantine hadn't been harmed by his magic, and he had seemed very fast. Not unnaturally so, but worthy of caution.

The other one darted in, lunging with his blade to test me. I batted at his wrist instinctively, like Roland had taught me, knocking his dagger free. I almost missed his partner jumping closer in an attempt to break my spine with a kick. But I arched my back and hit his thigh with an elbow, aiming for a pressure point. He chuckled throatily as he shook off the pain, dipping his head at me in approval. I swept up the fallen dagger, baring my teeth at him. I wanted to catch these punks and dump them in front of the Conclave myself, proving my credibility, and saving the wolves.

I feinted an aggressive flurry of swipes at brown eyes, reading their response. As expected, his blue-eyed partner lunged forward, but I was ready for it this time. I swung my knife at his face and managed to slice off his scarf. As it fell to the ground, I struggled to make out his features as he darted backwards into the shadows. Which meant I didn't see the kick from his partner as it clipped my jaw, almost knocking me out. Stars sparkled as my vision swirled, and then another kick caught me in the solar plexus, knocking the breath out of me as I fell.

He kicked me three more times, and all I could do was curl up as I tried to catch my breath and steady my vision. I felt a sudden movement and tensed for another blow, preparing myself to grab his boot and yank him off balance.

But nothing happened. Then I noticed it. Shouting. I sat up, hissing as liquid fire trailed down my ribs and forearms from the knife wounds. My attackers were gone, but I spotted the scarf I had cut away from blue eyes near my feet. I winced as I scooted closer, finally swiping the ragged fabric off the ground with bloody fingers. I closed my eyes and gritted my teeth as I tried to take a deeper breath. It didn't feel like the stab had torn a vital organ, but I needed to get it checked out just in case. I clamped a hand over it, resigned to my position as I struggled again to draw a full breath. There was no way I could escape, hobbling with cracked or broken ribs and leaking blood all over the place. They would see me from a mile away.

Without a sound, Roland was suddenly kneeling over me. I blinked in disbelief, almost shouting in surprise as I stared into his crimson eyes. His face was drawn and haggard and he looked to be struggling to ignore the blood covering me. Because part of him wanted to lick it up. He looked both disgusted at that idea, and like a junkie fighting a quick fix.

But the part of Roland that I knew best recognized that his student had been injured and was now bleeding out in the grass. Luckily, that part of him won.

"Assassins," I wheezed, holding out the scarf. I didn't even bother to ask how he had snuck back in to the Vatican grounds. He was obviously using his vampire powers, which was not good at all. Especially with me covered in blood. Which was why I was trying to distract him with the scarf. Give him a familiar task. Hope it beat his instinctive craving.

He took a big whiff as the sound of pounding feet neared. "I can track them," he whispered lighter than the breeze. And then he was just gone. I didn't even hear his clothing rustle. I quickly shoved the scarf in my pocket. I didn't want to give up the only real evidence we had found. I remained still as the shouting and footsteps grew closer, hoping my white hair would let the Shepherds recognize me as not an immediate threat.

Crispin rounded the corner of the prison, sword out and face grim. He spotted me, snarled, and hurried my way. He stared down at me, face a mix of emotions, but predominantly angry. Then he noticed my wound. He helped me up, glaring out at the surrounding night for danger.

"What happened?" he growled, not looking at me.

"Assassins," I groaned, telling him the same thing I had told Roland a second ago. "Wearing all black." I didn't mention the scarf, just in case any of the Shepherds were in on it. "I didn't get a look at their faces, but I tried."

He scanned the area more cautiously at this bit of news, but it was apparent they were long gone. "Damnit, Callie," he cursed. "What the hell am I supposed to do now? It's obvious you weren't just out on an evening stroll, dressed all in black," Crispin snarled at me just as Windsor and Fabrizio rounded the corner of the prison behind him, spotting us.

"How did you find me?" I asked, accepting his help to get to my feet. I kept my hand clamped over the wound and still held my dagger at my side, trying to look non-threatening.

"Your room was empty, and we knew you had returned from the city earlier. There was only one place we told you not to go, so when we couldn't find you or Roland in the obvious places we decided to come here."

I nodded tiredly, opening my mouth to explain.

He cut me off. "We found two dead guards at the prison entrance or we would have been here sooner. Someone tried to break in..." he glared down at my bloody dagger and I groaned in disbelief at the silent accusation.

"You've *got* to be kidding me..." I muttered as Fabrizio and Windsor appeared behind Crispin. "I was fucking stabbed! Did the dead guards have blood on their blades? Match it to mine and I'll gladly turn myself in," I rolled my eyes. This was just incredible.

"I don't believe it was you, Callie. I'm just pointing out how it *looks*..."

I nodded in defeat.

He growled in a steady stream of commands. "Rooms, now. We *told* you this was off limits! The one place you had to leave alone!" he seethed, sounding furious at the world in general. That he was forced to punish me, seeing no way around it.

Windsor piped up, studying me acutely. He didn't look pleased either, but he did look surprisingly more compassionate than normal. "Without her, they might have succeeded, Crispin. She distracted them," he said, glancing down at my wounds. "You okay?"

"I'm fine. The stab wasn't deep. I just need some bandages to stop the leaking."

Fabrizio leaned closer, speaking for the first time. "Where is Roland?" It didn't sound like concern for a friend. It sounded like a cop interrogating a suspect.

"Out for dessert?" I offered, exasperated at the bipolar emotions the Conclave bred into their Shepherds. Trust. Distrust. Trust. Distrust. Friends. Not friends. Rinse and repeat every three minutes. All three of them leveled me with serious looks. "He stayed in the city. Check your logs. I returned alone," I said, wincing as my wound stretched wider at the long explanation.

Crispin whipped out a cellphone and tried to place a call. I assumed it was Roland, since no one answered him. He hung up and rounded on Windsor.

"Take Callie to her rooms and see that her wounds are dressed. Keep her under guard, and keep calling Roland. I already heard he didn't return through the gates, so he has to still be in the city. Fabrizio and I will go comb the city, check his apartment," he sighed, frustrated. "Any of his known locations. Have the other Shepherds check every nook and cranny of the Vatican." He eyed me. "For ninjas dressed like her." I had watched all three of them for signs that they had witnessed my romantic display with Roland, but I didn't see anything even remotely suspicious. Damn. But Crispin's comment about knowing I had returned alone meant we were definitely still under surveillance. Bastards.

"I'm back on house arrest? I just saved the wolves from murder!" I argued.

Crispin held up a hand. "Or... you killed the guards," he said in a soft tone, holding out a hand for me to give him my blade. I did, grumbling under my breath.

"This place really sucks..." I groaned as Windsor led me back to my room, unsmiling.

I just hoped Roland was alright because I now had zero chance of saving the wolves or leaving the Vatican. Roland was on his own.

46

I stood before the Conclave, returning their milky, judgmental glares without blinking.

"What were you doing last night?" Daniel demanded, even though I was sure he had been briefed before he saw me. If he hadn't spent half the night debating the merits of declaring me guilty of a crime I had actually prevented. The Conclave seemed to excel at half-assed criminal procedure.

"I don't know if I can say it in simpler terms," I seethed angrily. "I ignored your demand to leave the investigation alone and went to question the wolves. I was attacked by two assassins in black clothes. I hurt them a little. They hurt me a little. They fled. I survived. But bled a little."

Several members of the Conclave grumbled hotly, but Daniel held up a hand. "And you ran into... ninjas?" he asked in a mocking tone. "Not wizards? Nothing supernatural?" he frowned, no doubt disappointed in my lacking hand-to-hand combat skills. I hadn't mentioned that I'd been distracted by trying to make a positive ID after I cut off his scarf. I hadn't even told them about the scarf. I no longer trusted anyone but Roland, the blood-sucking vampire. Someone here was a dirty liar. It was the only thing that made sense.

I lifted the bottom of my black long-sleeved shirt, revealing the bandage wrapping my waist, since they hadn't bothered to use magic to heal me. Maybe as a lesson of some kind. Then I showed them my forearms, which were wrapped in fresh gauze to cover the knife wounds I had earned. "They fought well. Got lucky. Had better weapons."

"And where is Roland?"

I shrugged. "He got lucky in town?" I watched all of their faces, trying to ascertain if any of them looked aware of our romantic act, belying that they had been spying on us. I saw nothing. They actually scowled at my flippant comment, not appreciating my humor. "He's not feeling well. He needed some time to pray over his murdered friend. He wanted a crepe." I sighed dramatically, throwing up my hands. "I don't know where he is. He asked for privacy, and being a good student, I obeyed him and tried to make one last ditch effort to help those girls."

But I was terribly nervous about the truth, because I hadn't heard back from Roland. He hadn't called, and I hadn't been able to leave my rooms, guarded all night until Windsor woke me to be rushed to this meeting. I had failed. Because it was time for the trial. Roland was gone, and the girls were going to be condemned. I just knew it.

"I've known Roland for over fifty years, and he's never taken a... sick day," Richter said.

I found myself surprised to hear Roland was that old, but dismissed it as Daniel spoke.

"Well, they didn't succeed in their ultimate mission, whoever they were. Your dagger was not the murder weapon, and you obviously didn't stab yourself."

I couldn't help myself. "It's truly frustrating when the evidence doesn't fall the way you like it, right?" His face turned that lovely shade of purple I loved so much. To think I had almost liked the guy during our first meeting. But to even mutter a comment about me stabbing myself being a plausible option brought out the bitch in me.

"I think this ordeal only proves that we need to proceed with the trial. Immediately. Before anything else can go wrong. Before their partners break into this room and try to free them."

"There you go with the objectivity again. Calling them partners without evidence is pretty slick. Almost as slick as convicting two little girls without proof." I clapped my hands delicately.

Daniel turned to Windsor, barely containing his rage, but knowing that if he resorted to arguing with me further he would only increase how ignorant he looked before his peers. "If Miss Penrose speaks one more time, you have permission to send her out and lock her up until we have time to coddle her."

Ohhhh, I almost commented on that, but managed to take a breath instead. Windsor grimaced, not happy with the order, but he gave a nod. Then he shot me a look that both spoke of his resolve, and begged me not to test it.

I gave him a much more polite nod than I had given anyone else this morning. Then I sat down, studying the faces of the Conclave, this crew of blind old wizards who thought they knew what they were doing. If I was running the show, I would have made sure they had beneficial areas of expertise. Technological. Military. Police. Shifter experience. Ex-Shepherds.

As I studied them, I realized a startling thought. They were a bunch of scared old men. Sure, they were wizards, but had they earned their position by playing politics or had they paid with scars? Even if by scars, did that mean they were a table of grumpy, ignorant brutes? The world was a different place now than from twenty, ten, even five years ago, and these men refused to adapt.

And were willing to execute two innocent girls in order to maintain their strip of power.

The real killer had wanted to silence the girls, but why? It was the night before the trial. It made no sense. They had to be aware that their conviction was a forgone conclusion. There was no need to risk exposure like they had. Unless... the girls *knew* something.

None of that mattered now. Two guards had died last night, and I didn't have a chance standing against the forces before me. They wanted a culprit, not the truth. The Shepherds were done being lenient. Because everything that had happened in the last few days had made them look horribly incompetent. And I had only shone a big spotlight on that fact. The other visiting Shepherds were now patrolling the grounds, ready for anything. Two of them even guarded the door to the Conclave, just in case of more ninjas.

As if on cue, Fabrizio entered the room with the wolves in tow, followed a minute later by Crispin and two middle-aged men. One had dark, slicked back hair, and was young, tall, and handsome, but had a nervous slouch. The other was ten years older with thinning hair and plump, bearded cheeks. His eyes darted around like a cornered rat, searching for a hole to hide in. The girls looked healthy, but exhausted, practically quivering with fear. Then I realized why. They were crying, but not making a sound. They were magically gagged, prevented from speaking.

Instinctively, I wanted to kill everyone at the front of the room. Gagging the defendants? Not even giving them a chance to speak? But then I thought about it. The two witnesses were Regulars. The Conclave didn't want the wolves saying or doing anything that might reveal the truth and scare the living hell out of the Regulars. Because that would prove the Vatican knew magic was real, and all hell would break loose.

Their only other option was to let the girls talk, and then kill the witnesses after they heard the truth. So in a way, this was the Conclave saving their lives in exchange for their testimony. But this was only acceptable to me if they later escorted the Regulars out, and then let the girls speak their side of the story. Before any verdict was called.

I hadn't seen the girls clearly before, since they had either been covered in filth and ruined makeup or hiding in the back of a cell before Roland transported them here.

They weren't cleaned up for a dance or anything, of course, but I saw enough to recognize their potential beauty. Both were dark-haired and vibrant, one taller, one shorter, but both with an exotic look to them. The shorter one had a round, innocent face, and thick brown hair. The taller one had harsh cheekbones and full lips I would have murdered for.

They didn't need makeup, but if they applied some, they could have convinced a priest to challenge his vow of celibacy. It was no wonder why they had been kidnapped in the first place. They could have been sisters – not identical, but similar enough to pass. Like Claire and I.

I rubbed my arms absently, my injuries itching as I locked eyes with the them, wondering which was Tiffany and which was Jasmine. Their eyes moistened in recognition, and the fear I saw made my stomach lurch.

They were silently begging me to save them.

All I wanted to do was look away, but that would have been cowardly. I shot them a sympathetic look, trying not to break down in tears. I rubbed at my arms again, using the motion to distract me from my anxiety, trying to jumpstart my brain to come up with a solution that could save them.

The first witness, the younger, handsome one, was called to the stand. "My name is Alberto Esposito. I was on my way home from work..." he shot suddenly guilty eyes to the seven officials staring down at him. "L-lighting a smoke in the alley. I heard voices and laughing. It sounded like women, so I approached." He looked suddenly guilty again, as if fearing God was about to smite him for considering picking up girls in an alley. The Conclave members didn't give him an inch, which made me smile faintly. "Anyway, as I n-neared the corner the laughter stopped and I heard something crash into a dumpster."

I realized I was leaning forward, trying to catch a lie. Maybe he really was a witness.

"I turned the corner and saw one woman trying to get up off the ground and another woman slam into a wall and not get up. An old man was glaring down at her as if he had shoved her. I was about to intervene when the first woman jumped to her feet, there was a scuffle, and they both fell to the ground." He lifted his eyes in shame. "I... I ran after that, calling the police."

The bastard was lying, or had seen something he couldn't understand – Freaks – and had filled in the gaps with something that made sense.

The Conclave deliberated on this in murmured silence, letting the witness squirm for a few moments before dismissing him back to his seat, thanking him for his time. He shot the girls a discreet look of disgust before slinking away from the podium. He even moved like a pathetic weakling. I hated him.

I almost fell over at their dismissal of the witness, literally holding myself to the chair, shaking in outrage. What the hell kind of a performance was that? No questions? No evidence? No analysis? Just a Regular reciting his description of a supernatural murder, when he wasn't even aware of the supernatural world? For all he knew, for all anyone knew, he had witnessed a battle of lightning and his brain had short-circuited, shuffling the events into a neat little box that he could comprehend.

This was the whole point of a courtroom. To have cross examination. Evidence to corroborate eye witness accounts. Otherwise, any witness could say whatever they wanted and get someone punished for a crime that may have never happened.

This wasn't *he said she said*. This was real life, and the Conclave was treating it like a tabloid magazine speaking the gospel.

Means. Motive. Opportunity. Those were the three cornerstones of an investigation. So far, they only had opportunity. They knew Constantine's throat was slashed, but they hadn't found a weapon, simply figuring anyone with claws would do in a pinch. I was seeing red, but knowing that Windsor would toss me out on my ear, and that the Regular witnesses were still present, I didn't speak. I just sat there, fuming.

For the millionth time, I wondered where Roland was and if he had found and murdered the assassins. If not, these two were about to die, and I might just die beside them, because I couldn't imagine a world where I didn't stand up in their defense.

Don't get me wrong. If they were guilty, I would have been the first to hop on the execution train, but I had seen the video from Haven. Now, I hadn't taken that as gospel either. I had come to the Vatican looking for proof to counteract the video I had seen, expecting the Conclave to have at least something incriminating.

But I had found nothing.

Even without knowledge of the video, I would feel the same way right now. Because the Conclave had their collective thumbs up their asses and were trying to quickly brush a murder under the rug, sacrificing two basically-adolescent werewolves to do it.

I scratched my arms again as I replayed the events of the attack last night. Roland had vamped out, or at least started to. Maybe he had found the assassins after. Crispin and Fabrizio had obviously failed to catch him. Or I would have heard something by now. Maybe right now he had the evidence to clear their names, but since he had vamped he couldn't risk making his way onto the property. Maybe he had found the real killer, drunk his blood in one vigilantic gulp, and was in the middle of a violent transformation.

Even if he managed to enter the Conclave right this moment to clear their names, he would only be condemning himself. I knew he didn't care about that and would do it in a heartbeat. That's just the way he was. But he wasn't here.

It sure put me in an impossible situation. If I had to choose who to save, would it be Roland or the wolves? I realized my answer, and had a hard time looking at the wolves after that. But I still made myself do it, lending them as much mental support as I could through my gaze.

I realized they had already called the second witness to the stand, and he was halfway through his story. I scratched my arms again, annoyed. Were my wounds infected? Or just irritated by the gauze? I dismissed the thought, staring down the baker. He had been taking out the trash behind his bakery, a few doors down from the altercation and had seen the whole thing. He couldn't describe it as specifically, but he had seen a lot of bodies moving. One of the girls had sliced Constantine's throat before both fell to the ground. No one mentioned a fourth person.

I frowned as I found myself rubbing my arms again. I lifted back my sleeve, searching for a rash. Blood was seeping through the gauze, but I froze as I noticed something else.

My arm hair was standing up on end. I blinked, the sounds of the courtroom fading in my ears. I realized something was causing the sensation of pebbling flesh, as if my body was trying to give me a warning. Then I recognized what it was and my heart shuddered in both excitement and fear. There was a humming power in the room. I casually glanced back, sweeping the room, fearing to find Roland, because I recognized Haven's amulet was near. Very near.

I wondered again why no one else seemed to notice it.

But Roland wasn't here. I was the only one in the audience. So why was I sensing the amulet? I followed the faint whisper of power and realized I was staring at the first witness.

I frowned in confusion. Was Roland hiding behind him somehow? The witness turned to look at the wolves with a disgusted look. I saw a flash of gold under his shirt, the chain of a necklace.

Time seemed to slow as I stared. I didn't know how, but he was wearing Roland's amulet. My heart stuttered to a stop. That meant... he had taken it. Roland had followed the assassins back to their lair and come face to face with more than just two of the dirty scarf killers. This witness was one of the assassins. Or worked with them.

And in the space of a second, any chance of me becoming a Shepherd evaporated. Because if I had to choose Shepherds over Roland, they were in for a rude awakening.

I didn't remember standing, but realized everyone was staring at me and that a maniacal cackle filled the courtroom.

Callie had officially lost her shit.

And it was *funny*, goddamnit.

47

I flung out my hand and a ball of fire screamed through the air, straight at the younger witness. Windsor threw up a hand, deflecting my attack in a shower of flaming droplets that ignited several chairs and a painting on the side wall in a violent splash. Before I had time for another strike, Fabrizio had launched himself off of a table and tackled me to the ground, knocking over several chairs in the process, cutting off my apparent laughter. I struggled, fought, kicked, screamed and bit his arm, but it was no use. He was too strong, and his magic smothered me like a wet blanket. I heard a loud hiss of steam and the smell of smoke grew fainter. Windsor had thought to use water to douse the flames. I felt Windsor lend Fabrizio some assistance, helping to block my magic. I heard a hammer striking the table.

Daniel roared. "How *dare* you attack an innocent man!" he shouted as Fabrizio lugged me to my feet. I was a breath away from using my Angelic magic, knowing they stood no chance if I tapped into the Whispers, as Angel had called them. My silver powers... "Lock her—"

"NO!" Crispin shouted, and the room went abruptly silent. I didn't care. I had eyes only for the two so-called witnesses. They were plants. Their pals had tried to kill me last night, and almost succeeded. If I hadn't decided to go against the Conclave's wishes, we would have added two wolves to the list of the dead. But why did they want them dead last night rather than this morning? I cocked my head at the younger man, wondering if his hair would look shaggy if not slicked back. I was baring my teeth at him like a wild animal, and Fabrizio was cursing.

I ignored him.

They stared at me with perfect masks of horror, but their lying faces wouldn't fool me. Crispin was standing between us, and I realized that he had frozen them in place with magic. They weren't necessarily horrified at my attack. They were horrified because they couldn't move and they didn't understand why. Let alone the crazy white-haired bitch who had flung fire at them with her bare hands. Crispin stood against the full might of the Conclave, panting.

"Maybe we should ask why Callie suddenly decided to attack the witness with a Molotov Cocktail. She must have had a reason to suddenly lose her mind." He glanced back at me, eyes uncertain, but hoping he hadn't just traded his career to back up a laughing lunatic. I distantly approved of how he had cleverly described my magic as a homemade bomb.

I was more surprised by his support, snapping me out of my mania. I nodded woodenly, regaining control of my emotions, but unable to fully process my surprise that Crispin was vouching for me. Finally, an ally when it was too late to matter. I took a deep breath and jerked my arm free from Fabrizio who muttered a dark warning under his breath.

"I don't want to kill you, but I will, Callie. Tread carefully," he breathed, eyes regretful.

"Check his forearm," I told Crispin, pointing at the witness. "I cut the assassin last—"

The door to the back of the room opened and two Shepherds walked in with Anthony the Antipope strutting behind him, and two of his guards wrapping up the procession. The Shepherds looked uncomfortable, as if they had been placed in an impossible situation. They couldn't very well deny the Antipope. Hadn't he left yesterday? Well, he was back now. Even though he didn't know about magic and had no business here, the Shepherds had no reason to deny him, and it would look suspicious if they tried. But I was pretty sure they would be in trouble for letting him in here, especially with the near murder that had just happened. We were a wild bunch.

Everyone stared at the arrivals, dumbfounded. Then the Antipope smiled, clapping his hands delightedly. The sinister grins on his guards curdled my blood.

The Antipope cleared his throat dramatically. "You didn't think I was aware of your dirty secret, did you?" He held up a phone, the volume on full blast. A second later, the phone blared with the agonized sounds of a man screaming, cursing, and threatening to rip throats out. It sounded familiar, but I was too stunned by their sudden arrival that all I could do was stare. "I showed this to your men outside and told them it would go live, if they didn't let me enter," Anthony said, pausing the video. He nodded at the two Shepherds. "Wise choice, boys."

What was on that video that would permit the Shepherds to allow him entry? Torture?

"What is the meaning of this?" Crispin demanded, growling as he stormed up to him.

The Antipope held out the phone, which Crispin accepted.

I was close enough to see the video as he clicked play. I almost threw up. Roland sat chained to a chair, fangs out, shying from ultraviolet light that was sporadically blasted at him like a torturous strobe light. His necklace was gone. The UV light sizzled against his skin each time the beam hit him. No one in the room spoke, the screams echoed off the walls.

I slowly swiveled my head to check on the Conclave, to read their thoughts. Maybe their ancient, milky eyes couldn't even see the video, but they had to recognize their own Shepherd's voice. Which was when I noticed that the two witnesses looked like entirely different people. Physically the same, but their faces were smug. If Fabrizio and Windsor weren't still blocking my magic, I would have burned every enemy to cinders. I briefly considered letting in the Whispers but hesitated. Would that only make matters worse? The Antipope's next words made that a resounding *yes*.

"Don't worry. I have other copies," he said, motioning for a sick-looking Crispin to share the video with the Conclave, who were collectively leaning out of their seats, murmuring in agitation. Crispin handed over the phone, his hand shaking as he told them what they were hearing. Apparently, the Conclave *couldn't* see that well.

"We found him snooping around our hotel last night," Anthony's voice echoed in the crowded courtroom. "Well, my security team did. And lucky I have them, or I'd be dead right now. He was quite adamant about that," he added, punctuating Roland's threats on the video that the Conclave was huddled over, even though they couldn't see it.

But they sure heard it. Some weren't even trying to look, merely turning an ear to the phone. They looked nauseated. I focused back on the witnesses and their victorious grins. Did that mean the assassins I had run into were part of the Antipope's security detail? That didn't make any sense. Why had they tried to infiltrate the prison? Well, they hadn't had this video yet, but what did they have to gain by killing the wolves a night early?

The Antipope rubbed his arms excitedly as the video ended and the Conclave finally looked up at him with wild, white eyes. "He killed one of my flock and must answer for that. It's very simple. You are going to excommunicate these demons," he sneered, indicating us magic users, "and your false Pope will endorse me as his immediate successor. I don't care *how* it is done, but... *thy will be done*. Or this goes public. And if anything... unfortunate happens to me, this goes public. One of your own... *Shepherds*, assaulting me in the middle of the night and proven to be a monster on camera." He leaned in, clicking his tongue. "For the second time, one of your monsters has killed, but you can't cover this one up unless you meet my terms. What would the world say if they learned their Pope employed monsters?"

I considered his words. It would be the end of the world. Finding out monsters were real would cause a panic. But that the Vatican had known about it all along?

Armageddon.

"You will deliver these monsters to me and my men tomorrow morning, or else. I'll send you the location one hour before. Oh, and I require Master Temple's generous donation prior to my rise to the Papacy," he said with a smile. "To continue God's work during the transition."

I could tell that he honestly believed he was doing the right thing. He wasn't power hungry, he believed we were evil. He abhorred monsters, and it literally sickened him to learn of the Vatican's dark underbelly. "I will cleanse this house of God," he promised.

"Now, give me back my men," he demanded, pointing at the two witnesses. After a jerky nod from the Conclave, Crispin obeyed, escorting the two arrogant fuckers to the Antipope. They smiled as they approached him, but Crispin's face was as white as a sheet. His eyes locked onto the Antipope with as much hatred as I had ever seen one human give another. On their way by, the younger witness pointed his thumb at me. "She's one of them, too." This close, I recognized those cold blue eyes. One of my attackers from last night. The other witness was unfamiliar.

I bared my teeth at him and Fabrizio clamped a calloused palm on my shoulder.

Anthony's lip curled up in disgust, forgetting all about our pleasant conversation yesterday. Well, darn. I'd really wanted him to like me. I guessed I would just have to kill him instead. "Then she will join the others when you deliver them to me tomorrow," he promised.

Then the group left, and I fell into my chair, mind reeling. It looked like I didn't need to fear running from the Conclave tomorrow. Because they were about to have a new Pope and the entire club would be dissolved.

But Roland was still in danger, and I no longer had to worry about being a good girl. I just needed to somehow get the girls out of here before I went *Kill Bill* on the Antipope.

Windsor cramped my style by locking me up in the prison along with the wolves. And with seven unstable Shepherds and seven terrified Conclave wizards glaring me down, I decided to be a good girl and let them. The wolves were also used as leverage against me. One wrong move, and they died. Instantly.

I could always use the Whispers to get out of my prison cell, knowing that there was no way they had anything powerful enough to hold me. They would have no reason to lock up an Angel. It would go against everything they stood for.

Even the Conclave wasn't that ignorant.

I had demanded to know why I was being treated like a criminal when it had been proven that I was at least partly right in judging the witnesses as liars.

"Because we know you would run at the first opportunity. Either because you had been told not to, or to go after Roland. The lying vampire!" Daniel spat before dismissing me.

❦ 48 ❧

I paced the walls of my cell for the fiftieth time.

Turns out, the Conclave did have cells strong enough for an Angel. A *Fallen* Angel. It was also wizard-proof, which was the reason they had chosen it for me. It was just dumb luck that it also happened to block my Angelic blood. I hadn't said anything, not wanting to draw attention to my rare gift. Even a broken Conclave got something right twice every hundred years.

The Whispers were silent to me, and for the first time, I missed them.

"*Motherfuckingmilkeyedshitweasels,*" I growled for the hundredth time, thinking of the Conclave. It was my new mantra – one that heralded new beginnings of peace and prosperity.

Over the bloated carcasses of the Conclave and the smoldering ashes of the Antipope.

I had been here for a long while, but since I had been patted down and relieved of anything electronic or non-fabric, I had no way to break out or wield the power of reading the time.

Windsor hadn't found the scarf, which I had very neatly folded in my panties, fearing they would pat me down before the trial. I had chosen the better undergarment for my pointless ruse, because he had made me remove my bra. The wires inside could be used for all sorts of sneaky things when wielded by a hormone-infused, raging, psychopathic wizard with a vendetta.

The scarf had been small enough that he hadn't felt it, or had wisely chosen not to comment on a little extra cushion on a woman's rear.

Turns out that Windsor, the emotionless sociopath, wasn't all that dumb after all.

Seeing that scarf would have resulted in questions. The big one being, *why had I purposely withheld evidence?* I had studied the cross sewn into the ratty, ivory scarf in my rooms last night, dredging up what little I knew of it. It wasn't the modern-day crucifix seen on churches, but an ornate, red *plus* sign – narrow at the joints and flaring out at the tips. The Cross Pattée. The symbol had been used numerous times throughout history, so it could have signified any number of organizations. Was it an old group or something the Antipope had adopted for his private security team?

Windsor had checked on me a few times, and even gave me a brief update a few hours ago.

Roland had been officially ex-communicated for failing in his duties as a Shepherd as well as hiding his cursed blood from the Conclave. Even though it was pointless to do so, since the Conclave and Shepherds were scheduled for disbandment and execution tomorrow. Sure, the Shepherds could storm the gates and kill Anthony – no matter the army the Antipope had at his disposal, nothing would stop fourteen furious wizards – but that wouldn't stop the video from hitting the web. Which would destroy not only the Conclave, but the Vatican.

Windsor had delivered this news in an emotionless tone. Maybe he suffered from shock? Perhaps he realized that his unconditional support of the Conclave's ignorance had brought his life screeching to a halt, resulting in this cold cruel world thunder-stomping his genitals.

Or did his calm presentation reveal a lack of concern – that maybe he was involved?

Because someone had fed Anthony a lot of classified information. The question was *who?*

I was obviously somewhat bitter about the whole thing, so I repeated my mantra again.

"*Motherfuckingmilkeyedshitweasels ... Ohhhhmmmmm...*" There. I felt better already.

I suspected each Shepherd for different reasons. But I had found an equal number of reasons to trust them. I didn't like any of the Conclave, but I trusted Roland's research into their past. If he said he found nothing, that was that. But they were still supreme shit-stains, incompetent on a level I still struggled to fathom. *Criminally* incompetent, and worse, too proud to admit it.

The Conclave was in a quandary. The only way to preserve the Vatican was to cave to a tyrant with blackmail power. Not just submit, but elect him the Grand Poobah. The Pope-est with the Most-est.

I wasn't anywhere near Tiffany and Jasmine – their cells were in the shifter section, which was far enough away to prevent girl talk. No one but us three were housed here, so I was basically in solitary confinement, left all alone in my own wizard-proof, Fallen Angel-proof cell.

When I had quizzed the robot known as Windsor on how long they expected to keep me locked up since we were all in the same boat, he had blinked at me and then walked away. I wondered if he considered me the catalyst to this whole thing and no longer saw me as a human.

I still couldn't understand how they had gotten Roland, and how the witness had gotten his amulet. Was it just a trophy to him? How had a vanilla human bested Roland? And why was a piss-ant thug awarded such a prize? Was it because he had volunteered to be a witness against the girls? Or a tip for accidentally leading the vampire back to their lair?

I also had no idea how a witness had been one of the assassins I fought last night. Hadn't they been kept under watch? This just led me in circles – to one of the three Shepherds. Or one of the Conclave. Then again, how would the Conclave explain keeping tabs on a citizen of Rome? Maybe they had kept an eye on him, but it wasn't like they could have arrested him and held him in custody. Witnessing a murder wasn't a crime. I frowned.

And since it had happened in the city, shouldn't the Roman Police – the Carabinieri – have handled it? I paused, congratulating myself on pulling that name out of my ass. "Callie is an infinite source of wisdom," I said out loud, pretending the echoes represented an adoring crowd.

Solitary confinement was not healthy for me.

Back to the police angle. There would have been all sorts of questions after a murder in an alley in the heart of Rome. Unless the Conclave used their Vatican pull to put pressure on the Carabinieri and they had caved. That made sense. I sighed, going back to the witnesses.

One was a waiter, and the other was a baker.

At least, that's what everyone had been led to believe.

A twisted part of me hoped that the Conclave was going over each of these same questions, and realizing their fatal mistakes, but I doubted it. They probably had an excuse ready for each one, or at least someone else to blame.

I was getting pissed again. Mantra time.

"*Motherfuckingmilkeyedshitweasels ... Ohhhhmmmmm...*"

"That seems like a highly inappropriate prayer on such holy ground," a familiar voice murmured from outside the door.

I blinked, recognizing Fabrizio's voice. Where had Windsor gone? "It's soothing. You should really try it. You just think of the Conclave and free-speak whatever comes to mind. Kind of like speaking in Tongues. Then you just add *Ohm* to it to make it meditative. But I guess you could substitute *Amen* instead."

I had given up on personally hating the three Shepherds. They were just doing their job.

Or one of them was behind it all. I didn't really care anymore. Not about the Conclave or the Shepherds, anyway. They could burn for all I cared. I just wanted to save the girls and Roland. That was enough for me.

Fabrizio coughed. "I'm only good at group meditations."

I cocked my head, frowning. "You're welcome to come on in. I'm not busy." Why not try?

I was stunned to hear a key unlocking the door, but I kept my calm in case he had a dozen armed men behind him pointing rifles my way. Maybe he was the mastermind behind it all and had decided it was gloating time. I very subtly angled my toes, preparing to dart out of the cell.

So I could access my magic and flay everyone in the hall alive. If it cost me a few bullet wounds or a scorched patch of skin from wizard's fire to save Roland and the girls, I would gladly pay it. The door swung open, revealing an empty hall. Freedom was only feet away.

I didn't move.

"It stinks in there. Come on out and I'll give your foul-mouthed mantra a try," he called out, sounding as if he was standing a few feet back and to the side from the door. "I killed the cameras, by the way. Didn't want anyone seeing me here."

Fearing a trap, I slipped off one of my Darling and Dear boots, which had been blocked from magic while in the prison cell. I did this quickly and silently, hating myself. Then I kissed one of them lovingly, almost wanting to cry, as if tossing out my own flesh and blood. With supreme will, I threw it through the open door, ready to jump out after he used up his first attack.

The boot hit the ground unharmed. I almost gasped in relief. Das boot lives!

Then a calloused hand flashed into view, snatched the boot, and disappeared.

❧ 49 ☙

My maternal instincts kicked in and I stormed out of the cell, certain he wasn't going to kill me after all. I found Fabrizio sitting on the floor, back against the wall, cuddling and stroking my boot possessively. He stared at me and hissed, "My preccciioooousssss," imitating that creepy character from the Lord of the Rings.

"Give me back my shoe, you creep!" I snarled at his grin.

He held it out, squinting at it with a thoughtful assessment before grunting and tossing it at my feet. "Cute boots. Might want to shack up with someone soon, though. Your infatuation is bordering on dependency."

"They were a gift."

"I don't even want to ask how you got a pair of those," he waved a hand, literally not wanting to talk about them.

I cocked my head. "You know about—"

"Those who shall not be named, yes," he said in a louder voice, poking fingers in his ears.

I frowned at him. "Fine. Not important anyway. What the hell are you doing here? Did someone forget to plug Windsor into the wall to charge?"

He grinned, leaning forward, careful to keep his hands in plain sight. "Speaking of Windsor, your hipster mantra really got under his skin. I even heard him muttering it under his breath as if he was trying to understand it." I blinked at him, waiting. He sighed. "Right. How about answering a few questions? If I like the answers, you're free to go." He glanced down at his watch. "We have twenty minutes until Windsor is finished charging. Your call."

I didn't let anything show on my face, but I opened myself to verify that I was indeed able to touch my magic. I didn't actually touch it, just verified nothing was in my way.

It was there, waiting for me. The Whispers reached out to me with a loving embrace, their seductive chant almost sweeping me under. I muted them – not quite understanding how – careful not to let the mental juggling show on my face. If Fabrizio was here to kill me, he sure had an odd way of going about it. That didn't mean I dismissed the possibility. I would have taken a similar approach if I were in his shoes. If he wanted to joke around and put me at ease as part of his master plan, I would play along, secretly vigilant to even a sliver of danger.

Fabrizio sighed. "My ass is falling asleep here."

"You cuss a lot for a Shepherd."

He held up a finger. "Only when off duty, or scheduled for execution in the morning. And I don't cuss nearly so much as my girlfriend." A ghostly look passed over his face, as if realizing he may not ever see her again. He concealed it quickly, returning to our conversation. "All have sinned and fallen short of the glory of God," he quoted to justify his potty-mouth.

"You turning a new leaf, or have you always been a closet-cusser?"

He shrugged. "I repent weekly, but I find cursing keeps my blood pressure down."

"Salads do that, too," I offered, smirking.

"Wait till you get out of your teens – when life punches you in the teeth. Then we'll talk about salads, Girlie. And..." he added, slapping his stomach, "I'm *Italian!*"

I rolled my eyes. "I'm well out of my teens, thank you very much, Gramps. I graduated High School three whole *years* back. It was like, forever ago."

He blinked at me, appalled. I burst out laughing. It felt surprisingly good, almost making me forget the situation. Just like that, my laughter died, and I sat down warily. He wore a metal bracelet I didn't remember from before.

He saw my attention and grunted, rattling it. "Blocks my magic. Didn't want us running off to do something stupid. We all go down with the ship, apparently."

My eyes widened. "What?"

He nodded. "You could kill me where you sit. As easy as stealing candy from a baby."

I studied him, not entirely buying it. "Questions. Shoot," I said instead.

"Okay. Why did you attack the witness? Alberto?"

"I felt Roland's necklace on him." I readied myself to kill Fabrizio if he so much as twitched. "The one that zapped you," I added.

Fabrizio frowned. "We put them both through a metal detector. He had a plain gold chain, but I checked it myself. No amulet, and much smaller than Roland's strange vampire trophy." Those words seemed to hit him for the first time. "It's not a trophy, is it?" he growled, shaking his head.

"No, it's not a trophy. But what the hell did I sense, then? I felt it. A slight vibration to the air. Almost a hum. It's unique, trust me." I wasn't going to share what it allowed him to do.

Fabrizio closed his eyes, mumbling under his breath, and I readied myself to kill him. His eyes shot open and he stared at me as if I *had* struck him in the forehead with a hammer.

"Crispin," he whispered. "Crispin was standing beside Alberto..." He looked ready to vomit. As if someone had just reached inside and torn out his guts.

I blinked at him, recalling the details. Was he right? *Crispin* had been wearing the amulet? He had stayed close to the witnesses the entire time. But he had defended me from the Conclave, arguing on my right to attack the witness. Then he had glared at the Antipope. "That... doesn't make any sense."

Fabrizio still looked sick, but animated at the same time, connecting dots. He lifted his wrist. It was shaking. "Guess who made us put these on?" He sounded disgusted that he hadn't seen it sooner. Unbelievable. Crispin had taken out the Shepherds in one fell swoop. "We searched the city last night... We separated to divide and conquer. He could have done it. Caught Roland. Especially if he learned... that he had become a vampire."

I felt tears building up. Was this a nightmare? Had Crispin taken Roland out because he was a vampire? But the Antipope had Roland. Why would Crispin give Roland to the Antipope? Because I'm paranoid, I tried to remember where Fabrizio had been during my attack on the witness. This could all be an elaborate misdirect. But... he hadn't been near them. Then he had tackled me. I would have felt it that close, practically touching me.

Then I remembered. The amulet had *zapped* Fabrizio. He *couldn't* have touched it. I didn't know why it hadn't zapped Crispin, but the facts clicked into place. The *why* didn't matter.

Saving my people was my only goal.

A set of keys hit the ground and skidded to my feet, but I didn't look down, keeping my eyes on him, very, very alert for an attack. But... he looked broken. Betrayed. A dead man walking.

Fabrizio slowly nodded at me. "Be sure to knock me out before you go, just to remove any doubt from your mind about me. I still have to live here if you save us, Girlie," he winked sadly. "Take the girls with you. Go save our boy, or we'll all be crucified tomorrow."

He saw the doubt in my eyes, and grumbled, jangling his bracelet pointedly. Seeing that it didn't sway me, he slowly climbed to his feet, holding his hands out before him in a submissive gesture. I stepped back, ready for anything. Then he calmly walked into my cell, for sure cutting off his access to magic. "Happy? I still think you should hit me, Girlie."

He still stood close to the door, but only as if remaining close enough for me to hit him. I was confident I could kill him before he could cross the barrier.

I blinked at him. "Why trust me? You think the girls are murderers."

He shrugged. "Maybe that's what we need. Three crazy bitches who would do anything for their friend. You're the perfect level of crazy. You've consistently broken every rule we've given you, all to find out the truth. No matter the cost. We'll need that asset to get him back. This is our last chance to get out of this. If you fail, or sit here doing nothing, we'll all die tomorrow. You have nothing to lose..." he grinned, "and everything to prove. Your sense of *right* is more important than your sense of *faith*. Some of us may flinch at doing what needs to be done. Too used to the rulebook." He met my eyes approvingly. "But I don't think you will. He's also *your* mentor. And..." he wiggled his bracelet, reminding me he couldn't use his magic. "Only Crispin has the key to take these off."

I struggled for a response, his comment about my mentor piercing my heart like a stiletto. "But... he's a vampire now..."

Fabrizio guffawed. "In our line of work? Could have happened to any of us over the years. Plus, if I'm going to trust a vampire, I'd prefer my first one to have spent decades as a man of God... Now, it's a long drive—"

I held up my hand. "How does your magic-tracking software work?" He frowned, and then pulled up his phone, showing me an app connected to a geo-locating service. "Use enough magic, the system spots it. That's about all I know. Windsor designed it. Not good with the people thing, but great with technology. I'm secretly convinced that he's a cyborg, but he's an automaton for God, so I roll with it."

"The same could be said about many at the Conclave," I muttered, earning a chuckle. But I still wasn't sure about Windsor. Maybe he had joined Crispin in exchange for a new keyboard.

I took a deep breath, deciding now was the best time to try it. I motioned for him to follow me out of the cell, extending an olive branch. I also needed to be able to see his phone. He frowned, but obeyed. I knew magic would set off the tracker, but I had another idea. I opened myself to the Whispers, and sighed as the silver power washed through me like a gulp of hot chocolate. I made a tiny Gateway to the opposite side of the room, convincing myself I needed it more than anything in the world. A silver oval the size of my fist winked into view and Fabrizio gasped. I glanced at his phone and saw absolutely no alarm. Fabrizio did the same, shaking his head.

"Damn, Girlie! What the hell was th—?"

I socked him in the jaw, knocking him out cold as I released the Silver Gateway. I scooted him into the cell, locked the door, and tugged my boot back on. Then I picked up his phone and jogged down the hall, eyes up to check the security cameras, even though Fabrizio had supposedly disabled them. They were all off. I knew this because I had noticed their blinking green lights on my way in with Windsor.

I found a small room with medical supplies and decided to replace my bandages since they hadn't bothered healing me. I rolled up my sleeves and replaced the saturated cloth around my arms and waist. Then, as an afterthought, I used the rest of the roll on my forearms, tying it off with my teeth. The added protection couldn't hurt. It was messy, but it would suffice.

Now it was time to calm some terrified wolves and then convince them to help me save a vampire.

I freed the girls, who had been napping in a cute spooning position on the stone floor. It looked like their werewolf healing ability had taken care of their injuries. Or, they'd been healed at some point in their incarceration, the Conclave not keen on keeping even suspected murderers in pain. Not concerned enough to provide them a bed, though.

The shifter cells were made with pure silver that had to be worth a fortune. Then, since silver was a softer metal, the metal bars had been inscribed with runes that could have knocked out a Cave of bears. Then they surrounded the silver cage with very thick marble that was also carved with runes. Must be a juicy story, there, because this was overkill.

They stared at me warily, probably exactly how I had looked when staring at Fabrizio. Close up, they were even more impressive than I had thought from the trial.

"Get up. We're leaving. Roland's in danger. Are you hurt? I could use the help, but I can't afford a liability."

"What the hell is going on?" the taller one demanded.

"Either way, you're free to go, but getting out on your own will be no piece of cake," I said, dropping the keys and turning my back on them. I smiled as I heard them scrambling to their feet and out to safety before I had taken two steps.

I made no sudden movements, not knowing how in control they were. In general, but also because they had spent a week locked up. "We don't need your help, but thanks for freeing us. Your job here is done. Tell us where Roland is and we'll get him," the taller one said.

I blinked, and then turned to face her. "*Excuse* me?"

"Where is he?" the shorter one begged, but her pretty lips were curled up in a snarl, as if hungry to start tearing the flesh from anyone standing between her and Roland.

"He saved our lives," the taller one said. "We'd do anything for him. We didn't ask for this," she said, waving a hand at her boobs. She was wearing clothes, but her motion had literally only indicated her ta-tas. I arched a brow and she realized how it had looked. "We didn't ask to be raped and turned into werewolves," she amended, "but if we can use it to help Roland, point us in the right direction and say *sic 'em*," she snarled. Then, as an afterthought, "Please."

I just stared at the two of them. "You do realize that I was there, right? That I helped save you? I kicked serious ass in that fucking bakery, even though Roland claimed the kills, I deserve a little goddamned respect. I'm the one that fucking found your location, tracked down the bastards, spent hours on the phone, spoke to all the bartenders." I took a step forward. "Me, not Roland. He was busy recovering from an earlier werewolf encounter. And here I am again."

They shared a look. "I don't remember seeing you there, but I did see you in the cells after, checking up on the other girl. I'm sure you're a great assistant to Roland. Callie, right? I think he mentioned your name a few times," she admitted. "My name is Tiffany, by the way."

The other one nodded in agreement. "Jasmine," she offered.

"Now, where is he?" Tiffany pleaded.

I was going to kill them. "*Assistant?*" I hissed. He had *mentioned* my *name* a few times? "I smashed a full pot of coffee over the tall werewolf's face!" I snarled, recalling the rescue.

Tiffany's face grew hard, obviously appreciating the amount of pain I had given her rapist.

"I'm sure that helped Roland immensely," Jasmine said, placating my anger, looking desperate to drop the conversation and go after Roland.

I was going to save Roland *just* so he could tell them how much of a badass I was. I seriously contemplated delaying our rescue just so he could suffer a few minutes longer in recompense for this bullshit. I couldn't believe this. I had spent *days* tracking these two down, but did they remember me? No. They just remembered the guy who carried them out of the bakery, tossed them in the back of *my* truck, then into a shifter *prison cell*, and then onto a jet to head to *Rome*. Where he left them to fall into *this* mess.

Men!

I took a deep breath so as not to kill my sidekicks, and prepared to open up to the Whispers again, focusing on my desperate need to find Roland. Because need was the key.

"Why does your butt look so puffy?" Tiffany asked me, startling me out of my focus.

I realized what they were talking about and ripped the scarf out of my pants. Then I tied it on my face, covering my nose and mouth. Maybe it would be useful to fit in. Enough for a casual glance, anyway. And this way these two mutts wouldn't see my permanent snarl.

"Gross! Did you just tie panties onto your face?" Jasmine gasped.

I rounded on them, ready to lock them back up in their cell. They flinched back a step, eyes flickering nervously in response to my sudden movement. Their eyes seemed to notice the scarf itself for the first time, widened, and then they snarled, going from nervous to murderous in a blink. "The killer wore that," they said in unison.

I tugged the scarf down, taking a threatening step forward. "I fucking *know*?" I hissed. "I stole it from one of his associates after they jumped me last night. By the way, I *stopped* them from coming to kill you in your cells! With my impressive *assistant* skills. You're welcome. *Again*."

They shared an uncertain look, as if wondering how far to trust me. I lowered my voice and tried to relax my shoulders into a less threatening posture, taking a deep breath. They were understandably scared to see the scarf again. That was all. "I intend to use this as a disguise to get close enough to kill the rest of them. Because I would do anything to save Roland. If you have a problem with that, I'll toss you back in your hotel suite and let the fucking Conclave take care of you." Okay, calm had flown out the window somewhere in the middle of my tirade, but we needed to stop fucking around and save Roland.

"We want blood for what they did to Constantine, and what they're doing to Roland," Tiffany said. I took her for the alpha of the two, but the shorter one – Jasmine – wasn't weak by any means. If anything, she looked to be in less control of her emotions, more unpredictable.

I nodded and turned my back on them, opening myself to the Whispers again. They purred in my ears, nothing specific, but encouraging sounds, desperate to be used. I just hoped I knew enough about them to get the job done, since my usual magic might set off the Shepherd's wards.

With a hiss of need, I ripped open a hole in reality, the Whispers calling to me with their seductive song. The Gateway was huge, easily big enough for us to walk through side by side, almost touching both walls of the hall. Through the silvery sheen, like a wall of mist, was a thicket of trees. I saw an old, broken church a hundred feet away, and grinned, stepping through the Gateway.

I glanced over my shoulder after checking for immediate threats and saw the looks on their faces. "Don't worry. It's not really silver." With sighs of relief, the werewolves followed me, finally realizing that this panty-faced secretary might just have a trick or two up her sleeve.

Or her ass. Whatever.

The Whispers had answered. *Need* had brought me here. No one could hide from me if my need was great enough, and I needed to save Roland. He was family. Three short trees concealed the Gateway from our target, so I left it open in case we needed a quick escape. We stared through the trees, spending a few moments to check our surroundings, study the church, count the patrolling guards, and try to figure out where we were. None of the guards noticed our presence. I focused on the Whispers, realizing they were repeating the same thing over and over. Something I could understand, but not necessarily English. More a feeling.

Double blades slowly formed in my fists as I followed their advice, pulling deep on my need for a stealthy weapon. What I now held in my fist was like a roll of quarters with blades poking out between my fingers, the sharp edges starting just beyond my knuckles. They extended a good six inches, thin enough to pierce armor, and strong enough to slice metal if I so chose. They weighed practically nothing.

I focused again and they disappeared. How freaking cool was that?

"I'm fucking Wolverine," I whispered to myself. My long hair hung free like a white cape down my back, easy to notice. Unacceptable. Without hesitation, I called back my new blades and chopped it off at my jawline. I tucked what was left under my scarf. Tiffany watched my sacrifice, an eerie smile stretching across her cheeks. She gave me a slow, approving nod, sensing something significant – a call to war, perhaps. I tried not to think about my loss.

Anything for Roland, I thought, my blades winking out of existence effortlessly.

I glanced down at Fabrizio's phone, saw no magic alert, and made sure it was on silent before pocketing it. The church ahead was old and obviously in neglect. I could tell that it had once been a sight to behold, but that had been a long time ago. It was just a skeleton now. A poor choice for the Antipope. Then again, if he was using it to hide a prisoner vampire, maybe this wasn't his home spot. Just a convenient place to hide a prisoner. We faced the back of the church, and I counted three guards. They were alone, not working in pairs. They held assault rifles like they knew how to use them. Poor guys. Maybe I should offer them some company.

"We're a few miles outside of Rome," Jasmine whispered, pointing at a distant hill behind us, the thin blanket of clouds in the sky not hindering our view. I grunted softly, not really caring exactly where we were. I'd just wanted to estimate how quick the response time would be. Then again, if Fabrizio had been lying, the Shepherds could always Shadow Walk to us once they sensed the magic flying. Or they were wearing those fancy bands Crispin had made them put on.

With a thought, I urgently whipped Fabrizio's phone out of my pocket and tossed it back through the Gateway before releasing it. I hadn't considered that the Conclave might track Fabrizio's missing phone after they found him in my cell.

I realized the two wolves were staring at the departed Gateway in awe. "We're really sorry for doubting you. We didn't know you were there. Please forgive us," Tiffany said.

"And thank you for saving us, Callie," Jasmine added.

"Yes, thank you, Callie. We're in your debt."

I leveled them with my game-face, which probably looked cool as hell with my scarf. "I want you to kill every sonofabitch in that building other than Roland. We don't stop until every *heart* stops. Do that and we're even."

In response, Tiffany took a sheepish step closer and readjusted the scarf on my face. "Sorry, it was bothering me," she murmured. Then she assessed me again, nodded, and stepped back.

In my head, I listed the *cons* of killing her. It was only one line, but it was a big one. *Roland would be displeased.* The two had given me plenty of *pros*, so I didn't bother with that list.

Luckily for them, they chose that moment to explode into werewolf form. I checked to make sure no guards had noticed before turning back to study them. They were different than the wolves from St. Louis. These were the Kansas City variety, a taller, longer, leaner version of wolf with a thick mane, barrel chest, and a much longer snout. They were both black as midnight, but thankfully Jasmine had shifted into a slightly shorter wolf. Their eyes had a crimson glow to them, which I had never seen before, definitely not from the wolves who had made them.

In short, they looked like my own personal Hellhounds.

And that was just fucking dandy for what I had in mind. Because I was going to deliver the Antipope and Crispin to Hell tonight. And I was much happier with my sidekicks unable to talk.

I realized I was smiling, thirsty for blood. I told them my plan, and they nodded eagerly.

I was beyond giving two shits about the Conclave's pristine name. We were going to do this Kansas City style. Brutal, dirty, and memorable. A story to be whispered for years.

"Whisper," I chuckled to myself. "Let's go hunt," I murmured. Without a sound, they ghosted off on their own, just like I'd advised, and I picked the closest guard, slipping through the night like just another shadow.

51

The body slipped to the ground at my feet, not making a noise as I cushioned his fall. That was my third kill, and I felt nothing about it. I had checked them for radios, but they all seemed to have malfunctioned. Idiots. They wouldn't even know what hit them.

I used my new blades to trick a side window open, and then risked a quick glance inside, seeing only a dark, empty hallway outside the main nave. The building was much larger than I had thought, stretching further with another wing to the right as I faced the back of the building.

More places to hide. I climbed through the window without a sound, landing on the balls of my feet and crouching down in the shadows. I waited in silence, letting my night vision adjust. A lone guard peered into the hall, and seeing it was clear, began to walk my way. I ducked under a low table, lying flat on my back to hide my white hair as he approached. I held my breath and waited.

His steady footsteps were almost silent, but I still tracked him. At the perfect moment, I curled up into a sitting position as he swept the area ahead of him with his rifle. I stood, stepped up behind him and released my breath in a whispered, *"Sinner,"* as I opened his throat, spraying blood everywhere. My other hand simultaneously struck his wrist, paralyzing it like Roland had taught me so he couldn't pull the trigger. I guided his silent death to the ground as if concerned he might hurt himself.

I had sliced deeply enough to sever his vocal cords, eliminating the chance of a sound. I shoved him under the table into the spot I had just warmed up for him.

Four, I thought to myself. I had killed four men so far. I didn't feel bad about it, which concerned me on a distant level. A very distant level, because this was all about saving Roland.

My best friend. I may as well have been reaping weeds.

These men had lost all rights to human decency. They were vermin. Stained. No mercy was owed. Just justice from my silver blades. Swift. Silent. Final. They were working with the Antipope, and had begun this whole thing. Constantine's killer had worn one of these scarves on his face. The same one now on mine. The red cross.

I could still smell the previous owner's scent on the fabric covering my mouth, but I ignored it, knowing it was poetic justice to disguise myself as one of their own. I sliced off my victim's scarf and wiped it in his blood before dropping it back onto his chest.

Then I moved, circling the nave and trying to get a feel for the layout. I reached an intersection and came face to face with a guard. I sliced the tendons in the wrist holding his rifle while simultaneously upper-cutting my other twin blades into the soft palate under his chin, straight through his mouth. I felt no give, as if merely stabbing mashed potatoes. He gagged as the blades severed his tongue, staring at me in disbelief. "*Sinner,*" I whispered, letting his body softly fall to the floor.

That had been close. I needed to be more careful or one of them was going to manage pulling the trigger and giving away our element of surprise. I stared past him down the hall and saw another guard thirty yards away, his back facing me as he watched the front of the church. I was about to sneak up behind him when a dark form flashed through the air, decapitating him in a silent fountain of blood. A second, smaller wolf padded up to the body and lapped up the blood. Her ears swiveled and she looked up at me. She sniffed the air, but I tugged down my scarf just in case.

Her eyes flashed red in the darkness as I waited for recognition. Her blood-soaked tongue popped out of her mouth and she panted. A sign of relaxation. I took a slow step to a nearby door and glanced through. The nave, where mass would have taken place. I looked back to the wolf to let her know where I was going, but she was gone.

I snapped my scarf back into place. Six guards down, by my count. I was sure the wolves had taken down more, but to my knowledge at least six were dead. There couldn't be that many left, and no alarm had been raised. I carefully pressed the handle, thankful it didn't squeak. Then I ducked inside and crouched low in the shadows of a pew. The door hadn't creaked. Was God giving me an assist?

I quickly swept the scene before me for guards, but saw none. Only one man stood in the room, and he was at the pulpit, staring up at a massive, ornate stained-glass window, his back to me. The window stretched almost from floor to ceiling, several stories high, and depicted angels, saints, Jesus, and other religious icons – so that during Mass, the congregation would stare at the bishop as he preached, limned by beauty. I hadn't noticed the window from outside, the building angled just enough to miss it. The man had no idea I was here. The Antipope.

Then I realized he wasn't staring at the window.

A man hung from glowing chains shackled to each wrist. The chains reached up to either wall on unlit chandeliers, leaving him to dangle before the center of the stained-glass window twenty feet off the ground. Where a crucifix would ordinarily have hung, the center of attention.

A display of triumph.

Roland.

My vision flashed silver as rage threatened to consume me, the Whispers urging me to burn the place to the foundation, snatch up Roland, and flee. With or without the wolves. I shoved their song away, taking a slow, measured breath so as not to reveal my presence.

Several other doors lined the walls, all points of entry or exit, all cloaked in shadows. I might not be the only one hiding in wait. But none of the other guards had shown an interest in sneaking through the shadows, confident in their numbers and this secret location. A broken church in disrepair. The Conclave had no reason to come here. There were dozens or more churches just like this all over Rome.

I stared up at Roland and his chains. What were they made of? Was he bait?

He had been tortured, his chest a fan of blood, weakening the almost-vampire.

Or maybe he was full vampire now.

At the sight of his blood, my fury leapt back to life. Here was my mentor, the man who had given his life for the church. And now he had given up his soul to save two wolves — hiding the fact that he was a vampire so he could do one last act of justice — even when no one had seemed to welcome his aid. He had been tortured and strung up.

My White Knight.

I realized I was no longer hiding, but standing in the center aisle. I didn't remember moving. I began to walk, feeling as if I was watching my body from above as it advanced. Pews crashed in my wake and my shoulders seared with lava as wings like dry ice abruptly flared out behind me. The already weakened wooden pews shattered as they slammed into the walls, hopefully blocking the doors. The ground smoked beneath my boots.

Anthony spun, eyes wide at the sudden cacophony. He took an instinctive step back as he saw me, flinching. More pews crashed into the walls as I stormed closer in calm, deliberate steps. Roland lifted his head slightly, eyes entirely red as they locked onto me, but they fluttered closed and his head sagged back down. I flung out my hands, severing the chains in a shower of sparks, commanding the Whispers.

They purred delightedly in my mind, eager to be of use.

Roland began to fall, but I lifted my hand as if cupping water for a drink. A silver cloud appeared beneath him, swiping ornate candleholders and a gilded Bible from the table below him before gently catching him and settling him down. I released the power, never slowing my measured advance to the pulpit. I was now only ten feet away from my target. The source of my wrath. My redemption.

"How..." Anthony stammered, "how did you do that?" he rasped, eyes flicking to my wings. "How did you find us? No one knows this place!" he whimpered.

I smiled, taking a few more steps. He couldn't see my icy grin behind my scarf. I didn't care. His anxiety would soon cease. Roland groaned again.

"Those chains were forged by Angels to stop vampires..." he rasped. He cast a look over his shoulder at Roland, not hiding his disgust. "Which I didn't believe existed before last night."

I considered the chains. I wasn't an Angel, but I was pretty sure I had Nephilim blood. Which meant I probably shouldn't have been strong enough to break a Heaven-forged chain. But I just had. I did have a drop of Angel's blood in my system. Maybe that was why. I spread my wings high above my back. I could feel the power required to maintain the wings draining me. I wasn't strong enough to keep this up for very long. It was time to end this shit-show.

Anthony collapsed to his knees, jaw hanging open in awe. "You... you're an *Angel?*" he whispered in awe, finally recognizing me with my new hair style.

"Where is the video, *child?*" I asked in an arctic air of command, not bothering to answer him. "I will not have the church sullied, but you shall have your just reward. As will the vampire."

Roland's just reward was survival. The Antipope's just reward was to die for his crimes.

Anthony nodded numbly, reaching into his pocket to pull out a flash drive. "Slide it over," I said. "Being too close to my celestial form will destroy your mortal body." I glanced back at the shattered pews for emphasis. He slid it over to me hurriedly, not daring to deny an Angel. He began muttering a prayer.

"Swear to God that this is the only copy. Angels can sense lies," I warned, capitalizing on his assumption. He was sobbing as he nodded vehemently. His eyes were wondrous, as if seeing the Pearly Gates behind me. I slammed my boot onto the flash drive, obliterating it. Then I flicked my finger and a droplet of silver flew, igniting it in a ball of white flame, melting it in seconds.

"Doing a service to God via a crime is unacceptable. Why did you murder the man in the alley, and what did you steal from the Vatican?"

Anthony began desperately shaking his head, climbing to his feet. "I didn't murder anyone, and definitely didn't steal. The Ten Commandments forbids it." he protested. "You may have a false impression of me from my threat to the Vatican. But this man," he pointed, "is not a child of God. He is sired by Lucifer. What other explanation can there be? He feasts on the blood of others to survive!"

"We can't be blamed for our father's mistakes. And in his case, he was infected. You have no idea the sacrifices he's made. Why he became a vampire," I seethed, panting. Roland had given up everything he valued to save two lives. His career, soul, and life goals. Giving up God was a requirement. "You couldn't even begin to fill his *boots*. He is the most pious man I know."

The Antipope frowned, as if suddenly seeing me in a new light. "Is that so?" he asked, picking up a crucifix from the floor as he began walking closer to Roland, who hissed in pain.

"Stop or die," I warned, taking a step closer, wanting to give him the chance to see the error of his ways. Not that I was unwilling to kill him, but I wanted to test my ability to use reason over power. This man wasn't a killer. Just misguided. He genuinely thought he was in the right.

He lowered his crucifix to stare at me. "You, an Angel, would kill a man of the cloth to save demonspawn?" An epiphany flashed in his eyes, and I watched as a film of resolve came over his features. "You have Fallen..." he whispered in defeat, his dream becoming a nightmare. His shoulders sagged, likely realizing that a Fallen Angel wouldn't hesitate in killing him, and that he didn't stand a chance. He realized he was facing his end.

I pressed my momentary advantage before he did something stupid. "Where are the rest of your guards? I know there are more."

"With their commander, Olin Fuentes."

"Describe him." Maybe he was already consecrating this holy ground with his blood.

He paused, eyes taking in my scarf. I could see the questions in his eyes. Why was I wearing it if I didn't know who led them? And why was an Angel wearing it in the first place? "Tall, older man with short white hair. Spiked." I hadn't run into anyone by that description.

"Where does Crispin fit into this?"

His shoulders steadily straightened, as if coming to a conclusion he didn't like. "He delivered the vampire to me." I could tell there was more to reveal, but his face grew into a scowl as he found his backbone. "You've *Fallen*." He spat it like a curse.

I ignored his declaration, my arms suddenly cold at hearing confirmation of Crispin's deceit.

I could see it now. Roland hunting the assassins. Runs into Crispin and sees an ally, a way to finally prove that we had been right about the wolves. Crispin double-crosses him somehow and delivers him to the Antipope, likely killing one of the guards to make it look like Roland had murdered him. Roland wouldn't have vamped out in front of Crispin unless he had to. Was it possible that Roland hadn't yet drank blood? No wonder he looked so weak.

He hadn't had his first kill. He wasn't a full-blown vampire yet.

Much of it was still foggy, but I was confident in the fact that Crispin had used Roland's trust as a dagger in the back. The question was *why* deliver him to the Antipope? Was it all to convince the Antipope to blackmail the Conclave? He'd had the amulet at the trial, though. Maybe he had done it to get the necklace for himself, knowing what it was. The amulet was only worth anything to vampires, and I knew Crispin wasn't a vampire because Roland had told me that a vampire can always sense another vampire.

The major hole in that hypothesis was that the amulet was fairly new to the equation.

It didn't answer why Constantine had been killed, the wolves framed, the file secretly delivered to us, or how the Antipope had entered the equation in the first place. Crispin fit for all of that, but what was his motive? He was First Shepherd. And Roland had vouched for him.

What had changed in Crispin? Why ally with a weakling Antipope?

The stress was too much, and my wings abruptly vanished. I groaned, but managed not to pass out. Anthony gasped, but all I could do was stare through him as I struggled against the pain – the dissection of Roland's fall. How pointless it all was.

What kind of man could betray a brother so easily? Roland didn't trust many, and Crispin had been one of the few he said he trusted with his life. Crispin had played Judas, betraying Roland with a kiss to deliver him to the Antipope. Manipulating Roland's trust was the only way Crispin could have beaten him. Otherwise Roland would have killed him with either his magic or vampire abilities. Or both.

Roland groaned, and a surge of adrenaline hit me. I was racing towards him when a flash of motion from the corner of the room launched towards me. The assailant almost hit me with a ball of fire, but I dove, rolling closer to Roland's table as it splashed against the wall.

Well, it looked like magic was fair play now.

52

Crispin stepped into the light near Anthony, obviously frustrated at his near miss.

The Antipope turned from the sudden flame to the new arrival, eyes wild. "What is the meaning of this?" he demanded of Crispin. "Kill her! She's a Fallen Angel! A demon!"

Crispin's lips thinned with distaste at the lack of respect. Then he punched Anthony in the mouth, sending him crashing to the floor. He spat on his face as the Antipope stared up at him, whimpering in pain and confusion, begging and pleading through bloody lips.

Well, maybe the two *weren't* working together. This place was beyond fucked up.

"You beat me to it," I growled at the traitor. "Why did you kill Constantine?"

He just laughed.

"Are you working with Olin Fuentes? The Commander?" I tapped my scarf. I wanted at least some answers before I killed him. I slipped my hand behind my back, placing my fingers on Roland's flesh. He flinched and I almost let out a sigh of relief. He wasn't dead yet.

Crispin snorted. "Constantine was sniffing too close to my hobbies." At my impatient look, his smile turned gloating. "He saw me meeting with the Sanguine Council."

I ran with that for all of two seconds before giving up. "You're not a vampire..."

This made him laugh harder. "Bingo." He mimed shooting me with a finger gun.

"Look," I snarled from under the scarf, the fabric shifting at the expulsion of breath. "I'm *really* fucking tired. Exhausted. I had to cut my hair off. Break out of prison..." I trailed off, not hiding how weary I was. "Just get to the bragging already. Then I'll do my bit."

He nodded, amused. "Hair looks nice, by the way." I rolled my eyes. He pointed at my scarf. "I killed one of those bastards a few years ago, kept his scarf as a keepsake. I decided to wear it when I killed Constantine – an ironic disguise to kill a Shepherd." His eyes were distantly pleased at the memory. "I'll admit I was just as surprised as he was when he tried to blast me with fire and it failed. I had no idea the damned scarf nullified magic," he chuckled. His eyes grew predatory, finished with the trip down memory lane as he jerked his chin at my scarf. "Too bad it won't save you. I'd always intended to slice you to death the old-fashioned way."

I could only stare. The scarf blocked magic? What the hell kind of magic was that, and why hadn't I heard of them before? "Why leave the wolves alive?" I asked instead, wanting to hide my surprise.

"Perfect scapegoats. Mentally scarred, hated men, unstable monsters. Take your pick. But then you had to go and ruin everything."

"Why the Vampire Council?" I asked, the pieces of the puzzle rattling uselessly in my mind. He wasn't a vampire, so why hadn't Roland's amulet zapped him? A sinking feeling developed in my stomach. "Do you know Haven?" I asked. Had Haven set this whole thing up?

Crispin cocked his head. "Never heard of him." He had no reason to lie. Not after what he had just admitted. "Immortality, of course. Taking down the Conclave will earn me a high position. You've seen how broken the Conclave is. The rest of my life is determined. To sit in a castle playing nice with monsters. We deserve more. I deserve more. Do you have any idea how much I've sacrificed?" He was shouting, panting. "To live like this for the sake of a group of doddering old men, too scared to step out of their precious fortress. Always forced to obey their command, when swift military strikes could solve the problem. No. If that is all that is left to me, to end up like Constantine, I choose the monsters. Better perks of the job."

He let out a breath, calming himself. I was floored. To hear such things from someone Roland had considered a brother... I knew Shepherds lived a long time, so it wasn't the immortality candy that had attracted him. It was... the Conclave itself. Holding him back, not letting him do his job. He wanted fame. Recognition. He was throwing a... tantrum because he didn't feel *appreciated?* It was almost laughable. He cleared his throat. "But to take down the Vatican, *and* the Conclave? Priceless."

"What did you steal from them?"

He hesitated, looking momentarily startled. "I thought you two had done that," he murmured thoughtfully. Then he shrugged it off, as if it wasn't relevant. "It was just an old Bible. Nothing dangerous. That's why I thought it was a misdirect for something else. No matter."

I shook my head. "How did you know about him?" I asked, pointing a thumb over my shoulder towards Roland.

"I bugged him." He grinned smugly. "Heard every conversation he had. But the best one was his talk with the Daywalker, admitting his *curse.*" He mimed finger quotes with the last word, his sneer pitiless. "Oh, and your raunchy night at the hotel was a close second. Even though you ruined the good part with a swim," he chuckled. "To find out that the most stoic of us had taken what I wanted..." he growled, clenching his fists, "and had the nerve to *bitch* about it! Pushed me over the edge. I reached out to my contact with the Sanguines, of course. She promised me my eternal reward if I could use Roland to break the Conclave."

He took a calming breath. "Too bad you're both going to die. I'm sure the Sanguines would have enjoyed two ex-Shepherds on their payroll, but I can't have any loose ends." He withdrew Roland's amulet from beneath his shirt, smiling adoringly. "Thought I was made when this thing zapped Fabrizio and not me. Perks of killing Constantine, I guess. That, and working with the vampires so much recently must have tricked it into thinking me an ally." He dropped it back under his shirt. "Looks better on me anyway," he admitted.

The Antipope was openly sobbing now, shaking his head in horror at the onslaught of information. Vampires. Werewolves. Crispin glanced down at him, pulling back his foot as Anthony reached for it. He laughed at the old man. "I even infected this poor bastard with werewolf saliva after he began asking too many questions. Almost exposed me. So I turned him into what he hated most in the world. Poetic justice." He bent over the Antipope, smirking. "Spoiler alert. You're a *monster*." Anthony gasped, tugging back his sleeve, eyes wide.

So, that was why he had been scratching at his arm... But why? Just for chaos?

I didn't realize I had spoken out loud.

Crispin shrugged. "Fun. Chaos. Whatever." He studied the scarf on my face with a greasy smirk. He pointed at it with one finger. "I had no idea your... *assassins* were in the game, let alone that they were working for *him*," he said, kicking the Antipope without making eye contact. The old man wheezed in pain, not having anticipated it, too focused on the red welts on his forearm. "This bastard almost ruined everything I had worked so hard for, sending the assassins to take out the wolves before their proper trial. The witnesses were a surprise. Even I didn't suspect them. But then I saw Roland leaning over you last night after their attack, sniffing that scarf. I was watching the whole time." He took a step forward, grinning. "You should know that I almost killed you, but I didn't want to risk Fabrizio or Windsor seeing anything. Then Roland fled, still wearing my tracker – which had finally dried off. I partnered with him to hunt down the assassins, and then double-crossed him, sensing my opportunity to break the Conclave. Trust can get you killed." He smiled down at Anthony. "The Antipope had no idea who he had gotten in bed with." He bent over to slap his knees, laughing suddenly. "The Temp—"

The stained glass cracked as a sniper round pierced it, whisking over Crispin's shoulder and hammering into the podium in the center of the pulpit. Crispin had been saved by his own laugh. He was already running as another round struck him in the side, shattering the priceless window behind me, but then he disappeared into the shadows near the door he had first appeared from.

I was covering Roland with my hands as the stained glass fell all around me, the larger shards biting into my neck and hands. When the sound stopped, I turned to see the light of the full moon shining through the gaping hole in the wall where the window had been...

Shining down on Anthony. A full moon. "Shit," I swore. His body began to spasm and twitch.

The halls filled with gunfire as I yanked Roland from the table and out of the sniper's line of sight. Wolves howled in the church, sounding as if a war was erupting along with the gunfight. But first, Roland.

Or all of this had been for nothing.

53

Roland groaned at his sudden movement, then hissed when his body crashed to the floor. I did my best to kick the glass out of my way as I dragged him behind me. Crispin was still nearby, we had a sniper on our ass, and the Antipope was about to turn into a werewolf.

And that was just in *this* room.

The bark of gunfire was more sporadic now, as if the wolves had escaped. With each new spate of bullets, a breath of relief escaped my lips. As long as I heard gunfire the wolves lived. I was pretty sure I knew who wore the scarves, now. Crispin had said *Temp...* before the bullet had interrupted him. My money was on Templar Knights. Templars, for crying out loud!

I didn't give a flying fuck if they were Shriners or Angels. If they shot at us, they died.

I placed my hand on Roland, checking his status. He stirred, so I slapped him in the face. "Wakey, wakey." His eyes shot wide open, irises entirely crimson. "You *know* me, Roland. Get the hell up, you lazy bastard. The Scooby Doo-ettes need us." His fangs popped out at mention of the wolves. He shivered involuntarily, breath ragged as he slowly sat up, sniffing the air in my direction, sensing my bloody wounds. I slapped him again. Harder. "Friend, not food," I scolded.

"And I had such high hopes for you..." a new voice echoed in the room. I spun to see a tall silhouette of a man striding down the center aisle, his boots clicking like a drumbeat. I lifted my hands, ready for a fight as Roland struggled to overcome his injuries – all while fighting an inner battle against the monster inside him. The one that craved only blood.

The situation was quite ridiculous if you thought about it. Here I was, sitting beside...

My Shepherd-pire, Roland.

Anthony the Antipope-wolf.

Crispy McFangLover.

And... *this* sum'bitch.

I recognized the man from Anthony's description. "Olin Fuentes. Templar," I snarled as he stepped into the light of the full moon.

His pale eyes took in the blood splatter from where the sniper round had almost killed Crispin, his lips thinning. "I'll deal with him later. The bastard sabotaged our radios or I would have had him sooner. But *you*..." he said, finally looking at me, "could have been something truly special. Instead, you choose to aid a vampire." He sounded disappointed, eyes flicking to Roland.

He was handsome. He wore black military fatigues and boots. He had a rifle hanging over one shoulder, the hilt of a sword over the other, and big-ass pistols on each hip. Lucky for him, his hands were still empty. A similar scarf to mine hung around his neck like a bandana. I met his gaze, holding out a hand for Roland to stay back. "If you want to get to Heaven, you have to raise a little Hell."

He was silent for a moment, and then he burst out laughing. I hoped the gunfire still echoing in the distant wings of the church meant that the wolves were leading his men on a good chase.

Or a game of *hide-and-seek-and-die*. One of my personal favorites.

The Antipope was whimpering and groaning, but still not shifting. It was only a matter of time. Sometimes the first shift was fast, sometimes it wasn't. I wondered if he was mentally fighting it, considering himself too holy to be tainted. Either way, it was a plus right now.

"We both know you're no Angel, Callie. I've watched you. You could be something great."

I grunted. "I don't think I like you very much." I deliberately studied him up and down. "Yep. I'm sure of it. You nauseate me."

"You stand against Templars with only two fledgling werewolves and a virgin vampire?" he asked, disappointed. "You don't stand a chance. I've been killing this filth for centuries."

Centuries? At least he had confirmed it for me. "Templar, eh?" I shrugged. "Those old dudes who hold weekly meetings after the Alcoholics Anonymous crew clears out?" I smirked. "Cool, man. And you worked for this poor bastard, right?" I pointed my thumb at the Antipope who was still struggling against his first shift. "Good call, working for a werewolf. Except now you're unemployed, I guess." Olin's forehead furrowed at my mockery. "Could you stay standing just like that for a few more seconds? I have a new trick I've been dying to try. I'll introduce you to God. Briefly, before he casts you back down to hell."

"I work for *God*, impudent child." He pointed at the Antipope. "He was a client, a means to an end. He's not my only path to success. For fun, let's pretend you're right. A fledgling acolyte of the Vatican who shows up in Italy without any travel itinerary or documentation, found in an abandoned church with dead bodies everywhere." I shivered to hear he knew I had no identification on me. How the hell had he found *that* out? "And the Antipope dead at her feet. Because you can't leave him alive. I'm sure you know this. Not after what he's seen."

I stared at him, not having thought about it in that light. But he was partially right. The Antipope might not *have* to die, but he *would* become one of the things he hated, a werewolf. Would he still want to tell the world, or would he have a sudden change of heart? I knew if he continued his threats the other Shepherds would take him down, but they would also give him the choice to flee and start a new life. I wasn't holding out much hope of him taking that offer.

Olin must have sensed my unease. "Your Shepherds are broken. They've gone soft. Gray. But the world is black and white. Us versus them. Children of God versus Monsters. *That* is my purpose. To hold the line or break it. The Templar Creed. To cleanse the world of the stain—"

A blast of fire roared up from the shadows, interrupting him as it raced towards the both of us. My black fan materialized on instinct, absorbing the fire and quenching it with a hiss of steam.

Roland hissed from behind me and a bar of red light as thick as my torso erupted from his palms, seeming to draw in shadows and darken the room. The air around it was distorted, the ground hissing underneath as it struck the far wall where the attack had originated. Crispin.

Roland hadn't heard about the scarf, but his blast winked out, the room brightening.

Knowing it probably wouldn't do any good, I flung out my hand at the same target, calling upon my wizard magic. Spears of razor sharp ice erupted over every surface like a mouth of teeth. I released it, panting. I didn't play with ice very often but with an unseen target – and Roland already casting his own hellish fire – I had decided to give it a try. Maybe I would get lucky and cause Crispin to slip and fall on his ass as he tried to flee on a sudden skating rink.

Roland let out a hunting scream, taking off after Crispin. "He has a key and your amulet, Roland!" I shouted, hoping he heard me. We would need that key to release the Shepherds from their bracelets. If Crispin had it on him. Roland disappeared without acknowledging me. I glanced over to check on the struggling Antipope, who seemed unaware of the chaos. Then I turned to assess the crispy Templar. Instead, Olin wore his scarf over his mouth and was lowering his rifle in my direction. Damnit. Forgot he had a scarf, too.

I spun my fan into place as his rifle coughed bullets at me. I crouched down low, not wanting him to hit my boots. Legs were important too, but the boots actually came to mind first for some reason. The feathers of my magical fan absorbed the onslaught, but he must have been using high caliber rounds, because the fan inched closer with each hit, forcing me to feed it more power.

I imitated Roland's spell as the Templar's gun clicked empty, and I flung out a bar of solid light at him. He grunted as it struck him in the chest, slicing his gun in half, but not harming him at all. The beam blasted a hole through the wall behind him and I heard a brief scream. I released my power, stunned to see the scarf's power in action. He should have sported a charred hole in his chest. He hadn't been lying. But... the scarf hadn't saved his men from my silver blades.

The main door to the nave burst open behind Olin and a guard screamed from behind his scarf as he ran towards us. A wolf leapt from the shadows behind him to tackle him to the ground and rip off his head. I realized the gunfire had ceased.

Olin grunted at his fallen soldier. Then he turned back to me, absently brushing at his chest as if to remove some crumbs. "Magic can't touch us," he said, indicating our matching accessories.

"For fuck's sake! Just die already," I cursed. He tossed his rifle pieces to the ground and threw a dagger almost casually behind him, striking the wolf in the side. She yelped as the blade sunk into her ribcage, smoking. Silver. The bastard.

He stalked my way, holding two more daggers, now.

"I'm going to enjoy this," I taunted, striding closer in a fighting stance, the ends of my wrist bandages hanging loose. "Magic might not touch you, but I'm betting you're not immune to an ice-cold bitch," I said with a dry smile, my silver claws slowly extending from my knuckles.

The silly shit thought I was referring to myself. How cute.

The unseen, shorter of the two wolves hammered into his back. Jasmine. I had spotted her limping up behind him, obviously injured, but taking advantage of the element of surprise. Her claws ripped into his back as she bit down on his neck. He flung her away with inhuman strength, quickly enough to avoid having his neck ripped out. She flew, crashing to the floor and slamming into the splintered wreckage of the pews. She whined, struggling to climb to her paws.

The sound of tearing fabric and a guttural howl made me spin back to the pulpit.

Popewolf was ready to join the party.

54

Damn it. Like I didn't have enough shit to deal with.

"I am never coming back to Italy!" I shouted loud enough for the Shepherds in Vatican City to hear me. I spun as I heard racing footsteps behind me, long enough to see Olin flee the room, clutching at his neck with one hand. "Coward!" I screamed.

Jasmine had climbed upright at the introduction of a new werewolf, but he was still completing his shift, roaring in pain as he grew – much larger than either of my two wolves. I pointed at the knife sticking out of Tiffany's ribs. Jasmine limped over to her and yanked the blade free with a yelp of pain as the silver touched her tongue. Tiffany shuddered in relief and they brushed muzzles with each other before she also climbed to her feet. They turned to look at the Antipope-wolf, and then me. They would only die here.

I pointed at the fleeing Templar. "Kill," I growled. "I've got this one."

They did, and I turned to fight the Antipope-wolf by myself. He stood on two tree-trunk thick hairy legs. No traditional wolf shape for him. *Noooo,* he had to jump straight to his beast form, a bipedal werewolf that looked more man than wolf. It was also the more dangerous form. Maybe his struggle in fighting his shift had forced the wolf to fight harder for dominance, resulting in mega-wolf.

He was easily seven-feet-tall and covered in reddish brown fur. He roared at me – the only other living thing in the room – with teeth as long as my fingers, spittle flying from his lips. Looked like he was waiting for me to confess my sins.

"Take me to church, Fido," I cackled, opening myself to the Whispers. The silver blades extended from my knuckles. Twin blades in each fist. I stared down at them, making them longer, like small swords. They didn't weigh any more than the daggers, and I could use the extra distance.

I could have blasted him with fire, killing him quickly with my magic. But I needed him alive. To confess his crimes to the Conclave. Well, *need* was a strong word. Let's go with...

I didn't *want* to use magic.

I wanted to torture him into submission. Maim him. *Break him.*

This was personal. This right-bastard had threatened to destroy the Vatican for personal gain. I didn't much care for the Conclave, but there were plenty of good people at the Vatican. And this motherfucker thought to blackmail them with Armageddon? Threatening to terrify the entire world so he could become Pope?

Nope.

I felt like getting my hands dirty. Even if I was injured – my wounds had broken open at some point – and tired. *So* damned tired. The bandages on my arms were thick with blood and my side was wet. I buried the pain and squared off with the hulking monster.

I screamed as I raced at him. "*Sinner!*" I hissed, eager to play with the Whispers.

He roared back, swinging a massive claw at my face. He was clumsy, but incredibly strong. I slid to my knees, wincing at the pain it caused my stab wound, but gritted my teeth, ignoring it. His claw obliterated the podium and I raked his forearm with my silver claws. Flesh and hair burned upon contact, and I was showered with his blood as he snarled in surprised pain.

Since I was still sliding, I lashed out with my other claw and chopped off several of his toes before climbing back to my feet with a groan. He howled, hammering his fist down at me. I wasn't fast enough, and his full strength clipped my tailbone, bouncing me off the ground. I rolled as his other fist slammed into the floor in an attempt to squash me flat.

I scrambled to my feet, but my legs gave out and I slipped in the puddle of his blood I had made. I tried again, and barely succeeded. His toeless back paw struck me in the chest, sending me flying ten feet. But luckily, my claws had been in the way, stabbing the full length of the four silver blades into his foot at the same time. He howled in agony, crashing to the floor as he tried to yank his foot away, even though I was already well clear of him.

He scrambled back to his feet, hopping on one foot and eyes dancing with both pain and rage. I did the same, panting heavily, confident he had managed to crack some of my ribs. We stared at each other from across the room, assessing weaknesses and formulating our plans of attack. Like two lions fighting over a fresh kill.

A dead body landed with a boneless splat between us and Roland sauntered in behind it, shirtless and covered in blood. His necklace stuck to his chest. He held his head back with his mouth open, his arms flung out to the side. He laughed, and the moonlight glinted off his fangs.

He looked happier than I had ever seen him.

We both stared at him, completely forgetting our fight. I glanced down at the mutilated body and recognized Crispin's dead eyes staring in my direction. His neck sported a savage hole as if Roland had simply torn out his throat. My stomach quivered at the thought. Not that I cared about Crispin's inhumane execution, but that my friend had literally ripped out his throat.

Roland finally lowered his head and shuddered, glancing down at his victim. The smile slowly drained from his face, as if only just realizing what he had done. *How* he had done it. There was no pity for Crispin in those crimson eyes, but shame had moved in.

Looked like he was a vampire, now.

The wolf made a chuffing sound, as if sniffing the vampire. Roland glanced up, saw the wolf, and black claws erupted from his fingers. He crouched and flew through the air in an impossible jump, slicing across the wolf's face and planting his feet on the shoulders, riding him down to the ground. Then he began to punch and stab with his claws, ignoring the pain as the wolf clawed at his back. Roland's wounds closed almost as fast as the wolf could inflict them.

I didn't realize I was running until I was right beside them. I reached out to the Whispers and clamped Roland's shoulders with a sudden silver gauntlet, flinging him away. My vision wavered as the werewolf groaned. I used another cord of power to latch onto the head of a nearby statue, and brought it crashing down on top of the Antipope. The ten-foot-tall marble depiction of Jesus crashed into him and broke in half with a cloud of dust and debris.

The Antipope didn't move. A second went by, and I saw the unconscious werewolf's chest rise with labored breath. His body shifted back to human and I let out a sigh of relief.

I turned to see Roland standing directly beside me, glaring at the wolf in a daze.

"You alright?" I rasped. Then my legs gave out.

He caught me as I fell, guiding me down to the ground. He brushed a bloody hand across my forehead, wiping back my hair in a loving gesture. He tugged down my scarf, his smile radiant and nightmarish. "You saved me," he whispered. He glanced back at Anthony. "And you saved him. That was... smart. I lost control..." he admitted.

I shrugged, trying to focus on his crimson eyes. I heard a faint clicking noise, but Roland was still staring at the werewolf, enveloped in his world of self-loathing.

"I need you to tell the girls how badass I am. Either that or I'll have to kill all three of you."

He blinked and then turned back to me, frowning. "What?"

I jerked my chin up, indicating for him to turn around. His head swiveled, his arms tightening as they clutched me protectively. His amulet hit me in the mouth and I almost retched, trying to spit the bloody necklace out. I shoved him back, weakly propping myself up.

Two wolves stood before us, a safe distance away so as not to appear threatening. They whined, crimson eyes locked onto Roland. I'd heard their claws on the floor as they approached.

Roland let out a relieved sob and flung out his arms. The wolves bounded up to him and I scooted away with an indignant squawk before they could trample me. They slammed into him, knocking him onto his back before slathering him with doggie kisses, whining and whimpering as they hopped back and forth excitedly, burying their heads in his chest in frantic motions.

Just imagine a puppy seeing his mom for the first time in a few days and you'll understand. Except these were killer werewolves, and he was a vampire covered in blood.

"Gross. Please stop," I asked, trying to speak over Roland's laughter at being tickled.

The three turned to face me and I hesitated at the sudden lack of joy in those six crimson eyes.

"Sorry, just the blood... and the wolf thing. And the vampire thing," I said in a softer tone.

The two wolves dipped their heads at me, stretching out their front legs like they were bowing. I blinked, and then gave them a careful nod. The wolves went back to licking Roland and I let out a sigh. Whatever.

I climbed to my feet, grunting as I clutched my side. I heard the sound of the wolves shifting back and turned to see the two bloody, naked girls nuzzled against Roland's chest. He let out a very appreciative sigh. I quickly averted my eyes, turning my back to assess the Antipope and make sure he hadn't died during the bloody threesome.

My how far a Shepherd can fall, I thought to myself.

I cleared my throat politely. "What happened to the Templar?"

"He escaped," one of the girls growled angrily. "We couldn't track him for some reason. He threw a smoke bomb of some kind and we couldn't get through it."

I turned to look at them. Roland was staring at me. "Wolfsbane," we said in unison.

I kicked a bent, bloody crucifix on the floor. "The Conclave could be here soon. We should gather the scarves. Can't leave them just lying around." The girls left the room as if it had been a command, gathering up the scarves from the countless dead bodies in the church.

A few minutes later, they returned, handing the scarves to Roland. He stood, frowning down at them for a few moments before wadding them up in a bundle and tying them off on his pants. I watched as he bent over Crispin, staring into his lifeless eyes. Then he used a bloody finger to write a word on Crispin's forehead. I moved to read it.

Traitor.

"Why not write *Sanguine?*" I asked. He met my eyes without speaking and I nodded in sudden understanding. Roland was a vampire now. Pointing the Conclave at the Sanguine Council wouldn't be good for his future.

"*Traitor* is enough," he said. "Did I hear you say something about a key?" he asked.

I had almost forgotten about it. "He made the Shepherds put on bracelets to block their magic. Fabrizio said Crispin had the only key."

Roland checked his pockets and then grunted. He withdrew a small key and set it on Crispin's chest.

We made our way over to the Antipope. Roland stared down at him for a few seconds, and then casually flung out his hand. A maroon web settled over Anthony's head, sinking into his flesh. It disappeared, and Anthony's breathing seemed to come easier, his body relaxing. I arched a brow. "To make sure he stays asleep until the Conclave arrives," he said as he bent over the man and wrote something on his forehead.

Werewolf.

I nodded. "Let's get the hell out of here," I muttered, eyeing the destruction. "Since you've been pretty much useless tonight, why don't you take us home?" I told Roland. He grunted and his version of a Gateway – a vertical pool of blood – erupted before us, leading into our training room at Abundant Angel Catholic Church in Kansas City.

I let out a sigh of relief. Home.

"Callie's hole is nicer," Jasmine commented. I blushed red at the phrasing.

Tiffany cuffed her shoulder. "Don't talk about a woman's hole like that!" she chided. But she did inspect the Gateway and nod her agreement. "Hers was shiny, but I didn't like the color. Silver," she shuddered. "Yours will suffice, Roland."

As I stepped through the Gateway, I spoke casually. "Roland?"

"Yes, Callie?"

"I need you to tell these mutts how much of a badass I am. They have the misconception that I'm your assistant. It's in your best interest to rectify that."

Roland sighed. "But you're such a good assista—"

The silver claws erupted in my fists, cutting him off.

"And you forgot to compliment her new haircut," Tiffany added sternly.

Roland blinked at her, then turned back to me, frowning. "You cut your hair!" he gasped.

Tiffany sighed. "*So* much worse. You have no idea."

Jasmine piped up, wrapping an arm around my shoulder. "Don't worry, Callie. He will learn. We'll teach him." She eyed Roland doubtfully. "Eventually."

"And we saw enough to classify you as a badass," Tiffany said with a tired laugh.

I released the blade. "Damn right. I'm going to sleep on that couch. Wake me and die," I said, shambling over to the couch, knowing I didn't have the strength to walk one step further.

"Sweet dreams, Callie," they said in unison.

"I really like your hair. It looks... very nice," Roland tried.

I'd kill him after my nap.

55

I had slept for a long time. Twelve whole hours. I hadn't bothered to look at a clock, simply taking Roland's word for it. I had woken up from a dream. A revelation. Something I had seen but forgotten from my experience with shifter reefer.

A dark, murky alley, and Abundant Angel Catholic Church rose before me. Arthur, our new janitor-slash-security guard lay sprawled on the ground, stabbed to death with a crucifix that the murderer had left behind.

The church itself was smoking. Not on fire, but as if the stone itself was hot to the touch, creating smoke as soon as air touched it. A large cross was buried into the earth just to the right of the steps beside the statue of the angel that had been there as long as I had known the place.

The cross was made of smoldering coals and held together by red, crackling chains of darkness. No flame licked the air, but the cross of embers was barely being held together by the magical chain. Each time it threatened to crumble, the chains flared darker, shifting to hold it together at all cost.

Roland knelt before it, muttering in a dried, rasping breath, praying to God in Latin over and over again, as if he had been doing it for days without rest, food, or water.

As if he was the only one holding the cross together.

The chains were his. The last of his power.

"Roland!" I shouted in disbelief, unable to move my body.

His head flinched, and he turned briefly, making me gasp. He was crying blood and had no eyes. He recognized my voice though, and burst out crying and laughing.

"Save me..." he rasped, and then he fell face-first to the ground, and the cross began crumbling as his magical chains evaporated.

I had woken up covered in sweat, panting at both the memory and the understanding of it. The vision had been a premonition. A warning of Roland becoming a vampire, but still trying to hold the church together all by himself. To save him. I only managed to calm down after a long, hot shower. I didn't tell Roland about it, wanting to see what else came back to me first, because I had a suspicion that it wasn't the only thing I had seen.

The wolves were eating upstairs, waiting for us as Roland and I chatted, enjoying our last few minutes in the church. We sipped coffee, reminiscing over embarrassing stories from my early days training in this very room.

Roland had healed me while I slept, not bothering to ask me first. I was still surprised to see he was using magic, even though it did look different, with the red tint to everything. Hopefully he hadn't stained my soul healing me, but I didn't really care if he had.

Roland had reached out to Fabrizio, telling him what had happened. I had apparently been talking in my sleep, saying *meatball* and *friend* enough times to give Roland the hint that he was trustworthy. Their conversation had gone well, because Roland had smiled while telling me about it. Fabrizio had been very grateful to find the key on Crispin's chest.

Neither of us knew where the Conclave stood on the events, and we didn't care. Fabrizio had still been at the scene when Roland called. He had unofficially taken over Crispin's place as First Shepherd, but he had promised to tell the Conclave the truth, that we had saved the day and Crispin had been behind it all. He agreed that it would be wise for us to stay out of town for a while until the chaos died down.

Fabrizio was adamant that he would fight tooth and nail for Roland's name to be cleared, but wasn't sure if Roland would ever be welcomed back into the Conclave. Too much had happened.

Windsor had even stolen the phone to apologize to Roland directly, repeating several times that he didn't care that Roland was a vampire, and if the Conclave ever ordered him to take Roland out, he would quit. Period. A lone tear had escaped my mentor's eye as he told me about it, so it was enough for me.

The Antipope was the newest guest in their prison, and would likely be given a fair trial. In exchange for his cooperation.

I hadn't wanted to risk running into Claire and Beckett at my apartment, possibly getting their freak on, so Roland had invited Arthur down to our secret compound. I had inadvertently given a job to the homeless man a few months ago after offering him sanctuary at the church. Now he was a permanent fixture, and was as dedicated as any soldier defending a castle.

After the shock had worn off – discovering that the church held secret sublevels full of deadly weapons and training gear – I had given him a list of things to pick up from my apartment. He had returned with a big bag an hour ago, enough items for a long journey – I knew not where. We were all going to take a trip. Somewhere far, far away. Even the wolves were joining us. One big happy family.

We planned on doing fun things. Like sightseeing, going out to eat, and researching how best to destroy the Templars. Roland needed time to adjust to his new life, and I just needed a break. The girls did, too.

I arched a brow at Roland as I hefted the bag Arthur had delivered on my shoulders, ready to leave. He nodded, following me up the stairs. "Were they serious about wanting to change their names? And *those* names? Because it's going to be hard to get a fake ID for them."

Roland sighed, nodding. "Paradise and Lost. Their old names are dead. They don't want to put their families at risk, or to find a way to explain their sudden rebirth."

I shook my head. "Still, *Paradise* and *Lost?*" I emphasized.

He scowled at me. "I'm a vampire. They are my familiars. It sounds perfectly cliché."

I rolled my eyes as we exited the secret door into the church proper. "Alright, Richter."

He frowned. "What?"

"If you want cliché, change your name to Richter Belmont." He blinked at me, not understanding. "Castlevania. The Vampire hunter who became Dracula?" I asked. Nothing. "Never mind. Forget I said anything."

I trailed a hand across the walls like a loving embrace. This might be the last time we were here. This was a Conclave-sanctioned church, and with neither of us being attached to them anymore, this might just be goodbye. Roland also looked nostalgic, but resolved. He was more bitter about it than

I was, which was saying something. I heard him mutter *Richter* to himself a few times, as if trying it on for size.

I chuckled as I placed my hand on the door leading outside. I opened it to find two charming FBI Agents waiting for me. They did a double-take, and then their faces hardened.

"Miss Penrose?" I nodded warily. "You're wanted for questioning about events in Italy."

56

I almost turned and ran. How the hell had they learned about Italy? Roland placed an arm around my shoulder, staying in the dark shadows of the church as he spoke. "She has been with me. What's the problem?"

"She was seen at a hotel in Italy, and is wanted for questions related to an attack at a church a few nights ago. Also, the disappearance of Bishop Anthony Gregory Gutierrez."

Roland grunted. "That's ridiculous. We went out that night, remember?" he asked me. "You called an Uber and they took us home. Pull up your bank statement on your phone."

I blinked, nodding dumbly as I pulled out my phone and logged into my account. Sure enough, Claire's Uber ride was shown as *pending*. As was a charge at a bar. I showed it to the Agents, trying to turn my anxiety into a look of concern.

"Is this some kind of identity theft thing? I hear there's been an uptick lately," I said, sounding alarmed. "And did you say a bishop?"

The Agents shared a very thoughtful look. Roland frowned at the Detectives. "She certainly hasn't had time to visit Italy, for what, a day? How long is that flight, anyway?"

They didn't look pleased, but finally nodded. "We'll look into that. We'll be needing a copy of that bank statement once it posts." He eyed the bag in my hand. "I would advise against leaving town."

The other Agent sized up Roland, as if trying to get a better look since he was still in the shadows. "And your name?"

Roland's tone grew decidedly less polite, almost icy. "I am but a humble priest, but you may call me Richter Belmont." I almost choked, but he continued. "Unless you have proof that her passport was stamped in Italy, this young woman can do as she pleases," he growled. The Agents actually took a step back at the menace in his voice. When he spoke next, his voice almost had a syrupy quality to it. Soothing. Enticing. Bewitching. "You have no reason to be concerned with us... You should drop all interest in either of us."

The two Agents slowly nodded, eyes dazed. "You're right. Not her. Impossible..."

"What led you to suspect her?" Roland pressed in that same hypnotic tone.

"Anonymous tip..." one said, slurring his speech. The other Agent was openly drooling.

"Thank you for your time. Have a safe drive back to the office," Roland said in a normal voice. They nodded and stumbled down the stairs, returning to an SUV parked near the entrance.

I rounded on Roland when they were out of earshot. "Did you just use the *Force* on them?" I asked, incredulously.

Roland grinned proudly. "I guess so..." he admitted. Neither of us voiced that he shouldn't have been able to do that as such a new vampire. Was it because he had been turned by Haven, a Master Vampire?

"And how the hell did you know about the Uber?" I demanded, face blushing at the memory of Claire and Beckett.

He shrugged. "Arthur said he found a note from Claire on top of your wallet with some cash, thanking you for the Uber and the money. I shoved them in your bag."

I watched as the FBI Agents pulled out of the lot. "Who told on me? Crispin?"

He sighed. "Or the Templar. Olin Fuentes."

I growled murderously. "Let's get out of here."

"Baaaaah, baaaah," a voice bleated from down the hall, sounding like a sheep. Roland and I spun to see Nate Temple poking his head out of our super-secret Shepherd door, the one that led down to our training area.

"Nate?" I gasped, ignoring his attempt at humor in bleating at the Shepherds like a sheep.

"How did you get in there!?" Roland bellowed.

Nate stepped into the hall, winking mischievously. "Sweet hair, Callie. Love it." He turned to Roland, who was growling at Nate's subtle comment. I almost burst out laughing at that. "I wanted to swing by and return something." He seemed to wilt slightly under our twin glares. "I... well, I kinda stole a book from the Vatican. A Welsh Bible. I needed it for something, but now I'm finished with it. I hoped Roland could return it without a fuss. Since he's cool with the Conclave."

"*How?*" I asked, feeling a migraine coming on. "You and Alucard were in the room with us!"

Nate shrugged. "A dragon pal of mine helped me. Yahn. He's really sneaky and can turn invisible. Those old goats never even knew he was there!" he chuckled. Seeing our faces, he cut off abruptly. "Look, I knew they wouldn't let me in there to have a look, so I borrowed it. It's nothing dangerous. I just had a translation issue I needed to verify, so I needed the original. Trust me, I know how to handle books. I run an arcane bookstore. No harm done. But I am sorry," he said, dipping his head at Roland.

The hallway was silent for a few tense moments, and I prepared myself to physically bar Roland from killing Nate. But wonder of all wonders, Roland began to laugh. Nate looked like he would rather have been yelled at. He shot me a desperate look, as if to ask if Roland had snapped.

I smiled at Roland, making sure he was okay, but he was clutching his sides, shaking his head at the irony. I turned back to Nate. "We... well, we don't work for them anymore." And I told him. About Roland. The fight. Everything. He stared back, stunned.

"Wow." Nate studied Roland for a second, smirking. "Holy vampire, huh?" he teased.

Roland let out a sigh. "I have no idea. But a vampire, yes."

"We're taking a long break," I told him, nudging my bag with a boot. Then another thought hit me. I leaned in close to Roland and asked him in a whisper. He leaned back, studying my face. "I'm not your boss, Callie. I think you can make your own decisions." He was smiling.

I turned to Nate and asked him. His wolfish grin was answer enough, but he nodded. We walked back to the outer door, Roland telling Nate about the two wolves.

"I'd really like to meet them if that's okay?" Nate asked.

Roland glanced at me and I nodded. "I'll go start your car, old man." He grunted and the two of them went off in search of Paradise and Lost. I had my hand on the door when I saw a car skid into the parking lot. Claire jumped out as if intending to invade the church, Beckett hot on her heels. I groaned. Couldn't a girl run away in peace?

With a resigned sigh, I opened the door just before she barreled through it. Claire squeaked in surprise. I grinned instinctively at her reaction. She was a shifter bear now – she needed to act a little tougher. Not wanting to prolong the inevitable, I spoke. "How was your wild date?" I steeled myself for the answer.

They shared an embarrassed look and then burst out laughing. I kept the smile plastered on my face, not understanding what was so funny. Claire skipped up to me and gave me a big hug, whispering into my ear. "Not my type." Then she leaned back and held out her palm for Beckett to back up. He did and Claire turned back to me, speaking softly.

"My hormones were a little out of whack in Alaska. I might have spoken in haste. But spending time with Beckett a few nights ago just confirmed that I'm not into flings. He's a great guy, but not for me," she said suggestively.

Then she turned back to Beckett. "You may approach now," she said, haughtily.

He rolled his eyes, turning to me. "Hey, Callie. Glad you made it home okay."

I smiled, holding out my arms for a hug. He accepted and it felt nice.

"You ready to go, Callie?" Nate asked from behind me.

Beckett stepped away from me, giving Nate a carefully controlled smile, but the tension was obvious. Nate walked up and smiled. "Hey, Claire." Then he held out a hand to shake with Beckett. "My name's Nate."

I knew Beckett well enough to sense the jealousy. But I didn't have the energy to make him feel better. Hearing he had spent the night with Claire had bothered me for days. This was just Karma giving me a pat on the back.

Maybe I would get to finally make up my mind about this billionaire from St. Louis. Both professionally and personally.

"I don't know when we'll be back, but I'll be in touch," I told Claire, ignoring the desperate curiosity in her eyes. "Take care of yourself, Roland," I said, sensing his presence behind Nate.

Roland grinned from the shadows. "You too, Callie." He gave Nate a respectful nod. "You too, Temple. Take good care of her, or I'll have to take good care of you..." he said with a dark grin. Still pleasant, but a warning not to do me harm.

I rolled my eyes. "Let's go, rogue," I said, guiding Nate back inside the church, knowing we wouldn't be taking a car where we were going. Wherever the hell that was.

"You're never going to believe what I found, Callie..." Nate said, his eyes twinkling.

I was ready for some mystery. "Show me," I said, smiling at him. "I might have a thing or two to show you as well..."

*Callie Penrose returns in **ANGEL'S ROAR**... Turn the page for a sample!* **Or get the book ONLINE!** *http://www.shaynesilvers.com/l/137537*

SAMPLE: ANGEL'S ROAR (FEATHERS AND FIRE # 4)

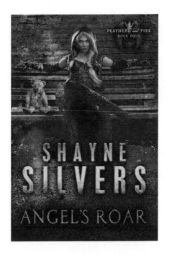

T
he rickety bench was cold and uncomfortable, still wet from the chilly downpour of rain earlier. Claire was studying the brick wall behind our bench while my eyes focused on the gang of thugs across the street. Sirens wailed in the distance, but they weren't anywhere near us.

Because police didn't typically patrol this part of town. They only came if someone called them, and even then, they would arrive armed with assault weapons, riot gear, and body armor. Gangs owned these streets. Police actually discouraged vehicles from coming to a complete stop at the stop signs, because gangs were known to target obedient drivers. Follow laws too closely here and you were liable to see the barrel of a shotgun pointing at your face from outside the window. New age highway robbery.

I took a deep breath, tucking some stray hair back under my hood. Even though the heavy rain had ceased, constant drizzle still fell from the leaden-gray night sky.

I heard the hiss of air brakes from a nearby Greyhound bus and the heavy scent of exhaust was like a stale perfume in the air – almost enough to overpower the smell of wet trash and refuse. This part of town was neglected, forgotten. At least the rain attempted to wash away some of the grime. The beautiful skyline in the distance was a mockery of the poverty festering here.

Almost like this place wasn't a part of Kansas City.

But it was.

I studied the street of leaning brownstone homes before us, marking the parked cars lining both sides of the street. Many of the bulbs in the lamp-posts were broken – whether they had burned out or been shot out by local hoodlums, I wasn't sure. Regardless, they hadn't been replaced. I clenched my fists as I watched the thugs breaking into the cars, stealing the stereos and any other valuables inside. They did this without shame, unconcerned with anyone witnessing their crime.

On the upside, the distant sirens wouldn't be close enough to save these assholes from me.

"What is the... *Chancery?*" Claire asked thoughtfully, pointing at some graffiti on the wall.

I shrugged, continuing to watch the brazen thieves. "Someone really ought to tell them about an *eye for an eye...*" I mumbled.

"What about this one? Think it's talking about Nate?"

I ignored her, not wanting to talk about Nate Temple. I leaned forward, gritting my teeth as the thugs shattered another car window, laughing as they congratulated each other. What if the owner of that vehicle had kids? That would fuck with their sense of security in the morning when they were getting ready to leave for daycare.

"Oh! I think this one's talking about *you*—"

"Please stop, Claire," I said in a tight voice, turning to face her. I was getting annoyed with her fascination with the graffiti. She didn't seem concerned about the hoodlums across the street, just the shitty graffiti. She was pointing at a section on the brick wall behind us. It was a crude sketch of a fist – two blades extending out from between the knuckles. A halo floated above the fist, like some kind of logo.

I jolted in recognition. It *was* about me.

How had anyone heard about *that?* I had first used those blades months ago, but that had been in Rome, not here in Kansas City. It was pretty obvious the sketch was referencing me, unless we had an Angelic Wolverine in town that I hadn't yet met.

Seeing that image, scrawled on a shitty wall in a shitty part of town made me uneasy. Like a sniper had me in his sights.

I stood hastily, my eyes latching onto one of the other graffiti tags Claire had pointed out. *Chancery wuz here.* I frowned, dismissing the street art. *Stupid name*, I thought to myself. "These assholes are pissing me off," I said, openly glaring at the seven hoodlums.

Sinners... a soothing purr filled my ears.

My skin pebbled instinctively at the sensation, but I no longer flinched when they spoke to me. The *Whispers* were something to do with the Angelic blood flowing through my veins. They offered constant commentary to my life, like my own personal narrator. Sometimes they were pleasant, other times obnoxiously creepy. Like someone was staring through my eyes and passing judgment on these thieves. I muted them. I didn't need them for what I had planned.

I felt Claire standing beside me, watching me with concern. I waved a hand and put on a shallow smile. "Just tired," I said. "And pissed."

Her breath puffed out before her face in a brief cloud. "Are they Freaks?" she asked, scrutinizing the thugs.

I nodded, tightening the straps of my small backpack so it wouldn't be a hindrance in a fight. "Saw some fangs. And that one ripped a door off with one hand," I said, pointing openly. Two of the thugs were now watching us, their predatory gazes full of warning. Two young women shouldn't be out alone in this part of town at this time of night. And they definitely shouldn't have any hobbies remotely related to the automotive industry.

It was a threat. They were strong, hardened, dangerous men. And we were two cute blonde women, obviously in the wrong part of town on the wrong night. We weren't welcome.

Claire openly snorted at their silent threat and their eyes narrowed, lips pulling back into snarls. "I'm bringing Teddy," she said, waving a small white teddy bear towards the dangerous thieves. "It's only fair to warn them. Did you bring your scarf?"

"I'm not a Knight Templar," I murmured disgustedly under my breath, not wanting to think about the scarf I had stolen from them in Rome. The one that blocked magical attacks.

Claire shrugged. "It's more for *their* benefit," she said, waving her white teddy bear at them more blatantly. "To give them fair warning of what we *really* are." I nodded absently.

The stuffed animal to let them know she was really a shifter polar bear.

She turned the bear to face her. "Right, Teddy?" she asked it, staring into its button eyes.

"Right, Clairebear," she answered herself in a tinny voice.

I shot her a baffled look. "Really?" I shifted my eyes to study the bear, thinking. "If you're going to talk to a stuffed animal, shouldn't you at least make his voice deep and rumbly?"

"My bear, my rules," she said defensively. She jerked her chin at the thieves, her green eyes twinkling with anticipation. I turned to see them now forming a line. Brass knuckles glinted in the dim lamplight on a few pairs of hands. Others sported outright claws, proving my point about them being Freaks, and that they didn't have a sliver of concern that anyone might see them. People kept their heads down in this part of town. Even if they didn't know about Freaks – supernatural beings – the Regular criminals were ruthless enough. The wrong look could earn you a bullet and a shallow grave.

I rolled my shoulders, plucking out my Crucifix necklace so it could hang freely before me. Maybe Claire had a point. It *was* only fair to warn them. Then I stalked closer, shoving my hands in the pockets of my Darling and Dear coat.

Claire chuckled at my necklace, matching my stride. "There. *Now*, they've been warned."

I grunted. I wasn't particularly religious – at least I didn't attend Mass like a good little Catholic girl or anything. But... I had *seen* things. Been shown that I literally had some kind of bond with Heaven. My father had been a Nephilim, and I'd once had a minor Angel blood transfusion. So... it felt kind of childish to deny that the Crucifix didn't hold power. Still, it made me feel like a poser.

Because I was no saint.

"Hey, boys. Like my teddy bear?" Claire asked, pouting her lips.

A tall, pale, gangly man stepped forward. Water dripped from the stubble on his chin as he sneered back at Claire, ignoring me. "The only teddy I want to see is you in skimpy lingerie in the back of my truck, where I can show you where a tiny woman like you belongs late at night. On her back—"

I shoved my fingers in my ears in anticipation, right before Claire exploded into a massive white polar bear. She was easily ten feet tall, and her roar threatened to shatter window panes in the nearby homes. Her thick, snow-white fur whipped back and forth as she shook off the misty rain.

Like any woman should do in a similar situation, she slapped the offensive little prick.

I'm pretty sure he was a vampire.

And I'm pretty sure she broke his spine in three places.

At least, it sounded like muffled firecrackers had erupted under his skin before he flew back into one of the cars, shattering the windshield. He groaned in a very unmanly way, staring up at the misty night with wheezing, shallow breaths. Surprisingly, the car alarm didn't go off. Then again, maybe the thugs had somehow deactivated them. Made sense. Hard to rob a whole street full of cars if all the alarms were going off.

The street was silent as the other thugs stared at us in stunned shock. "One Brokeback vampire, served cold. *Sooo* cold," I chuckled.

Clairebear made an amused chuffing sound.

I pointed at the teddy bear – miraculously still gripped in Claire's massive claw. "We're not really into foreplay, but we did try to give you a heads up," I said, shifting my finger from the teddy bear to Claire. "Practically a flashing sign, really." I was mildly surprised that the werewolves in the back hadn't noticed her scent. Maybe they hadn't ever met a shifter bear.

"And what the fuck are *you*? A Ninja Nun?" a squat bald man asked me, his jowls quivering like a wet plate of tapioca Jell-O as he indicated my Crucifix. A few of his crew chuckled, but the rest frowned thoughtfully.

I let my hood fall back to reveal my unique white hair, and the single braid hair extension I had chosen for the night's activities. Most Freaks in town had seen a video of me kicking demon ass with my long white hair and recognized me by it. Those who hadn't initially laughed along with their pals froze, their previous hesitation now confirmed horror, but the leader just stared, not noticing their reaction or recognizing me. At least *some* of them recognized me.

"Have you heard about our Lord and Savior?" I asked in a soft tone, shaking out the thick, white braid. I had cut my hair off at the jaw recently, and the familiar weight of the extension made me feel more... me, I guess. I missed it, so had picked up an extension for nights like this when I was bored.

I took a casual step closer, my polite smile turning menacing as I flashed my teeth.

"Because he sure as fuck's heard about *you*," I said.

The three furthest away turned and ran. "It's her!" one of them screamed as he fled, tossing his brass knuckles to the street in a sign of surrender.

Sometimes, it was nice for a girl to be recognized. To have a reputation.

Claire didn't let them get very far before tearing after them on all fours, her teddy flopping in her paw at the sudden motion, splashing through the puddles and ruining the beautiful white fur. I smiled at the remaining hoodlums.

"Oh, no. Whatever shall I do?" I said in mock fear.

Get your copy of ANGEL'S ROAR online today!
http://www.shaynesilvers.com/l/137537

*Turn the page to read a sample of **OBSIDIAN SON** - The Nate Temple Series Book 1 - or **BUY ONLINE**. Nate Temple is a billionaire wizard from St. Louis. He rides a bloodthirsty unicorn and drinks with the Four Horsemen. He even cow-tipped the Minotaur. Once...*

(Note: Nate's books 1-6 happen prior to UNCHAINED, but they crossover from then on, the two series taking place in the same universe but also able to standalone if you prefer)

Full chronology of all books in the TempleVerse shown on the 'BOOKS BY SHAYNE SILVERS' page.

TRY: OBSIDIAN SON (NATE TEMPLE #1)

There was no room for emotion in a hate crime. I had to be cold. Heartless. This was just another victim. Nothing more. No face, no name.

Frosted blades of grass crunched under my feet, sounding to my ears like the symbolic glass that one would shatter under a napkin at a Jewish wedding. The noise would have threatened to give away my stealthy advance as I stalked through the moonlit field, but I was no novice and had planned accordingly. Being a wizard, I was able to muffle all sensory evidence with a fine cloud of magic—no sounds, and no smells. Nifty. But if I made the spell much stronger, the anomaly would be too obvious to my prey.

I knew the consequences for my dark deed tonight. If caught, jail time or possibly even a gruesome, painful death. But if I succeeded, the look of fear and surprise in my victim's eyes before his world collapsed around him, it was well worth the risk. I simply couldn't help myself; I had to take him down.

I knew the cops had been keeping tabs on my car, but I was confident that they hadn't followed me. I hadn't seen a tail on my way here but seeing as how they frowned on this kind of thing, I had taken a circuitous route just in case. I was safe. I hoped.

Then my phone chirped at me as I received a text.

I practically jumped out of my skin, hissing instinctively. "Motherf—" I cut off abruptly, remembering the whole stealth aspect of my mission. I was off to a stellar start. I had forgotten to silence the damned phone. *Stupid, stupid, stupid!*

My heart felt like it was on the verge of exploding inside my chest with such thunderous violence that I briefly envisioned a mystifying Rorschach blood-blot that would have made coroners and psychologists drool.

My body remained tense as I swept my gaze over the field, fearing that I had been made. Precious seconds ticked by without any change in my surroundings, and my breathing finally began to slow as my pulse returned to normal. Hopefully, my magic had muted the phone and my resulting outburst. I glanced down at the phone to scan the text and then typed back a quick and angry response before I switched the cursed device to vibrate.

Now, where were we?

I continued on, the lining of my coat constricting my breathing. Or maybe it was because I was leaning forward in anticipation. *Breathe*, I chided myself. *He doesn't know you're here.* All this risk for a book. It had better be worth it.

I'm taller than most, and not abnormally handsome, but I knew how to play the genetic cards I had been dealt. I had shaggy, dirty blonde hair—leaning more towards brown with each passing year—and my frame was thick with well-earned muscle, yet I was still lean. I had once been told that my eyes were like twin emeralds pitted against the golden-brown tufts of my hair—a face like a jewelry box. Of course, that was two bottles of wine into a date, so I could have been a little foggy on her quote. Still, I liked to imagine that was how everyone saw me.

But tonight, all that was masked by magic.

I grinned broadly as the outline of the hairy hulk finally came into view. He was blessedly alone—no nearby sentries to give me away. That was always a risk when performing this ancient rite-of-passage. I tried to keep the grin on my face from dissolving into a maniacal cackle.

My skin danced with energy, both natural and unnatural, as I manipulated the threads of magic floating all around me. My victim stood just ahead, oblivious to the world of hurt that I was about to unleash. Even with his millennia of experience, he didn't stand a chance. I had done this so many times that the routine of it was my only enemy. I lost count of how many times I had been told not to do it again; those who knew declared it *cruel, evil, and sadistic*. But what fun wasn't? Regardless, that wasn't enough to stop me from doing it again. And again. And again.

It was an addiction.

The pungent smell of manure filled the air, latching onto my nostril hairs. I took another step, trying to calm my racing pulse. A glint of gold reflected in the silver moonlight, but my victim remained motionless, hopefully unaware or all was lost. I wouldn't make it out alive if he knew I was here. Timing was everything.

I carefully took the last two steps, a lifetime between each, watching the legendary monster's ears, anxious and terrified that I would catch even so much as a twitch in my direction. Seeing nothing, a fierce grin split my unshaven cheeks. My spell had worked! I raised my palms an inch away from their target, firmly planted my feet, and squared my shoulders. I took one silent, calming breath, and then heaved forward with every ounce of physical strength I could muster. As well as a teensy-weensy boost of magic. Enough to goose him good.

"*MOOO!!!*" The sound tore through the cool October night like an unstoppable freight train. *Thud-splat!* The beast collapsed sideways onto the frosted grass; straight into a steaming patty of cow shit, cow dung, or, if you really wanted to church it up, a Meadow Muffin. But to me, shit is, and always will be, shit.

Cow tipping. It doesn't get any better than that in Missouri.

Especially when you're tipping the *Minotaur*. Capital M. I'd tipped plenty of ordinary cows before, but never the legendary variety.

Razor-blade hooves tore at the frozen earth as the beast struggled to stand, his grunts of rage vibrating the air. I raised my arms triumphantly. "Boo-yah! Temple 1, Minotaur 0!" I crowed. Then I very bravely prepared to protect myself. Some people just couldn't take a joke. *Cruel, evil,* and *sadistic* cow tipping may be, but by hell, it was a *rush*. The legendary beast turned his gaze on me after gaining his feet, eyes ablaze as his body...*shifted* from his bull disguise into his notorious, well-known bipedal form. He unfolded to his full height on two tree trunk-thick legs, his hooves having magically transformed into heavily booted feet. The thick, gold ring dangling from his snotty snout quivered as the Minotaur panted, and his dense, corded muscles contracted over his now human-like chest. As I stared up into those brown eyes, I actually felt sorry...for, well, myself.

"I have killed greater men than you for lesser offense," he growled.

His voice sounded like an angry James Earl Jones—like Mufasa talking to Scar.

"You have shit on your shoulder, Asterion." I ignited a roiling ball of fire in my palm in order to see his eyes more clearly. By no means was it a defensive gesture on my part. It was just dark. Under the weight of his glare, I somehow managed to keep my face composed, even though my fraudulent, self-denial had curled up into the fetal position and started whimpering. I hoped using a form of his ancient name would give me brownie points. Or maybe just not-worthy-of-killing points.

The beast grunted, eyes tightening, and I sensed the barest hesitation. "Nate Temple...your name would look splendid on my already long list of slain idiots." Asterion took a threatening step forward, and I thrust out my palm in warning, my roiling flame blue now.

"You lost fair and square, Asterion. Yield or perish." The beast's shoulders sagged slightly. Then he finally nodded to himself in resignation, appraising me with the scrutiny of a worthy adversary. "Your time comes, Temple, but I will grant you this. You've got a pair of stones on you to rival Hercules."

I reflexively glanced in the direction of the myth's own crown jewels before jerking my gaze away. Some things you simply couldn't un-see. "Well, I won't be needing a wheelbarrow any time soon, but overcompensating today keeps future lower-back pain away."

The Minotaur blinked once, and then he bellowed out a deep, contagious, snorting laughter. Realizing I wasn't about to become a murder statistic, I couldn't help but join in. It felt good. It had been a while since I had allowed myself to experience genuine laughter.

In the harsh moonlight, his bulk was even more intimidating as he towered head and shoulders above me. This was the beast that had fed upon human sacrifices for countless years while imprisoned in Daedalus' Labyrinth in Greece. And all that protein had not gone to waste, forming a heavily woven musculature over the beast's body that made even Mr. Olympia look puny.

From the neck up, he was now entirely bull, but the rest of his body more closely resembled a thickly furred man. But, as shown moments ago, he could adapt his form to his environment, never appearing fully human, but able to make his entire form appear as a bull when necessary. For instance, how he had looked just before I tipped him. Maybe he had been scouting the field for heifers before I had so efficiently killed the mood.

His bull face was also covered in thick, coarse hair—he even sported a long, wavy beard of sorts, and his eyes were the deepest brown I had ever seen. Cow-shit brown. His snout jutted out, emphasizing the golden ring dangling from his glistening nostrils, and both glinted in the luminous glow of the moon. The metal was at least an inch thick and etched with runes of a language long forgotten. Wide, aged ivory horns sprouted from each temple, long enough to skewer a wizard with little effort. He was nude except for a massive beaded necklace and a pair of worn leather boots that were big enough to stomp a size twenty-five imprint in my face if he felt so inclined.

I hoped our blossoming friendship wouldn't end that way. I really did.

Because friends didn't let friends wear boots naked...

Get your copy of OBSIDIAN SON online today!
http://www.shaynesilvers.com/l/38474

*Turn the page to read a sample of **WHISKEY GINGER** - Phantom Queen Diaries Book 1, or **BUY ONLINE**. Quinn MacKenna is a black magic arms dealer in Boston. She likes to fight monsters almost as much as she likes to drink.*

TRY: WHISKEY GINGER (PHANTOM QUEEN DIARIES BOOK 1)

T he pasty guitarist hunched forward, thrust a rolled-up wad of paper deep into one nostril, and snorted a line of blood crystals— frozen hemoglobin that I'd smuggled over in a refrigerated canister—with the uncanny grace of a drug addict. He sat back, fangs gleaming, and pawed at his nose. "That's some bodacious shit. Hey, bros," he said, glancing at his fellow band members, "come hit this shit before it melts."

He fetched one of the backstage passes hanging nearby, pried the plastic badge from its lanyard, and used it to split up the crystals, murmuring something in an accent that reminded me of California. Not *the* California, but you know, Cali-foh-nia—the land of beaches, babes, and bros. I retrieved a toothpick from my pocket and punched it through its thin wrapper. "So," I asked no one in particular, "now that ye have the product, who's payin'?"

Another band member stepped out of the shadows to my left, and I don't mean that figuratively, either—the fucker literally stepped out of the shadows. I scowled at him, but hid my surprise, nonchalantly rolling the toothpick from one side of my mouth to the other.

The rest of the band gathered around the dressing room table, following the guitarist's lead by preparing their own snorting utensils—tattered magazine covers, mostly. Typically, you'd do this sort of thing with a dollar-bill, maybe even a Benjamin if you were flush. But fangers like this lot couldn't touch cash directly—in God We Trust and all that. Of course, I didn't really understand why sucking blood the old-fashioned way had suddenly gone out of style. More of a rush, maybe?

"It lasts longer," the vampire next to me explained, catching my mildly curious expression. "It's especially good for shows and stuff. Makes us look, like, less—"

"Creepy?" I offered, my Irish brogue lilting just enough to make it a question.

"Pale," he finished, frowning.

I shrugged. "Listen, I've got places to be," I said, holding out my hand.

"I'm sure you do," he replied, smiling. "Tell you what, why don't you, like, hang around for a bit? Once that wears off," he dipped his head toward the bloody powder smeared across the table's surface, "we may need a pick-me-up." He rested his hand on my arm and our gazes locked.

I blinked, realized what he was trying to pull, and rolled my eyes. His widened in surprise, then shock as I yanked out my toothpick and shoved it through his hand.

"Motherfuck—"

"I want what we agreed on," I declared. "Now. No tricks."

The rest of the band saw what happened and rose faster than I could blink. They circled me, their grins feral...they might have even seemed intimidating if it weren't for the fact that they each had a case of the sniffles—I had to work extra hard not to think about what it felt like to have someone else's blood dripping down my nasal cavity.

I held up a hand.

"Can I ask ye gentlemen a question before we get started?" I asked. "Do ye even *have* what I asked for?"

Two of the band members exchanged looks and shrugged. The guitarist, however, glanced back towards the dressing room, where a brown paper bag sat next to a case full of makeup. He caught me looking and bared his teeth, his fangs stretching until it looked like it would be uncomfortable for him to close his mouth without piercing his own lip.

"Follow-up question," I said, eyeing the vampire I'd stabbed as he gingerly withdrew the toothpick from his hand and flung it across the room with a snarl. "Do ye do each other's make-up? Since, ye know, ye can't use mirrors?"

I was genuinely curious.

The guitarist grunted. "Mike, we have to go on soon."

"Wait a minute. Mike?" I turned to the snarling vampire with a frown. "What happened to *The Vampire Prospero*?" I glanced at the numerous fliers in the dressing room, most of which depicted the band members wading through blood, with Mike in the lead, each one titled *The Vampire Prospero* in *Rocky Horror Picture Show* font. Come to think of it...Mike did look a little like Tim Curry in all that leather and lace.

I was about to comment on the resemblance when Mike spoke up, "Alright, change of plans, bros. We're gonna drain this bitch before the show. We'll look totally—"

"Creepy?" I offered, again.

"Kill her."

Get the full book ONLINE! http://www.shaynesilvers.com/l/206897

MAKE A DIFFERENCE

Reviews are the most powerful tools in my arsenal when it comes to getting attention for my books. Much as I'd like to, I don't have the financial muscle of a New York publisher.

But I do have something much more powerful and effective than that, and it's something that those publishers would kill to get their hands on.

A committed and loyal bunch of readers.

Honest reviews of my books help bring them to the attention of other readers.

If you've enjoyed this book, I would be very grateful if you could spend just five minutes leaving a review (it can be as short as you like) on my book's Amazon page.

Thank you very much in advance.

ACKNOWLEDGMENTS

First, I would like to thank my beta-readers, TEAM TEMPLE, those individuals who spent hours of their time to read, and re-re-read the TempleVerse stories. Your dark, twisted, cunning sense of humor makes me feel right at home...

I would also like to thank you, the reader. I hope you enjoyed reading *WHISPERS* as much as I enjoyed writing it. Be sure to check out the two crossover series in the TempleVerse: **The Nate Temple Series** and the **Phantom Queen Diaries**.

And last, but definitely not least, I thank my wife, Lexy. Without your support, none of this would have been possible.

ABOUT SHAYNE SILVERS

Shayne is a man of mystery and power, whose power is exceeded only by his mystery...

He currently writes the Amazon Bestselling **Nate Temple** Series, which features a foul-mouthed wizard from St. Louis. He rides a bloodthirsty unicorn, drinks with Achilles, and is pals with the Four Horsemen.

He also writes the Amazon Bestselling **Feathers and Fire** Series—a second series in the TempleVerse. The story follows a rookie spell-slinger named Callie Penrose who works for the Vatican in Kansas City. Her problem? Hell seems to know more about her past than she does.

He coauthors **The Phantom Queen Diaries**—a third series set in The TempleVerse—with Cameron O'Connell. The story follows Quinn MacKenna, a mouthy black magic arms dealer in Boston. All she wants? A round-trip ticket to the Fae realm...and maybe a drink on the house.

He also writes the **Shade of Devil Series**, which tells the story of Sorin Ambrogio—the world's FIRST vampire. He was put into a magical slumber by a Native American Medicine Man when the Americas were first discovered by Europeans. Sorin wakes up after five-hundred years to learn that his protege, Dracula, stole his reputation and that no one has ever even heard of Sorin Ambrogio. The streets of New York City will run with blood as Sorin reclaims his legend.

Shayne holds two high-ranking black belts, and can be found writing in a coffee shop, cackling madly into his computer screen while pounding shots of espresso. He's hard at work on the newest books in the TempleVerse— You can find updates on new releases or chronological reading order on the next page, his website, or any of his social media accounts. **Follow him online for all sorts of groovy goodies, giveaways, and new release updates:**

BOOKS BY SHAYNE

CHRONOLOGY: All stories in the TempleVerse are shown in chronological order on the following page

FEATHERS AND FIRE SERIES

(Set in the TempleVerse)

by Shayne Silvers

UNCHAINED

RAGE

WHISPERS

ANGEL'S ROAR

MOTHERLUCKER (Novella #4.5 in the 'LAST CALL' anthology)

SINNER

BLACK SHEEP

GODLESS

NATE TEMPLE SERIES

(Main series in the TempleVerse)

by Shayne Silvers

FAIRY TALE - FREE prequel novella #0 for my subscribers

OBSIDIAN SON

BLOOD DEBTS

GRIMM

SILVER TONGUE

BEAST MASTER

BEERLYMPIAN (Novella #5.5 in the 'LAST CALL' anthology)

TINY GODS

DADDY DUTY (Novella #6.5)

WILD SIDE

WAR HAMMER

NINE SOULS

HORSEMAN

LEGEND

KNIGHTMARE

ASCENSION

PHANTOM QUEEN DIARIES

(Also set in the TempleVerse)

by Cameron O'Connell & Shayne Silvers

COLLINS (Prequel novella #0 in the 'LAST CALL' anthology)

WHISKEY GINGER

COSMOPOLITAN

OLD FASHIONED

MOTHERLUCKER (Novella #3.5 in the 'LAST CALL' anthology)

DARK AND STORMY

MOSCOW MULE

WITCHES BREW

SALTY DOG

SEA BREEZE

HURRICANE

CHRONOLOGICAL ORDER: TEMPLEVERSE

FAIRY TALE (TEMPLE PREQUEL)

OBSIDIAN SON (TEMPLE 1)

BLOOD DEBTS (TEMPLE 2)

GRIMM (TEMPLE 3)

SILVER TONGUE (TEMPLE 4)

BEAST MASTER (TEMPLE 5)

BEERLYMPIAN (TEMPLE 5.5)

TINY GODS (TEMPLE 6)

DADDY DUTY (TEMPLE NOVELLA 6.5)

UNCHAINED (FEATHERS... 1)

RAGE (FEATHERS... 2)

WILD SIDE (TEMPLE 7)

WAR HAMMER (TEMPLE 8)

WHISPERS (FEATHERS... 3)

COLLINS (PHANTOM 0)

WHISKEY GINGER (PHANTOM... 1)

NINE SOULS (TEMPLE 9)

COSMOPOLITAN (PHANTOM... 2)

ANGEL'S ROAR (FEATHERS... 4)

MOTHERLUCKER (FEATHERS 4.5, PHANTOM 3.5)

OLD FASHIONED (PHANTOM...3)

HORSEMAN (TEMPLE 10)

DARK AND STORMY (PHANTOM... 4)

MOSCOW MULE (PHANTOM...5)

SINNER (FEATHERS...5)

WITCHES BREW (PHANTOM...6)

LEGEND (TEMPLE...11)

SALTY DOG (PHANTOM...7)

BLACK SHEEP (FEATHERS...6)

GODLESS (FEATHERS...7)

KNIGHTMARE (TEMPLE 12)

ASCENSION (TEMPLE 13)

SEA BREEZE (PHANTOM...8)

HURRICANE (PHANTOM...9)

SHADE OF DEVIL SERIES

(Not part of the Temple Verse)

by Shayne Silvers

DEVIL'S DREAM

DEVIL'S CRY

DEVIL'S BLOOD

Printed in Great Britain
by Amazon